HOPE RUN

STEPHEN OSBORNE

JERRY,
HOPE YOU ENJOY IT.

ISBN: 978-1-63491-084-2

Published by BookLocker.com, Inc., Bradenton, Florida.

Printed on acid-free paper.

BookLocker.com, Inc.
2016

First Edition

Tuesday, September 5, 1950
Scioto County, Ohio

From the front seat of the school bus, Mike watched her as she carefully closed the front door, walked down the porch steps, and down the dirt path toward him, clutching a brown paper bag in her left hand. Her multicolored dress looked homemade and nearly touched the ground. Her long, dark hair was tied back in a double ponytail.

As she tentatively stepped onto the bus, the driver greeted her with a smile and a cheery 'good morning'. She smiled back shyly and looked around as if she couldn't decide whether to stay on the nearly empty bus or run back to her house.

Mike patted the seat beside him. "You can sit by me."

She looked his way, smiled, and then looked toward the rear of the bus.

He stood up. "You can sit by the window if you want."

The driver, a heavy-set, middle-aged, man in bib overalls and a baseball cap, said, "Take a seat, honey. We need to get moving."

Mike moved into the aisle. She smiled again, slid past him, and sat by the window.

"I'm Mike Harrison," he said as he sat next to her on the bench seat. "What's your name?"

In a voice barely above a whisper, she replied, "My name is Mary…Mary Bryant." She smoothed her dress.

"I like your dress," he said, looking at her face.

She smiled again, and said, matter-of-factly, "No you don't. But thank you."

He looked at her paper bag. "What're you having for lunch?"

"Bologna sandwich and an apple I picked from our tree this morning."

"You like peanut butter and jelly sandwiches?" He became more animated. "I make really good ones. My mom taught me."

She nodded. "Yes, I do."

"Okay, how about this? Every day I bring you a peanut butter and jelly sandwich—plenty of room in here." He tapped his Roy Rogers lunch box with his forefinger. "And every day you bring me an apple."

"Okay, but the apples will only last a few more weeks—maybe a month." Her eyes sparkled.

"When the apples run out, the peanut butter and jelly sandwiches run out."

She smiled and extended her right hand. "It's a deal."

He took her hand. It was soft and warm, reminding him of something. "I do like your dress," he said.

She smiled again but didn't reply.

"My mom died," he said, watching her eyes.

Her smile disappeared. "When?"

"Three weeks ago, today."

"Oh." She pointed south. "You live in the white house down that way—close to the road?"

"Yeah. How'd you know?"

"My mom told me."

"Your mom knew my mom?"

"She went to see her once last summer and invited her to go to church with us, but your mom didn't want to."

He watched her eyes some more. "You scared about starting school?"

"A little."

"Me, too—a little."

They were silent as the bus turned left onto Hope Run.

At length, he said. "My dad lives with me now."

She patted his hand. "I'm sorry about your mom." Reaching behind him, she tucked the tag back inside his shirt collar.

In the 1950's, Scioto County, Ohio was the poorest county in the state, with many families living on welfare, eking out a living on small farms, cutting timber and using their mules to snake logs out of the many local 'hollers', or 'junking' scrap metal just to feed their large families. The more industrious ones did all of the above.

Located in the foothills of the Appalachian Mountains, the county is split in half by the Scioto River, which empties into the Ohio at Portsmouth. In August, one could find many poor families wading in the muddy Ohio and Scioto River bottoms, 'tubbing' fish—mostly carp—that had been trapped in shallow pools by the receding water.

There were still some good paying jobs—the steel mill, the stove foundry, the shoe factory, the atomic plant—but those jobs were dwindling. Along the narrow two-lane county roads, and back in the 'hollers', one would find an stark contrast between the nice homes of those who had good jobs and the run-down shacks of those who didn't.

There had been better times. In the '20's, Portsmouth was a growing city, boasting several shoe factories and two steel mills. At one point, there was even a professional football team called the Portsmouth Spartans, which eventually became the Detroit Lions.

The population of Portsmouth began its decline at the start of the Great Depression, and by the '50's had lost nearly twenty-five percent of its population as businesses failed or moved out. The population of Scioto County suffered a similar decline as many residents headed north to Columbus, Cleveland, and to automobile plants in Michigan.

Monday, May 28, 1962
Ocean Beach, California—near San Diego

Mike Harrison sat in the sand, watching a surfer in a wetsuit try in vain to get up on his board. The beach was nearly deserted. School was still in session in California.

Maybe I'll take up surfing.

After watching for several minutes, and deciding that surfing looked too difficult—and dangerous, he got up and roamed the beach, stepping around seaweed, and dodging the cold water as it repeatedly rushed at him and then receded. As he considered going back to Whittier, grabbing Norma West, and heading back south—maybe to Mexico, or even farther, his attention was drawn to the music—Aker Bilk's instrumental, 'Stranger on the Shore'. *How appropriate.*

The music was coming from a large transistor radio sitting in the sand beside a beach chair occupied by a woman with long red hair, wearing large sunglasses and reading a book. He watched her put the paperback in her lap, take a sip from a can of beer, briefly stare out at the ocean, and then return to her book.

He stopped ten feet in front of her, seeing that she was tall, thin, attractive, and somewhat older; definitely not a teenager. Maybe mid-twenties; maybe thirty. She didn't look up.

When he stepped closer, she glanced up briefly, and then re-focused on her book. He turned left, walked ten paces north, turned around, and walked past her, counting ten paces to the south. Finally, mustering the courage, he turned again, walked back to her and stopped. Raising her sunglasses to her forehead, she looked at him, revealing a splash of freckles across her nose and cheeks.

"Move along, sonny," she said, firmly.

He turned north again, counted ten paces, pivoted, and returned. Her somewhat conservative, one piece, royal blue swimsuit didn't cover her freckled, shoulders, which were turning pink.

Standing in front of her, he said, "I've been told that light skinned people shouldn't spend a lot of time in the sun."

She placed her sunglasses atop her thick, auburn hair. Her eyes smiled, though her face didn't. "Haven't you also been told that children should be seen, not heard?"

"Actually, I have." After a slight bow, he turned and walked ten paces south. Returning, he stood in front of her again.

She lifted her sunglasses again. "What?"

He said nothing.

"Now you're getting creepy."

"I just wanted to be seen, not heard."

She stifled a laugh. "You're blocking my sun."

Taking that as an invitation, he plopped down in the sand beside her and looked out at the water. She continued pretending to read.

"My name's Mike—Mike Harrison," he ventured, looking up at her.

She put down her book and, after a 'Lord, help me' look toward the sky, extended her hand. "Debbie Blanco."

"You don't look Italian." He didn't let go of her hand.

She showed him her left hand. "I'm not, but my husband is."

He dropped her hand and looked around. "Is he here?"

"No." She pointed at the ocean and smiled. "He's about five thousand miles that-a-way."

"Where's that?"

"Okinawa. Third Marine Division. His name is Frank Blanco. Gunnery Sergeant Francis Blanco, lifer, USMC." The smile disappeared as she saluted the ocean. "Semper Fi."

"You don't sound happy about being married to a Marine."

"Probably be more so if he was ever home." She looked down at him. "Do you have a story, or are you just a stalker?"

"It's a long story—and I'm not a stalker."

"I'm sure all stalkers say that. How old are you, eighteen—nineteen?"

"Eighteen."

"Where are you from? Alabama? Tennessee?"

"Ohio."

"Your accent sounds...southern."

"Well, I'm from *southern* Ohio. We don't say 'y'all'; we say 'you'uns'."

She laughed. "Does your mommy know you're here?"

"Don't have one."

"I'm sorry." She studied his face, looked out at the ocean, and then back at him. "Listen, I'm having a party tonight. Wanna come?"

"Sure. Where and when?"

She turned and pointed. "See that tall pine and the shorter one next to it with the dead branches?"

"Yeah."

"See the house in between?"

"Green roof?"

"Yep. That's where I live." She tore a page from her paperback and scribbled down an address. "Seven or so." She returned to her book.

It was nearly seven-thirty when he arrived at her small ranch-style house and parked on the street. He noticed a '58 Oldsmobile under the carport but saw no other vehicles near the property. After re-checking the address, he knocked.

She greeted him in a thin, green, cotton dress that stopped a few inches above her knees. Large, white buttons adorned the front, top to bottom, which led him to recall a conversation he'd had with his friends, John and Tim. They had come up with the theory that going on a date with a girl who was wearing a dress that buttoned down the front significantly improved your chance of scoring. Mike had never had the opportunity to test the theory.

"Am I early?" he asked, noticing that the dress matched her eyes.

She grinned. "Right on time. Something to drink?"

"Uh…beer, I guess."

"Come on. You're just in time to watch the sunset."

She opened two bottles of Schaefer and handed him one, saying, "The one beer to have when you're having more than one." Seeing that he was puzzled, she said, "That's their slogan—and jingle." She sang it to him and laughed. "I could be arrested for contributing to the delinquency of a minor."

On her back patio, she indicated a high-backed wooden bench, and said, "Sit." He sat; she sat next to him. They sipped their beers, occasionally glancing at each other, but not talking. The sun sank into the ocean two beers later.

He looked around. "Your other guests...?"

She shook her head and snapped her fingers. "Shucks, I forgot to invite anybody else. You disappointed?"

He shrugged but didn't reply.

"Ready for another beer?"

Confused, he drained his bottle and handed it to her.

When she came back, she sat closer to him. "Getting chilly," she said. "I should get a sweater." Without waiting for a response, she leaned in and kissed him on the lips.

He kissed her back, but feeling himself respond, pulled away. "That's not what I came here for."

She stood up and, hands on hips, glared down at him. "Just what the hell did you come here for?"

"Uh...companionship, I guess. Maybe I should leave." He stood up.

She shook her head and laughed, waving him back to the bench. "You a twink?"

'A what?"

"You know—homo...gay...queer?"

"No. Just the opposite, I guess. My life would probably be simpler if I was."

"So, what's your story?"

"It's a long one."

"So, I decide to cheat on my husband—for the first time *ever*, believe it or not—and I get picked up by an eighteen-year-old what—virgin who wants to stay pure?"

He stared at a crack in the concrete floor. "Not a virgin; far from pure."

She smiled, mussed his hair, and sat back down.

"Should I leave?" he asked.

"Of course not. Now you have me intrigued, and I want to hear your long story since I apparently have all night. Let me get my sweater."

Four more beers each later, she held up her hand. "Enough. We'll have to take this up in the morning. I'm too buzzed to concentrate, and your story is starting to confuse me."

Too drunk to argue, he gazed at her through glassy eyes. "I can stay, then?"

"Of course you can stay. In fact, I insist on it, since you're not of legal drinking age in California, and you're plastered."

"Thank you," he slurred.

Tuesday, May 29

A headache woke him up at six AM, and seemed to be getting worse by the minute. At six-thirty, he gave up and eased himself out of bed. That vodka hangover from last summer was nothing compared to this.

After quietly rummaging around in the kitchen, he found the coffee and made a pot. Wearing only swim trunks, he poured himself a cup and headed to the beach. It was cool and foggy, but pleasant and deserted—except for the gulls.

He finished his coffee and waded out to where the cold water was waist deep and lapping up to his chest. Looking back toward the beach, he didn't see the huge wave that broke just behind him and knocked him flat on his face. As he stood up, the undertow swept his feet from under him and his face was in the water again.

Spluttering and wiping salt water from his eyes, he waded ashore, found his coffee cup, and headed back to the house, some two hundred yards away. Debbie was standing on the patio with a glass of red liquid in each hand, and a beach towel over her shoulder.

As he grabbed the towel, she said, "Bloody Marys, best hangover cure known to man—or woman."

He took one and gulped half of it. His lips, tongue, and throat burned.

"Too spicy?" she asked.

Eyes watering, he shrugged and downed the rest.

"How about bacon and eggs?" she asked.

"No bacon. But eggs and toast sound good."

"You Jewish?"

"Uh…no. Why?"

"I thought everybody liked bacon."

"If I tell you why I don't eat bacon, will you promise not to laugh?"

"Sure."

He told her; she laughed.

As they ate breakfast, Mike asked, "What if word gets back to your Marine husband that I stayed overnight? Will he hunt me down and beat me to death with his bare hands?"

She giggled. "He might if he finds out. But I don't even know any of my neighbors, so there's no reason for anyone to say anything."

"How long have you lived here?"

"Eight years."

"And you don't know any neighbors?"

"Waved at one of them once, but she didn't wave back." She laughed. "Actually, since this is the only house on the block that isn't vacation property, I don't have any regular neighbors."

"But still, if I had an awesome looking wife like you, and was going to be gone for a long time, I think I'd maybe have a buddy look after her—if not to see if she was cheating—at least to make sure she was all right."

She raised an eyebrow. "I look awesome?"

"You know you do."

"Thanks, but I don't think Frank would do that. And if he did I could always say it was my little brother, Sean, who's about your age."

"Where's he live?"

"He's just finishing his freshman year at USC. He rarely visits." She took their empty plates to the kitchen and brought more coffee. "Now, about your story."

"I wanna hear yours, first. How'd you end up with a Marine?"

She took a sip and stared out the window at the ocean. "He wasn't a Marine when I fell in love with him. We grew up together in Riverside, up near L.A. Dated the last two years of high school. He enlisted the day after graduation and shipped off to Korea right after infantry training. Ever heard of the Chosin Reservoir?"

"Nope."

"Well, it's part of the Marine Corps legend—along with the halls of Montezuma, the shores of Tripoli, and the sands of Iwo Jima."

"I've heard of those places."

"Anyway, Frank was at the Chosin Reservoir—the 'Frozen Chosin', as the Marines call it. Came back with a Bronze Star, frostbite, and a different personality, but I married him anyway." She shook her head. "He went there a PFC and came back a Sergeant E-5, so he decided to re-enlist. Didn't make me happy, but..." She sipped and stared some more. "His first duty station after Korea was Camp Pendleton, which is right up the coast, so I convinced him to buy this place—with my parents' money."

"What year did you get married?"

"Fifty-three. Our eighth anniversary is coming up soon."

"No kids, huh?"

"No. He brought it up once, but I insisted we wait 'til he's home more—which may be never, since he seems to want to be gone all the time."

Mike thought about his father. "His personality changed, you said?"

"That's part of how he changed. He didn't want to be home. There were other things—nightmares, bouts of heavy drinking, sitting and staring as if he was in a daze or something. After a couple of years, the nightmares dwindled, the drinking moderated, but he still didn't wanna stay here. Marines get orders to different places every couple of years, but, aside from Camp Pendleton, he had options such as MCRD, which is five miles from here."

"What's that?"

"Marine Corps Recruit Depot. That's where they train kids your age how to kill, swear, and talk dirty, with efficiency." She smiled and sipped. "He could have been a drill instructor there. Or, he could have gone to Barstow, which is only a couple of hundred miles from here, or Twenty-Nine Palms, which is even closer, and he could have come home on some weekends. Instead, he's gone to Quantico, Virginia; Camp Lejeune, North Carolina; and Okinawa. He'll be there 'til August."

"He could choose?"

"Not always. But as a senior NCO, he's had some options—especially at re-enlistment time."

"You couldn't go with him?"

"I could have gone to North Carolina and Virginia, but he didn't ask me to. And…I wasn't really interested. I like it here."

"That's sad."

"Yeah. I'm thinking about divorcing him when he comes back. I'll feel guilty if I do, but I don't think he'll make a big deal of it. Shit, for all I know, he could have himself a little Okinawan girl, doing his laundry and taking care of his other*…needs*, right now. I've heard stories." Even her frown was sexy. "Sometimes I think he'd rather be back in the Chosin Reservoir, freezing his ass off, watching his buddies die, and fighting for Corps, Country, and God, than be here with me. You ever heard of a place called Vietnam?"

"No."

"Well, I don't know much about it, myself, except that North Vietnam is communist, and South Vietnam is democratic, they're fighting, and we have advisors over there teaching the South Vietnamese soldiers how to fight. Anyway, that's where Frank wants to go when he gets back from Okinawa."

Mike looked out at the beach where a blonde woman, with a big black dog on a leash, was playing tag with the waves. "None of my business, but does he...hit you when he is home?" he asked, thinking about his parents.

"No. I don't think I'm important enough to him for that. And he knows I'd murder him in his sleep if he did."

"Your parents...?"

"Died in a car accident on the PCH up near Morro Bay two years ago. Sandwiched between two semis in the fog. Frank didn't even come to the funeral. Said he couldn't get leave, but I never believed that."

"And you don't see much of your brother?"

"Being born ten years apart, we don't have much in common. Might see him during the summer, might not."

"Friends?"

"Not many. I work at the MCRD PX a couple of days a week. Go out for a beer once in a while with the other employees."

"I could be your little brother for a few days."

As she poured more coffee, her face lit up. "Yes, you could. Hey, I could take you sightseeing."

"What days do you work?"

"Wednesdays and Fridays, but I'll call in sick. We could go to Disneyland, Knott's Berry Farm, Catalina Island..."

"Maybe a Dodger game," he interjected.

"Sure. I don't care that much for baseball, but I could eat hotdogs and pretend we're on a date."

"Brothers and sisters don't date."

"I said we could pretend. But now, I want to hear your story, starting over and leaving nothing out. You rambled and went back and forth a lot last night, and I had trouble concentrating. I'll make us another Bloody Mary and we'll go out to the beach."

"Didn't you get enough sun yesterday?" He looked at her red face and shoulders.

"Don't start with that shit. You're supposed to be my little brother, not my father.

"Better slap on some sunscreen, Sis."

"Fine."

On the beach, he slathered Coppertone on her back and shoulders, handed her the tube, sat down in the sand, sipped his drink, and looked out at the ocean. She dropped down beside him and looked expectantly at him.

Tuesday, August 1, 1961
Scioto County, Ohio

As he turned left onto Hope Run, Mike looked at his watch. It was eight-thirty, giving him only a half hour to be in the locker room, dressed, and ready for practice. He hit second gear and punched it, peeling rubber, and enjoying the throaty roar of the twin glass-packed mufflers on his '55 Chevy.

'Tossin' and Turnin'' by Bobby Lewis, a song that had topped the charts for nearly a month, was playing on WIOI. He switched to WNXT and caught the baseball scores. The Cincinnati Reds, looking for their first National League pennant since 1940, had beaten the

Chicago Cubs 5-4. A four-run seventh inning, highlighted by Jerry Lynch's two-run pinch double, had spelled the difference. The Reds were still a half game behind the L.A. Dodgers.

In the American League, Roger Maris and Mickey Mantle were chasing Babe Ruth's record of sixty home runs, set in 1927. Maris now had forty and Mantle thirty-nine.

Mike listened absently to the news. Politicians were still talking about the failed Bay of Pigs invasion in Cuba. Also, there was a crisis brewing in Berlin. Apparently, the East Germans were planning to put up a barrier in East Berlin to keep their citizens from escaping to the West. The Cold War was heating up. So far, it had been a rough first year for President Kennedy.

He switched back to WIOI, only to hear the obnoxious Blackburn's Market commercial.

In the locker room, his focus was not on baseball, rock 'n' roll, or world events. It was on football, as today was the first day of practice at Scioto Central High School, home of The Fighting Shawnee. Mike, going into his senior year, had been the star running back on last year's 7-2 team, which had finished third in the South Central Ohio Conference, behind the powerhouses Waverly and Wheelersburg.

At 6'2", 200, he was ten pounds heavier than last year when he had rushed for 1250 yards, scored 16 touchdowns, and caught a dozen passes for over 200 yards, in a 'three yards and a cloud of dust' offense that would have made Woody Hayes proud.

His goal this season was to make Woody Hayes proud enough to offer him a scholarship to The Ohio State

University. He'd had visits from several Ohio schools, last year, but no offers.

The temperature outside was already in the eighties, with the high humidity making it feel even hotter. Inside the locker room, it seemed just as hot, and the stale jock strap and dirty sock smell lingering from last year, combined with the smell of a roomful of sweaty teenage bodies, was already assaulting his nose. It was going to get worse as the season progressed.

He looked around the room, quickly counting heads. Fifty kids, trying out for the forty spots on the team. He saw only one person he didn't recognize—the guy sitting in the corner by himself, looking almost too old to be a student. The girls would surely find him attractive, with his dark wavy hair, olive skin, Roman nose, and pearly white teeth. *Movie star good looks.*

As Mike contemplated introducing himself, the coach walked in and bellowed, "What died in here?" Everyone chuckled; no one answered.

Paul Hauser had been the football coach at Scioto Central since the school initiated the program in 1957. After the team struggled the first two seasons, he was able to turn it around, and post winning records the last two years.

Hauser, who had been a running back at Ohio University in the early fifties, was thirty years old, but his rapidly thinning hair and protruding stomach made him look older.

The coach looked around the room and said, "Listen up." Everyone got quiet. "One of these years, we'll have funding—and enough bodies turning out—to have a JV team. We have pads and practice jerseys for all of you, but right now, we have forty uniforms, which means we'll have to cut some of you. However, with the expected dropouts, injuries, etc., I'm sure everyone in this room, who wants to play football, will get the chance before the season's over."

He cleared his throat and continued. "As most of you know, Billy Sorenson, our quarterback the past two years, has graduated. But fortunately, we have a replacement that will allow us to do some different things with the offense, and maybe—just maybe—compete with Waverly. Tony, would you stand up?"

The 'movie star' stood, shrugged, and looked up at the ceiling. He was taller than Mike, and lanky, looking to be about 6'4", maybe 180 pounds.

"This is Tony Duvardo. His family just moved here from Detroit. Fortunately, they bought a house in our school district, which means we get him for his senior year. Tony was an outstanding quarterback up there, and is already being recruited by Michigan, OSU, and several other big-time schools."

The players applauded politely as Tony sat down. The coach continued, "This will allow us to change to more of a pro-style offense. Long story short, we'll throw the ball more."

Mike was beginning to feel sick. More throwing meant less running, which meant fewer opportunities for him to impress college recruiters. He glanced at John Breech, a senior and a three-year starter at both offensive and defensive tackle. John shrugged and mouthed, *"What the hell...?"*

John, who had been Mike's close friend since first grade, was also looking for a football scholarship. At 6'4",

240 pounds, his blocking from the left tackle spot had been one significant reason for Mike's success at running back.

Last year's backup quarterback, Tim Crabtree, was staring at the floor, his face expressionless. Tall and thin, his best sport was basketball, but he had been counting on getting a shot at the starting quarterback job. He had been an adequate, if not spectacular, backup to Billy Sorenson the past two years. He and Mike were also close friends.

"Now," the coach continued, "the Full House T formation we used in the past will be replaced by the Pro Set, using a split end, a flanker, and two running backs. The playbook is going to be expanded considerably. Everyone who makes the team will be expected to know every play." He looked around the room, allowing his gaze to fall on Mike, and stay there. "The other piece of good news is that the Pied Piper is with us for another year."

Everyone looked at Mike, who met the coach's gaze; no one laughed; several players applauded.

The coach didn't look away. "Remember, you're playing for the name across the front of your jersey, not the number. Now let's get out there and get started. Two laps, some conditioning exercises, and we'll get down to business."

Thirty-four-year-old Matt Riley was the basketball coach at Central. He was also the assistant football coach even though he had played no college football. He was popular with the students, especially the girls. In appearance and in mannerisms, he reminded Mike of the actor, Paul Newman.

After warm-ups, he took Mike aside. "I know you haven't been asked to do much pass blocking, but with the new system, that's going to be a big part of your duty as fullback."

"Whatever it takes, Coach." Mike looked at the ground. "But, why the hell does he single me out like that? I've always been a team player."

"He knows that. But what I've noticed is that the two of you seem to enjoy antagonizing each other. Coach Hauser is fully aware that we won't win this thing without you."

"I think we can win it without the new guy. Just handing him the job and building the playbook around him, seems…unfair, and…reckless."

"It's possible we'd win without him, with all the returning starters we have. But he gives us a much better chance. We all love Tim, but I've seen this kid throw a football. I swear to God, Mike, I've never seen anyone throw it as well. If we keep him healthy, we're going to put up some big scores."

Great. He looks like a movie star and plays quarterback like Johnny Unitas.

Coach Riley glanced at Coach Hauser, who was looking their way. "Look, Mike, I know you're thinking you're getting screwed here, but this is the offense of the future—at all levels. At some point, even Woody Hayes is going to have to start throwing the ball more. Even *he* is going to need a fullback who can pass block. And…I hear he's aggressively recruiting this kid."

"It is what it is, Coach." Mike glanced up at a small dark cloud that was about to obscure the sun, and then concentrated on a dandelion in front of his feet.

"By my calculations, you got your hands on the ball about twenty-five times a game last year. That number will be lower, but not as low as you might think. We'll still have to run the ball; just not as much. That third running back will now be a wide receiver, and there are pass plays that involve you coming out of the backfield."

Mike simply nodded.

"Mike, we have a good team, but we're loaded with seniors. This'll be our last shot for several years."

"It'll be fine, Coach. You don't have to convince me of anything." He jerked a thumb over his shoulder in Coach Hauser's direction. "And you can tell him I'll be the least of his problems."

"Atta boy. And, if you put on a few more pounds, some schools just might be looking at you as a linebacker. That might be your best shot at OSU, anyway, since they already have a pretty good stable of running backs. Any way you can get there, right?"

Mike nodded. "Any way I can get there, Coach."

"Let's get to work." The coach clapped him on the back.

Saturday, August 5, 1961

Another hot and humid day.

Taking a break from cutting grass, Mike had WNXT blaring the Reds' game on his transistor. As Cincinnati came to bat in the bottom of the second, trailing the Pittsburgh Pirates 6-0, play-by-play announcer, Waite Hoyt, was speaking in the monotone he always used when the team was losing. "Have fun; have a Burger", he said dourly, referring not to a hamburger, but to a popular local beer.

Gus Bell was in the process of grounding out to the second baseman when the phone rang. Remembering that the Bryants were supposed to have a phone installed today, Mike assumed it was Mary.

"Hi there," he heard her say.

"Oh, you got the phone, huh?"

"Yep."

"No shit? That's great."

"Don't talk dirty, but yeah, it is. Just think, when I met you, we had no electricity. Five years ago, no indoor plumbing. Now we have a telephone, and I can call and pester you anytime I want. Hey, listen, do you wanna come over and help us can beans? We just picked a jillion of them."

"I thought maybe you wanted me to come over for a couple of hours of wild sex."

She laughed and asked innocently, "Is that an appropriate amount of time for that sort of thing?"

"I think so."

"Well, you can dream about it, but in the meantime..."

"I'll be there in about an hour."

If asked, he would have trouble describing his relationship with Mary. While John and Tim were his close friends, he spent more time with her than either of them. She wasn't his girlfriend. They'd never dated, or even kissed, but, to everyone who knew them, they were a couple.

Mary was easily the most attractive girl in school, with her big brown eyes, long dark hair, and slim figure, which was now filling out in the right places. Her parents, Joe, and Rose belonged to a conservative, 'old time' Baptist church. They didn't allow her to wear makeup—or dresses that exposed much more than her ankles. And, going on a date was out of the question. Mike was attracted to her as more than a friend, but, fearing her father's wrath, he wasn't sure how to handle it.

Mary's parents had moved to Scioto County in 1948. They farmed—actually gardened—about five acres, mostly hillside—a mile up Hope Run from Mike's house. In addition, her father worked at the stove foundry in Portsmouth.

Mary and Mike always sat together on the bus, until he finally got his '55 Chevy. After he got his car, her father reluctantly permitted her to ride to school with him. Once football season was over, she also rode home with him. "As long as you bring her straight home," her father had said.

Mary was a straight A student and Mike, though not a terrible student himself, used her as a tutor and a motivator to keep his own grades up. They had spent eight years of grade school together, and—at her insistence—had taken nearly every class in high school together.

Exactly an hour after their phone conversation, he headed north on Hope Run toward Bryant Holler. On the way, he listened to Portsmouth's dawn to dusk top forties radio station, WIOI, playing Del Shannon's 'Runaway', followed by what he knew would be ten minutes of commercials. He tuned to WNXT. The Reds were losing 10-5 in the seventh inning. He passed the run-down Mail Pouch Tobacco barn on the right and turned left onto the dirt road leading to Mary's house, carefully avoiding the ruts and potholes.

Bryant Holler was narrow for the first hundred yards and then opened up into the bowl-shaped area that was the Bryants' property. There was no garage or driveway. The dirt road, which stopped at the front yard, had been widened to allow the school bus room to turn. The Bryants' '53 Ford Country Squire station wagon was parked in front of the house, a large, white, two-story, in need of paint. The house had a homey appearance, though, with both a front and back porch, a large flower garden in the front yard, and evergreen shrubs around the front porch.

There was no one in the front of the house, but Mike heard conversation and laughter coming from the back, as Sam, the family beagle, came to greet him. He scratched Sam behind the ears and followed him, finding the whole family on the back porch.

Mary and her six-year-old brother, Joshua, were sitting on the edge of the high porch with their bare feet dangling. Between them was a bushel basket nearly full of green beans. They were snapping and stringing the beans, throwing the scraps in one bucket, and the beans in another. Mary was correcting Joshua, who seemed to get confused as to what went where.

Farther down the porch, her fourteen-year-old sister, Becky, her twelve-year-old brother, Jimmy, and her nine-year-old sister, Esther, were working on another basket of beans, while three-year-old Mark played in the dirt below Mary's feet. On a large table next to the back door, her mother, Rose, was stuffing quart Mason jars full of green beans, as her father, Joe, added water, topped off each jar with a teaspoon of salt, and screwed on the lids.

Mike waved his hello to the family, sat down next to Mary, nudged her, and began snapping beans. Without a word, she nudged him back, beamed at him, and continued working.

He looked out at the rear of the property. The flat area was larger here than in front—about two hundred feet. Dozens of chickens were pecking at the grass in a fenced area beyond the large back yard. Inside the fence was the chicken coop. To his right ran a creek, which emptied into the larger Hope Creek that snaked its way along Hope Run. On the other side of the creek were a small barn, a corncrib, and a hog pen with a large hog lying underneath a black oak tree. The hog would be dead and hanging in the smokehouse by Thanksgiving weekend.

Mike had participated in the hog butchering last year; it wasn't a pleasant undertaking. First, Joe shot the hog between the eyes with a rifle and then quickly slit his throat to bleed him out. Then, laying the hog on a wooden platform, they poured boiling water on him and scraped off the hair with kitchen knives. Using a chain hoist and a singletree, they hung him upside down by his Achilles tendons on a 2x8, which extended out from the front of the smokehouse. There, he was gutted, quartered, salted, and hung inside. Not much was wasted. The feet were pickled and the head was used to make souse meat which was commonly referred to as head cheese. Nauseated by the whole process, Mike hadn't knowingly eaten any pork products since.

"You should have been here when we castrated him," Mary had told him with an impish grin. "You've probably never heard anything squeal that loudly."

"I'm sure I'd squeal loudly, too," Mike had retorted.

Above the hog pen and the barn was a large cornfield. To his left was the smokehouse sitting atop the cellar, which had been cut into the hillside. Above that was a large potato patch, an area containing other vegetables and more corn.

Rose Bryant looked up from her work, smiled at Mike, and asked, "How are you, Michael?" She was tall, slim, in her late thirties, with long, dark hair that was beginning to show some gray. Mike recalled how beautiful she had been when he first met her nearly eleven years ago. Six kids later, she was still attractive. He also recalled that, from day one, she had treated him as one of her own.

"Fine, Mrs. Bryant," he replied. "How about you?"

"I think I'm getting a touch of arthritis, but I'll be fine, God willing." She showed a hand with two crooked fingers. Her eyes sparkled.

Joe Bryant looked up from his work. "Thanks for comin', Mike." Tall and thin, he reminded Mike of Henry Fonda in *The Grapes of Wrath*. He was wearing sweaty work clothes and an even sweatier cap with a John Deere logo. Of course, he had no use for a John Deere or any other tractor, as it would tip over if one tried to plow the hillside with it. The Bryants had two mules that they used for plowing and hauling.

Mike thought about this past spring when he had tried his hand at using the turning plow. It was hard work and an embarrassment to him that Mary could do it better. The mules responded immediately and efficiently to her commands of 'Gee' and 'Haw', but ignored those same commands from him, forcing him to keep letting go of one handle or the other to pull on the reins. Her cuts were straight and parallel; his weren't. She gloated; he quit plowing.

"No problem, sir," Mike replied. "I probably would have come by anyway. Always nice to see you folks." It was true, and it wasn't just to see Mary. He enjoyed hanging out with the family and playing ball with the kids.

"Same here, Mike." Joe glanced at Mary and then looked back at Mike. "I was thinkin' maybe you could get your two buddies together and help me with a job."

"Dad…no!" Mary interjected. "I didn't ask him over for that. Besides, he has football practice."

"It won't hurt to ask him, Mary. He can always say 'no', and there won't be no hard feelins'." He re-focused on Mike. "No Saturday practice, right?"

"Not unless Coach decides to change it."

"We have what we call an association meetin' of several of our churches, and it's my job to set this thing up. One of our members has a piece of flat pasture jist across the river in Kentucky we can use. We gotta clean it up, cut down some small bushes, and build a stage. We'll need to set up a tent to use as a concession stand to sell pop and sandwiches—and to let people get outta the hot sun from time to time.

"This thing's comin' up the 17th through the 20th of this month, so I gotta git goin' on it. I have a couple church members lined up to help with the carpenter work. I figger with three healthy football players with strong backs, we can probably knock it out in a day. I'm thinkin' this comin' Saturday—week from today."

Mike looked sideways at Mary, who looked back and shrugged. "I'll talk to John and Tim and see what they have to say. I'm sure they'll help as long as it doesn't interfere with football." He dropped a bean down Mary's back. She squirmed, shook it out the bottom of her shirt, and backhanded him on the shoulder. Her mother looked up and smiled.

"The church has allowed me sixty bucks to pay you and your friends for this," Joe continued. "It ain't a lot, but twenty bucks apiece should come in handy."

Mike nodded. "Gas money. I'll check with the guys and let you know."

With the baskets empty, Mike got up to leave.

"Stay for supper, Michael," Mrs. Bryant said. "We'll be eating in about an hour."

"Thanks, but I need to get home in case Dad calls. He may need me to work tonight. Said he had an employee he might have to send home sick. Some other time, though?"

"Anytime, Michael, but wait a minute." She went into the kitchen and returned several minutes later with a large paper bag. "Some roasting ears, beans, and tomatoes. Healthy eating."

"Thank you Ma'am." He hugged her and waved at the family.

Jimmy caught up with him in the front yard. "Did you hear they're starting grade school football next year?"

"Yeah, I heard about that."

"Well, I wanna try out for quarterback. You think you could work with me a little bit on that. I can't seem to throw a decent spiral."

"You *really* think your dad'll let you play football?"

"Well, a lot of the practice is during school hours, and I have a whole year to convince him." He put his hand on Mike's shoulder and grinned. "You could help me with that, too."

Mike looked him up and down. Jimmy was tall for a twelve-year-old, but skinny. “What are you, 5’10”, maybe 130 pounds, soaking wet? Maybe you should concentrate on basketball.”

“I can gain some weight.”

“Let’s see your hand span.” Mike put his left hand up to compare it with Jimmy’s right. Mike’s hand measured just over 9 inches, spread from the tip of his thumb to the tip of his little finger. To his surprise, Jimmy’s hand span was longer. “Definitely a quarterback, which I’m not. But I’ll show you what I know. Do you have a football?”

“Just the one you gave me a couple of years ago, but it’s pretty well shot; won’t hold air. I thought maybe you’d bring one.”

“Hard to throw a spiral with a football that won’t hold air.”

“I know.”

“Well, next year’s a long way off, but it won’t hurt to get an early start.” Mike patted him on the shoulder. “I’ll bring a good football.”

Mike was back on Hope Run, heading home, and listening to Sam Cooke doing ‘Cupid’. Looking in his rearview mirror, he noticed a red Corvette convertible coming up quickly behind him. As it got closer, he recognized Tony Duvardo, who honked twice and signaled him to pull over.

He found a spot where they could pull off the narrow road, got out, and walked back to the Corvette. Tony sat smugly behind the wheel.

“Yours?” Mike asked.

“Yeah. It’s kind of my bribe for not making a fuss about moving to this backwater.”

"New?"

"Yep, '61." He got out and opened the hood. "Fuel injected 283, 316 horse. It's really quick. I guess Dad got a deal since it's the end of the model year."

"What does your dad do for a living?"

"Oh, he's a big-wig at the steel mill."

"Where do you live?"

Tony pointed his thumb north, over his shoulder. "All the way at the end of Hope Run."

"Oh, the ritzy houses by the golf course?"

"Yeah."

"Different world, almost." Mike looked under the hood. "Pretty sweet. Probably get laid a lot, driving around in this thing."

"No back seat, but I'll figure something out," Tony replied, with a wink that Mike found obnoxious. "Wanna take a ride?"

"Can't, really. I need to get home. May have to work tonight."

"Where's work?"

"My dad owns a bowling alley in Portsmouth."

"Oh, Harrison Bowl? I drove by it after I picked up my car this morning."

"Some other time, then."

Mike drove away thinking he should be nice to his quarterback. There was something about the guy he couldn't bring himself to like, though. *Big city attitude? Maybe. And he talks funny.*

The phone was ringing as he walked through the front door. It was his father.

"Just as I thought, I had to send Andy home—hell of a summer cold, I guess. Sicker'n a dog. We're busier than I thought we'd be, and I'm having some problems with lane three."

"I'll be there in about a half hour, Dad."

Harrison Bowl was busy for a Saturday afternoon in August. As Mike walked in, he noticed eight of the ten lanes were running, with only lanes two and three not in use. The cool air was a sharp contrast from the hot, humid air outside. *Probably why it's busy.*

Marsha Christensen, the bartender/cook, was busy in the kitchen. His dad was in the process of giving out lane two to a teenage couple. "Mike, you wanna look at three or take care of the counter?" was his father's greeting.

"I'd rather fix a pinsetter than smell stinky shoes." Mike crinkled his nose.

"They don't stink if you spray them right."

Without replying, Mike headed for the back where he was greeted by the familiar *clack, clack* of AMF 8230 pinsetters in operation. Of the ten pinsetters, number three was the lemon, as it repeatedly malfunctioned.

It didn't take long to diagnose the problem. A typical AMF pinsetter would hold 20 or 21 pins. With 10 on the pin deck, there would be 10 or 11 being fed to the top by a large pin wheel, which was the source of the clacking noise. The pins would then be dropped onto a conveyer belt and distributed to the proper position. The problem with three was that the pin distributor, which ran along an almost triangular track, was not feeding the pins properly into the spotting cups, resulting in a massive pile-up at the top.

Mike climbed on top of the machine, cleared the pile of pins, and moved the distributor two teeth farther along on the track, ran it around the track by hand several times, and then tightened the clutch. He cycled the machine with the reset button; it seemed to work fine. After running it through a half dozen more cycles without a problem, he cleaned the grease off his hands and headed back up front.

"I think it's good, Dad. May need to replace the distributor belt. I can do that tonight if we're not too busy." he said.

"You know...if this football thing doesn't work out, you can make a living as a pinsetter mechanic."

Mike responded with a short laugh. "It could come to that."

"I'm serious. Maybe working for me wouldn't be that great, since I can't afford to pay a good mechanic, but in a bigger house, you could make 150-200 bucks a week—with benefits. Of course, you'd have to move to a big city like Columbus or Cincinnati, but you'd make close to what I make busting my ass here eighty hours a week."

"You like it, though. I don't." *Can't wait to get rid of me?*

"Yeah. Better get your ball and throw a few on three just to make sure it's working all right. We may get busy tonight."

Though Mike had quit league bowling after one year of juniors—averaging 190 at the age of fourteen—he still bowled from time to time and was still quite good at the sport.

After throwing a few warm-up balls, he began throwing strikes. Walking back off the approach after the sixth in a row, he looked up to see Al Lewis standing behind the bench with his arms folded, and the ever-present unlit cigar in his mouth. A tall, thin, nearly bald man in his forties, he was one of the top bowlers at Harrison Bowl. He bowled league three times a week, coached the kids on Saturday morning, and was a fixture at the Saturday night pot games. He had spent many hours helping Mike with his footwork, hand position, follow-through, and other technical aspects of the game. His best advice, however, had been "Never eat your french fries with your bowling hand."

"The last five shots looked like the pins fell exactly the same way every time," he said.

"Did you ever smoke one of those things, Al?"

"Yeah, but not here; not lately. They stunk up the place and your dad bitched at me." He dropped the cigar into a trash can. "You know if this football thing doesn't work out for you..."

"Not much money in bowling, though."

Al shrugged. "There could be more than you think. Not much on the pro tour, but there are always suckers around willing to bowl for money."

"Well, if the football...*thing* doesn't work out, we'll talk."

"How's football practice?" his father asked as Mike was changing his shoes.

Mike stood, brought his fists to his chest with his forearms parallel to the floor, and leaned slightly forward. "Learning to pass block."

"Well, you know they're not gonna have him throw the ball on every down. You'll get your chances."

It was their last conversation of the day.

Though he and his father rarely talked, Mike had—primarily from conversations with his grandfather—pieced together some basic information:

Don Harrison was a World War II veteran of the U.S. Marine Corps. He had participated in the 'Island Hopping' campaign in the Solomon Islands, and received the Bronze Star for bravery, along with a Purple Heart, after taking two bullets in his left leg. He was sent home with a permanent and pronounced limp in the spring of 1943. His wife, Anna, gave birth to Mike on Valentine's Day, 1944.

Anna divorced Don in 1948, and Mike lived with her until 1950 when she died of breast cancer. Shortly before she died, Don moved back into the house on Hope Run to look after her and Mike during her illness.

He never talked about the war, the divorce, or his wife's death. Once, Mike asked him why they had gotten divorced. His reply was, "I was an asshole, and she..." He never finished the sentence, and they never discussed it again.

Though he took responsibility for Mike's basic needs, he was not Ward Cleaver. He rarely initiated a conversation, almost never displayed affection, and seemed uncomfortable in Mike's presence.

Don had gotten involved in the bowling 'culture' in the late '30's when he took a job as a pin boy at a now defunct bowling alley on Second Street in Portsmouth. Though the place stank of cigar smoke, sweat, and stale beer, the people were friendly and fun to be around. He found himself hanging out at the place even when he wasn't working. Aside from earning a nickel a line for setting pins, he was permitted to bowl free. He took advantage of that, and with a little help from some of the better bowlers, became a very good bowler. At the age of eighteen, he was carrying a 200 average in leagues with adults. In 1939, he enrolled at Ohio University in Athens.

But, with the promise of a job at the steel mill, he dropped out in 1941 and proposed to Anna. They were married Thanksgiving weekend. In March 1942, he joined the Marines.

After recuperating from his war wounds, he went back to work at the steel mill and purchased the small house on Hope Run on the G.I. Bill. Over the years, he expanded and modernized it, installing indoor plumbing, a bathroom, and a third bedroom. In 1948, the Rural Electrification Program came to Hope Run, allowing him to wire the house. He bought electric appliances and had central heating installed just in time to move out, leaving Anna and Mike in a house that was exceptionally modern for Hope Run.

By 1951, he was able to save and borrow enough money to buy a vacant building in Portsmouth big enough to house ten bowling lanes, a bar, and a kitchen. Working nearly all the hours the bowling alley was open, he did little more at home than sleep. His hard work paid off, and by 1961, business was good, as regular bowlers preferred the homey atmosphere of Harrison Bowl to City Lanes across town.

For the first few years, he took Mike to work with him when Mike wasn't in school. During those years, Mike, in addition to doing odd jobs such as taking out the trash, did most of his homework and much of his sleeping in the office. But in 1955, at the age of eleven, he insisted that he could be home alone. His father didn't object, but a year later had him working part time.

When Mike started high school, Don gave him the choice—football or baseball. "Basketball's out," he said. "We're too busy here in the winter."

Even though he had done well in Little League, and really liked baseball, Mike—primarily because of lobbying from John Breech—chose football.

With his father working long hours, Mike did all the cooking and house cleaning. While Don managed to take off work some Friday nights during football season to attend games, there were no father-son talks, no playing catch, no gestures of affection, and rarely any discussion about Mike's future.

Sunday, August 6

The Reds were in Pittsburgh for a doubleheader. After yesterday's loss, they held a slim game-and-a-half lead over the Dodgers.

Having worked late, Mike slept in until eleven. His dad was gone—presumably to work. Mike was in the process of scrambling eggs when the phone rang; it was John Breech. "Hey, did I wake you up?"

"Not really. Had a long night at the bowling alley, though."

"Why don't you come over and watch the Reds game? Tim's coming over, and I have two six-packs of Burger sitting in the fridge. It's three-two, all I could get, but it's still beer."

"What channel is the game on?"

"WLW-T in Cincinnati."

"I didn't know you could get that channel. I sure can't. All I get is snow and shadows of people."

"We moved our antenna up the hill. The reception ain't great, but it's watchable. We can even get some Columbus channels, now."

"So, where are your parents?"

"They're in Columbus visiting my aunt. Took both my little brothers with them and won't be back 'til tonight. It'll be just the three of us and twelve bottles of beer."

"See you in an hour."

John greeted Mike at the front door with a cold beer. Tim was already there, sitting on the couch with a half-empty bottle in his hand. He saluted Mike with the bottle.

It didn't take long for the conversation to turn to football and Tony Duvardo. "What do you think of our new quarterback?" John asked Mike.

"Looks capable. Sure as hell can throw a football."

"Lot better than I can," said Tim.

"That ain't saying much," said John.

Tim gave him the finger.

"Just as long as everybody realizes that you're the leader of this team, not him," John said. "The players respect you, and we don't even know this guy."

"Respect?" Mike made a face.

"Of course. If we had to go to war, we'd expect you to lead us into battle." He chuckled. "Wouldn't that be something?"

"I'd probably get us all killed. Besides, the quarterback should be the leader of a football team."

"Was Billy?"

Mike didn't reply.

John sipped his beer, watched Vada Pinson single to right field, and said, "Look, you've broken up fights, settled disputes, got guys back together with their girlfriends…"

"Got bullies to quit bullying," Tim chimed in.

"Just because I hate controversy."

"Remember the kid you beat up in fourth grade?" John said. "He pushed Mary down on the playground."

"Yeah, Billy…somebody."

"Billy Cooper. Remember you had to stay in at recess?"

"Yeah."

"Do you remember that over half the class stayed in with you 'til the teacher made us all go out?"

"I didn't ask you to do that."

"Didn't have to," said Tim.

"You also have influence with the coaches," John continued. "Remember the salt pill thing, when Hauser wouldn't let anyone drink water during practice? He said we should just take the salt pills instead. Remember what you said? You said 'I'm no scientist, Coach, but sweat has to be at least 99 percent water, and since we're all sweating like crazy, the water has to come from our bodies and it needs to be put back in'. Have you noticed that we've had water on the sidelines for every practice and every game since then?"

"That was Mary's idea, by the way. And now Hauser calls me the Pied Piper."

"Maybe it fits—and it's not really an insult. Since grade school, Mike, you've been in charge. At recess, you organized the games and made the rules. We all just did it your way."

"Didn't anybody resent that?"

"If anybody did, they didn't say anything. Of course, sometimes it bugged me when you picked Mary ahead of me."

"She was a better athlete than you," Mike smirked.

"Screw you." John chuckled. "And remember, we'd play touch football at recess, and every once in a while you'd make it a point to throw the ball to the scrawny guys who couldn't catch, just to make them feel like they were in the game? Same thing in basketball; you included everybody."

"What if I don't want to be your leader? And what's the point of this, anyway?"

"First of all, you have no choice. You're our leader; deal with it. Secondly, I don't like this new offense."

"I know. You'd rather run block so you can knock people on their asses."

"Yeah, that's true." He laughed. "But most of the guys don't like it and don't trust this new guy to run it. He'll probably be throwing the ball all over the field, throwing interceptions and shit. Remember what Woody Hayes said?"

"Refresh my memory." Mike knew exactly what he was going to say.

"He said, 'When you throw the ball, three things can happen and two of them are bad'. That's what he said. We have a good team this year, and I don't want to see it screwed up by some hotshot from Michigan. Fucker's a Catholic. I don't know why he doesn't just go to Notre Dame."

Mike shook his head. "So, I'm supposed to do what... go to Hauser and tell him to make Tim the quarterback?

"Of course not. Tim sucks."

Tim elbowed him in the ribs, causing him to slosh his beer on the couch.

"Shit, I'm gonna be in trouble," John said, as he rubbed the couch cushion with his shirttail. "But anyway, Mike, maybe you could suggest we run the ball more. Have you even looked at the playbook? It's ninety percent pass plays. It's not gonna work."

"I've memorized the playbook, and I think you're wrong," Mike said. "We'll put up a lot more points with this guy throwing the ball, and—no offense to Tim or Billy—he can throw it a lot better than anyone I've seen at this school, and even in this conference." He drained his beer. "Be glad he's not going to Notre Dame. With him as their quarterback, they'd kick our asses.

"And…I don't have nearly as much influence with Hauser at you think. In fact, he hates me. So, let's you and me just work on our pass blocking and see what happens."

John was adamant. "But you have more influence with the players than Hauser does. You get into it with him and walk off the team, most of the players go with you."

"Well, that's not gonna happen. Could you just get us another beer? I'd like to watch the ballgame."

After watching the Reds lose 9-4, Mike finished his third beer and said, "Gotta go home and take a nap. Beer makes me sleepy."

"Makes me fart," said John.

"Everything makes you fart," Tim quipped.

"Oh, I almost forgot," Mike said as he stood up. "What're you guys doing Saturday?"

John sighed and looked at the ceiling. "What're we doing Saturday, Mike?"

After he told them, Tim snickered. "Do you think that'll get you into Mary's pants?"

"No, shithead. And you don't have to do it."

"What time are we doing it, Mike?" John asked as he and Tim exchanged amused glances.

"I'll let you know. Thanks, guys."

Mike drove home listening to Curtis Lee's 'Pretty Little Angel Eyes', and thinking about Mary. When the commercials came, he switched to WNXT, as game two was getting ready to start.

He didn't take a nap. Instead, he brushed his teeth, gargled away the beer smell, grabbed a football, and headed for Bryant Holler.

The Bryant family were just piling out of the station wagon when he arrived. Home from church, he assumed.

He got out of his car, tossing the football from hand to hand. "Came to teach Jimmy how to throw a football," he said, looking Joe Bryant in the eye.

Joe stared at him, but couldn't hold back a smile. "I ain't said I'd let Jimmy play football."

"Just in case." Mike smiled back. "By the way, I got Tim and John to help me, so we're good for Saturday. What time?"

"I'll be there at six in the mornin'." He took a piece of paper from the station wagon. "Made a map. Can you read my hen scratchin'?"

Mike looked at the map. "I think I can find it."

"Okay." Joe turned to Jimmy. "Change your clothes. I'll give you an hour, and then you got work to do. But I ain't said you can play football."

The family went into the house; Mary stayed behind.

"Boy," she said. "I wish I had as much influence with Dad as you do."

"You probably have more than you realize."

"I just wish he'd join the 20th century, Mike. Just look at how the other girls dress, and then look at me." She opened her hands and looked down at her dress. "I know we don't have the money to buy me fashionable clothes, but mine are so...frumpy. My friends are too nice to say anything, but I know what they're thinking."

"What they're thinking is: 'I wish I was Mary Bryant, because she's the prettiest, sexiest, and smartest girl in school', and the guys are all thinking, 'I'd fall in love with *her* for half an hour'."

She laughed. "I thought you said that took two hours."

He put his forearm on her shoulder. "For me, not them. Listen, your parents are good people."

"I know that. But I should be allowed to go on dates. You know I've never been to a school dance."

"You don't even know how to dance."

"I've watched *American Bandstand.* I can dance."

"Oh, yeah?"

"Sure. Becky and I dance sometimes—when the parents aren't around. One day last week, we were doing the Twist; doing it just as well as those kids on TV."

"I asked your dad once if I could take you to a dance and he gave me a lecture about how dancing is immoral."

She nodded. "Prelude to the sex act, the church calls it."

"Let's dance, Mary."

She backhanded him on the shoulder. "I could be a cheerleader."

"You'd look great in one of those skimpy little cheerleader outfits."

"Yeah, well, we'll never know. Do you know what the girls call me? 'Virgin Mary'."

"I've heard that. But you know what I think? I think there are lots of girls—and guys—who are virgins and pretend they aren't. And vice versa, of course."

"So...?"

"You can't tell the players without a scorecard."

"Apparently, Eve Phillips doesn't pretend to be one. You know what they call her."

Uncomfortable now, he asked, "What?"

"They call her 'Easy Eve'. She has a reputation, you know. I'm sure you've noticed how she dresses and how she walks."

Even more uncomfortable now, he said, "Maybe she's just pretending."

She looked sharply at him. He averted his eyes.

"You slept with her didn't you?" She was glaring at him, now.

Why is it I can look my dad, teachers, and coaches in the eye and lie, but not her?

"I didn't sleep with her," he mumbled, now looking at his feet.

"Fine. You...*screwed* her."

Being that it was the first time he'd ever heard her use that expression, his first impulse was to take advantage of a rare opportunity and say, 'Don't talk dirty', but deciding that now wasn't the time to play that game, he kept looking at his shoes.

Though he'd gotten as far as third base a couple of times with Connie Parsons, he'd lost his virginity to Eve in the back seat of the Chevy after the Valley game last year. Then, after the spring dance in April, he offered her a ride home. She lived ten minutes from school, but it took them two hours to get there.

When Jimmy emerged from the house, Mary was still staring at Mike.

"All right, Mary," he said, finally looking back at her, "you can be the pass receiver and I'll show Jimmy how to throw the ball."

"Sure!" She pointed at her feet. "These are the only good shoes I own, my dress is dragging the ground, and you want me to play football."

"Well, just go change."

She glared at him again, and then turned and went inside, slamming the door behind her.

Five minutes later, she emerged in a tight pair of jeans, a tee shirt that likely belonged to Jimmy, and—quite obviously—no bra. All Mike could do was stare.

Calmly, Jimmy asked, "Where's Mom and Dad?"

"Where *are* Mom and Dad?" she corrected. "They went up the holler to pick blackberries. They were holding hands, so I figure they'll be a while."

"Good thing." Jimmy shook his head. "Those must be last year's jeans. You probably should give them to Becky. And you're stretching my shirt in the wrong places."

Mike was still gawking.

"I'll be right back," Jimmy said, as he ran into the house.

When he returned thirty seconds later, Mike was trying not to look at Mary.

"I got Becky looking out for the parents. You're welcome, Mary," Jimmy said, giving her an exasperated look. "We'll have to do this out on the road, since we can't go to the back yard, now."

"Let's play," said Mary, displaying her best fake smile.

Forcing himself to avert his eyes, Mike said, "All right, Jimmy, you hold the ball slightly to the back half, fingers on the laces." He demonstrated, and handed Jimmy the ball.

"No. Spread your index finger a little more—and your pinky. That's it. Now bring it back with your palm facing forward, and as you throw it let it go with a little flick—like you're flicking a booger off your index finger with your thumb." He threw the ball to Mary, who caught it easily.

"That's disgusting," she said as she tossed it back.

Jimmy threw several wobbly passes to Mary.

"More booger flick, Jimmy," Mike said, trying not to look at Mary.

"Yuck. Still disgusting," she said.

After a half-hour, Jimmy was throwing good spirals to Mary, who caught nearly everything he threw. Finally, she threw a perfect spiral to Mike and smiled triumphantly. "We have to quit. Jimmy and I have work to do."

"I thought your folks didn't believe in working on Sunday," Mike quipped.

Doing her best Eve Phillips impression, she sauntered up to him, breathed softly into his ear, and whispered, "*We have two mules, a cow, a pig, and some chickens. They don't know it's Sunday. They just know they're hungry.*"

He could feel her right breast brush against his right arm as she leaned closer. *"And, oh, the cow produces milk on Sunday, just like every other day of the week."*

Too flustered to respond, he was beginning to get the feeling in his groin that was about to embarrass him. As he turned to walk away she said, “Wait. There's something I've been meaning to ask you.” She leaned in, breathed softly into his ear again, and whispered, *“Some people think the Washington Monument is some sort of a phallic symbol. What do you think?”*

Even more flustered, he quickly got into the Chevy, leaving her smiling and waving as he drove off.

Mike was restless. The Reds had won the second game of the doubleheader 3-2 behind the pitching of Jim O'Toole, and maintained a half-game lead over the Dodgers. He had listened to the last three innings with his mind continually wandering back to Mary.

He turned on WIOI, which was playing an Everly Brothers oldie, ‘All I Have to Do is Dream’. He couldn't get the image of Mary in that tee shirt out of his head.

After roaming the house for twenty minutes, he clicked on the television but saw nothing that interested him. He rarely watched TV, spending his evenings either listening to a Reds game or listening to music. When the dawn-to-dusk radio stations went off the air, he had several he could listen to. Sometimes he would tune to WBZ in Boston and listen to Bruce Bradley. Sometimes it would be Dick Biondi at WLS in Chicago. Both were 50,000-watt ‘clear channel’ stations that, unlike WIOI, featured more songs than commercials.

Some nights, when the Reds weren't playing, there were other baseball games. He could listen to Bob Prince announcing the Pirates games on KDKA, or Harry Caray doing the Cardinals games on KMOX. Caray had a terrible habit of mispronouncing players' names, but, in some ways, was a refreshing change from Waite Hoyt, who could be very bland. Mike could get the Cleveland Indians games, but the American League bored him.

It was Sunday, it wasn't dark, all the ballgames were over, and he was depressed. It wasn't just carnal thoughts of Mary that was bugging him. For some reason, Sunday afternoons always depressed him. He felt like an orphan. *I wonder what it would be like to have a little brother or sister to fight with.*

"Maybe I should get a dog," he said aloud.

To un-jumble his brain, he headed out the back door to take a walk. Off to his right was the highest hill on Hope Run, nearly 300 yards up a steep, narrow path to the top. He had created the path over the years and ran it quite often to stay in shape; today he walked.

In the winter, when the trees were bare, he could see the roof of Mary's house from the top. Not in August, though. All he saw was a couple of crows halfway down the other side of the hill working on a small animal carcass, and a frightened squirrel scampering up a black oak tree.

Still restless, he went home and made himself a peanut butter and jelly sandwich, grabbed a Pepsi, and went out to the back porch. He considered calling Eve, but after today's exchange with Mary, could generate no enthusiasm for it.

He ate half his sandwich, and then threw the other half to a squirrel that was hanging out in the back yard, staring at him. After downing half the Pepsi, he went back inside, grabbed the open vodka bottle from his father's liquor cabinet, and poured himself a generous portion into a glass, adding two ice cubes and the remainder of the Pepsi. He then poured water into the vodka bottle, hoping his father wouldn't notice. Back on the porch, he looked for the squirrel. It was gone, as was the sandwich.

He downed his drink and made himself another.

Monday, August 7

Mike awoke with a severe hangover. He took four aspirin, and stood in the shower, running cold water for half an hour, before getting dressed and heading for practice.

Still nauseated after warmups, he promised his body that, if it would refrain from embarrassing him by barfing on the football field, he would refrain from putting vodka into it, ever again. Apparently, his body agreed to the deal; the nausea subsided.

The offense began by working on deep routes. Tony showed off his strong and accurate arm by hitting receivers in stride on several throws. They then worked on screen passes and draw plays, with Tony executing nearly every play flawlessly. From the chatter Mike was hearing from his teammates, he could tell they were warming up to their quarterback. After taking a screen pass all the way to the end zone, he looked at John Breech, who was giving him two thumbs up. *We have a team that can beat Waverly.*

After practice, Tony caught up with Mike in the parking lot. "Wanna take that ride in the 'Vette now."

Unable to think of an excuse, Mike said, “Fine. Let’s go. I’ll show off my Chevy tomorrow.”

“What’s so special about a ’55 Chevy?"

“You'll see. Let’s drive into town and I’ll introduce you to my Dad.”

They crossed the Scioto River at Lucasville and headed south on U.S. 23 toward Portsmouth. As soon as they hit an open stretch of road, Tony punched it. Mike watched the speedometer quickly go to 60, 70, 80, 90, and nearly 100 when Tony suddenly braked. Mike looked up.

“Highway Patrol,” Tony muttered.

Mike turned and watched as the patrol car came after them, lights flashing, siren blaring. Tony pulled over and waited.

After looking at Tony’s license and registration, the officer said, “Duvardo, huh? I heard about you. The football player from up north, right?”

Tony nodded. “Yes, sir.”

After spending five minutes in the patrol car with Tony’s documents, the officer came back. “I’m going to let you go with a warning this time.”

“Thank you, officer. It won’t happen again.”

“Make sure it doesn’t. Dead people can’t play football. And we all know the Buckeyes are going to need a quarterback in a couple of years.” He looked at Mike. “You’re Don Harrison’s boy, right?”

Mike nodded. “Yes, sir.”

“Maybe you could help him stay out of trouble.”

Mike nodded, again, but said nothing.

Tony eased the Corvette back onto the highway and quietly drove the speed limit all the way to Portsmouth.

Don Harrison was sitting behind the counter, shuffling through a stack of papers, when Mike and Tony walked into the bowling alley. No one was bowling, but the bar was busy with lunch patrons. After Mike introduced him to Tony, he said, “Order lunch. I’m buying.”

Mike walked back to the kitchen, gave Marsha their order, cheeseburgers and french fries, and then kissed her on the ear. She blushed and waved him away.

Ten minutes later, they were eating lunch at a concourse table. Don joined them. “So, how are you adjusting to living in the sticks?” he asked Tony. “Must be quite a change for you.”

“Well, I have to say it’s different, but I’ll get used to it,” Tony replied. “Great burgers, by the way.”

“Fresh ground every day from the New Boston Meat Market,” Don said. “How’s the team look?”

“Well, we’ve only had a week of practice, but there are some good players on the team.” He looked at Mike. “But...no niggers on the team, though. Those black boys can really run. Be nice to have one or two as wide receivers, at least.”

Mike glared at him. “Yeah, and I bet you wish Cotton was a monkey. We have no *Negroes* in our school, period. No colored people; no Jews that I know of; no Hindus; no Muslims; no slant-eyed Japs. Not a whole lot of Italians either for that matter—or should I say, ‘wops—or dagos’? I think we’ll be okay,” He washed down the last bite of his cheeseburger with his last gulp of Pepsi and stood up. “Gotta go, Dad; left my car at school.”

Don glanced at Tony, who was looking down at the table with a scolded child expression, and then turned to Mike. “I’m gonna need you to do some telephoning and postcard addressing this week and next.” He waved the sheets of paper. "Gotta get my bowling leagues organized. They're my bread and butter, you know."

"I know. You say that every year."

"It's true every year."

"How about I start Wednesday after practice?"

"That'll be fine. You going by Mary's house?"

"Maybe."

"Say 'hi' for me."

"Who's Mary?" Tony asked.

"Just a friend. Let's go."

"We'll take a ride in my car, tomorrow," Mike said as he got in the Chevy.

Tony drove away without hearing him start it up.

Mike drove home listening to Roy Orbison's 'Running Scared', followed by the usual ten minutes of commercials. He considered stopping by Mary's house, but decided to go home, do laundry, and take a nap.

Two hours later, after doing the laundry and skipping the nap, he parked the Chevy in front of her house.

Sam greeted him, and then bounded around to the rear of the house; Mike followed. Mary was sitting on the squeaky glider on the back porch with her long legs curled up underneath her, reading a book, and wearing her usual baggy shirt, baggy blue jeans, *and* a bra. He sat down next to her but said nothing. She looked at him, flashed the fake smile, and returned to her book.

He looked to his left at the potato patch. "Potatoes look like they're dying."

"It's August. They'll be ready to harvest in a month or so." She didn't look up.

"Whatcha reading?"

"*To Kill a Mockingbird.*" She still didn't look up.

"What's it about?"

"It takes place in the South, so I assume it's about racism." She still didn't look up.

"So, what's wrong with killing a Mockingbird?"

"Some people think it's a sin." Though she still didn't look up, he was sure she was only pretending to read, now.

"Where's the family?"

"Mom's watching her soap opera, the kids are upstairs fighting over a board game, and Dad's still at work." She looked at him warily.

"Wanna take a walk?" he asked.

Still wary, she replied, "I'll get the cow."

"Oh, Babs? You take her up to the meadow by the swimming hole, right?"

"Yeah. I promised Dad I'd take her this afternoon." She looked at the sky. "I was just waiting for a little more shade."

Babs, a large Holstein with a huge udder and four extremely long teats, emerged from the barn first. Mary followed holding on to a long chain attached to Babs' collar. "Wanna take her?" she asked, handing Mike the chain.

That was Babs' cue to head down the path leading to the meadow. Mike followed, holding on.

"Does she ever get...like...belligerent?" he asked, quickening his pace to keep up. "From the look of those horns, she could do some real damage."

"Only when she is in heat, which could happen any day now," she teased.

"Any day now?" He looked warily at the cow.

She laughed. "Ok, sissy, it'll be a while. She's actually pregnant now, so you're safe. Probably won't gore you today."

"Good."

"A lot of people de-horn their cows, but I hear it's very painful. We couldn't do that to Babs."

Their 'walk' was no more than a quarter of a mile up the holler to the meadow, where Mike hooked Babs' long chain to a stump as she began grazing in earnest.

The meadow was mostly a field of clover, with a few weeds and saplings here and there. At the bottom of the hill opposite the creek, was a cluster of tall horseweed. Behind that was a raspberry patch the Bryant family had recently picked clean.

They sat on a log by the nearly dry creek bed and silently watched Babs graze.

Mike broke the silence. "Where would Babs go if we didn't tie her up?"

"Not far. But Dad's concerned that she might wander into the woods and get herself hurt. She's not going to run away from home, though."

"Why doesn't your dad just fence this in, so you don't have to tie her up?"

"This is not even our property. Our property line ends at about that big white oak tree." She pointed.

"Whose property is it?"

"Nobody around here knows. Probably some old guy who doesn't even know he owns it; or maybe he's dead and his family doesn't want it. Dad's talked about fencing it anyway; maybe next summer. Lots of people around here use land that doesn't belong to them. We go back into the hills there and cut firewood. Dad and Jimmy hunt all over these hills during squirrel season. You don't hunt, though, do you?"

"We don't even own a gun."

"Dad has several. He let me shoot his twelve-gauge shotgun, once. My shoulder was sore for a week."

Silently, they watched Babs eat and switch flies with her tail. Recalling the summer of '55 when he and Mary—with a little help from Becky—had dammed the creek to create the swimming hole, he asked, "Been swimming lately?"

She shook her head. "Not since the fourth of July, when you went with us. Water's stagnant, anyway—and low, since we haven't had any rain lately. Besides, I never go without you."

"Why? Jimmy could keep the critters away from you."

"It's not about critters." Their eyes met; hers sparkled.

He thought about the swimsuit she had worn that first year. Even though it was baggy, formless, and very long, her father had been reluctant to allow her to wear it. The one she wore this summer wasn't much better, resembling one of the dowdy gym outfits the girls were required to wear at school. To Mike, she still managed to look sexy.

"How'd Babs get her name, anyway?" he asked.

"Oh, you remember the TV show, *The Life of Riley?*"

"Sort of remember watching it when I was little."

"There was a daughter named Barbara. They called her Babs, and, for some reason, Dad thought it was a good name for a cow."

"Kind of an insult to the TV Babs, huh."

"She'll never know."

More silence.

"What was yesterday all about?" he finally asked.

She feigned innocence. "Football?"

"No, it wasn't. You know what you did to me."

She laughed. "Sorry. But why did you think you needed me for your little lesson? You and Jimmy could have just tossed the ball to each other."

Mike thought about it for a moment. "Didn't need you; just wanted you. And it wasn't about Jimmy. It was about you and me—and Eve."

"Then why did you ask?" She sighed. "Look...what I did was stupid, and Dad would have killed me if he'd seen me."

"What would he really do? Would he hit you?"

"No. He spanked me once when I was five. I was so traumatized he promised never to do that again."

"Was it as traumatic as when I told you there was no Santa Claus?"

"Almost." She laughed. "Speaking of cruel... Anyway, he hasn't hit me since. He once told me that Grandpa—God rest his soul—used to beat him a lot. Beat him with a switch or a belt for little things like forgetting chores or not doing them satisfactorily—or quickly enough. He told me about the time Grandpa handed him a pocket knife and told him to cut a switch that would be an appropriate punishment for taking too long bringing water from the well. Dad brought back a two-foot stalk of horseweed. Grandpa punched him in the mouth. I don't think Dad ever got over that. I think he forgave Grandpa but didn't seem to want much to do with him."

"When did your grandpa die?"

"Same year as your mother—1950. February, I think. Grandma died three months later. Seemed like—with him gone—she didn't think she had a reason to live."

"That's sad. How about your mom's parents?"

"Moved back to Kentucky that same year. Mom has four brothers and two sisters back there, and—by my last count—I have twenty-five cousins. We visit once or twice a year. It's kinda depressing."

"How's that?"

"They're both in ill health. And the area itself is depressing—all the poor people. Middle-aged men dying of black lung from working in the coal mines."

"So, you basically lost all your grandparents in the same year—the same year my mom died. Why didn't I know this?"

She shrugged. "You never asked."

After a reflective pause, he asked, "So, does your dad hit the other kids?"

"Rarely. And when he does it's just a swat on the rear-end to get their attention. You've heard the mantra 'Spare the rod, spoil the child'. Disapproving looks from Dad seem to work just as well. By the way, how's your Dad?"

"He's fine, I guess; we don't talk much. Your dad was in the war, right?"

"He was drafted, but never sent overseas."

You had an uncle who died in the war?"

"Uncle Paul. He died at Anzio—in Italy. That was before I was born. How's your grandpa?"

"I should go see him; it's been a while."

"How's your new quarterback?"

"He's very good."

"He's Catholic, right?"

"Yeah, that's what I hear."

"I remember several years ago hearing that, in the Catholic religion, the priest gets to sleep with the bride before the groom does."

"Who told you that?"

"Some girl, at church. I think some people in the church still believe it."

"You know it's bullshit, right?"

"Of course, but don't talk dirty. That was when I was just learning about sex."

"Who'd you learn about sex from?"

"Same girl. Turns out she was wrong about a lot of things."

"I could teach you a couple of things."

"Teach me what you learned from Eve?"

He shook his head. "Walked right into that one."

More silence.

"So, tell me about this church thing you got me into," he finally said.

She frowned at him. "I didn't get you into a *church thing*. You could have just said 'no'."

"No, I couldn't have."

"Did you want to say 'no'?"

"Not really."

"Anyway, you're just helping set it up. You won't have to listen to any preaching, you heathen. Heaven forbid."

"I've been to church before."

"Weddings and funerals?" She rolled her eyes.

"No. I remember going with my Mom when I was little. I'd sit and squirm for an hour or so, and then we'd go for ice cream. As I remember, it wasn't so bad."

"Our church is a little different. It might be two hours if you're lucky. It might be three or four. It depends on how long they want to sing, and how many preachers want to preach. And we rarely get rewarded with ice cream."

"Why so many preachers?"

"Okay…the services at our church are only on the third Sunday of each month. The services in Ironton are the first Sunday, South Shore on the fourth, etc. So, each church has services once a month and all the preachers go to church every Sunday, and each church has its own preachers, so you have these spare preachers. Plus, each church will have more than one. They don't go to seminary school. If they decide that they are 'called' by God to preach, and the church elders agree with them, they are allowed to preach. You might have six or eight at one service, but fortunately, they won't all want to preach. So, you don't know how many are going to preach until they are done. They aren't paid, by the way, not even the Moderator of the Church.

"It seems like, with the adults, it's 'the more preachers, the better'. The kids get restless, but we get in trouble if we get too fidgety. But anyhow, the church isn't necessarily meant to be kid friendly. That's why I just stay at home and watch the kids some Sundays, and Mom and Dad go alone."

"What about Sunday School?"

"They don't believe in Sunday School. Don't believe in musical instruments in church, either. They do a thing called 'line-singing' where one person says the line and everybody else sings it. Actually, it sounds cool. You should go with me sometime."

"Is that because they don't have song books, or because they're illiterate."

She shouldered him off the log, causing him to land hard on his rear end in the grass. "No, you jackass. It's a tradition going way back to Scotland a couple or three centuries ago. Are you making fun of our church?"

"Of course not." Sitting in the grass, he smiled up at her with an expression of innocence. "Is jackass a dirty word?"

"No. It's an animal—like a mule—or a mule-headed person, like you." She smiled and then shrugged. "Might have been about illiteracy in the beginning. I should read up on it."

"Maybe I will go with you sometime, but you know I'll be looking at my watch after a couple of hours, hoping they're done before the ball game starts."

"Certainly wouldn't hurt you to go. Missing the first few innings of a game wouldn't be a disaster, either." She smiled. "You and I could go for ice cream on the way home."

"Sounds good."

"About the other thing…" She stuck out her hand and helped him off the ground. "We've been buddies since first grade. We should probably just keep it that way." She pulled him to her, and kissed him on the mouth. He felt a quick but unmistakable flick of her tongue.

He cleared his throat and quipped, "Buddies don't kiss like that."

"We do." She flashed her fake smile.

Hearing *plop, plop*, they looked out at Babs, as she fertilized the grass.

"You know, that's going to be part of your job, Saturday," she said, grinning at him.

"Cleaning up cow shit?"

"Don't talk dirty, but yes."

"I won't tell the guys 'til we get there.

Tuesday, August 8

The Reds had lost to the Cardinals, Monday night, and were now in a virtual tie with the Dodgers for first place.

After practice, Mike and Tony got into the Chevy. Tony looked down at the 'four-on-the-floor' Hurst shifter and said, "Whoa!" When Mike started it up, he heard the throbbing of the engine and the growl of the glass packed mufflers, and said, "Whoa!" again.

Mike drove out to Hope Run. "Not likely to be any cops out here," he said, as they crossed a one-lane wooden bridge. He stopped and pointed ahead at a white oak tree with a branch hanging over the road. "See that tree? That's a quarter mile from right here. Time me."

Tony nodded and looked at his watch. "Wait!" he said.

Mike revved the engine; it roared; the car shook.

Tony said, "Go!"

Mike popped the clutch; the tires screamed. Red lining every gear, he was just shifting into fourth when he passed the tree at a hundred and ten miles per hour. He braked quickly, and turned around in the Neumann's driveway, just short of another one-lane bridge that crossed the deepest part of Hope Creek.

He recalled his first 'romantic' encounter—a half-hour make-out session with the Neumann's youngest daughter, Sandy, under the bridge, in the summer of '58. It turned out to be his only such encounter with her, but it was memorable.

Sandy had graduated in May and moved out, leaving her elderly parents alone in a rundown little house a mile from their nearest neighbor.

Mike glanced at the house, seeing an older model Oldsmobile parked under the carport, but no sign of life.

He headed back toward the school, driving through the lingering smoke. "What was my time?"

"Not sure, since I was plastered to the seat back." Tony looked at his watch. "Twelve or 13 seconds, I think. What's the story with this thing, anyway?"

"It used to belong to a guy who raced it at the Raven Rock Drag Strip pretty regularly. It apparently started as a stock 265 with an automatic on the column. He had it bored out to somewhere close to 400 cubes, stroked—whatever that means—added a new manifold, three deuces, four-speed tranny, positraction rear end. I don't know a lot about engines, or cars in general—but I know it's quick enough. I had to install a new exhaust system, so I had the glass-packed mufflers put on. They don't help the car's performance, but they sound good."

"Yeah, they do."

"Anyway, the guy was killed in a boating accident on Lake White a couple years ago. His family just wanted to get rid of it. My grandfather bought it for five hundred dollars. I've heard the modifications alone cost way more than that.

"When I turned 16, I did a lot of begging and pleading. He agreed to sell it to me, on time, with the stipulation that, if I blew the engine, he'd take it back. I take him a few bucks every time I go to visit him, just to keep him happy. He would never have driven it anyway."

"Better not blow the engine, huh?"

Mike grunted but said nothing.

"Also, you shouldn't pop the clutch like that."

"Why?"

"You lose traction. Spinning wheels just burn rubber. Probably costs you a second in your quarter time. Also, with all that torque, you could do some real damage to the rear end."

"Well, I don't plan on doing any racing, anyway."

They were silent until Mike pulled up next to the Corvette in the school parking lot. As Tony opened the door, he looked at Mike and said, "Maybe we should go back out there some day and see who can get to that tree first—or the bridge."

"Maybe we should," was Mike's unenthusiastic reply. *Why do I feel the need to impress this guy, anyway?*

Wednesday, August 9

The Reds had lost again to the Cardinals, Tuesday night, and were now a full game behind the Dodgers.

After practice, Mike decided to go see his grandfather.

Tom Harrison had retired from the steel mill in 1958. He lived alone in a small house on Front Street in Portsmouth, a twenty-minute drive from the Harrison's house on Hope Run. He'd purchased the house after the '37 flood, and—with the help of his wife, Molly, and his teenage children, Margaret and Don—renovated it. Margaret married and moved to Cincinnati in 1939, the same year Don went off to college.

After Molly's death in 1947, Don suggested that Tom move in with him, Anna, and Mike on Hope Run. He declined, citing the fact that the house wasn't big enough for all of them, and that all his friends were in Portsmouth.

Mike didn't remember his grandmother, but was well aware that his grandfather still missed her. Though several women had passed through his life over the last 14 years, he had never remarried. He had just turned 68 last month, but his upright posture, full head of salt and pepper hair, and bright eyes belied his age.

He greeted Mike at the door with a handshake. "Glad you could come, Mikey."

"Sorry I haven't been by lately, Gramps."

"That's okay. I know you're busy with football. Your dad came by this morning for coffee before he went to work." He shook his head. "He sure puts in a lot of hours."

Mike shrugged. "Yeah I know, but it seems to be what he wants to do."

"You blow the engine in that car yet?" Tom asked.

"No, Gramps. It's parked in your driveway, as you can see."

"You know when they bore out an engine like that, the walls…"

"I know, I know, Gramps. We've talked about that a hundred times."

"Change the oil regularly? Check it every time you gas up?"

"Yes, sir." *Sometimes.*

"I do mean check it yourself."

"Yeah." *Rarely.*

"Remember our deal. I'm serious. If you blow that engine…"

"I remember, Gramps."

"Okay. I was getting ready to have lunch. You hungry?"

"Sure. Peanut butter and jelly?"

"Of course."

'By the way, before I forget, here's twenty on the car."

His grandfather took the bill and tossed it on the kitchen counter.

"Do you even know how much I've paid you so far?" Mike asked.

Tom tapped himself on the right temple. "I've got it all right here."

"So, how much is it?"

"I'll let you know when it's paid off. How's Mary?"

"Mary's fine. I see her about every day."

"You two getting serious?"

"Funny you should ask. We decided to just be friends."

"I had a friend like that once. Our forty-fifth wedding anniversary would have been this past June."

"So, why didn't you ever re-marry, Gramps?"

Tom finished making the sandwiches and handed one to Mike. "You know, I've dated several women since your grandmother died. Every time I kissed one of them...or anything, I felt like I was cheating on her. I haven't stopped seeing women, but I've stopped kissing them." He laughed. "Does that make any sense to you?"

Mike shook his head. "It might when I'm your age."

"You'd be lucky to have what I had."

They ate, silently.

"What about Dad and Mom?" Mike ventured. "They didn't have much, did they?"

"Every time I ever tried to talk to him about that he clammed up. He's a very troubled man—your father. I'm sure it's not easy watching your friends die in a war. Your mom used to tell me about his nightmares, but you were probably too young to remember them. I got the impression that—after the war—they still loved each other, but just didn't like each other much."

Mike nodded. "I asked him about the war a couple of times, but he wouldn't talk about it."

"All I know is that I had thirty-one great years married to your grandmother, and I'm telling you, you'd better hang on to that little girl, Mikey."

Mike finished his sandwich and stood up. "I'd better go, Gramps, or you'll have me proposing to Mary on my way home. Like I told you, we decided to be just friends—buddies."

"Doesn't work that way, Mikey."

Saturday, August 12

The Reds were now a game and a half behind the Dodgers. It was not looking good. The Dodgers were playing well, while the Reds seemed to have some issues with their pitching staff. Reporters were accusing manager, Freddie Hutchinson, of overusing his starters.

Mike picked John up at 5:15 AM, and Tim, ten minutes later.

"God, I'm sleepy," John said as he curled up in the back seat. "I was out with Carolyn 'til after midnight."

"Get any?" Tim asked.

"None of your business, but no." He sat up and slapped Tim gently on the back of the head.

"Couldn't find an extra small rubber, huh?"

John slapped him again but laughed.

"Sandy and I went to the drive-in," Tim volunteered. "Saw *The Guns of Navarone*. It was pretty good."

"You get any?" asked Mike.

"None of your business, but no," Tim replied with a grin.

"Probably didn't see much of the movie, huh?" John quipped.

"No, but it must have been good; it got awards and stuff. So, that brings us to Mikey. How did you spend your Friday night? Milking cows with Mary?"

"No, asshole. Actually, I went out with Eve. First time I'd seen her all summer."

Tim and John both snickered.

"What?"

"Guess we don't have to ask if you got any," Tim said.

"Hey, she's a nice girl; I like her."

"How many times did you like her last night?" John asked.

Mike didn't respond.

Turning onto U.S. 23, he paid the fifteen-cent toll to cross the Ohio River via the U.S. Grant Bridge.

"We're in Kentucky. Act like hillbillies," John said.

"We're already hillbillies. Crossing that river doesn't make us any different," Mike replied.

After making several wrong turns, they found the road they were looking for. "See, I was right," John said. "We should have made that turn fifteen minutes ago."

"So you were right about something for the first time in your life," Tim retorted.

"Second time. The first time was when I said you were a shitty quarterback."

"At least I won't have to worry about a football scholarship," Tim scoffed. "There are academic scholarships I can get."

"What about you, Mike?" John asked. "What if you don't get that OSU football scholarship?"

"Plan B would be to get an offer from Ohio U, or UC, or Bowling Green or somebody," Mike said after a short pause. "There is no plan C. I have zero interest in college if it doesn't involve football. I'd maybe go to Cincinnati or Columbus and get a job as a bowling alley mechanic. Dad says I can make good money at that."

"That sounds like a plan C to me," John said. "I feel the same way about college, though. If I can't play football, I'm not really interested."

They spotted Joe Bryant's station wagon parked alongside the road behind an older Ford pickup. Mike parked behind the station wagon and looked at his watch. It was nearly 6:30.

"I was 'bout to give up on you boys," Joe said as he shook hands with each of them.

"Couple of wrong turns. Sorry," Mike replied.

"No problem. More daylight makes it easier to see the cow pies you're all about to clean up." He handed them each a shovel and pointed to a large field to the right. "Up 'til yesterday, this was a pasture. We'll have somewhere around four hundred people next weekend—maybe more, maybe less, dependin' on the weather. Probably less on Thursday and Friday."

"What do you do if it rains?" John asked.

"Well, we can set up more tents if it's jist a little rain. If we get thunderstorms, we cancel and end up doin' church business later. Forecast says hot and humid—no rain."

"Who's going to tear it down?" Mike asked.

"I was plannin' on askin' you boys to help me with that on the twenty-sixth, but Mary told me you had a scrimmage against West Portsmouth that day, so I got people to help me. It'll be a lot easier to tear down than put up."

Joe introduced the boys to Cliff and Hiram who were dressed like twins, wearing gray bib overalls and Caterpillar caps. They were, obviously, not twins. Hiram was short and muscular; Cliff was tall and thin. *Mutt and Jeff.* They each had a cigarette in one hand and a cup of coffee in the other.

"They're the carpenters," Joe said. "We got a truckload of lumber comin' in a couple of hours. They'll need help unloadin' it." He cut the barbed wire fence between two posts. "Let's go; we're burnin' daylight." He chuckled. "Heard that on *Rawhide*. Sounded good."

By noon, with all the cow manure cleaned up, small shrubs cut down and removed, and the lumber stacked in a neat pile, they broke for lunch. Joe pulled an ice chest from the back of the station wagon. In it were sandwiches and soft drinks. "I appreciate your help, boys. You worked your butts off this mornin'." He handed ham and cheese sandwiches to Tim and John. "Long way to go, though." He smiled as he handed Mike a peanut butter and jelly. "Better be right; Mary made it."

Mike inspected the sandwich. "So, what happens here for four days?"

Joe took a swig of his Pepsi. "It's a yearly get-together of all the churches in the association. Worship and fellowship. See that creek over there? We're lucky there's enough water in it for baptisms, 'cause we expect several of them. We'll have services every day, and conduct some business; publish minutes of the business meetin's. People write obituaries of members who died in the past year, and we put 'em in the minutes. For me, it's a little vacation, seein' people I ain't seen in a while. But we're doin' the Lord's work at the same time."

"Will Mary be here?" Mike asked.

"She'll be runnin' the concession stand. You could help her if you want; no pay for that."

Mike shrugged. "If she wants my help, she'll have to ask."

"I'll tell her that. Let's get at it, boys; lotta work to be done, still."

By eight PM, they had cut the grass, lined up three portable toilets under a poplar tree and loaded scraps of lumber back onto the truck. The two carpenters wearily shook the boys' hands and thanked them.

Joe handed Mike sixty dollars—two twenties and two tens—and said, "Appreciate your help." He shook hands with each of them.

Mike handed John and Tim each thirty dollars and said, "Let's go home, guys."

In the car, Tim spoke up. "What's this? It was supposed to be twenty apiece."

"Just take it and shut up. You guys worked your asses off," Mike said. He looked at the fuel gauge. "I'm gonna need gas. You can pay for a fill-up if you want."

"So, you gonna work the concession stand with Mary?" John asked.

"Only if she asks."

"You know she will," said Tim.

"Maybe that'll get you into her pants," John chimed in.

Mike reached over and tapped him on the back of the head, but smiled.

Sunday, August 13

The phone awakened Mike at ten AM.

"So, you gonna do it?" Mary asked.

He yawned. "Do what, Mary?"

"Help me at the concession stand. Dad said…"

"My brain must have been fried from busting my ass for 14 hours."

"Thanks for doing that." She hesitated. "So…you didn't mean it?"

"Sure, I meant it; but only Saturday and Sunday, though. The other two days I have practice, and then I have to help my dad at the bowling alley."

"That's okay. Saturday and Sunday are the busy days. You wanna come over later and play ball with the kids?"

"What will you be wearing?" Before she could answer he asked, "How come you're not in church?"

"The kids didn't go, but Mom dragged Dad out of bed. I don't think he felt much like going; looked really beat. C'mon over and we'll have hotdogs for lunch."

"Are they all-beef?"

"Of course. And…I'll be wearing my usual frumpy clothes."

"That's disappointing."

They played wiffle ball with a bat and ball Mike had bought for them in the spring.

Mike took Joshua and Esther on his team—with the usual rule that Mike wasn't allowed to pitch—while Mary took Jimmy and Becky. The result was the same as always, as Mary, Jimmy, and Becky played as if it was game seven of the World Series. With six-year-old Joshua not being able to catch or hit and Esther doing the pitching, Mary's team won all three three-inning games by lopsided scores. As usual, Mike allowed three-year-old Mark to swing the bat a few times, but, as usual, he never made contact. He seemed to prefer playing in the dirt, anyway.

It was after four when Mike begged off playing a fourth game and decided to go home. "To do what?" asked Mary.

"Listen to the ball game." *Call Eve.*

"You could do that here. You could eat supper with us here; even stay overnight if you want. You could even live here."

"Yeah, that'd be a great idea. Maybe you and I could share a room—even a bed." He rolled his eyes.

"Don't go home, Mike," she implored him. "I know you hate being alone."

He shrugged. "Fine, I'll stay. Turn on the radio. WNXT." The Reds' game was getting ready to start in San Francisco.

Fifteen minutes later Joe and Rose Bryant arrived home from church. “Staying for supper, Michael?” she asked.

Mike nodded. “If it’s okay.”

Smiling broadly, she said, “Kill us a chicken, Jimmy.”

The whole family sat watching TV, with Mike and Mary sitting thigh-to-thigh on the couch. Mark was sound asleep on Mike’s lap by the time *Bonanza* started. Mary smiled at Mike, picked Mark up, and headed upstairs. When she returned, she sat even closer. Mike looked at her father, and then at her mother. Neither seemed to be paying attention to them.

He left when *Bonanza* was over and was home in time to catch the baseball scores on the late news. His father, who always closed the bowling alley early on Sundays, was already in bed. The Reds and Dodgers had both won, setting up a big series in L.A. starting Tuesday.

He sat staring mindlessly at the TV for the next hour, thinking about Mary and her family. Over the years, she had told him the family history:

Joe Bryant grew up in the ‘20’s and ‘30’s in Harlan County, Kentucky. He dropped out of school after the sixth grade, and spent his teen years working on his father’s small farm, and—off and on—at a local coal mine.

The Bryants were devout Baptists, rarely missing church, which was where he met Rose. Early on, their courtship consisted of sitting together at church and holding hands afterward under the watchful eyes of her parents. On her seventeenth birthday, they were finally allowed to go on their first unchaperoned date. They were married a year later.

By 1948, Rose, out of fear for her husband's health and safety at the mine, insisted they move. With two kids and another on the way, Joe agreed.

They moved to Scioto County, bringing his ailing parents with them, and acquired the five-acre parcel of land off Hope Run by paying the back taxes. With the help of neighbors and friends from church, they cleared the land, built the house, and the dirt road leading to it.

After many years of eking out a living farming the land, and using his mules to snake logs out of the many hollers on Hope Run for a local sawmill, he landed a job at the Ohio Stove Company in 1957. Their sixth child, Mark, was on the way.

Despite numerous layoffs, things got better for the Bryant family. Lately, remembering their own lean years, he and Rose were giving much of their produce to poor Hope Run neighbors.

While they both thought some of those neighbors would be doing better if the simply got off their couches and did more for themselves, they realized that many of them were in ill health, uneducated, or both. Some struggled with alcoholism, which seemed to know no social or economic boundaries.

"Judge not, lest ye be judged," Joe had told Mary.

Saturday, August 19

The Reds were back in first place, two games ahead of the Dodgers, who had lost five in a row while the Reds were winning five in a row, including a three-game sweep in L.A.

Mike picked Mary up at seven AM. Her double ponytail reminded him of that first day he met her. The short sleeved, ankle-length, yellow dress put Buddy Holly's 'Peggy Sue' into his head. They loaded the Chevy with coolers full of Coke, 7UP, and Barq's Root Beer. What looked to Mike like a hundred homemade sandwiches were wrapped and packed in another cooler, along with two boxes of Milky Way candy bars.

"We may be throwing sandwiches away," Mary said. "Some people bring their own lunch; others don't eat. Some members who live close by, have people over to eat afterward. You never know." She was clutching a five-dollar bill in her left hand. "We have to stop somewhere for ice. Why are you looking at me? Is something wrong?" She looked down at herself.

"Definitely not," Mike replied.

She smiled at him and smoothed her dress. "C'mon, buddy. Let's go to work."

They arrived at the pasture at just after eight AM. Mike drove the Chevy across the shallow ditch where the fence had been cut, and parked behind the concession tent. After helping Mary set up, he noticed Joe Bryant, and a balding, middle-aged man he didn't recognize, setting up folding chairs on the stage. When Mike went to help, Joe introduced him to Elder Jesse Tackett. "He's the Moderator of our church."

"Mary's football player?" the man asked, as they shook hands.

Mike sighed. "That's me, I guess."

"Okay," Mary said to Mike when he returned to the concession stand. "Pop and candy—fifteen cents. Sandwiches—a quarter."

The crowd began showing up at nine o'clock. At ten, a man on the dais began the line singing that Mary had told him about. He had to admit that, although it was different, it sounded good—almost festive.

"Why can't men and women sit together?" he asked Mary.

"Tradition, based on something in the Bible. Women can't preach, can't lead the singing, can't cut their hair, or wear makeup."

"You don't need makeup, and I'd be upset if you were to cut your hair, but I do see some ladies out there who look like they've cut theirs. I see some that I would swear are wearing makeup."

She put her head on his shoulder. Her hair smelled like lilac. "You like my hair?"

"Of course."

"Anyway, some cheat, just like regular people." She smiled at him. "Judge not."

"So…men and women are sitting together out front. What's that about?"

"Well, some of them aren't even members. This church is not like other churches. You can't just walk in off the street and say 'I want to be a member'. You have to be 'born again'. Once you convince the Elders of the church that you are ready, they take you down to the creek—or river—and baptize you. They don't just sprinkle you with water; they completely submerge you."

"What if the water's cold?"

"Mom and Dad were both baptized in January. Said they had to break the ice before they could do it."

"Makes me shiver just to think about it."

"Strangely, they said it didn't feel that cold."

"I can't imagine that. Why didn't they just wait for spring?"

She shrugged. "Just didn't want to, I guess. The important thing is that you and I can sit together because we're not members. In fact, we're just children. And children should be seen, not heard." She nudged him.

"People our age can't join?"

"There have been cases where seventeen-year-olds have been baptized, but not many. I'm certainly not ready for that." She laughed. "And we both know you're not."

"You're right about that," he conceded. "You don't get paid for this, huh?"

"Nope. It all goes to the churches. They all need money since—unlike other churches—there's no tithing. People give what they think they can afford, which is zero for a lot of them. In fact, some are so poor that the church sometimes takes up collections just for them. Preachers don't get paid, but there's still church maintenance and repairs, plus heating and light bills."

People were constantly coming up to the small card table they were using to display their wares, saying "Hello", and introducing themselves to 'Mary's football player'.

"Mary's football player?" Mike finally asked. "What's that about?"

"I've told people about you, but never said you were *my* football player." She shrugged and smiled. "Sounds nice, though."

"I feel like a sideshow freak. They seem to be more interested in 'Mary's football player' than what we're selling."

She smiled and mussed his hair. "Get over yourself."

A preacher came to the pulpit and began speaking softly and slowly. After a few minutes, his speech was neither soft nor slow. Mike couldn't understand what he was saying, but could tell it was being said with an enthusiasm that was shared by the congregation. In the middle of the sermon, the preacher left the stage and began shaking hands with the congregation. A woman on the dais stood up and began pacing in front of the other women. She was shouting something Mike couldn't understand. Another woman joined her, and then another.

Singing began again and the preacher finally ended his sermon. After a short break, the ritual was repeated with the next preacher—and the next. There was a constant line for the portable toilets.

By three PM, the proceedings were coming to a halt. Mary and Mike had sold nearly everything they had brought. They sat in the grass under a tree munching on the last two peanut butter and jelly sandwiches and sharing the last root beer.

"That was interesting," he commented as he looked out at the dwindling crowd.

"You gonna come back tomorrow?"

"I thought you people didn't work on Sundays." He suppressed a smile.

She whispered into his ear, "*Don't start*."

Sunday, August 20

The Reds had won their sixth game in a row. With the Dodgers losing again, Cincinnati now held a three game lead.

Sunday at the pasture was a repeat of Saturday, except it was busier—and shorter. Mary and Mike ran out of everything by one o'clock. Joe Bryant came by, helped them pack up, and shook Mike's hand, thanking him profusely.

"I have grass to cut, and a neglected house to clean," Mike told Mary on the way back.

"Yeah, and a ball game to listen to," she said, looking out the car window at the calm waters of the Ohio River. "It's okay, though. You deserve a break from me."

"I really don't need a break from you." He did, though, as his brain was, again, in the process of dropping about three feet.

After dropping her off, he went home and stared at the phone for several minutes before calling Eve.

Saturday, August 26

The Dodgers had ended a ten game losing streak Friday night by beating the Reds 7-2 behind the pitching of Sandy Koufax, to pull within two games. That was game one of a big four-game series in Cincinnati.

The bus for West Portsmouth left at eleven AM for a one PM scrimmage. The Scioto Central players had to dress at their school and ride the bus in full uniform, which made the bus more crowded than normal. Mike was the last one on the bus. The only seat available was the front seat, next to Tony, who asked, “How’s Mary?”

Mike gave him a stare. “You don’t even know Mary.”

“I’ve heard about the Mike and Mary saga,” Tony smirked.

“There’s no saga. She’s one of my best friends, and that’s it.”

“What if I were to ask her out?”

No longer trying hiding his irritation, Mike said, “Mary doesn’t go out. Let’s drop it.”

Tony held up his hands. “Okay, it’s dropped.”

The scrimmage went well for the Shawnee. On offense, Tony looked sharp completing passes all over the field. Mike took advantage of the half-dozen chances he got to run the ball. Neither he nor Tony played on defense. While Tony wasn’t likely to play at all on defense, Mike expected to play nearly every down as an inside linebacker, once the season started.

West Portsmouth had had an upper echelon team last year with a 6-3 record. But, judging how the Shawnee dominated the scrimmage, Mike figured their regular season game would not be close.

Back at Central High, Coach Hauser held a short meeting in the locker room.

"All right. I don't want you guys to get too cocky, but you looked pretty good out there. I have to compliment the offensive line, especially. I couldn't find a grass stain anywhere on Tony's uniform. And that's a good thing. First cut is going to be the end of the week. Work hard." He clapped Mike on the shoulder as he left, but said nothing.

Tuesday, September 5

The Reds now held a three-game lead over the Dodgers.

First day of school. Mary bubbled with an enthusiasm that Mike didn't share. Sitting in a classroom six hours a day had never appealed to him, though it would be good, he figured, to see classmates he hadn't seen since May.

He had spent Labor Day with the Bryant family, while his father and grandfather had gone to Cincinnati to visit Mike's Aunt Margaret. They asked him to go along, but he declined, not wanting to deal with Margaret's husband, Ted McMahon. *Obnoxious little drunk.*

On the way to school, as they listened to WIOI, hearing Elvis' new hit, 'Little Sister', Mike said, "Speaking of little sisters—since Becky's in high school now—we should let her ride with us."

Mary smiled and patted him on the thigh. "Becky can ride the bus."

Jack O'Brien was the American History teacher at Scioto Central. He was small—about 5'2"—not much over a hundred pounds. He greeted Mike warmly in the hallway and asked about the football team. Aside from being an outstanding teacher, he was friendly, outgoing, and witty. Occasionally he would join Mike, John, and Tim in the cafeteria and talk sports. Mike had nicknamed him Jack Spratt last year, and now everyone called him that. His effeminate mannerisms had sparked rumors about his sexual preference, but none of the students seemed to care. Everyone simply liked Jack Spratt. Having taken American History as a junior, Mike would not have him for class, this year.

Tony Duvardo, because he needed the credit, did have to take American History. Apparently, the curriculum in Michigan was different. Right away, he made it obvious that he didn't share Mike's affection for Jack Spratt."

"So, what's the deal with this funny looking little history teacher?" he asked Mike after practice.

"What do you mean, deal? He's a good teacher and a good guy."

"Queer, ain't he?"

"Don't know; don't care."

"Gives me the creeps."

"Queerness is not contagious, as far as I know."

"He still gives me the creeps."

Mike shrugged. "I don't think he'll be putting the moves on you; deal with it."

Mike was home from practice and making himself a sandwich when Mary called.

"How was practice?" she asked.

"Fine," he answered. "I practiced blocking for the star. Wish I could play more defense in practice so I could knock the shit out of the star."

"Don't talk dirty, but I thought you said he was okay."

"Just gets on my nerves." He told her about his Jack Spratt conversation with Tony. "Fu…" He stopped in time. "Intercourse him."

She laughed, but said, "Quit that. Let's change the subject. There's a new girl in our homeroom, named Norma West. Moved from Portsmouth; dresses kinda provocatively. Did you notice her?"

"Barely." *How could I not?*

"Bet she'll give Eve some competition. Sorry. Judge not."

"How's Babs?"

"I just brought her back from the meadow and milked her. Maybe Saturday the three of us…." She laughed. "She misses you, I think."

"Maybe, if I'm not crippled from Friday night's game. You going?"

"Dad says he'll drop me at the home games if you'll bring me home—straight home, he emphasized."

"You may have to wait half an hour or more after the game, what with showers and listening to whatever Coach wants to bitch about."

"That's okay. Dad trusts you."

Friday, September 8

The Reds still held a one-game lead over the Dodgers.

Scioto Central played their first game of the season against New Boston at home, winning 35-7. Tony threw for nearly 300 yards. Mike took advantage of what opportunities he got on offense, taking a screen pass thirty yards for a touchdown, and gaining sixty yards on ten carries. He also played well on defense, making, by his count, at least a dozen solo tackles.

When he came out of the school building, Mary was sitting on the front fender of the Chevy. Standing next to her was Norma West.

He checked her out, trying not to be obvious. She was short—about 5'2"—with short, dark hair, and large breasts that made her appear top-heavy. Her jeans fit snugly against her round posterior. She smiled at him through large, dark eyes. *Built like a brick house and beautiful.*

Mary introduced them and said, "She's waiting for Tony."

"He played well, tonight," Mike said, briefly returning Norma's smile. Looking back at Mary, he asked, "Ready to go?"

When he parked the Chevy in front of her house, she leaned over and kissed him on the mouth with enthusiasm. Somewhat surprised, he kissed her back. She tasted like grape Kool-Aid; her hair smelled like lilac. He glanced at the house, seeing no one, as 'This Magic Moment' by The Drifters played on WLS.

After they made out for several minutes, he glanced toward the house, again, and then put his hand on her thigh, slowly moving it upward. She gently pushed his hand away and opened the car door.

"Sorry," he said.

"Goodnight, Mike," she said with a quick smile. "See you tomorrow.

Saturday, September 9

The Reds had beaten the Cardinals while the Dodgers were losing to the Giants, giving the Reds a two-game lead.

As he parked in front of the Bryant's house at five PM, Mike noticed that the station wagon was gone. Sam greeted him and then ran to the rear of the house. Mike grabbed the transistor radio from the seat and followed him, finding Mary on the back porch glider reading a book.

He sat down by her and looked out at the potato patch. "Potatoes look even worse."

"Well, you know the story. About ready to harvest."

"Where is everybody?"

"They went to a church service in Kentucky for some guy who's sick. They do that a lot. If a member's not able to go to church, they take the church to him—or her. Probably won't be back 'til eight or so."

"Why didn't you go?"

She smiled up at him. "I had to wait for you, silly."

"Whatcha reading?"

"*The Great Gatsby.*"

"What's it about?"

"It takes place on some ritzy island in New York, so I assume it's about rich people. You should read more."

"I read."

"You read what?"

"I've read all the *Chip Hilton* books."

"I read a couple of chapters of one of those books," she scoffed. "Let's see...they're about this perfect-in-every-way high school athlete who always leads his team to victory despite adversity."

"Actually, he doesn't win all the time. Sometimes they lose in spite of his heroics. Kinda like me."

"You should read serious literature. You might learn something. And, by the way, don't forget you have that book report due by the middle of next month."

"Yeah, something about mice."

"It's *Of Mice and Men.* I have a copy."

"Why do you have a copy?"

"It's a classic."

"Wanna take a walk?"

"I'll get the cow."

Noticing that the grass in the meadow had been overgrazed around the stump, he tied Babs to a sapling farther back near the hill. Sam came trotting up to Mary as she and Mike sat on the log. She scratched him behind the ears. He rolled over for a belly rub; she obliged.

"Must be nice to be a dog," Mike said.

"You want me to scratch you behind the ears and rub your belly?"

"Or rub something."

She giggled. "Quit it."

"The mules get to graze here, too?" he asked.

"Yeah, that's Jimmy's job."

He tuned the radio to WIOI. The Drifters were doing 'Please Stay'.

"Sorry about last night," he ventured.

"Why? I'm sure it's normal—raging hormones and all that. I might have been disappointed if you hadn't tried anything."

"You know I didn't…"

She cut him off. "I sometimes wonder what you want from me, Mike. Do you even know why you made it a point to have me sit with you on the bus all those years ago?"

Mike chewed on a blade of grass, realizing that he wasn't in trouble for trying to feel her up, but for apologizing. Trying to lighten the mood, he said, "Well, you were really hot—for a first grader."

"Don't make stupid jokes. What if I'd been a boy? Would you have wanted me to sit by you?

"As I remember, the Payne brothers were on the bus, already. That should answer your question."

She considered this. "By the way, it wasn't a request; it was an order, which I obeyed."

"You didn't want to sit by me?"

"I was glad you did that—and still am. But…for over ten years, we rode the bus together and you wouldn't let anybody sit next to me. I remember one fight on the bus when you got paddled by the bus driver because some kid sat down next to me and wouldn't get up."

"Wasn't a fight. I just moved him." He watched Sam dig for something under a briar patch.

"Remember that time in fourth grade, when Billy…somebody…?"

"Billy Cooper. He pushed you down on the playground; I kicked his ass. I had to stay in at recess for a week, but it was worth it."

"Why was it worth it?"

"Maybe I just didn't like Billy Cooper."

"I wasn't the only person he bullied. How many times did you beat him up?"

"Once was enough. He quit bullying people after that—at least at school. Only real fight I ever had."

"You know, if my father did allow me to date, no one would ever ask me out. Do you know why?"

"Because you're so ugly?"

"No, Mike. And you're still not funny. Even the ugly guys wouldn't ask me out. They'd be afraid you'd beat them up. Everybody thinks of me as your possession."

He crushed an ant that was crawling up his arm but said nothing.

"Last night was the first time you ever tried…anything." She continued. "It's like you don't want me, but don't want anyone else to have me."

"Would it have made you feel better if I'd been more persistent? What if I'd felt you up while you were trying to stop me? I'll tell you what…you'd have been really pissed off and I'd have hated myself. Look, I'll put a notice on the bulletin board, Monday, stating that I don't own you, and that anybody who wants to can ask you out. How's that?"

She didn't answer; just stared at the hillside.

He got up to leave. "Tony will probably be the first guy to do that. Of course, we both know what your dad will say."

"Mike, I just want there to be…us."

"There will always be us."

"Will there ever be...just us?" She stood and put a hand on his shoulder.

Is this about Norma West?

He put his hand on hers. "I didn't come here to fight with you."

"Why did you come here?" He could hear the agitation in her voice.

"To spend time with...my best friend. I should go home, Mary?"

"Yeah, you should go home...or to Eve's house, or..." Fighting back tears, she pushed his hand away.

This is about Norma West.

"See you Monday," he said, evenly.

She looked up at him. "I guess I'll be riding the bus, huh."

"Not if you don't want to."

He went home and called Eve.

Monday, September 11

Mike turned on WNXT radio and listened to baseball scores and the news, as he got ready for school. The Reds had beaten the Cardinals 5-2, while the Dodgers were losing their third in a row to the Giants. Cincinnati was now looking good with a four-game lead.

Carla, a category five hurricane, was about to make landfall somewhere in Texas. Iraqi warplanes had attacked the Kurds who lived in the northern part of the country. *What's a Kurd? Something to do with spoiled milk?* He smelled the milk before pouring it on his Cheerios.

As he was finishing his cereal, the phone rang. It was Mary. "I…don't want to," She said.

"Don't want to what?"

"Ride the bus."

"I'm really glad. See you in a little bit."

When she got into the car, she smiled tentatively at him. "Mike, let's forget about the other night. I just get confused, sometimes…about us."

"Me too, Mary." He squeezed her hand; she squeezed back.

Friday, September 15

The Reds now held a five-game lead over the Dodgers.

The Shawnee played Portsmouth East at Sciotoville. Because it had rained all day, and the field was muddy, Mike figured he'd be carrying the ball a lot. He figured wrong, however, as Tony threw the ball 31 times, completing 23 for 250 yards. Mike did carry the ball nine times for 65 yards, and played well on defense, intercepting a pass and forcing a fumble. The Shawnee won 30-14.

It was nearly eleven PM when Mike reached his car back at Scioto Central. Norma West was sitting on the front fender.

"Waiting for Tony?" he asked.

She smiled, hesitantly. "Waiting for you."

He checked her out. She was wearing a dark colored, tight, knee-length skirt and a white blouse that buttoned down the front. The top two buttons were unbuttoned, showing more cleavage than he'd ever seen—except for a couple of middle-aged fat women he'd noticed at the bowling alley.

"What did you have in mind?"

"A ride home—or somewhere."

"How'd you get here?"

She showed him a thumb.

"You're shitting me."

"No, I'm not. It's easy. All I have to do is show a thumb and a little bit of thigh."

"You should be careful with that."

"Yeah." She smiled up at him.

"Your parents let you stay out late?"

"My dad won't know since he lives in California. My mom is out with a *friend*, and may not be home tonight. How about you?"

"I get home when I get home." He opened the passenger door. "Let's go."

He drove north on 104. Gene McDaniels' 'A hundred Pounds of Clay' was playing on WLS.

"You taking me home?" she asked.

"I don't even know where you live."

"Right there." She pointed at a small yellow house on the left as they passed it.

"I guess not, then." He continued north for several miles and turned right onto a dirt road leading to the Scioto River. Carefully avoiding the ruts, and overhanging tree limbs, he eased the Chevy into a clearing by the riverbank. Kids came here frequently to make out, but tonight, they had it all to themselves.

Elvis was singing a new hit, 'His Latest Flame'. Mike parked, turned off the engine, but left the radio on.

"So...I thought you were going out with Tony," he ventured.

"Once was enough."

"Oh yeah? Good-looking guy, great car, star of the football team. What more could a girl want?"

She looked out the window, and then back at him. "He was too aggressive. We weren't in the car five minutes before he had his tongue in my mouth and his hand in my crotch."

Mike cleared his throat. "Didn't like that, huh?"

She sighed. "You obviously don't understand girls at all."

Silence.

"How do you like our school?" he asked, at length.

"It's okay. Smaller than PHS, but maybe that's a good thing."

"So, why'd you move?"

"My parents got divorced, sold the house in Portsmouth, and Dad moved to California with his new woman. Mom got a job at the Atomic Plant up near Piketon, and decided to move closer to work, so she's renting the house on 104."

"Have any brothers or sisters?"

"No, it's just me and Mom. I wish it was just me and Dad, but it didn't work out that way. Maybe I'll move to California after graduation."

"You and your mom don't get along so well, huh?"

"Not really."

"So, why didn't you go with your dad?"

"He didn't ask me to. He went with his girlfriend, so I figured I'd just be in their way."

"Our situations are somewhat similar."

"How's that?"

"I'm an only child. Mom died and Dad probably wouldn't miss me if I was gone."

They sat silently, listening to the Corsairs singing 'Smoky Places'.

"I've been here before," she said, gazing at him.

"Doing what?" he smirked.

"Watching submarine races." She leaned in and kissed him.

They 'watched submarine races' twice, leaving at one AM. On the way back, she asked, "Did you ever take Mary there?"

After a quick glance at her, he concentrated on the road, saying nothing, feeling guilty.

"I get it," she said.

Tuesday, May 29, 1962
Ocean Beach

"So…that's what got you in trouble?" Debbie asked.

"No. I think I got away with that one."

"Ready for another Bloody Mary—or a beer?"

"No, thanks."

"Well, I'm having one. I'll be right back."

"I probably drink too much," she said when she returned.

"So...why do you drink so much?"

"I like myself better when I'm drunk."

"Must be a reason for that."

"Must be. You gonna harass me about it?"

"No, Ma'am."

"Good."

Monday, September 18, 1961
Scioto County

The Dodgers had won Sunday, reducing the Reds' lead to three and a half games. The magic number was still eight.

Both Mary and Becky were waiting on the front porch when Mike pulled up in the rain. Mary didn't look pleased.

Smiling, Becky got into the back seat. "Thank you, Mike. You remember how long that bus takes to get to school, don't you?"

"Yes, I do." He returned her smile.

With a sigh of displeasure, Mary said, "Mom says, if she can't ride with you, I can't either."

Mike shrugged. "I don't see a problem. Do you?"

"I guess not."

It had rained all day and was pouring when school let out. After waiting for half an hour, Coach Hauser canceled practice. Mike chauffeured home a carload of players who normally walked, then decided to visit his grandfather.

"Why don't you just move in with Dad and me?" Mike asked as he toyed with his can of Pepsi.

"Why would I? I have my friends here and I can take care of myself. Let's wait 'til I'm decrepit and sickly. That'll come soon enough."

"Maybe I need the company."

"My being there would probably screw up your love life."

Mike laughed. "Not as long as I have a back seat in the Chevy."

"You be careful with that, Mikey"

"I always am."

"How's Mary?"

Mike sighed. "Mary's fine; we're still just friends."

His grandfather shook his head. "I went bowling the other day with Virgil and Jerry. Had a 180 game. Kicked their asses."

"Oh yeah? Dad make you pay?"

"He tried not to, but we insisted. You should probably spend more time with him, you know."

"I know, but he works all the time. And we never have anything to talk about, anyway."

"You could start by talking about sports. Maybe some other subject will come up."

"Seems like he's not comfortable around me—and I'm not real comfortable around him."

"Yeah, I know what you mean."

They made small talk about school, football, and baseball. "I played a little high school football. Did you know that?" Gramps said.

"Tell me about it." He'd heard the story several times.

"Believe it or not, there was a time when I was young and full of piss and vinegar like you and Mary."

Mike laughed. "Is it all right if I tell Mary you said she was full of piss and vinegar?"

"Better not. Anyhow, it was before the war...the first war. We didn't have all the padding you guys have. No helmets, either. The only special equipment we wore was a piece of leather covering our ears. Even that was optional. I played end and was mostly a blocker. Didn't throw the ball as much in those days as they do now; in fact, hardly ever. I think I caught three passes in the two years I played. I saw a couple of guys get hurt really bad, so I decided it wasn't worth the risk. Did you know that there was some serious talk of banning the sport, at that time?"

"I read about that."

"Several players died. A lot of others were crippled or brain-damaged. Anyway, I quit and concentrated on baseball." He smiled. "Couldn't hit worth a damn, but I was a decent pitcher.

"Doesn't seem that long ago. Seems like the years just zip along. You're a teenager with all these hopes and dreams for the future; next thing you know, you're an old man waiting to die."

"Is there some grandfatherly advice there, or are you just feeling sorry for yourself?"

"I don't know. I'm not much for giving advice, but you should plan for the future—maybe make sacrifices now."

Mike sighed. "With Mary, you mean?"

"Among other things. You know, Mikey, when I was your age I thought I knew everything. I'm sure it's the same with most kids. Old people like me keep trying to keep kids from repeating our mistakes, but they never listen."

He went to the kitchen window and looked out at his small backyard. It had stopped raining. "Just the prattle of a useless old man with nothing to look forward to but dying." He turned to Mike, grinned, and rubbed his nose. "Hope they remember to shave the top of my nose before they put me in the casket."

Mike laughed. "You've got a lot of good years left, Gramps."

"Bullshit. So far, I'm managing my aches and pains, but there seems to be a new one every day. I'm not worried about dying. What I worry about is getting to the point where I can't take care of myself—shit my pants and whatever. I remember what it was like with my father...helpless as a newborn baby the last six months of his life. When I get to that point I'd like you to shoot me, please"

Mike chuckled. "That's still against the law, I think. Listen, Gramps, I gotta go; homework. Why don't you come to the game this Friday? Dad'll pick you up."

"We'll see. Maybe. You take care, Mikey."

"You too."

Friday, September 22

The Reds' magic number was four.

Scioto Central played at home against Piketon, with both Tom and Don Harrison in attendance. Ronnie Stone, the Shawnee's regular kick returner, was out with a sprained knee. Mike asked to take his place on the opening kick-off. Coach Hauser initially shook his head, and then said, "Oh, what the hell? Take it all the way back."

Mike did just that—ninety-five yards worth.

On his way back to the bench, he looked up to see his father and grandfather standing up with the rest of the crowd, applauding politely. He found Mary who was jumping up and down and screaming. Mike waved; she waved back. Standing next to her was Norma West, who also waved at him.

The Shawnee won the game 56-14, with Tony throwing for over three hundred yards and four touchdowns. Neither he nor Mike played in the fourth quarter. Tim Crabtree finished the game at quarterback, throwing one pass and completing it for twenty yards and a touchdown.

Mary was waiting alone for Mike in the parking lot. Looking around, he was relieved that Norma was nowhere in sight.

On the way home, they quietly listened to WBZ in Boston. The Chantels did 'Look in My Eyes'.

Finally, Mike ventured, "I saw you with Norma West. You two getting to be friends?"

"She seems nice. I figured, being new, she probably needed a friend or two." She was looking straight ahead. "Doesn't seem to like her mother much, though."

Mike said nothing.

In front of Mary's house, she looked at him briefly, kissed him lightly on the lips and opened the door. "Good night, Mike," she said softly.

She knows.

Saturday, September 23

The Magic number was still four, as the Reds had lost Friday night and the Dodgers had won.

At his father's request, Mike spent the morning at the bowling alley, doing pinsetter maintenance and cleaning in the back end. Having parked the Chevy by the back door, he decided to give it a thorough cleaning, also.

As he was cleaning the chrome, his father emerged with lunch, consisting of the usual cheeseburgers and fries.

"Mike, did you hear what happened last night?"

"We won a football game. What else happened?"

"A kid ran off the bridge on Hope Run by the Neumann place."

"God, that's fifteen or twenty feet down. Did he die?"

"Yes. They say he went through the guardrail at a high rate of speed. Souped-up '57 Chevy."

"Who was it?"

"Kid from West Portsmouth by the name of Clayton. I believe I met his dad—not sure, though. I've met a lot of people. Anyway, I hear kids drag race up there a lot, but nobody said that's what he was doing."

"The Neumanns moved out, I hear."

"Yeah, last week. Moved to Columbus. Living with their oldest son. I forget his name."

"Kenny, I think."

“Yeah, that’s it.” He slapped the top of the Chevy. “You need to be careful in this thing.”

“I will.”

“Your grandfather shouldn’t have let you have it.”

“I’ll be careful. Who’s minding the store?”

“Andy and Marsha are here. It’s well covered.”

They ate lunch in the front seat of the Chevy.

Thinking about his recent conversation with Gramps, Mike said, “Hey, Dad, since Andy and Marsha have it covered, we could take a break. Maybe go down by the river and watch the boats. Shoot the shit.”

Don looked briefly at him, shrugged and stuffed the last two french fries into his mouth. “Why not? I’ll be right back.”

Several minutes later, he returned with two large drink cups with lids and got in. “Let’s go. Wanna pick your grandfather up on the way?"

Mike shook his head. "No. That's okay."

Mike parked on Front Street, and they walked to a small park area on the bank of the Ohio River, just west of the U.S. Grant Bridge. Across the river was a steep, wooded hill. Kentucky.

They sat on a park bench, and Don handed his son a drink cup. Mike popped the lid; there was beer inside. “I thought about putting vodka in there, but decided beer was safer,” Don said with a wink.

Mike’s face turned crimson. “Just once.”

“I know. So...what do you want to talk about? Problems with Mary.”

Mike sighed and sipped his beer. “Does everything have to be about Mary?”

“No, it doesn’t. What else you got?”

Mike watched a barge slowly make its way under the bridge. *I guess we're not gonna talk about sports.* "I asked you about you and Mom, once. You gave me the short answer, but I'd like to hear more."

"You won't get the long answer. What else you got?"

Mike tried not to voice his exasperation. "Okay. How come we never went to church?"

"You went a few times with your mother. I just wasn't interested."

"So, you're an atheist?"

Don took a sip of beer. "No, I'm not. Listen, I admit I never did like the idea of getting out of bed on Sunday morning, getting all dressed up and hanging around a bunch of phonies and hypocrites. But, really, I just don't believe in churches." He took another sip. "They're all right for some people, I suppose. For some it's a social thing, something like a bowling league is to me and my customers." He looked briefly at Mike, and then back at the river. "Maybe the bowling alley *is* my church."

"No phonies or hypocrites at the bowling alley, huh?"

Don laughed. "At least they pay me for the privilege."

Mike looked at him. "You don't do *that* much."

"What?"

"Laugh."

Don met his gaze, but then looked away. "No, I don't."

"So...do you believe in Jesus?"

"I believe in the teachings of Jesus, as I understand them. But...you know what Gandhi said?"

"What?"

"He said, 'I like your Christ. I do not like your Christians. They are so unlike your Christ'.

"When you look back at Charlemagne, the Crusades, the Spanish Inquisition, witch hunts, the Puritans escaping religious oppression in England so that they could come to the new world and become the oppressors; slavery... Hell, even Hitler used Christianity as justification for killing all those Jews.

"Mind you, I'm not talking about all Christians. In fact, I'd say the majority of the ones I've met are kind and generous—people like Joe Bryant. What I object to is people forcing their religion on others. I can't sell beer on Sunday, because..." He stopped and cleared his throat. "Sorry. I didn't mean to make a speech."

"It's okay. I didn't know you were a religious scholar, though."

"I'm not. I was planning on majoring in World History in college. Retained a little of what they taught me. Sometimes I'm sorry I dropped out."

"Why did you?"

"Didn't like being away from your mother. Got the opportunity to settle down with a good paying job."

After some hesitation, Mike said, "So, you and Mom loved each other at that point."

Don's face went blank as he stared at Mike. "I've always loved your mother, Mike."

Mike decided to keep pushing. "But you joined the Marines."

Don shrugged. "Well, Pearl Harbor happened. I wanted to fight the Japs. Like so many others at the time, I was really pissed. I hated leaving your mother; just felt it was my duty."

After a short silence, Mike asked, "Do you pray, Dad?"

"I've been known to. Can't say I was ever answered. Listen, Mike, why don't you talk to Joe about the religion thing? He apparently has faith, which is something I'll likely never have. And he's way more knowledgeable about the Bible stuff than I am."

Mike nodded, doubting that Joe Bryant had ever heard of the Spanish Inquisition—or Charlemagne. "What about Charlemagne, Dad?"

"Ask your history teacher."

Mike debated with himself, and took a sip of beer before asking, "Will you…tell me about the war?"

His father stared at Kentucky as Mike watched him. Belatedly, he began. "You want to hear about the war? What the Japs did? What we did? You want to hear about the guys lying with their guts hanging out, screaming for their mommies? You want to hear about guys who were crippled, maimed, paralyzed, blinded…?"

Mike started to speak, but his father held up a hand and continued. "You want to hear about my squad leader, Sergeant Yoder? He stepped on a mine. His legs were gone, and despite all the blood, I could tell that his…genitals were also gone. He begged me to shoot him. I pointed my rifle at his chest, but couldn't pull the trigger."

A man on a passing barge waved at them; Mike waved back.

Don stood up, slowly walked around the bench, looked down at Mike, and sat back down. With a distant look in his eyes, he spoke again. "I remember going ashore at Guadalcanal assuming I was going to die, which is pretty much the only way to get through something like that. I remember being disappointed that I'd survived."

"Why?"

"The survivors had to witness the carnage. Lying there with two bullet holes in my leg, waiting for a corpsman, seeing the guys who needed him more—and seeing the guys who were beyond help, wondering why I survived and they didn't. At the same time, wondering if I was going to bleed to death before I got attended to. It's a weird feeling when you're about to go into shock from blood loss."

"You can stop now, Dad," Mike said.

"You don't want more war stories, Mike? I can tell you what some of our guys did to Jap prisoners."

"No. And I'm sorry I brought it up."

"Oh, I guess you wanted the Hollywood version."

"Sorry I brought it up," Mike repeated.

"That's okay. Now let's get back to the real world," He drained his cup and crushed it between his hands. "To be honest, I was a terrible husband, and we both know I'm not much of a father. So maybe I shouldn't even be giving advice, but here it is, for what it's worth. And it has nothing to do with religion or war." He paused. "Let's say there's an overweight person who wants to lose a few pounds, standing in a cafeteria line picking out his dessert. His choices are a big piece of cake with ice cream, or an apple. It may not be quite as tasty, but he knows the apple is the wisest choice. It all depends on how badly he wants to lose weight, and how much self-control he has."

"That's related to Mary and me, right?"

"You spend time with her and you get yourself all...worked up. Instead of going home and heading for the phone to call Eve—or the other girl—maybe the wisest choice would be to just grab a *National Geographic*, or whatever, and head for the bathroom. It all depends on how badly you want to keep Mary Bryant—and how much self-control you have."

"I didn't know you knew about Eve—or the other girl. Her name's Norma."

"Yeah, that's the name I heard. Mike, you're a celebrity of sorts. People notice what you do."

"Me?"

"Yes. And a person hears a lot of gossip in a bowling alley. Probably about the same as one hears after church. Kids tell parents; parents tell other parents.

"Listen, Mike, sowing your wild oats is okay—if that's all you want. But we both know that's not all you want. We both know you want Mary Bryant. But when you finally get around to deciding you're ready, she just might not be available."

Mike studied his beer. "Uh…do you have a lady friend, Dad?"

"No one you should meet, if that's what you're getting at. Lots of women pass through the bowling alley. Nothing serious."

"So, those nights when you come home really late, you're out with a woman?"

"Yeah, sometimes."

"Would you want a serious relationship?"

"Hell no. It'd be hard to find a woman who'd put up with me, anyway. Maybe when I'm your grandfather's age, I'll think differently. Anything else on your mind, Mike? I should get back to work."

"Not really, but maybe we could do this again sometime. Or maybe we could go to a Reds game."

"Season's about over, Mike. Maybe next year."

Back at home, Mike called Mary. "Want some company for church tomorrow?"

"You sick?"

"I told you I'd go sometime, and tomorrow is sometime. Where's church?"

"South Shore."

"Good. There's a Dairy Bar on 23."

"Pick me up at 7:30. What're you doing now?"

"Gotta cut the grass and clean house," he lied. "See you tomorrow."

He hung up the phone and stared at it for several minutes, debating whether to call Eve or Norma. Finally deciding on neither, he ran the hill twice.

Back in the house, he picked up a *National Geographic* from the coffee table.

Sunday, September 24

The Reds and Dodgers both had won Saturday night, leaving the magic number at three.

Mike dragged himself out of bed at seven AM, and was at the Bryants' house shortly before eight.

"Sorry I'm late."

"I planned on that; we have time," said Mary, as she straightened his tie. "Becky and Jimmy are going to ride with us if you don't mind. It gets really crowded in the station wagon."

"No problem."

"They can ride back home with the parents, and you and I can go for ice cream."

The church was a white, wood-frame, structure with no steeple. The inside was a single room. To the rear, occupying nearly half the room, was a large dais for the members, and a podium for the preacher. As before, the female members sat on the right, the men on the left. There were several rows of wooden benches for the congregation. Mike and Mary sat in the last row, by the door.

"Where's the restroom?" he asked.

"Outhouse in the back." She patted his hand.

The 'line singing' was pretty much the same as before, but easier for Mike to hear. He still couldn't understand the preaching, but the membership was really into it. As before, several women stood up and shouted, sounding hysterical.

After what seemed like a day and a half, he looked at his watch. It was almost noon. Mary patted him on the hand and whispered, "Not much longer."

She was right. Shortly after noon, it was over except for the handshaking, the hugging, and people coming by to meet 'Mary's football player'.

The Bryant family stayed for dinner (lunch) at the home of a local church member. Mike and Mary went for ice cream.

"So, the preaching—was it rants or chants I was hearing?" Mike asked as they turned onto U.S. 23.

"Maybe some of both—and a little fire and brimstone—admonition. A lot of quoting or paraphrasing Bible verses."

"What were the women shouting about?"

She laughed. "They were just happy."

"It just didn't sound like sermons I've heard before."

She looked askance at him. "How many sermons have you heard?

"I've heard a few sermons on TV."

"Ugh. My dad doesn't think much of TV preachers."

"Why is that?"

"He says they're just in it for the money. Fleecing old people out of their Social Security checks, and giving them the impression they need to—or can—buy their way into heaven. The preachers get richer, the old people get poorer, and the eye of the needle stays the same size."

"That sounded like a sermon, Mary."

She laughed. "Women aren't allowed to preach."

"Why?"

"It's in the Bible, somewhere. 'Obey, serve, and remain silent'." She studied his face. "Mike, whatever relationship you and I have is not about my parents' church. It's just about you and me. You can go to church with me, go to a different church, or go to no church at all. I just want there to be...you and me."

"There will always be you and me. But please don't just ...'obey, serve, and remain silent'. That wouldn't be any fun for either of us."

She hugged his arm and leaned on his shoulder.

The Dairy Bar was located on the right, a hundred yards from the Ohio River. They took their ice cream cones and walked down a narrow path to the river.

"Did you know that, technically, if you step into the water in Ohio, you're in Kentucky?" Mary asked.

"No, I didn't."

"Well, it's apparently still in dispute, but Kentucky claims the whole river along its border."

"Shouldn't they call it the Kentucky River?"

"There's already a Kentucky River."

"Where is it?"

She laughed. “It’s in Kentucky.”

“So what does Ohio mean?”

“You want a geography lesson?”

“Sure.” He smiled at her. “Sunday School.”

“It’s an Iroquois name meaning Great River.”

"So...how about Scioto?”

“Well, there’s some debate about that. Some say it means hairy, others say it means deer.”

“Why the confusion?”

“Well, if you can imagine a white settler and an Indian standing on a cliff, trying to communicate, and they see a hairy deer drinking out of the river. The Indian points and says ‘Scioto’. Does he mean the deer, the hair on the deer, or the river, itself?”

“Could mean a hairy deer drinking out of the river.”

“I think that’d be more than one word. I have read, though, that, years ago, the deer were so plentiful that, in the spring when they shed their coats, the river would be clogged with deer hair.”

“Someone made that up.”

“Maybe.”

They watched the barges go by, heading toward Portsmouth, Cincinnati, and other towns along the way.

“We could go all the way to New Orleans on a barge,” he said. “You and I should just climb on one and see where it goes. It’d be an adventure.”

“Well, not today.” She smiled indulgently and licked the melting ice cream off the side of her cone. “But we could take a drive somewhere.”

“Where would you like to go?”

“Doesn’t matter.”

“Your parents will expect you to be home soon.”

"I'm with you, Mike. They think I'm safe." She looked up at him, giggled, and licked her cone some more. "Am I safe?"

Not if you keep licking that cone like that. "Of course, you're safe. But we should go home and change first."

The Reds were losing to the Giants, and the Dodgers were just getting started in St. Louis when they left Mike's house at 2:30 PM. He tuned the car radio to WIOI. Brian Hyland was singing 'Let Me Belong to You'.

"I just have to be home in time to milk the cow," she said.

"How is Babs, anyway?"

"Missing you, as always." She smiled.

He smiled back, indulgently.

"Where to?" he asked as he pulled out onto Hope Run.

"We could drive through the Shawnee State Forest. I remember Dad took us all swimming in Bear Creek Lake a couple of years ago. Can't remember how we got there, though."

"I think I can find it. Went there a couple of times with John and Tim." *And once with Connie Parsons.*

They entered Shawnee State Forest from State Route 73 by Union Elementary School, and after making several wrong turns on the unmarked dirt roads, they found the lake.

The leaves were just beginning to turn, with some yellow and some orange showing in the oak and maple trees. Shadows nearly blanketed the lake, a reminder that the days were getting shorter. A family of four was sitting at a picnic table, but no one was in the water.

"I bet the water's cold," Mary said as she hugged herself.

"We could jump in and find out."

"You first."

Behind the picnic table was a path leading to the top of a hill. He suggested that they walk it; she took his hand. *Holding hands after church.*

"Is this a date?" she asked.

"Nope."

She squeezed his hand. "Someday."

They climbed several feet up a maple tree and sat on a wide limb, admiring the view of the rolling hills of southern Ohio. In another month, it would be spectacular.

"So, if you and I ran off to Tahiti, your parents wouldn't mind, because you're with me?" he asked.

"They know we're not going to run off to Tahiti. They know we're both responsible enough not to do anything stupid."

After a silence, he asked, "So, have you made any definite plans about college?"

"Here's my plan." She leaned on him. "There's a journalism scholarship to OSU that I'm going to apply for. I'm going to win that, and then spend four happy years in Columbus with my favorite football player."

"And who would that be?"

She elbowed him gently in the ribs. "Seriously, what will you do if you don't get the football scholarship?"

"Seriously? Tony is more likely to get there than I am. I may end up playing somewhere else, but if no scholarship..." He shrugged. "I wouldn't be all that enthusiastic about college without football."

"Maybe you could get into coaching."

He shrugged again. "Maybe. I hadn't thought about that. Might be fun coaching kids."

She took his hand and looked at his watch. "I need to get home and milk Babs. It gets dark earlier, now."

Wednesday, September 27

The Cincinnati Reds had clinched their first National League pennant since 1940, Tuesday night.

The Yankees' Roger Maris had hit his 60th home run. Baseball Commissioner, Ford Frick had decreed that in order for the record to count it had to be done in 154 games. Maris's 60th came in game 159. Interestingly, it took Maris fewer plate appearances than Ruth to get to 60.

Mike had stayed up late listening to Bob Prince doing the Pirates broadcast as they shut out the Dodgers 8-0 in the second game of a twi-night doubleheader, giving the Reds a four-game lead with three left to play.

"They won the pennant!" Mary exclaimed as she closed the car door. "Aren't you excited?"

"Actually, I am. I'll probably cut afternoon classes every day of the World Series. You'll have to keep me updated on English and Physics."

"Maybe I'll cut classes too."

He rolled his eyes. "How many times have you ever cut a class?"

"It could happen. One of these days I'm gonna do something really stupid, Mike, and you'll be shocked."

"Won't happen." Mike glanced at Becky in the back seat.

Becky looked up from her English book. "Stupid people do stupid things."

They listened to Freddy Cannon doing "Transistor Sister" on WIOI.

At lunchtime, Mike spotted Jack O'Brien sitting alone in the cafeteria.

"Mind if I join you?" he asked.

"Of course not," the teacher replied cheerfully, as he pulled out the chair next to him.

After a few minutes of discussing football, Mike asked, "What can you tell me about Charlemagne?"

The teacher raised a brow. "What, specifically, do you want to know?"

"Well...his influence on Christianity, I guess. I remember he conquered the barbarians, controlled most of Europe..."

"Yes, well, he may have converted more people to Christianity than anyone. He didn't just conquer the barbarians. He gave them a choice—convert or die. Obviously, most converted; many died. Some say that wasn't what Jesus had in mind when he talked about spreading the 'good news'. Others...have a different view. Charlemagne was very popular with the Church, as you might imagine. Also, he's generally considered the primary role model for both Napoleon and Hitler."

Mike drained his milk carton. "So...Christianity was spread mostly by conquest, not by preaching the 'good news'?"

Jack pecked at his food with his fork. “That's been the case with most religions, I think. Why the sudden interest, Mike?”

Mike shrugged. “Just a conversation I had. I think you answered my question.”

“Good.”

“Uh…are you a Christian?”

The teacher hesitated. "Go to the library and look up Deism. A number of our founding fathers—Washington, Jefferson, Madison, Franklin—were Deists. Essentially, they believe that God created us, but doesn't interfere in our daily lives. There are many variations. Some believe in an afterlife and some don't. But most believe that He equipped us with the means to, collectively, solve our own problems. I lean toward that notion. Let's keep that between you and me, though.”

“No freedom of religion at Central High, huh?”

"Maybe more than you think. But considering my...situation, I just don't want to rock the boat."

Mike nodded. “So…what about evolution?”

“Maybe God and evolution are synonymous.” The teacher cleared his throat, dabbed his mouth with his napkin. “Are you all right, Mike? You seem…”

“I'm fine.”

“Listen…my beliefs work for me. I assume that Mary's parents' beliefs work for them. Methodists, Episcopalians, Jews, and Muslims all have beliefs that seem to work for them. You have to decide for yourself what works for you. Okay?

“Yeah.”

“How are you and Mary getting along?

”Great.”

"I'm so happy for you both." He gave Mike an inscrutable look, and then a quick smile. "You two belong together."

Friday, September 29

The Shawnee played an away game at Portsmouth Notre Dame. Mike sprained his ankle early in the first quarter while making a tackle, and sat out the rest of the game. Without him in the backfield to block and carry out play-action fakes, Tony struggled, throwing his first interception of the season.

Notre Dame, running the old style single wing offense, led 14-7 at halftime. Coach Hauser was livid. "I can't understand how losing one player can turn us into such a bad team," he ranted, looking at Mike, who was icing his ankle. "We can't throw the ball; we can't run the ball; we can't tackle; we..."

As the coach continued to rant, Mike hobbled over to Tony and knelt down beside him. "You need to roll out to the left where John Breech and Homer Phipps can protect you. Nobody gets by John. And Homer's pretty good, too." he said, barely above a whisper. "You *can* roll out to your left and make accurate throws, can't you? Won't make it in the pros if you can't."

"I can make the throws," Tony muttered without looking at him.

Mike looked up to see Coach Hauser staring at them. "If you're talking, you can't be listening," the coach said.

"Sorry, Coach," Mike and Tony said in unison.

Rolling to his left on nearly every pass play, Tony threw for nearly 200 yards, three touchdowns, and three two-point conversions, in the second half. The Shawnee won 31-21. They were now 4-0.

Saturday, September 30

Mike stayed home, keeping his foot elevated as much as possible. He listened to the heavily favored Ohio State Buckeyes tie TCU 7-7 in their first game of their season. He could imagine Woody Hayes ranting in the locker room.

At five o'clock, the doorbell rang. He yelled, "Come in!" It was Mary, smiling broadly.

"How'd you get here?"

"I walked." She held up a thermos. "Chicken soup."

Mike suppressed a laugh. "I don't have the flu or anything like that, just a sprained ankle."

"So, you don't want the chicken soup? I killed the chicken, myself." She made a cranking motion with her right hand. "Wrung its neck."

"Of course I want it, killer." He hugged her as he stood on one foot.

"You sit back down and I'll find a bowl."

"There's a tray table in the closet."

She sat on the couch, watching him eat. "Your house is a mess; needs a woman's touch."

"Well, it ain't getting one. It's fine."

"Isn't," she corrected.

"Mary, do you ever correct your dad's English."

She shook her head and laughed. "Impossible task."

As he settled in with his soup to watch the college football *Scoreboard* show, he could hear her rustling in the kitchen.

"Mary, stop cleaning my kitchen!" he commanded.

"Okay."

Ten minutes later, she was back. "All done. I'm afraid to look at your bathroom."

"I told you not to do that," he growled. "And the bathroom's fine."

She mussed his hair. "Shut up and eat your gruel."

"It's getting dark. I'll have to drive you home."

She stretched and yawned. "Maybe I'll stay all night."

"I'm sure your dad would draw a line there."

"Yeah, he would. Your dad can drive me home when he gets home."

"Sure. Four in the morning?"

"That late, huh?"

"If he's lucky. Sometimes the pot games go on all night long."

"Well, I'm staying a while, unless you want to get rid of me."

"No. I'm glad you're here."

She sat on the arm of his chair and mussed his hair. "I'm glad you're glad. Let's do some homework."

Two hours later, her father came to pick her up. As they were leaving, Mary said, "Wait, Dad, I forgot something." She ran back in and kissed Mike quickly on the mouth.

At eight PM, Mike was dozing in his chair when the phone rang. “It’s Tony. I’m coming over.” He hung up without waiting for a response.

Fifteen minutes later, he was knocking on the door.

“How’s the ankle?” He asked.

“Shitty. But I’m sure it’ll be fine by Friday. What’s up?”

Tony pulled a hand-rolled cigarette from his shirt pocket. “This’ll make you feel better.”

“I don’t smoke,” said Mike, shaking his head. “And you can buy them pre-rolled, you know.”

Tony laughed, pulled a lighter from his pocket, and lit up. “It’s not tobacco,” he said. After taking a long drag, he handed the cigarette to Mike, and then slowly exhaled blue smoke.

Mike looked at the joint. “Marijuana?”

“The finest; Columbian.”

“I couldn’t tell Columbian from ditch weed, but why not?” He took a drag and immediately had a coughing fit, feeling the burn in his throat.

Tony laughed. “You gotta hold it in,”

Mike tried again and managed to keep it in his lungs for two seconds before coughing violently. He handed it back to Tony who took another long hit.

Mike tried again with even more success, holding it in for close to ten seconds before coughing. “That’s enough,” he said, trying to blink away the smoke.

Tony took another hit, then wet his fingers, put the joint out, and stuck it in his pocket. “Gotta save that. Good stuff.”

“I’ve heard stories about this shit. Is it safe?”

Tony laughed. “Hell of a time to be asking, but it won’t kill you. Hasn’t killed *me* yet, anyway.”

Within minutes, Mike felt a strange sensation in his head, which seemed to be fuller, but, somehow, lighter than it had been. The pain in his ankle was still there but seemed insignificant.

"How long have you been doing this stuff?" he asked.

"Couple years."

"Ever play football, high?"

"Yeah, once. I scrambled away from pass rushers who weren't there, and didn't see defensive backs who were."

They both giggled.

"Maybe you should just quit it."

"Maybe, but I probably won't. I like myself better when I'm high. What'd you think of the Buckeyes game?"

"Looks like they need a quarterback." Mike giggled. *Why was that funny?*

The TV was on the NBC Saturday night movie, showing the musical, *Gentlemen Prefer Blondes*. Through the fog in Mike's brain, the movie suddenly seemed interesting, with Marilyn Monroe looking especially hot.

It seemed like ten minutes later when Tony spoke. "Even if I get there, freshmen don't play on the varsity, so it'll be '63 before I get my shot. Besides, I'm still considering Michigan. People talk funny down here."

"What do you mean by that?"

"You know you do. My dad says the guys at the mill sound like a cross between Jimmy Stewart and Tennessee Ernie Ford." He tried, unsuccessfully, to imitate the Southern Ohio drawl, and then giggled.

"That's funny," Mike said, also giggling. "Not accurate, but funny. We had a girl move here from Michigan a couple of years ago. She talked funny, just like you. It didn't take us long to get her talking almost like a normal person, but then she moved somewhere out east—Boston, I think. Can't imagine what kind of accent she has now."

They both laughed, and then concentrated on the movie. After what seemed like an hour, Mike looked at the wall clock. It was 8:30.

"People in Columbus don't talk like people around here, anyway," Mike said.

Tony shrugged. "I just don't feel like I belong here."

"It's 'cause you're an asshole." Mike giggled some more.

Tony frowned. "How's that?"

"You come around talking about 'niggers' and 'queers', driving your fancy new Corvette. Lots of poor people around here resent that shit." Mike concentrated on the TV, watching Marilyn squirm and wiggle her way through 'Diamonds Are a Girl's Best Friend'.

"So, you don't have any prejudices, Mister Perfect?"

"Yeah, I'm prejudiced against assholes." Mike giggled again, but Tony didn't.

"I hear she doesn't take regular baths," Tony commented as Marilyn finished her song. "She douses herself with perfume to kill the smell."

Picturing himself in a bathtub with Marilyn, Mike didn't reply.

"So, you think everybody around here likes niggers and queers?" Tony asked.

Mike waved him off. "You don't get it and probably never will."

"Enlighten me."

"It's 'niggers' and 'queers', now. But people like you don't stop there. It's fat people, skinny people, ugly people, poor people, crippled people, retarded people, actresses who don't take regular baths… You know what I think?"

"Tell me what you think."

"I think you're a bully. I've heard that bullies tend to be insecure, which makes me wonder if you have something to feel insecure about. Maybe your dad picked on you for pissing the bed when you were younger." *What am I doing?*

"You trying to pick a fight?"

Mike just looked at him.

"Because, if you are, you're not getting one. If I kick your ass, John Breech beats me to a pulp."

"First of all, don't ever think you could kick my ass."

"Never said I could."

"And John's not my bodyguard. I don't need one."

"You know, this stuff is supposed to mellow you out—relax you—not make you…belligerent."

Mike said nothing. They silently watched TV.

Mike spoke up. "I'm hungry, for some reason. You know how to make a peanut butter and jelly sandwich?"

"Well, yeah. Everybody does. Spread peanut butter on one slice of bread and jelly on the other and slap them together."

"That's not the way to do it. You mix the peanut butter and jelly in a bowl, and then spread the mixture on both slices of bread. Then you cut the sandwich diagonally."

"There a law that says that's the only way to do it?"

"Yeah, there is."

"You don't have anything like potato chips?"

"No, but I have peanut butter and jelly—and bread."

Tony shrugged and headed for the kitchen.

Five minutes later, he came back and handed Mike a messy looking sandwich.

Mike licked the excess jelly off the crust, looked at Tony, and shook his head. “You know anything about the Civil War?”

Tony shrugged. “Some.”

“I’ve always wondered why poor southern white men, who couldn’t afford even one slave, and didn’t have any need for one, fought and died to protect slavery. Did you ever wonder about that?”

Tony grunted. “Not lately.”

“Well, I have a theory about it. Did you know that, in 1860, a healthy young field hand—a young buck—would cost a thousand dollars or more? Allowing for inflation, that’s more than your fancy sports car cost your dad.”

“So...why did they fight?”

“Because they were thinking: ‘I ain’t much, but at least, I’m better’n ‘em niggers’. That’s the only explanation I can come up with. And now, a hundred years later, their grandchildren and great grandchildren still think the same way.”

“That relates to me, somehow?”

“Yep.”

“I’m not from the South.”

“It’s not about geography; it’s about attitude.”

Tony munched his sandwich and looked at the TV screen. “That Jane Russell sure has a nice pair on her.”

Mike nodded but said nothing. *Jane Russell does have a nice pair. So does Norma.*

“I guess you’re an only child, huh?” Tony asked.

“Yeah.”

“Me too. We should have been brothers.”

“No, we shouldn’t have.”

"Why not?"

"Because you're an asshole. And if we were brothers, I'd probably be an asshole, too. Either that or I'd be kicking your ass on a regular basis."

"Maybe I wouldn't be an asshole if I had a brother to fight with. And you know what? Maybe the poor whites in the South just didn't want the Yankees telling them how to live."

"Didn't want to be told they couldn't treat dark skinned people like farm animals—or worse?"

Tony didn't answer.

"You're a Catholic, right," Mike asked.

"Yeah."

"So, when you go to confession, do you confess to being an asshole? How many Hail Marys is that?"

There was no more giggling.

At some point, Mike fell asleep; at some point, Tony left. Mike woke up alone in the middle of the 11:00 news, not feeling good about himself. *Must have been the marijuana.*

He shrugged and hobbled off to bed.

Tuesday, May 29, 1962
Ocean Beach

Debbie spoke up. "I took a class at San Diego State on the Civil War a couple of years ago."

"Oh, yeah. Why?"

"Boredom, mostly. I've taken several classes, there. Anyway, aside from the fact that many of them were drafted, there are several reasons why poor Southerners fought in the Civil War. But I think a major one was fear of what four million freed slaves would do to them after all those years of mistreatment. In some states, the slaves outnumbered the white people. And...of course, they *really* didn't want the Yankees telling them how to live. Probably should have been two separate countries, to begin with.

"Also...Tony had a point about the marijuana. It makes most people mellow out, but it has a different effect on different people. It does make some people paranoid. But I think the reason you acted the way you did was because Tony scared you."

"What do you mean—scared?"

"Not physically."

Wednesday, October 4, 1961
Scioto County

Game one of the World Series.

The TV was on in the school cafeteria. Mike, John, and Tim sat at the nearest table watching the pregame show from a packed Yankee Stadium. The controversy over Maris, who had hit his 61st home run on the last day of the season still lingered.

Looking around the room, Mike saw about thirty students—mostly seniors—there to watch the game, along with half a dozen teachers.

The Reds started Jim O'Toole against Whitey Ford. As the Yankees took the field, Mary walked in, sat down next to Mike and grinned at him.

"No! You cut class?" he asked, incredulously.

"Sure, I did," she replied, still grinning.

"You'll go to hell for lying, Mary."

She sighed. "Okay, fine. I got permission. And I have our assignments." She waved a sheet of paper in his face and stuck it inside her Physics book.

Mike hugged her.

In the second inning, Tony walked in with Eve Phillips and sat at the table next to them. Eve smiled at Mike, but Tony didn't. "How's the ankle?" He asked, barely making eye contact. The two of them hadn't spoken since Saturday.

Mike considered apologizing for his tirade, but quickly rejected the notion. "I'll be ready to keep you from getting knocked on your ass, Friday."

Tony focused on the TV. "That's good to know."

O'Toole pitched well, but not well enough, as Whitey Ford shut the Reds out 2-0.

Mary left after the 7th inning to catch the bus. Coach Hauser delayed practice until after the game. Mike practiced on his sore ankle for the first time.

"So, you gonna skip class tomorrow?" Mike asked Mary as they sat on her back porch doing homework.

"No. One of us has to be responsible. But I'll get the assignments for you," she replied.

He looked out at the barn. "Thanks. How's Babs, by the way?"

"She's fine. Before long, the grass will be gone. Oh, and she misses you, of course."

"How about me, you, and Babs get together Sunday after the game?"

"You, Babs, and I," she corrected. "Would that qualify as a date?"

He shook his head, emphatically. "Nope."

Thursday, October 5

The Reds sent 21-game-winner, Joey Jay, to the mound to face Ralph Terry of the Yankees in game two.

Mike sat alone at the table closest to the TV, as John and Tim had decided to attend class. As he looked around the room, noticing that there were fewer people than yesterday, Tony and Eve walked in and sat down at his table. A few minutes later, Norma came in, smiled at Eve, ignored Tony, and sat down next to Mike.

Gordy Coleman hit a two-run homer in the top of the fourth to give the Reds the lead, but Yogi Berra tied it in the bottom of the inning with a two-run homer of his own.

Mike could feel Norma's warm thigh against his. He moved his leg; she slid closer.

Johnny Edwards put the Reds back ahead in the fifth with an RBI single. They scored another run in the sixth aided by Clete Boyer's error.

In the bottom of the seventh, Mary stuck her head in the door to say goodbye to Mike on her way to the bus. She looked at Norma, looked at Mike, waved, and left without saying a word.

Shit!

Norma and Eve left to catch the bus. Tony glanced at Mike and smirked, but said nothing.

Joey Jay pitched a complete game, four-hitter, and the Reds won 6-2, evening the series at a game apiece.

Friday, October 6

No baseball; travel day.

The Shawnee played at home against Portsmouth West.

Mike's heavily taped ankle felt somewhat better. He ran the ball four times for 22 yards and caught two passes for 24 more. Tony had a great night—24 for 29, for 325 yards, including an eighty-yard bomb to wide receiver, Larry Penn. Mike sat out the entire second half, as the Shawnee romped 42-10, to go to 5-0 for the season.

Everything seemed fine with Mary as they necked in front of her house. She was enthusiastic, but Mike made it a point to keep his hands away from her 'sensitive' areas.

Sunday, October 8

The Reds were now in trouble, losing 3-2 Saturday on Maris' ninth-inning home run off Bob Purkey, then being shut out 7-0 by Whitey Ford. A Yankee win Monday would give them the World Series.

At four PM, Mike sat down on the glider next to Mary, who was reading a book.

"Looks like the potatoes are gone," he remarked, looking out at the furrows of dirt that used to be the potato patch.

"Harvested them yesterday," she said. "My back's still sore."

"I would have helped."

"I know, but the World Series was on, so I didn't ask." She indicated a brown paper bag on the floor. "Potatoes for you—from Mom."

"Thanks. Where is everybody?"

"Watching TV, I think. We just got home from church a little bit ago."

"Whatcha reading?"

"*The Caine Mutiny.*"

"What's it about?"

"Considering the title, it's probably about a mutiny—maybe on a ship." She flashed a fake smile.

"Wanna take a walk?"

"I'll get the cow."

Mike looked out at Babs. "So, what'll happen to the calf?"

"Depends. If it's a boy, he'll probably be sold and end up as veal. If it's a girl, we might keep her and let her grow up to be a dairy cow. Or we might sell her to someone else for that. Females are worth a lot more than males."

"How's that?"

"Cows give milk; bulls don't. I don't know the exact numbers, but one bull can service hundreds of cows. One lucky one out of a hundred or so gets to be a bull. The rest end up on somebody's plate."

"How can he handle so many?"

She smiled indulgently and patted him on the knee. "If you had paid attention in biology class you'd know that cows are not like humans. They come in heat—or get horny, as you would call it—shortly after the calf is weaned. Once she gets pregnant again, that's it. Bulls are like teenage boys—ready to go anytime—but cows don't have recreational sex."

"So, I guess he doesn't have to take her out to dinner or bring her flowers huh?"

She slapped him on the shoulder but giggled. "I've seen them do it, you know. It takes about five seconds—wham, bam, thank you, ma'am." She giggled again.

"Where'd you hear that expression?"

"I don't know." She giggled some more. "Somewhere."

"So, if women were like cows they could slaughter about 99 percent of boys?"

"Theoretically, that would be enough to propagate the species."

"Who would fight the wars and hunt the wooly mammoths?"

"Women probably would have to do that. We'd probably keep the man in a cage, and bring him out when we needed him. Who knows? Maybe there wouldn't be any wars."

"Who services Babs?"

"You know the Rameys, about two miles up the road?"

"Yeah. Paul's a sophomore. Skinny guy; tried out for football, but didn't make it."

"They have a bull. We usually walk her there—or actually, she walks us, quickly, since she knows where she's going and why."

"What's the bull's name?"

"Barney, I think."

Mike looked quickly toward the house, and then kissed her; she kissed him back. He put his hand on her stomach; she left it there. When he slid it lower, underneath the waistband of her jeans, she gently pushed it away.

"So, what else do you want to talk about?" he asked.

"I hear Tony's dating Eve."

"Dating, or just..."

"Shush," she interrupted. "Does that bother you?"

"Tony and Eve? Of course not. Why would it?"

They were silent for several minutes.

"Girls get horny, too, you know," she finally said.

"And...?"

"And that doesn't mean we should act like Babs and go after the first...bull we can find."

"Because boys act like Barney?"

"Well, you know you do."

"You mentioned biology class."

"Humans are different. We're supposed to exercise some self-control. And, with us, there's commitment, affection, enjoying each other's company, not just sex."

"So, do you think Babs has any affection for Barney, or is it just, 'Get it over with and leave me alone'?"

“I suspect she has more affection for the mules than she does for Barney. She shares a barn with them, and sees him once a year.”

“Makes sense.”

She looked at the sky. “It’s getting dark. Do you have your homework done?”

“Yeah.”

“Good boy. What’re you going to do tonight? You could stay for supper.”

“Okay,” he said, figuring that if he left now, he wouldn’t be able to resist calling Eve—or Norma.

“This wasn’t a date, huh?” Mary asked.

“Nope.”

Monday, October 9

The Yankees scored five runs off Joey Jay in the first inning. Mike gave up and went to class.

The Reds were in their first World Series in 21 years. The Yankees were in their eleventh in thirteen. Obviously, it was an intimidating experience for Cincinnati. *Maybe next year.*

When Mike got to his car after practice, there was a note from Mary underneath his wiper blade, reminding him—again—that his book report on *Of Mice and Men* was due Friday.

After listening to the post-mortem of the Reds’ 13-5 loss, he stopped by her house, picked up the book, and headed home to spend the evening with Steinbeck.

Tuesday, October 10

Bleary eyed from reading and working on his report until one in the morning, Mike arrived at Mary's house ten minutes later than usual. Mary was waiting, but Becky wasn't.

"She think I wasn't coming?"

"Actually, you remember we were talking about Paul Ramey?

He nodded.

"Well…it seems Becky's a little bit sweet on him, so she wants to ride the bus with him."

"That skinny kid?"

"Shut up. He's cute, and he's the smartest kid in sophomore class. Did you get your book report done?"

"Almost. You should look at it."

"Yeah, I should."

"It was a sad story. Where'd the title come from?"

"We covered that poem in freshman English."

"You know I hate poetry."

"Well, it's from a Robert Burns poem called 'To a Mouse'. He's plowing up a field and plows up a nest of mice. As the story goes, he wrote the poem while still standing at the plow. 'The best-laid plans of mice and men often go awry'. Well, actually, he wrote 'The best-laid schemes o' mice an' men gang aft-a-glay'."

"I get the picture. Certainly true, but not much of a revelation."

He tuned the radio to WIOI. They listened to The Everly Brothers sing 'Ebony Eyes'.

"No game Friday," Mike said. "Maybe we could do something—if your dad will let us."

"You and I could do something?" Her eyes widened as she stared at him. "You mean like a date?"

"Yes, like a date. Don't have a heart attack."

"I'm about to. What'll we do?"

"Well, we could go to a movie in Portsmouth, and then maybe get a burger at the bowling alley. Or we could go to a drive-in restaurant, eat in the car, and neck like real teenagers do. Or just skip the food and go somewhere and neck."

She shook her head but smiled. "We'd better go to the bowling alley. You *will* have to ask Dad, though."

"What'll he say?"

"Actually, he and I had a conversation about this a few weeks ago. I told him that if you asked me out on a date, he should allow me to go. He said, 'If *Mike* asks you out, you can go'. So I figure he'll give you that stern look and say, 'You'd better have her home by ten'." She used the deepest voice she could muster.

"What'll I say?"

"You'll say 'How about eleven?'"

"And what'll he say?"

"Are you kidding? It's you, Mike. He'll say, 'Okay, make sure it's no later'n 'at'."

"What would he have said if I'd asked him a year ago?"

"He would have said, 'You two ain't goin' on no date. You're too young'."

"What's changed in a year?"

"Aside from the fact that we're a year older, I think he's come to the realization that, at some point, he's just going to have to let go."

"So, I'm supposed to...take over?"

"Well...kind of."

"Are you comfortable with that?"

"Always have been—kind of. I don't want another father, telling me how to dress and how to act. And I still want to do something with my life besides make babies. Maybe I could get into TV; be the anchorwoman on network news—a female Chet Huntley."

"More likely you'd just be getting coffee for Chet Huntley."

"Times are changing, Mike. You know...people in my family—and I have lots of family scattered all over Kentucky and West Virginia—they don't graduate from high school. The boys learn to read and write, quit school, and go job hunting. The girls start looking for a husband by the time they get to be teenagers, so they can start making babies. I have cousins my age who are already married and have children. One of them compared herself to a brood mare. I don't know of anyone in the family who has ever attended college. But fortunately, Mom and Dad want me to go. So, the real question is: Are you comfortable with that?"

"Yeah. I'd be disappointed, too, if you didn't go to college."

He parked the car; she took his hand.

"So...I could have a career, and you wouldn't mind helping with babies, changing diapers—if we were fortunate enough to have babies? You wouldn't mind helping with the cooking and cleaning?"

They have it all planned out. Best laid plans... He shrugged. "Well, I already do the cooking and cleaning. Never changed a shitty diaper, though."

"Don't talk dirty." She kissed him quickly.

"What if we end up at different schools?"

"I don't even wanna think about that. Come on; we'll be late."

Friday, October 13

No game. No practice.

"So, you told everybody we were going on a date, huh?" Mike asked on the way home from school.

"I'd have asked the principal to announce it over the PA system if I'd thought he'd do it," she quipped.

"He just might have. John said it was about time, and Tim shook my hand and congratulated me. Kind of stupid since it's just a date," he grumbled.

"Just our first date." Her eyes sparkled.

"Movie starts at seven-thirty." He smiled at her enthusiasm. "How about I pick you up at seven?"

"We won't have much time to go to the bowling alley. I have to be home by eleven."

"I negotiated it to midnight." Trying to mimic Joe Bryant's voice he said, "Okay, make sure it's no later'n 'at."

She laughed. "Do you realize it's Friday the thirteenth?"

"You superstitious?"

"You just never know what might happen, Mike."

At seven o'clock, Mike was sitting in the Bryant's living room talking football with Jimmy when Mary came down the stairs, wearing a powder blue calf length dress with a wide white belt that emphasized her narrow waist. The dress fit her just a bit more snugly in the hips and bosom than what she normally wore. Not tight, just snug in the right places. Her long dark hair, normally in a ponytail, now fell freely down her back and shoulders. She was carrying a white sweater on her arm. No makeup, no jewelry, no high heels, no stockings. She didn't need any of that.

He looked down at his open-collared shirt and jeans, realizing he was underdressed.

"Well?" she asked.

"New dress?"

"Yeah. You like it?"

"Should I go home and change?"

"No, silly. You look fine."

"Your parents know about the dress?"

"Mom helped me pick it out."

"What's your dad think?"

She looked cautiously around the room. "He hasn't seen it. You still haven't told me if you like it."

"I like it, and I like what's in it."

In the car, she asked, "What're we seeing?

"How about *Elmer Gantry*?"

"How about *not*?"

"That leaves *Lover Come Back*, with Doris Day and Rock Hudson, at the LaRoy. Starts at seven-forty-five."

"That sounds more like it." She hugged his arm. "Wow, this is a date, Mike, and you can't say it isn't."

He looked at her as he downshifted coming up to a stop sign. "Mary, I really don't deserve you," he said.

"I know, but you have me anyway, so deal with it, buddy."

They walked into a busy Harrison Bowl at ten-fifteen, and, in a matter of seconds, were swarmed by league bowlers. "Is this Mary?" they all asked. "You lucky dog," one man said as he looked Mary up and down." "It's about time you showed her off," another said.

"Now you know how I felt at your church," Mike said to Mary as Al Lewis pulled out a concourse chair for her.

Don came out from behind the counter and greeted her with a hug. "Good to see you, Mary. It's been a while."

"I'll see if I can rustle us up some grub," Mike said.

Tonight, as with most league nights, Penny Hilt was the bartender and Marsha was the cook. Penny was a borderline attractive, thirtyish, blonde, divorcee, with two pre-teen boys at home. Though she always looked slightly unkempt, she was friendly, outgoing, and popular with the customers.

She hugged Mike across the bar and said, "I'm a little busy, but I definitely want to meet that girl before you leave."

"You got it," he replied. "Is Marsha too busy to make us a couple of burgers, you think?"

"You know she'll drop everything to cook for you."

"Make the real customers wait, huh?"

"Of course."

Marsha greeted him in the kitchen with a hug. "It'd better be burgers and fries, 'cause I just put 'em down for you." She slapped him gently on the shoulder. "Get outa my kitchen. I'll bring 'em out. I want to say 'hi' to Mary. Haven't seen her since Willy's funeral."

Recalling the sad day in '57 when they had buried Marsha's husband, Mike bussed her cheek and went out to rescue Mary, who was still surrounded by bowlers. To his surprise, she seemed to be enjoying the attention.

"How long have you two known each other," one woman asked Mary.

"Since first grade," Mary replied politely. "It's our first date, though."

"Why in the world would you wait so long to take her out, Mike?" asked another.

"It's a long story, and I'm not telling it tonight," Mike replied as he sat down next to Mary.

They left at 11:30, allowing just enough time to get her home before midnight. "I don't want to turn into a pumpkin," she said.

"Maybe I should shoot for one o'clock next time."

"Don't push your luck," she responded dreamily, as she snuggled up to him.

"Here," he said. "Give me your hand." He took his class ring from his pocket and closed her fingers around it."

"Wow," she said.

"I never wore it, anyway."

She laughed. "Well, that's romantic."

"How long have you known me, Mary?"

"Good point."

His hand brushed her thigh as he shifted gears.

"Is my leg in the way?" she asked.

"No. It's in exactly the right place."

She didn't move it.

They stepped quietly onto the Bryant's front porch at 11:55. The house was dark except for one dim light in the living room.

Mary sighed. “I feel like Cinderella.”

“Would that make me Prince Charming?”

“Wrong fairy tale, Harrison, but…yes, you are my Prince Charming.”

“You think everyone’s asleep in there.”

“The kids are probably asleep. Mom and Dad are probably pretending.”

After a long goodnight kiss, she walked into the house at 11:59.

Saturday, October 14

Mike did laundry and cleaned house while listening to the Buckeyes thrash Illinois 44-0.

Mary called at five o’clock. “Whatcha doing, Prince Charming?”

“Scrubbing the bathroom floor, Snow White…or is it Cinderella?”

“Prince Charming was in Snow White. The Handsome Prince was in Cinderella. You can be whichever you want to be.

“Couldn’t I be both?”

“Handsome Prince Charming might be taking it a little too far, but…” She laughed. “Listen, we’re having a little corn-shucking party tonight. Wanna come join us?”

“What’s that?”

“Well, you know we don’t have harvesting equipment. We do everything by hand, including shucking the corn.”

“What time?”

"About seven. The Rameys will be here—and the Mitchells."

"Won't it be getting dark?"

"That's part of the fun. We'll build a big bonfire for light—and to keep us warm. Later, we'll roast marshmallows—maybe tell stories. Dad says that's the way they did it when he was a kid. Sounded like fun, so I talked him into doing it this year."

"I'll be there."

Sam escorted him to the rear of the house where a bonfire was rising into the semi-darkness on the other end of the yard. There was a large circle of folding chairs, lounge chairs, and blankets around the fire. Inside the circle, almost safely away from the fire, were two wooden sleds, piled high with corn the Bryants had picked by hand.

Joe Bryant greeted him with a handshake, and introduced him to the Ramey family—Paul being the only one Mike had ever met. Paul's father, Emmitt, was a short, skinny man with a long beard and sparse, brown teeth, wearing a very old looking fedora with a hole at the peak. His wife, Pearl, was pleasant looking, but much heavier than her husband. Her rear end barely fit into the lawn chair she occupied. Her teeth were so perfect that Mike was sure they were false. They actually seemed to glow in the firelight. Intermingled in the circle were the six Bryant children and the seven Ramey children. The little ones sat on blankets next to their parents.

Joe also introduced Mike to Simon and Lily Mitchell, an older couple who looked to be in their sixties. Simon was bald, short, and wide. A guitar leaned against his chair. Lily was a somewhat large woman with several warts on her face. When she smiled at Mike, the warts seemed to dance around.

Mike took a chair between Mary and Paul. Becky was on Paul's other side, sitting possessively close.

"I'm going to be suiting up Monday," Paul said to Mike. "I'm on the team."

"Hey, that's great, Paul. Who quit?"

"Coach kicked Donny Miller off the team for missing practice two days in a row."

"Donny never played much, anyway."

"I probably won't either, but it'll be fun just to be on the team."

"Yes, it will. Congratulations."

Mary stood up, walked around to Becky, and whispered in her ear. Becky looked up toward her parents, nodded, and then slid her chair a few inches away from Paul. Mary looked at her father, and then back at Becky, who sighed and moved farther away.

As the radio blared country music from the Grand Ole Opry, the adults reminisced about the good old days and bad old days in Eastern Kentucky. They talked about their religion and hardship. About relatives and friends who had died of black lung and from mining accidents. About moonshining, unsolved murders, and crooked government officials. About their ancestors and current relatives—sometimes with reverence, sometimes with disdain.

Mike had no family stories to tell.

After shucking all the corn and putting it in the crib for winter feed, they roasted marshmallows, talked, laughed, and told jokes.

Joe turned off the radio. Simon finished a story about an unfortunate acquaintance from his moonshining days with "shot him down like an egg-suckin' dog", and then picked up his guitar and began picking and singing Gospel songs. He did 'I'll Fly Away', 'The Old Rugged Cross', and a Hank Williams song, 'I Saw the Light'. His voice was pleasant but monotonal.

Putting down his guitar, he began singing 'Amazing Grace'. Led by Joe, others joined in. It seemed to Mike—as he looked around—that he was the only one over the age of five who didn't know the words.

They threw more logs on the fire as the air became chillier. Mike looked at his watch; it was ten o'clock.

Mary patted him on the arm, went into the house, and returned wearing a blue and white flannel shirt, and carrying a transistor radio and a flashlight.

"That my shirt?" he asked.

"Yeah. You left it last spring. You're not getting it back. I sleep in it, sometimes." She handed Mike the radio, took him by the hand, and led him down the path toward the meadow. He looked back at her parents, who were pretending not to notice.

She turned off the flashlight as they sat on the log. Looking back toward the house, he could see the fire and the shadows of people. No one in the backyard could see them.

Mike tuned the radio to WLS. The Lettermen were doing 'The Way You Look Tonight'.

They looked at the sky. A few stars were visible despite the bonfire. They looked at each other in the dark. He kissed her; she kissed him back. She still tasted like grape Kool-Aid. Her hair smelled like lilac and wood smoke.

“Interesting friends your parents have,” he said, at length.

“Simon’s a faith healer.”

“Really? Does that ever work?”

“I’ve heard it works for some people—people who have faith, I guess. He tried it on Jimmy’s tooth once.”

"Did it work?"

“No. Dad took him to the dentist the next day. Had to have a root canal; that worked.” She laughed. “I guess Jimmy didn’t have enough faith.”

Serenaded by Connie Francis’ version of ‘Hold Me, Thrill Me, Kiss Me’, they made out for several minutes, with Mike finally getting to second base, and heading for third. Her left hand briefly brushed against him before gently pushing his hand away. She stood up and rearranged her clothes.

“Time to re-join the party,” she said, breathlessly.

“We’ll have to wait a couple minutes,” he told her.

“Why?” She laughed. “Oh.”

Friday, October 20

The Shawnee were to play Valley at Lucasville.

“Did you hear what happened in Mr. O’Brien’s class, yesterday?” Mary asked Mike on the way to school.

“No. What?”

“Someone put a…a dildo on his desk.” Her face turned crimson.

“Let me guess. Sixth period?” Mike asked.

“Yes, it was.”

"Tony did it."

"What makes you think that?"

"Because I know him. So, what did Jack Spratt do?"

"We should stop calling him that, but I heard he just picked it up and put it in the trash. Didn't say a word; just started class as if nothing had happened."

"Good for him. And he doesn't mind being called that."

"Only because you gave him the name?" She shook her head. "You don't know it was Tony, though. You're just guessing."

"Pretty educated guess. I know him; he's an asshole."

"Don't talk dirty."

"Fine. He's a jackass."

On the way to Lucasville, Coach Matt Riley sat down next to Mike. "Ever heard of Bo Schembechler?" he asked.

"Yeah, he's an assistant coach at OSU."

"He's Woody Hayes' right-hand man, and he's going to be at the game, tonight."

"Scouting Tony, no doubt. You want me to keep making Tony look good, right?"

The coach sighed. "There's more to it than that, Mike. I met him once at a coaching camp; seemed like a good guy. Long story short, I sent him a letter about you, building you up—maybe more than you deserve. He replied by saying he'd heard about you, and since he wanted to take another look at the Duvardo kid, he'd look at you, also. Truth is they've already offered Tony, which means he's here primarily to check you out."

"Thanks, Coach. I'll do my best to impress him."

"Could be your only chance."

He impressed Bo in a big way, ripping off runs of 78 and 60 yards, on his way to 230 yards on 12 carries. On defense, he was all over the field, making tackles, and breaking up passes. He sat out the fourth quarter in a 63-16 romp. Tony put up big numbers passing and left the game the same time as Mike. There were no grass stains on his uniform. The Shawnee were now 6-0.

After the game, Coach Riley introduced Mike to Coach Schembechler.

"Great game," the Buckeyes' assistant said to Mike. "I can't be a hundred percent sure, since we have several kids to look at, but I think we're going to offer you. Not as a running back, though. Ferguson will be gone, but we still have Paul Warfield and Matt Snell, plus a couple of real good freshmen. I'm not sure about Coach Hayes, but I want you as a linebacker. You seem to have the right amount of controlled meanness for the position."

"I hope that's a compliment, Sir."

Schembechler laughed. "It certainly is, son. Listen, you keep your grades up and stay out of trouble, you'll be in Columbus next fall."

He shook Mike's hand and left.

Tears welled in Mike's eyes as he looked at Coach Riley. "Thanks, Coach."

The coach put his hand on Mike's shoulder. "You deserve it."

Mike looked at Coach Hauser, who stuck out his hand. "Congratulations, Harrison. Don't screw it up."

Mike gave Paul Ramey a ride home after the game. Because it was such a blowout, Paul had played most of the fourth quarter and registered a solo tackle and an assist.

"Congratulations, Mike," he said when Mike told him about Schembechler. "You know, I'd give twenty IQ points to be as good an athlete as you."

"That probably would be a bad move on your part. But just between you and I, you'd still be smarter."

"Between you and me," Paul corrected. "Sorry."

"Oh, it's okay. Mary does that all the time. She could star in a new TV series, *Mary Bryant, Language Cop*. You could be her faithful sidekick. Going after criminals like me."

Paul chuckled. "People who murder the language?"

"Yeah. I might make that trade, though, if it was possible."

"Really?"

"Maybe. I'd like to have the twenty IQ points."

"I'd like to be a better athlete. I feel like a...a jock trapped in a nerd's body."

Mike laughed. "Maybe you should just work on it. Put on a few pounds, run up and down the hills."

"You think?"

"Yeah, and if I studied harder, I could be smarter."

At length, Paul said, "Tony's kind of a bully, isn't he?"

"What'd he do?"

"Head-butted me once in practice. Gives me dirty looks all the time; makes snide remarks about how scrawny I am."

Mike took a while to respond, thinking about his marijuana-fueled conversation with Tony. "I'm not surprised," he finally said. "He's an asshole. Get in his face next time. He'll back off."

"You think?"

"Well, if he doesn't I'll pull him off you before he does too much damage."

"That's encouraging."

Mike couldn't wait to tell Mary about Schembechler. After dropping Paul off, he drove up Bryant Holler. The house was dark except for a faint light in the upstairs bedroom that Mary shared with Becky. He remembered a scene from a movie where a guy threw small pebbles at his girlfriend's window to get her attention. Reluctantly, figuring he'd probably break a window, he turned the Chevy around and went home.

Saturday, October 21

He called her at eight AM. "Hey, why don't I come get you; we can have breakfast here?"

"I've had breakfast. Some of us don't get to sleep all morning. What's going on? You never call me this early, Mike. Did you hurt yourself?"

"No, I just have some news."

"Just a minute." She put down the phone and yelled, "DAD!"

Seconds later, she was back on the phone. "Give me an hour."

"Nine o'clock, sharp."

"Okay, but I have to be home by noon. Chores to do."

In the car, Mary asked, "What's your news?"

"Not telling you 'til we get to my house."

In his living room, she grabbed his arm. "Tell me."

"No. Breakfast first, woman."

She let go and giggled. "Fine, I'll make you eggs and bacon?"

"You know there's no pig meat in this house."

"You know, Mike, the Rameys butcher cows about the same way; yet you eat hamburger. And you've seen what we do to chickens."

"What's your point?"

With a smile, she patted him on the head and went into the kitchen.

While he scarfed down eggs and potatoes, she sat sipping an overly sweetened and overly creamed cup of coffee.

"Can you even taste the coffee?" he asked.

"No, I hate the taste. Now tell me."

"So, why do you drink it?"

"Tell me!"

He told her about the game, and then about Coach Schembechler.

She jumped on him, nearly knocking his chair over. "I knew it! I knew it!" she exclaimed. "Everything's going to work out. We'll be in Columbus together." She pounded his chest. "Aren't you excited?"

"I am, actually." He grabbed her hands. "Please don't kill me."

"Sorry. Now I have to work hard on my scholarship."

"It's ten o'clock. What're we going to do for the next two hours?" she asked.

He tilted his head toward his bedroom. "I have an idea."

She rolled her eyes but smiled. “What are we going to do for the next two hours, Mike?”

“We’re going to run the hill.”

“Oh yeah? What hill, and why?”

Mike pointed out the kitchen window. “That hill and because I want to show you something. There’s a path all the way to the top that I run to stay in shape. And sometimes I run it because I’m pissed off or frustrated.”

“Don’t talk dirty,” she smiled.

“What? Pissed ain’t a dirty word. Come on.”

“It is, and don’t say 'ain’t'. Aren’t you sore from last night?”

“Yeah, a little; but this gets the blood flowing.”

She looked around the house. “Is your dad ever home?”

“Not much. Right now, the kids’ league is bowling, and he never misses that. Let’s go.”

They sprinted up the hill. She nearly stayed with him, falling only about ten yards behind by the time he reached the top. It took her a few minutes to catch her breath.

“C’mere, I want to show you something,” he said.

He took her by the shoulders and turned her forty-five degrees to the left. Standing behind her, he pointed over her shoulder. “You can see it better when all the leaves are gone, but if you look closely you can see it now.”

“My house!”

“Yeah, it is. Sometimes I come up here just to make sure it’s still there.”

She hugged him. “I can’t believe that, having known each other all these years, we haven’t been up here together.”

"You and I haven't spent much time at my house in all these years. We're always at yours under the watchful eyes of your parents."

"That's true."

"Sometimes I come up here and bat rocks for hours."

"Bat rocks?"

"Yeah, I don't use a regular baseball bat, because the rocks would ruin it. I took a 1x4, cut it thirty inches long, and whittled it down at one end to make a handle. Most times…" He paused. "It's kind of a stress reliever. Take my frustrations out on the rocks."

They walked twenty feet down the ridgeline toward Hope Run, and then another twenty feet down the other side of the hill to a flat area. He picked up a quarter-sized rock. "You see, there are lots of these. Heavy rain washes 'em down the ridge to this area. I bat 'em down the hill; toss 'em into the air and whack 'em like hitting fungoes. Hit 'em just right they go a long way. Sometimes I play a game, pretending to be the Reds against the Dodgers or the Reds and Yankees in the World Series. I hit for both teams and bat right-handed for the right-handed batters and left for the lefties. Sometimes I bat 'til I get blisters on my hands."

He pointed down the hill toward a clearing near the creek where the remnants of a small house stood. "I hear a family named Boyd farmed this side up 'til after the war. The parents both died, and the kids just abandoned the place and moved back to Kentucky to live with other relatives.

"All the tall trees have been logged out, so, you can see, there's a clear shot toward the house. Whether it's an out, a single, a double, a triple, or a home run depends on how far—and how straight—I hit it. See the two dead chestnuts?" He pointed. "They're the foul poles. Haven't done it since before football practice started, though. Not much free time."

"You and I should do that together sometime. It sounds like fun. I could be the Yankees."

He hugged her. "We'll have lots of days to do that."

Sunday, October 22

It was eleven AM and Don Harrison had gone to work. Mike was sprawled on the couch reading the newspaper. The seventh-ranked Ohio State Buckeyes had shut out Northwestern 10-0, Saturday. There was an article recapping the South Central Ohio Conference action from Friday night. Mike's name was prominent, as there was a sub-headline, asking, 'Was that Mike Harrison or Jim Brown out there Friday night?'

Hearing a car in the driveway, he looked out the window. Norma West was getting out of a beat up '51 Ford, her face looking red and puffy, and her hair looking like she had just gotten out of bed. He greeted her at the door. "You're a mess. What's up?"

"Thanks. You look nice, too." Tears ran down her face; a bruise highlighted her left cheekbone.

Mike escorted her to the couch.

"Coffee?" he asked. "I just made a pot."

"Yes, please."

"Cream, sugar…?"

"Just coffee."

After she took a sip, Mike looked at her cheek. “The assailant was right-handed,” he remarked.

“How’d you guess?” She smiled between the tears.

“Tell me who it was; I’ll go beat him up, right now.”

“Thanks, but that’s not why I’m here. I just want to hang out for a while. My mother’s boyfriend thought he had the right to discipline me. Spare the fist, spoil the child, you know.” She laughed. “I feel better already. May I stay awhile, please?”

“That your mom’s car?”

“Yeah, her jackass boyfriend will give her a ride if she wants to go somewhere.”

“Sure, but I don’t want any rumors to get started. Mary and I are in a really good place right now and I don’t wanna ruin it.”

Sounding disappointed, she said, “Thanks. I’ll be really discreet.”

He made up an ice pack; she lay back on the couch and held it to her cheek. He picked up the newspaper and moved to the recliner across the room. Five minutes later, he looked up; she was sound asleep.

The Cleveland Browns were playing in Pittsburgh, and the game was to be televised locally. He figured he’d watch the game, get rid of Norma, and then call Mary. Maybe whittle her a bat.

As the Steelers were kicking off to Bobby Mitchell, Norma woke up and said, “I need to use the bathroom.”

Mike pointed, and then returned his attention to the game as Jim Brown ran off left tackle for eight yards. Milt Plum followed with a pass over the middle for sixteen yards to Ray Renfro.

Norma returned, looking better. She sat on the arm of the recliner and leaned toward him, showing significant cleavage.

"See anything you like?" she asked.

"Of course, but..."

"No buts. Mary will never know." She began unbuckling his belt.

Norma left at halftime. The Browns won 30-28 with Mike barely paying attention.

The phone rang right after the game went final.

"We just got home. Had to eat at some old couple's house," Mary said. "How's my prince?"

"Uh...good. How was church?"

"It was...church. I miss you. Come for supper."

"I...I have to go to the bowling alley."

"Why?"

Can't look you in the eye. "Uh...problems with lane three again. They have a full house of league tonight."

"Okay, I'll see you tomorrow. I love you."

"I love you too, Mary."

He ran the hill three times and was exhausted, but felt no better. *I'm an idiot.*

Friday, October 27

Big road game tonight against the Wheelersburg Pirates who were still undefeated along with Waverly and Central.

Mary was unusually quiet on the way to school.

"You okay?" Mike asked.

"Yes, I'm fine, Mike," she replied without looking at him.

"I wish you could be at the game, tonight."

"Well, I can't."

That time of the month?

She was quietly polite to him the rest of the day, and didn't talk to him at all before getting on the bus.

He still had her in his head at the beginning of the game, and, for the first time all season, allowed a pass rusher to get to Tony and tackle him for a loss. He quickly helped Tony to his feet and apologized.

"You okay?" Tony asked him.

"Fine. I should be asking you," hc replied, shaking his head. "The guy was a little quicker than I thought. Won't happen again."

It didn't. With the offensive line playing well, Tony completed two long touchdown passes to Ronnie Stone. Mike was everywhere making plays on defense. And with five minutes to play, the Shawnee leading 24-16, and Wheelersburg out of time-outs, he carried the ball seven straight times for three first downs as they ran out the clock. Seven and oh, with the homecoming game against Northwest next Friday, and then the big game against Waverly.

Saturday, October 28

He knocked on the Bryants' door at nine AM. Joe answered and asked, "What's goin' on with you and Mary?"

"I don't know, sir. I need to talk to her."

"She's out back on the log takin' a break. We've been cuttin' firewood." He squeezed Mike's shoulder and went back inside.

Mary was sitting on the log, staring straight ahead, as Mike approached.

"Tell me what's wrong and I'll fix it, Mary," he said, as he sat down next to her.

She didn't reply immediately, just stared at the hillside. Finally, she exhaled forcefully and looked up at him through teary eyes.

"I called your house Sunday after you said you were going to the bowling alley, but you didn't answer. I just wanted to compare notes on the Physics homework…." She stopped and looked away. "Then, I called the bowling alley. You weren't there, hadn't been there, and weren't expected." Her voice was barely above a whisper, now. "Was Norma West at your house that day?"

"Mary, I can explain that. Her mom's boyfriend beat her up."

"I heard about that, but why did she come to your house?"

"I don't know, but I couldn't kick her out. And I must have been running the hill when you called."

"Why'd you lie?"

He didn't answer.

She whispered, *"Did you and Norma…?"*

"Mary…"

"DID YOU SCREW NORMA WEST?" she screamed. Putting her hands together as if in prayer, she whispered again. *"Did you?"*

Unable to look at her, he looked toward the house, seeing Joe Bryant walking toward them. "Better go on home, son."

Sunday, October 29

Mike went to visit his grandfather at noon.

As Gramps stood in the kitchen making their peanut butter and jelly sandwiches, he asked, "How's your dad? I haven't talked to him in a while."

"I haven't talked to him much, either. Seems okay, though. Still works all the time." He studied his grandfather as they ate. "Move in with us, Gramps."

"I'll be a burden soon enough, Mikey. But what's wrong with you?"

"You'll just say 'I told you so'."

"Probably." He shrugged. "About all I'm good for at my age. You blow the engine in your car?"

"No."

"Something going on with you and Mary?"

Mike told him the story.

Gramps sighed. "You're not the only teenager who screwed up a relationship because he couldn't keep his pecker in his pants. And you certainly won't be the last.

Give it some time and she'll forgive you, just like your grandmother forgave me."

"You?"

"Yeah, I was a horny teenager once, believe it or not. If she loves you, she won't let you go—as long as you don't make a habit of it."

They watched the Cleveland Browns beat the Cardinals 21-10 with Jim Brown and Bobby Mitchell combining for 230 yards rushing. Mike left, feeling somewhat better.

At home, he decided to take a chance and call her. Becky answered the phone. "She won't talk to you, Mike, but she said that, if you called, she'd be taking the bus from now on."

Friday, November 3

It had been a rough week for Mike, with Mary not even acknowledging his existence.

As he brought his lunch tray into the cafeteria, he saw her sitting with two girls from speech class—*and* Tony Duvardo. Mary seemed to be listening intently to something Tony was saying. She glanced at Mike, stone-faced, and then returned her attention to Tony.

Mike's first impulse was to smash Tony's face with his lunch tray. He resisted the impulse but fumed. *She's punishing me, and I deserve it. But sitting with Tony…?*

He found an empty table and ate alone.

Eve Phillips was Homecoming Queen, and Mike, as team captain, was supposed to be her escort, but he begged off and Tony was given the task.

Mike stood silently, impatiently, on the sideline during the festivities, just wanting the game to start so that he could hit people. He scoured the bleachers, not seeing Mary, but not expecting to.

On defense, he forced and recovered two fumbles in the first half. Tony threw three touchdown passes and the Shawnee led the Northwest Mohawks 24-0 at halftime.

As he sat ignoring Coach Hauser's halftime speech, an idea was forming in his head. He tried to beat it back, but it wouldn't go away.

His chance came midway through the third quarter with the Shawnee in possession of the ball at the Mohawks forty-five yard line. Tony had thrown two incomplete passes, making it third and ten.

Northwest had a 230-pound all-conference defensive lineman named Dan Sawicki, who was having no success lining up against John Breech. He moved to the other side and lined up against 160-pound end, Luke Craycraft.

Noting this, Tony looked back at Mike and pointed. Mike nodded.

As Tony backpedaled, Sawicki tossed Luke aside. Mike moved to make the block, while Tony confidently slid behind him, looking downfield. Mike made a feeble pretense of a block, and then allowed Sawicki to brush by him and plant his helmet squarely into Tony's chest, causing him to fumble as he went down in a heap. Luke quickly fell on the ball.

Tony stayed down for several seconds. Standing over him, Mike reached down to help him up and said, “Stay away from Mary, Tony.”

Tony ignored the hand, rolled over and stood up slowly. Before trotting to the sideline, he put his face close to Mike’s earhole. “I guess I’m not the only asshole on this team,” he said.

Mike felt a tap on his shoulder and turned to see David Wall who simply jerked his thumb toward the sideline. As he went to the sideline, hearing boos for the first time in his life, Coach Hauser confronted him. “I knew I’d have trouble with you. You’re done for the night.”

Helmet in hand, Mike moved away from the bench and knelt in the grass. What he had done made him feel no better.

Coach Riley knelt down beside him, and said, “Really disappointed, Mike. You’re not like that.”

Mike shook his head. “I don’t know why I did that, Coach.”

“You know why you did it; I know; Coach Hauser knows; your teammates know. Hell, there’s probably two or three hundred people up in the bleachers who know. And by the end of the game, there will probably be a thousand. But I never expected *that* from you.”

Mike stayed there, in that position, until the end of the game.

The Shawnee won 31-14 to go to 8-0.

No one spoke to him after the game. When he got to his car, Norma was waiting for him. “Mike, this is all my fault. I’m so sorry. I just didn’t think…”

“*We* didn’t think, Norma. Go home.”

He opened the car door but turned back as she stood teary-eyed, looking at him. With a loud sigh, he said, "You know something? You may be the only friend I have left, so let me give you a ride home. And I do mean just a ride."

He had the radio on WLS. 'Gypsy Woman' by The Impressions was playing. He glanced at her; she glanced back with an abused puppy look in her eyes.

"How's your mother and her boyfriend doing?" he asked.

"Fortunately, she dumped his ass. Unfortunately, she's got herself another drunken jerk."

"He hit you?"

"Not yet." She sighed. "What a mess we made, huh? Seems like everybody knows what happened. And it's all my fault. I'm really sorry."

"Who'd you tell, Norma?"

"Connie Parsons drove by your house that day, saw my mom's car, and put two and two together. I told her not to tell anybody. I thought she was my friend; obviously, I was wrong."

"Connie's a nice girl, but she's the biggest gossip in school. Just can't keep her mouth shut about anything. For a girl who's been around, you sure are naïve."

"Yeah, I guess I am," she conceded. "Haven't been *around* as much as you think, though."

"Why'd you come to my house that day?"

"I don't know, Mike. The car just took me there. I honestly didn't know where I was going when I left home. Look, I'm the new girl in school. Apparently, everyone knew you were off limits because of Mary. I…didn't know the…*whole* story."

He shrugged. "The story's been exaggerated." *Eve didn't think I was off limits.*

"Regardless, people will remember me as the slut who made a play for Mary's football player."

"Stop that."

He parked in front of her house on 104. "Friends, then?" she asked, as she squeezed his hand.

"*Just* friends," he replied. *Is that even possible.*

On his way back home, he tuned the radio to WNXT and caught the SCOC scores. Waverly had beaten Wheelersburg. The Tigers were now also 8-0.

He was sitting alone in front of the TV, watching the Ohio State-Michigan game at The Horseshoe. The Buckeyes broke the huddle; Tony Duvardo was the quarterback—confidently barking signals. He dropped back and heaved the ball downfield. A wide receiver caught the ball in stride and took it in for a touchdown. The camera panned the student section, focusing on Mary, who was blowing kisses toward the field.

He awoke and looked at the clock. Four AM. At four-thirty, he got up, turned on the TV, and watched the test pattern for an hour before going back to bed.

Monday, November 6

After a miserable weekend alone, he was expecting a miserable week at school. The Buckeyes had beaten Iowa 29-13, while the Browns had lost to the rival

Steelers 17-13. He had barely paid attention to either game.

He got looks and head shakes from classmates, but no one seemed to want to engage him in conversation. He was alone in a crowd of 500 people.

Not the Pied Piper, anymore.

In the locker room before practice, he asked Coach Hauser if he could address the team. The coach simply nodded.

Mike rose slowly and cleared his throat. "Guys, can I have your attention for just a sec, please?" The room got quiet. "I know I screwed up badly, Friday, and I want to apologize for that. To the coaches, the players, and especially to Tony, who trusted me to do my job. I let my personal feelings get in the way of that. And I want to assure you all that it'll never happen again. That's all I can say." Fighting back tears, he mumbled, "Thank you."

One by one the players came by and patted him on the shoulder pads, making comments such as, 'Hang in there', and 'Let's just win Friday'. Coach Riley patted him on the shoulder but said nothing. Tony Duvardo and Coach Hauser walked out of the locker room without even looking in his direction.

Friday, November 10

The one hundred eighty-sixth birthday of the United States Marine Corps, one of the few things Mike's father made a point of communicating to him every year. Mike never knew why it was important. *I should probably ask him.*

Coach Hauser called Mike into his office as the players were dressing for the game.

"I know the players elected you captain, but for this game, I'm overruling that," the coach said. "Tony is our captain, tonight. I hope you don't have a problem with it."

Mike studied the floor. "It's fine with me, Coach. I just want to get through this and win the game." *It's not really fine at all.*

Waverly, one of the larger schools in the conference, had a long-standing and very successful football program, which included a JV team. While Central dressed forty players for a game, Waverly dressed as many as seventy. This year they had a huge offensive line and a big, quick, running back named Evan Burke, who was drawing some attention from college scouts.

The Central locker room was unusually quiet before the game. Missing was the usual horseplay, towel snapping, and dirty jokes. Several players glanced at Mike, expecting him to make his usual encouraging speech. He looked at Tony, who was sitting alone with a football in his hand—shadow passing.

Reluctantly, Mike stood up and got everyone's attention. "Biggest game of our lives, guys. Let's take care of business." Several players asserted their agreement, but there was no rah-rah. *Quiet confidence—or fear of failure?*

Coach Hauser walked in; Mike sat down. After looking around the room, the coach made his shortest pre-game speech of the season: "This is what you've been busting your asses for since August. Let's finish it."

Mike looked up at the large, noisy crowd as the team ran onto the field. The bleachers were full. There were people sitting in the grass, and people standing along the chain link fence that circled the field. The largest crowd ever at a Central home game, by far. Halfway up, on the home side near the fifty-yard line, sat his father.

Waverly won the coin toss and elected to receive. After running the kickoff back to their thirty-five-yard line, they marched down the field, running the ball on every play; three yards, five yards, eight yards, converting four third downs along the way. Evan Burke took the ball in from two yards out for the first score, and then ran it in for the two-point conversion, to make it 8-0. They had used nearly ten minutes of the first quarter.

The Shawnee came right back, with Tony completing short passes and Mike gaining fifteen yards on two runs. The drive stalled at the Waverly fifteen yard line when, instead of running the ball on third and one, Tony threw a post pattern to Larry Penn, who was wide open, but dropped it.

Placekicking was not a priority in the Conference, as most teams usually went for two after touchdowns, and rarely tried field goals. The Shawnee, however, had an ace in Tommy Phillips, Eve's brother. Coach Hauser sent him in, rather than going for the first down. He got the ball just inside the left upright, making the score 8-3.

Waverly moved the ball on the ground, again, but Burke fumbled the hand-off at mid-field. Homer Phipps recovered it. Central couldn't take advantage of the break, however, going three and out. Tommy Phillips's punt went out of bounds at the Waverly fifteen.

The Tigers kept pounding away with the running game, essentially playing keep away. They went eighty-five yards, scoring another touchdown with five minutes left in the first half and led 14-3 after Mike stuffed Burke at the line of scrimmage on another two-point conversion attempt. Tony brought Central back again, scoring on a quarterback sneak from the half-yard line. The big play was a thirty-yard screen pass to Mike, who broke four tackles along the way. The halftime score was 14-10, Waverly.

Mike sat in the locker room with his eyes closed as Coach Hauser made his halftime speech. Like nearly every starter on the team, he was battered, bruised, and exhausted from going up against a larger, more experienced, and deeper team. He had noticed that only three players on the Waverly team played both ways, while Central had seven offensive starters who also played defense. Waverly also substituted more, keeping their players fresh, while Mike, John, and Homer Phipps played nearly every down on offense and defense.

Coach Hauser had Mike receive the second half kickoff, which he ran back to midfield. Two plays later, Tony completed a long pass to Ronnie Stone who was tackled at the two-yard line. Mike ran off left tackle behind John Breech for the touchdown, giving Central a 17-14 lead, the first time they had ever held a lead over Waverly.

Waverly moved the ball on their first possession of the third quarter, but on third and one from Central's thirty-eight, the Waverly left tackle, who had been beaten by John Breech all night long, false-started for a five-yard penalty. On the next play, Mike, correctly guessing draw play, fought off a block, and tackled Burke at the line of scrimmage. Waverly's first punt of the night landed on the ten-yard line and bounced into the end zone for a touchback with just over four minutes left in the third quarter.

Hauser called a time-out, and said, "I think we can run the ball on these guys. They've gone to four defensive backs."

The standard defense of the conference was a basic 5-4, featuring five down linemen, four linebackers, and two defensive backs. By pulling a lineman and a linebacker and replacing them with two defensive backs, Waverly was showing a defense that was more common in the NFL where throwing the ball was more prevalent. This alignment, however, was more vulnerable to the run. Tony didn't look pleased but nodded.

They lined up in the full-house 'T' formation they had hardly used since last season. With Tony alternately handing off to Mike and Lonny Williams, they marched down the field and were at the Tigers fifteen-yard line when the third quarter ended. The Waverly defenders, looking exhausted, straggled to the sideline. *Fifteen minutes and we've got 'em.*

On the first play of the fourth quarter, Mike ran the ball to the nine-yard line. First and goal. Lonny Williams ran the ball behind Mike's lead block to the five. Then, inexplicably, Tony threw two consecutive incomplete passes into the end zone.

Coach Hauser sent Tommy Phillips in to kick the field goal. He was still in Tony's face as Tommy split the uprights to make it 20-14, with just over ten minutes to go.

The Tigers, taking advantage of a weary Shawnee defense, marched right back down the field. Taking over six minutes off the clock, they scored, as Burke, dragging two defenders, ran it in from the four-yard line tying the score at twenty. They chose to kick the extra point, and were successful, putting them ahead, 21-20.

Mike took the kickoff and nearly ran it all the way back. He was hemmed in along the sideline and forced out of bounds at the Waverly twenty-one yard line. The crowd roared and began chanting his name.

"Just run the damned ball," Hauser yelled at Tony. Mike looked up at the game clock. Just over three minutes to go.

Using as much of the clock as possible, the Shawnee moved the ball to the thirteen on three runs. On fourth and two, Phillips made the clutch field goal putting Central back in the lead, 23-21 with thirty-eight seconds left.

On the ensuing kickoff, the Waverly return man was gang-tackled at his own nineteen. Lonny Williams ripped the ball out and Ronnie Stone recovered it. The Waverly Tigers were looking at their first loss in three years.

Coach Hauser called a timeout. "Just hold on to the ball, Mike," he said.

"They'll have to rip my arms off, coach."

"Believe you me, they'll be trying." He turned to Tony and grabbed him by the facemask. "Just give to Harrison!"

On the first play, Mike carried it to the sixteen, concentrating on holding onto the ball. The Tigers quickly called their first timeout. To the fourteen. Timeout. On third down, he was brought down inside the ten. The officials brought in the chains for a measurement. Less than a foot short of the first down. Waverly called their last timeout with fifteen seconds to play.

Coach Hauser said to Tony, "Give the ball to Mike. If he doesn't make it they'll have one play—two at the most—to go ninety yards."

In the huddle, Tony said, "I've thrown a touchdown pass in every game I've ever quarterbacked. They'll be concentrating on Mike. I want that touchdown pass."

"No, Tony!" Mike said in disbelief.

"Don't talk in my huddle, Mike. I'm the quarterback—and the captain—in case you forgot. Twenty-five, Z right, buttonhook, on two." He clapped his hands.

Nine players looked at Mike without budging. Tony had turned toward the line of scrimmage, but turned back and looked at Mike, expectantly.

Calling a time-out crossed Mike's mind, but he rejected it. *Tony's the captain.* He clapped his hands and said, "Make sure you don't block downfield; you'll get a penalty."

As they broke the huddle, Mike looked up at the noisy crowd. No one was sitting.

The play called for a play-action fake to Mike, who would run where everyone expected—off left tackle, behind John Breech and Homer Phipps. Ronnie Stone would split out to the right, sprint to the end zone, 'button hook', and wait for the ball. Tony would roll out in the same direction and toss the ball to Ronnie for an easy completion.

Tony took the snap, stuck the ball into Mike's belly, expertly yanked it out, hid it on his right hip, and rolled to his right. Waverly had ten men crowding the line of scrimmage, with one safety standing in the middle of the end zone. They saw no reason to cover Ronnie.

From the point where he was tackled, near the line of scrimmage, Mike rose to his knees to watch. His first thought was that Tony could practically walk into the end zone. There was no one near him. Ronnie was standing in the end zone, wide open, as the safety, just beginning to realize what was happening, sprinted frantically toward him.

Tony made a perfect throw, the ball coming at Ronnie, chest high. Ronnie, however, made the mistake of glancing at the defender while the ball was in the air, and was unable to re-focus on the ball in time. It slipped through his hands, and glanced up and to his right off his facemask, directly into the hands of the safety who picked it off, and ran past him up the sideline before he could recover.

Tony was blocked by a Waverly player but quickly recovered and gave chase. Mike was on his feet immediately, but was blocked in the back and fell on his face. With a facemask full of grass and mud, he watched helplessly as Tony steadily gained on the Waverly safety. No one else had a chance to catch him.

To Mike, both players seemed to be moving in slow motion, like they were running in quicksand, but Tony was gaining. At the twenty, he was three yards back. At the ten, he was closer. With a lunge, he caught the ball carrier inside the five-yard line and both players fell forward. The official, trailing the play by at least fifteen yards, saw Tony on top of the Waverly safety, who was holding on to the ball at the goal line. He raised both arms, signaling a touchdown.

Judging from the reaction of the fans in the vicinity of the goal line, it was the wrong call. Tony complained vehemently, holding his hands two feet apart, demonstrating that the ball carrier was down short of the goal line, but the official turned his back and walked away.

Mike looked around for a flag for the illegal block; there wasn't one. Both Central coaches were on the field screaming at the closest official and pointing to where Mike was on his knees at the Waverly fifteen-yard line. The official ignored them and ran off the field.

'When you throw the ball, three things can happen, and two of them are bad'.

Coach Riley grabbed Mike's arm. "Why did you let him do that, Mike?"

Mike jerked his arm away and went nose to nose with the coach. "I'm just a peon here," he hissed. "Why don't you go talk to your fucking quarterback slash captain? Or better yet, talk to Hauser."

Helmet in hand, he turned and hobbled toward the locker room. Looking toward the chain-link fence near the corner of the end zone, he spotted a solitary figure, standing still in the dim light, looking his way. *Mary? Not likely. Wishful thinking?* As he approached, the figure disappeared into the crowd as though it had been a mirage.

Tony Duvardo quickly changed into street clothes without showering, piled his uniform in front of his locker, and left without saying a word. The rest of the team sat, stunned, in the locker room.

"It ain't fair," someone finally mumbled.

Coach Hauser walked into the room, stared directly at Mike for several seconds. Mike stared back; the coach looked away.

"All right, leave your uniforms in front of your lockers," he bellowed out. "I want practice jerseys and pants washed and turned in within a week. If you're not coming out for basketball, clear out your lockers. No personal items; no stinky jock straps; no dirty socks." He turned and left without another word.

As Mike sat staring at his locker, John Breech plopped down next to him. "You played a great game, Mike. In fact, you played great all season."

They shook hands.

"You too, John. We'd have made that foot, by the way."

"No doubt, whatsoever. All you would have had to do was climb up my back." He wiped his brow with his sleeve. "We deserved better, didn't we?"

Mike studied the crack in the concrete floor. "I could have stopped him, John."

"I know. And I kind of understand why you didn't. You think we could have won without him?"

Mike shrugged. "Probably would have ended up the same. I think we'd have beaten Wheelersburg, but not Waverly. Wouldn't have been able to run the ball as well without the passing threat."

"You're probably right. But with Tim's attitude and Tony's talent, we'd have been unstoppable."

"Yeah."

Three lockers away, Ronnie Stone sat silently, tears streaming down his face. Mike looked at him and said, "Not your fault, Ronnie; let it go."

Ronnie didn't respond.

In the shower, Tommy Phillips stood under the water like a statue, blankly staring at the wall, and mumbling something about his sister.

"You almost kicked us to a championship," Mike told him.

"That son-of-a-bitch," he muttered as he continued to stare.

Norma was waiting for Mike by the Chevy. Eve was standing next to her. "Tony take off without you, did he?" he asked Eve.

"Looks like it. I had to stand in line for the bathroom. When I came out he was gone."

He looked at Norma, looked back at Eve, smiled ruefully, and shook his head. "Get in ladies; I'll give you both a ride home."

On the way, Eve said, "I'm really sorry about the game, Mike. The whole school's gonna be depressed."

"Not the end of the world, Eve; just a football game." He shook his head and exhaled loudly through clenched teeth.

"People were yelling nasty things at Tony when he came off the field."

"People have short memories, Eve. It'll all blow over in a few weeks." *Not likely.*

Tuesday, May 29, 1962
Ocean Beach

"You're getting awfully red, Sis," Mike told Debbie. "We should go in."

"Finish your story."

He took her hand and pulled her to her feet. "No. We need to take a break. I can't concentrate, right now."

"Okay. Let's do something fun. We'll go to Coronado Island. We can walk through the Del."

"What?"

"Hotel Del Coronado. It's a ritzy place where a lot of celebrities stay. Practically every president and big movie star since the 1880's has stayed there. Remember the movie, *Some Like it Hot?"*

"Yeah."

"Well, parts of it were filmed there. We could have lunch there—if you're buying."

"Fine, if you'll put on something that'll cover your red skin."

She mumbled something unintelligible and went into her bedroom.

Five minutes later she emerged, wearing a long sleeved silk blouse, blue jeans, large sunglasses, and a sombrero. "Happy?"

He smiled. "You look cute, Sis."

After seeing all that was worth seeing on Coronado Island, they toured 'Old Town', and were back at her house by four PM.

She popped open two beers and handed him one. "Sit. Finish your story. It was just getting interesting."

"Where was I?"

"You just lost a football game."

Saturday, November 11, 1961
Hope Run

When Mike rolled out of bed at ten AM, he could barely walk. He hobbled to the bathroom and checked himself out. A large bruise covered nearly his entire left rib cage, making it painful to breathe. His left forearm and bicep were also bruised from helmets that had been used like battering rams, trying to dislodge the football. And, it seemed like every muscle in his body was sore.

"I'll live," he mumbled. He took two aspirin, made coffee, and called his father at work.

"You need me tonight, Dad? Football's over."

"Just stay home and recuperate, Mike. They beat the shit outta you, didn't they?"

"Got in a few licks myself, Dad."

"You guys deserved better."

By noon, he finally worked up the courage to call Mary. Becky answered the phone. "She's still in bed, Mike. Says she's sick, but I think she's just being a bitch. Should I see if she wants to talk?"

"No. She knows she can call me if she wants to." *Not gonna beg.*

After taking a long, hot shower, he absently watched the third-ranked Buckeyes beat Indiana 16-7, and then decided to go by the bowling alley, since being home alone was too depressing, and hanging out with John and Tim would be even more so.

When he walked into Harrison Bowl at five PM, it was relatively quiet, as the league didn't start until seven. Two lanes were going with open bowling. To his surprise, his father came out from behind the counter and gave him a quick, awkward hug, but said nothing.

Elbert Travis, the owner of a local auto repair shop, was sitting in the bar drinking beer. Well-respected for both his expertise and his honesty, he had recently tuned up the Chevy. Looking up, he spotted Mike and hurried out to him. "Sorry about the game," he said as they shook hands. "Listen, I was about to call you at home. I got a deal for you."

"What's that?"

"I have a guy who wants your engine. Actually, he wants your car, but I told him you wouldn't sell it."

"You're right; I won't. Why doesn't he get his own engine? I need mine."

"Let me explain it to you. He wants to build something to take to the drag strip. I have a stock 265—totally rebuilt, just like brand new—at my place, kinda on consignment. Ain't paid for it, yet.

"This guy could buy that and get it modified and set up like yours, but it'd cost him big bucks. And they don't always come out as good as yours. I told him about your set-up and he wants it—the whole thing, with the manifold, three deuces. Whoever set your car up spent a lot of money.

"He's got a fifty-six, which your engine will fit right into. I figure he'll save a couple hundred; I'll make a couple hundred, and pay you a couple hundred. You'll have yourself an almost new engine that I'll guarantee for a year. It won't be as fast, but it'll get you where you want to go faster'n you need, and will get better gas mileage."

"I don't know."

"Hell, you don't race it or anything."

"I don't know, Elbert. Let me think about it."

"Don't think too long. He's looking around."

"I'll call you Monday."

"Okay." Elbert shrugged and went back to his beer.

Monday, November 13

Mary wasn't at school. Between classes, Mike found Becky and asked about her. She shrugged. "Says she's sick, but I don't know..."

"What do you mean?"

"I don't know, Mike. Maybe you should just come over, grab her by the face, and fix things. It's no fun at our house anymore. People miss you; Babs misses you."

Mike chuckled. "That's silly, Becky. What makes you think Babs misses me?"

"She just hasn't been herself. Yesterday, she kicked over a whole bucket of milk. She never does that. You know, animals can sense when something's wrong. So please...just come over and grab her by the face."

"Babs?"

She stifled a giggle. "No. Mary, you clown."

He shook his head. "It's not an easy fix. And Mary's not the bad person here. Tell the family I said 'hello', and that I miss them, too." He hugged her and looked down at her freckled face. "Tell Babs I miss her, too."

She smiled up at him. "I will."

When Mike walked into his sixth period physics class, Mr. Freeman, the teacher, handed him a note that simply read, 'Mike, I need to see you after school in my office' – Coach Hauser.

He wadded up the note, threw it in the trash, and muttered, "Fuck him". But by the time class was over, he decided to see what the coach had to say.

Both coaches were in Hauser's office. Coach Riley was leaning against the wall by the window. Hauser stood and extended his hand, but Mike ignored it and took off his shirt, exposing his bruises.

He had rehearsed his opening line. "I was just a peon out there with no authority to make any decisions, but I busted my ass on every play. Never been abused like that in my life. Every muscle in my body still hurts, and if you two called me in here just to bitch at me for losing the game you can both go f..."

Coach Hauser quickly held up both hands and said, "Whoa, big fella."

Mike took a deep breath; it still hurt.

"Before you talk yourself into trouble. I didn't call you in here for that. I called you in to apologize. If either of us is to blame for losing the game, it was me."

He looked at Mike, cleared his throat, and smiled. Mike stared back—speechless.

The coach continued. "The decision to make Tony the captain was a knee-jerk reaction on my part after what happened in the Northwest game. Chances are you would have acted like a captain if I hadn't done that. You would have said 'NO!', and that would have been the end of it."

"I did. Told me to keep my mouth shut in *his* huddle."

Coach Riley spoke up. "Mike, I saw what happened out there before that last play. If you had stood your ground, there were nine other guys who would not have broke that huddle."

"*Broken*," Mike whispered.

"What?"

"Nothing, Coach?" Mike sighed. "You're right. I made another bad decision. Seems like I've made a lot of those, lately." He focused on the back wall, which featured a blown-up photograph of General Patton with his ugly dog. "I could have stopped it. We had a timeout left; I should have called it."

"Let's drop that; it's done. We didn't call you in here to bitch at you," said Coach Hauser. "As I said, that loss was on me."

Mike looked back at the coach. "Have you talked to Tony?"

"I haven't, and probably won't, since I have nothing to say to him. He'll get his scholarship in spite of what he did. And it sounds like he'll be going to Michigan. That brings me to the real reason you're here. You and I have had our differences. But I want you to know that you are far and away the best football player I've had in my five years of coaching here."

Mike focused on the ugly dog. "Thank you."

"It's unfortunate that your...personal life has become so public. You made a couple of bad choices that, had it been anyone else, would likely have gone unnoticed. But keep in mind, you've been the..." He chuckled. "You've been the Pied Piper of Central High School since you first got here, and—like it or not—held to a higher standard than the rest of them.

"Now, both Coach Riley and I are going to write letters to Coach Hayes. You can even read them and correct our English if you want." He looked at Coach Riley who flashed a grin at Mike. "We're going to extol the virtues of Mike Harrison, the football player. Maybe we can help that scholarship offer along. Schembechler loves you. Hayes will, too."

Mike looked at Coach Riley, and then back at Hauser. "Thank you."

"Okay, that's all we have, except maybe you should get that bruise looked at. And…I hope to God you fix things with Mary Bryant. It'll make you a much nicer person." He rose and shook Mike's hand.

Having decided that the best thing to do was to trade his engine before something happened to it, he called Elbert as soon as he got home from school.

"I was about to call you," Elbert said. "We lost it. The guy found something else."

"I wonder what's going to happen next," Mike mumbled as he hung up the phone.

Wednesday, November 15

Feeling better physically and mentally, He blared the radio, as he drove to school, listening to Rick Nelson's 'A Wonder like You', and hoping Mary would be back to school after missing two days. Thinking back, he couldn't remember her missing even one day of high school.

She was sitting at her desk in homeroom, staring straight ahead, not communicating with anyone. Mike knelt down beside her. "Mary, are you all right?"

Without looking at him, she replied, "I'm fine. Just had a little stomach bug, I guess."

"Can we talk?"

"Now?"

"No. Let me drive you home after school."

She finally turned toward him. Her dark eyes looked vacant. With a nearly imperceptible nod, she said, "Okay," and turned away.

In the Chevy, she sat against the passenger door, looking out the window.

"Mary, just talk to me," he began, as he drove off the parking lot.

She gave him a look that seemed to be somewhere between rage and self-pity. "Okay, I'll talk to you. I want a divorce."

"What…?"

"For eleven years we've been like a married couple. My whole life has been 'Mike and Mary'. Everybody considered us to be a…a *unit*. It seems like I can't even get into a conversation with anyone without your name coming up. I want to be just Mary, now." She stared out the window.

Mike downshifted as he turned onto Hope Run, searching for a response. At length, he looked at her and said, "You know there's one way we were never really like a married couple."

Her eyes flashed as she turned toward him. "Oh, you mean the sex thing? What would have happened if I had given in to you? Would you have just humped me and dumped me? Would you have put me in the same category as Eve and Norma?"

He started to answer, but she stopped him. "I remember several times—ever since first grade—going home and telling Mom I was going to marry you. That was my plan—my only plan. I never thought about what it would be like after the wedding."

Mike could think of no reason to respond.

After a long sigh, she continued. "What you did got me thinking, and picturing myself married to you. Giving up my own career to have your babies. Sitting home fat and pregnant while you were out screwing somebody like Norma. How many girls were there, anyway?"

"Just the two."

"Can I even believe that?"

"I didn't realize you had such a low opinion of me."

"Well, I didn't realize you had so little regard for me. You know, girls have...erotic thoughts, just like boys. The difference was I didn't act on mine. I was saving it, not for marriage, but for you, Mike, because I knew that was what you wanted. At some point, I would have stopped pushing your hand away, and you know that."

Mike said nothing.

"Give me your hand," she said. Taking his hand, she closed his fingers around his class ring.

When he parked in front of her house, she turned to him and said, "I'm really sorry about the game, Mike. You deserved better; the team deserved better; the school deserved better."

"Yeah," he muttered.

She watched his eyes. "Don't look at me with those sad, blue eyes, Mike. We're not in first grade, anymore."

He drove home listening to Johnny Tillotson's 'Without You'.

Tuesday, May 29, 1962
Ocean Beach

Debbie interrupted him. "So…here's how I see it. She gave you a pass with Eve because she didn't think of her as a serious threat. Norma was a different story, right?"

Mike nodded. "From day one, I think."

"Eve was a just piece of ass. Norma was more than that."

He didn't answer. *Still is.*

Wednesday, November 15
Scioto County

At 5:30, he left for work. His arrangement with his father was that he work Wednesdays from six PM to ten PM, and Friday and Saturday six PM to closing, which could be anytime between two and five in the morning. Don worked with Mike on Friday nights but took Saturday nights off.

On 73, just outside West Portsmouth, listening to Marty Robbins' 'Don't Worry', he came up behind an elderly couple in a Model A Ford, going barely twenty miles per hour and hugging the centerline. "Pick a lane, Grandpa," he muttered.

Still reeling from his conversation with Mary, he changed lanes, downshifted to second and stomped on the gas. The tires screamed. Seeing an oncoming car less than a hundred yards away, he kept it floored, and was safely back in his own lane when he heard an almost imperceptible *bang* followed by a *whoosh.* Suddenly the car stopped accelerating. He looked at the tachometer; it dropped to zero. He looked at the oil pressure gauge; zero. Smoke and steam began billowing out from under the hood.

Not even surprised, he shifted the car out of gear and coasted off to the side of the road, getting as close to the guardrail as possible. The old couple in the Model A drove by without looking his way.

He put on his jacket and stuck out a thumb. A middle-aged man in a '57 Ford Fairlane picked him up almost immediately. "Breakdown, huh? Always been a Ford man, myself. Never had any luck with a Chevy," the man told him.

"I'll keep that in mind," Mike muttered, staring out the window.

On the way, he decided that he couldn't tell his father or grandfather. He'd have to find a way to get the car fixed without their knowledge, thinking he could talk to Elbert, who, hopefully, still had the Chevy engine.

When he arrived at Harrison Bowl, his father was lying on his stomach on lane three's pin deck. The sweep was down; tools were all around him. Karen Brannon, a part-timer was behind the counter.

"Broken bounce board—whatever that is," she said. "He's been working on it for an hour."

Mike quickly called Elbert from the office.

"You threw a rod," Elbert told him.

"So, my engine's gone, right?"

"Yep. Sure sounds like it. You checked the oil, lately?"

"Yeah." *No.*

"I can pick up your car, install that engine, and—barring anything unexpected—deliver it to your house by Sunday," Elbert told him. "One problem, though. It'll cost you six hundred and I'll need at least a hundred dollar deposit, and the rest of the money by Monday. The guy was gonna pick it up this weekend and put it in a '55 he just bought. If it's gone, he'll want his money."

"Can't put him off with hundred dollar deposit, huh?"

"Maybe a day or two, but...the guy's a real prick. Wednesday at the latest. I can salvage some parts—like the carburetor setup—sell them to cover my labor charge. But I'll need four hundred bucks by next Wednesday. Best I can do."

Mike sighed. "Can you lend me that '52 Pontiac you never drive?"

"Yeah, it still runs okay, I think. Not much for looks, though."

"Can you bring it by the bowling alley, tonight? And uh...keep this a secret?"

"Don't want your dad to know, huh?"

"Nor Gramps—especially not Gramps. I'll tell them you're tuning the Chevy up. They won't know what's under the hood."

"Mike, why don't you just tell your dad or your granddad? Borrow the money from one of 'em."

"I just can't do that, Elbert, but I'll get the money."

"You know, Mike, you can buy a nice car for that kind of money."

"I know. But that's not an option." He hung up and quickly headed to the back to help his father.

Friday, November 17

Al Lewis was sitting in the bar, flirting with Penny, and chomping on his unlit cigar between sips of beer when Mike arrived at work. Recalling Al's stories about big money bowling matches, Mike quickly took him aside. "You think you could set us up a doubles match for tomorrow night? I need money."

He told Al the story.

"Well, let me make some calls," Al said, rubbing his chin. "Maybe the Jensen brothers. They like action. They're both sporting 200 averages across town, but we can beat 'em. They block the lanes over there; averages are inflated. Four hundred bucks will get you back into your car, right?"

"Yeah."

"How about I propose a three-game doubles match for eight hundred—four hundred apiece?"

"I have no money to put up. Can we work something out?"

"I'll front the money, and if we lose, you'll owe me four hundred. But I'm sure we won't lose; these guys are suckers. If by chance they're not interested, I have a couple of other prospects. I'll let you know before the night's over."

"Thanks."

Al put his arm around Mike. "You sure you wanna do this?"

Mike nodded. "Only option I can think of. Gotta go to work, Al. Please don't mention this to Dad."

Two hours later Al Lewis confirmed their match with the Jensen brothers for Saturday night. "Can't be here 'til after one AM, though. Apparently, they have some action across town before that.

At midnight, after the league was finished, and a handful of bowlers were having one last beer in the bar, Mike said, "Why don't you just go home, Dad? I'll close up. In fact, I'll just go out and throw a few balls on lane three, since we had some problems with it tonight. Maybe I can make a couple of adjustments.

"If you're sure," his father said. "I rebuilt the spare distributor. Might be a good idea to put it on just to make sure it's okay." He went into the office, made a phone call, and then left quickly and wordlessly.

Ten minutes later, he called Mike to say he wouldn't be home. *Must be getting some.*

By one-thirty, the customers were all gone, and Mike had the place cleaned up and ready for the Saturday morning kids league. He locked up and—after changing the pin distributor—changed into his bowling shoes and went out to lane three to practice. Recalling what Al had taught him, he worked on his timing, ball speed and body alignment.

Lacquer finish on a bowling lane wears down to the wood after a time. With most of the experienced right-handed bowlers using the second arrow from the right as a target, the wear area would be in that vicinity, creating a track. The track wasn't always visible, but it was there. At Harrison Bowl, it was showing as a slightly darker streak caused by saturation of the oil that was applied daily. The better bowlers used this to their advantage since playing the track at the proper angle created a small but significant margin for error. Using the right ball speed and hand position, an experienced bowler could keep the ball in the track all the way to the pocket.

Once he got comfortable with alignment and ball speed, Mike spent a half hour working on spare shooting, spending extra time shooting at the ten pin, which, because of the angle, was the most difficult single pin spare for right-handed bowlers. When his thumb began to feel sore, he quit and went home, apprehensive about tomorrow night, but feeling good about his game—and the spare distributor.

Saturday, November 18

Mike listened to the OSU game while he cleaned house. The second-ranked Buckeyes beat Oregon in a non-conference game 22-12.

His current dilemma helped keep his mind off Mary. When the 'what if's' invaded his brain, he reminded himself of a quote attributed to Satchel Paige: *'Don't look back. Something might be gaining on you'.*

The pot games began at one AM, using lanes five through ten. Per Al's suggestion, Mike held lanes one and two—the toughest pair—for the doubles match with the Jensen brothers.

Pot game formats vary from city to city. At Harrison Bowl, they consisted of a number of bowlers—twelve in this case—putting three dollars in a pot each game. Bowling across six lanes, they would start on lane five, bowl the first frame, move to lane six for frame two, seven for frame three, etc., with the sixth frame being on lane ten, and then back to lane five for frame seven.

The scorekeeper, who had to be very attentive, sat at the middle score table. With twelve bowlers, the winner of each game would get twenty-seven dollars, the house six, and the scorekeeper three. The formula changed as bowlers dropped out, or new ones were added. Some nights, depending on who was winning, they would bowl as late as six AM. Some nights, one bowler would dominate, sending everyone home early. Some nights—aside from the house—the scorekeeper was the big winner.

Al Lewis won the first game by throwing a clutch turkey in the tenth frame. He was picking up his money when the Jensen brothers walked in.

"Jon and Dale, this is Mike," Al said. They shook hands, and Mike led them into the office.

"I don't want anyone to see any money," Mike said. "Let's leave it right here in the safe."

Jon Jensen produced a wad of cash, and peeled off eight one hundred dollar bills; Al Lewis did the same.

Mike stuffed them in an envelope and locked them in the safe.

With some desperation in his voice, Mike asked, "Can we keep this whole thing quiet? I'm sure you all know why."

All three nodded.

Mike turned on lanes one and two, allowing the Jensen brothers ten minutes of warm-up. Al joined them as Mike changed shoes in the office. When he came out, he was shocked to see Tony Duvardo talking on the pay phone by the front entrance. Tony looked at him, spoke quickly into the phone, hung up, and went out the door, leaving Mike staring after him. *With all the pay phones in town, why would he use this one?*

Mike would rather have kicked everyone out and locked the doors, but figured that someone would report that back to his father. Instead, he went around to each person in the building and made the same request: "If anyone asks, we're just bowling for fun. Okay?"

He then had Penny close the bar. She volunteered to keep score for them. The pot bowlers halted their game to watch the match.

The Jensen brothers struggled the first game, with Dale shooting 181, and Jon 189. Mike's 211 and Al's 206 gave them a forty-seven-pin lead.

The brothers came back strong the second game with Jon shooting 236 and Dale 212. Mike was steady with a 215, but Al missed two ten pins and dropped to a 189, leaving Mike and Al with a slim three-pin lead.

"Sorry about that," Al said. "Can't seem to carry the ten pin on lane two. Of course, I'm not supposed to miss it, either."

"Remember what you used to tell me about ten pins?"

"I told you a lot of things."

"One thing was that if you're leaving tens, starting about six inches farther back on the approach sometimes helps."

Al grinned. "Point taken."

The match turned into a rout the last game, as Mike started with a six-bagger, while Al went spare, spare, turkey, spare. The brothers, with two open frames each and no doubles after six frames, conceded, slammed their bowling balls into their bags and walked out.

"That went well," Al remarked as he counted out Mike's four hundred dollars in the office.

The other bowlers went back to their pot games and Mike went back to work, cleaning up the place and getting it ready for tomorrow, his stomach churning. *That was too easy.*

Monday, November 20

Elbert had dropped the Chevy off Sunday, as promised, and Mike paid him four hundred dollars right away. With the hundred he had paid in advance, he still owed a hundred but assumed Elbert could get at least that much by selling salvaged parts. The car ran great and Mike vowed to drive it like an adult.

At school, Tony was getting out of the Corvette as Mike drove up. Mike considered catching up to him and saying something conciliatory, but Tony looked at him, looked away, and walked quickly into the building. *It'll get easier for both of us, eventually.*

Coach Hauser called him into his office after school.

"Mike, I have letters from several schools including OSU and UC. These are not exactly offers. They want to set up campus visits and interviews. You can pick through them and decide which ones you want to visit." He shuffled through the papers. "Kent State, Bowling Green, Indiana. Since OSU is your first option, I can call and set something up for you if you'd like."

"Sure. Thanks, Coach. If OSU doesn't offer me right away I'll set up other visits, but that's the only one I'm interested in right now."

"Good. I'll call Coach Schembechler.

Saturday, November 25

The Ohio State-Michigan game.

At Mike's house, the three of them watched the second-ranked Buckeyes romp over Michigan 50-20 to go to 8-0-1, win the Big Ten championship and qualify for the Rose Bowl. They were not likely to pass top-ranked Alabama in the polls unless the undefeated Crimson Tide were to lose to rival Auburn next week.

"Just think, Mike, you could be playing in that game in a couple of years," John said.

"You, too," Mike said, absently.

"Tim, you could be a cheerleader."

Tim chuckled but called John an asshole.

"You look like shit, Mike," John said. "You okay?"

"Haven't slept much lately."

"Worrying about Mary isn't gonna help. And she'll get over it."

Mike grunted.

"Nothing you can do about the Waverly game, either."

Mike grunted.

At six o'clock, Al Lewis walked into Harrison Bowl and sidled up to Mike at the counter. "I don't want to alarm you, but I just found out there were several thousand dollars in side action on our match. Not as well kept a secret as I thought it would be."

"Shit!"

"No proof that you won any money, though. I'll lie like a rug for you if something does come up." He reached across the counter and squeezed Mike's shoulder. "Just thought you should know."

Thursday, November 30

The news had broken that the Ohio State faculty committee had voted to reject the Rose Bowl invitation, ending the Buckeyes season, and sparking rioting on campus. This was considered by many to be a slap in the face to Woody Hayes, and there was speculation that it would adversely affect his recruiting efforts.

"Maybe it'll improve our chances," John said during homeroom.

"Maybe," Mike replied as he looked up to see Coach Hauser enter the room, looking somber.

"Mike, we have to talk."

The coach led him into his office and closed the door.

"I need an honest answer, here." He picked up a sheet of paper from his desk. "I have a letter stating that there are multiple people willing to swear that you bowled for money and won several hundred dollars, a week ago Saturday."

"I..." Mike quickly considered his options. *They can't prove it. Al will lie for me. No one else saw the money. Who are these multiple people? Is Tony involved in it some way?*

"I am required to report this; I have no choice. Tell me it's not true and I'll be a hundred percent behind you, but if it is true..."

Mike stared at Patton's ugly dog. With tears starting to well up, he looked at the floor and replied softly, "Shit...I'm not gonna lie to you, Coach. It's true."

The coach looked close to tears, himself. "I was praying that it wasn't, Mike. You realize your football career is over. The NCAA is very strict about this. We can argue the merits of the policy all day long, but it is what it is. And...you can't plead ignorance. Participating in any sport for money makes you a professional athlete. I'm sure you've heard about Jim Thorpe. They took all his Olympic medals away because he'd made a few bucks playing baseball."

Mike nodded. "I suppose you had a meeting set up, already."

"I did, and I'll have to cancel that."

"I'm sorry."

"I'm sorry too, Mike, since I was kind of looking forward to attending some games and watching you play linebacker. I wanted to be able to look down onto the field and say 'I coached that kid'." He shook his head and exhaled forcefully through his teeth.

Realizing that he wouldn't be able to concentrate on class work, Mike went straight to his car and drove home, his brain in a fog.

Tuesday, May 29, 1962
Ocean Beach

"So, why did you admit it?" Debbie asked. "Assuming your friend, Al, wouldn't have finked on you, they wouldn't have been able to prove anything."

Mike shrugged. "I guess I just wanted the bullshit to stop."

"It's a stupid rule."

"I know, but I was fully aware of it. The coaches mentioned it several times."

"An attack of conscience?"

"Maybe. But...most likely, just the accusation would have kept me from getting offers, since I was kinda borderline, anyway."

"Borderline?"

"Probably ten-fifteen pounds too light and a step too slow. Thousands of guys like me out there. Big fish in little ponds. I'm not saying I wouldn't have made it if given the chance, but..." He shrugged.

"I assume there's more to your story."
"It gets worse."

Sunday, December 3, 1961
Hope Run

Mike barely noticed that Alabama had beaten Auburn 33-0, Saturday, sealing the national championship for the Crimson Tide.

Word had gotten out Friday about his losing his college eligibility. His classmates were mostly mum about it. Mary glanced fleetingly his way several times but said nothing.

His father merely shook his head when Mike told him. The chore he dreaded most was telling his grandfather; he was planning to do so today.

As he was finishing breakfast, the phone rang. It was John Breech.

"Did you hear?"

"Hear what?"

"Tony Duvardo's dead. They found his body by the dumpster behind the bowling alley this morning. Shot in the head."

"You're shitting me!"

"His car was still parked in the alley."

"Behind *our* bowling alley?" Mike asked, struggling to comprehend what he had just heard.

"Yeah. Not a lot of details, but they say maybe a robbery."

Mike's mind flashed back to Tony on the pay phone. "But what the hell would he have been doing there, and why didn't they take his car? Shit, I worked 'til five in the morning. Did they say what time?"

"No. That's all the details I got."

"Shit. Thanks for calling me, John. Talk to you later."

Mike turned on the radio to WNXT but got no more details than what John had given him, except that Tony had accepted a football scholarship to the University of Michigan.

Absently, he ran the hill. It was cold but dry. He stood at the top for an hour looking at Mary's house. When he closed his eyes, he could see her in that blue dress.

"I wouldn't have taken your car, Mikey," Gramps said as he mixed the peanut butter and jelly.

"It wasn't just that, Gramps. You warned me about Mary. I screwed that up. Now this..."

"Mikey, how many times have you heard someone say, 'If I could only go back and do it over, I'd do it differently'?"

"Lots."

"Well, since that's not possible, I can only suggest that, in the future, you work on getting it right the first time. Not that easy, I know. But...hey, you're young, smart, and good-looking. You'll be okay."

They ate silently.

"What do you think about this Tony Duvardo thing?" Gramps finally asked.

"Don't know. Kinda scary, being that it happened behind the bowling alley. And...I was working when it happened."

Gramps was looking out the kitchen window. "You don't think a bowler was involved, do you?"

Mike shrugged. "Tony did come in that night—the night I screwed everything up."

"Oh, yeah?"

"Made a phone call and left."

"Probably no connection."

Mike eyed his grandfather. "So honestly, Gramps, how are you doing?"

"Definitely slowing down a little, Mikey. Don't seem to have the energy anymore. Arthur is showing up in my joints, and if I don't watch what I eat, I get indigestion so bad sometimes I think I'm having a heart attack. I figure my prostate is about the size of a basketball. Getting old ain't much fun."

"Maybe you just need a woman."

Gramps scoffed but said nothing.

"Been to the doctor lately?"

"No, I hate doctors."

"Move in with us, Gramps."

"I'm thinking about it, Mikey. I'm definitely thinking about it." There was no enthusiasm in his voice. "I would think most seventeen-year-olds would love to be in your position—practically no adult supervision."

"Most seventeen-year-olds have never tried it."

Monday, December 4

Mike noticed a county sheriff squad car in the school parking lot as he drove up.

In homeroom, several students glanced his way as he walked in. Mary stared at him, smiled weakly, and turned away.

Mr. Barr, the homeroom teacher, took attendance, and then announced, "The following students are to report to the principal's office: Mike Harrison, Mary Bryant, John Breech, Tim Crabtree, Eve Phillips, Norma West."

Deputy Earl Hoch was sitting at Principal Thomas' desk. Mike recognized him immediately. Though not a regular bowler, he was a regular lunch patron at Harrison Bowl. Mike didn't know him well, but they had talked on several occasions. He recalled Hoch telling stories about his days as a running back at Portsmouth High School in the late '40's.

He nodded at Mike and then introduced himself to the others. Shorter and heavier than Mike, he had plain features, penetrating blue eyes, and a short flattop cut of his blond hair.

"I'm sure you all know about the unfortunate death of your classmate, Tony Duvardo. I'm looking for any information that any of you can give me to help with this investigation. I want to interview each of you individually, but you don't have to talk to me. If you have doubts, I encourage you to call your parents, but I want to assure you that, at this point, we're not accusing any of you of anything, and you can stop the interview at any time. Understood?"

They all nodded.

"For your information, this crime happened in the jurisdiction of the Portsmouth Police Department. The Sheriff's Department is just assisting in the investigation. And you six are not the only ones I'll be talking to. You will be called out of class one at a time, and I'll try to minimize the inconvenience."

He looked at Mike. "You're first. The rest of you can go back to class."

Principal Thomas left his office with the others, leaving Mike alone with the deputy.

Hoch picked up a sheet of paper. "I heard about your problem, Mike. Sorry."

"Nobody to blame but myself," Mike mumbled.

The deputy grunted. "Okay. I'll get right to it. At about eight AM, yesterday, an elderly gentleman walking his dog, found the body behind the dumpster in the rear of the bowling alley. Actually, the dog found the body. It's unlikely the man would have noticed it if he'd been walking alone. You worked that night?"

"Yes, 'til five AM."

"You left through the front door?"

"Yes."

"Did you take out the trash before you left?"

"Took it out around 12:30."

"You closed at what time?"

"Around five. A handful of pot bowlers won't generate much trash, so I always do it early. Gets me out the door sooner when they're done."

"Pot bowlers?"

Mike explained.

"You saw nothing unusual in the alley when you took out the trash—like a red Corvette?"

"I didn't see a car of any kind. And, I'm sure I'd recognize Tony's Corvette."

"Yeah, you probably would. Your dad didn't work that night?"

"No. He works the day shift on Saturday."

"Did he know Tony?"

"He met him once, back in August. Don't think he's talked to him since." Mike shrugged. "Can't say for sure."

"So, Tony didn't frequent the bowling alley?"

"No, sir. At least not when I was there."

"What's your relationship with Mary Bryant?"

Taken aback, Mike hesitated. "Relationship? Not much of one right now. Did you and Dad talk about that?"

"No, we didn't. I heard rumors. Just want to get my facts straight."

Mike looked out the window, noticing that a light snow was falling. "Mary has been my best friend since first grade. We dated; it didn't work out."

"Did the Duvardo kid get in the way?" the deputy asked with a blank stare.

Mike stared back. *My dick got in the way.* "My problems with Mary had nothing to do with Tony, and aren't...relevant to your investigation."

"Really? How about the Northwest game?"

"Word gets around, doesn't it?"

"Yes, it does."

"I could tell you I just missed a block, but you wouldn't believe that—any more than anyone else did."

"Do you want to continue with this now, or pick it up later—or talk to your dad?"

Mike glared. "I have nothing to hide! My...breakup with Mary had *nothing* to do with Tony!" He took a calming breath. "After the breakup, I saw him talking to her at lunch and got pissed off and stupid. At the next practice, I apologized to Tony, the coach, and the team. That's all there was to that."

"Did Mary and Tony date?"

Mike shook his head. "You don't know Mary's father. The only person allowed to date Mary was me."

"How so?"

"He's a very conservative Christian, and very protective of his daughter. I've known the family since I was six. I've spent a lot of time with them, and they trust me…or did."

The deputy looked at his notes again. "Your dad own a gun?"

"Not that I know of. I think he got enough of guns during the war."

"Yeah, I gathered that. And you?"

"Never fired one in my life."

"Okay, Mike, I'm done. I'd appreciate it if you didn't discuss this interview with classmates 'til I've talked to them."

"So we can't coordinate our stories?"

"Something like that."

"Am I a suspect?"

Hoch smiled. "What's that they say on the hokey detective shows? 'I suspect no one; I suspect everyone'." The smile disappeared. "You did have motive and opportunity, but so did several others. The fact that it happened behind the bowling alley—while you were working—kinda puts you in the spotlight. But right now, I'm just gathering evidence. The city police will probably want to interview you at some point."

"That's fine. But...motive? Nothing that happened made me want to kill him. And I didn't. I wanted to kick his ass after the game, but didn't have the energy."

The deputy nodded and glanced down at his notes again. "Mind if I ask you one more question, just out of personal curiosity?"

"Go ahead."

"Do you think Tony's dumb call in the Waverly game was related to his problems with you?"

Mike thought about it. "I don't think that had anything to do with me. He wanted a touchdown pass. In fact, he made a couple of questionable play calls earlier in the game, trying to get one. I can only tell you that he made the perfect call—and executed the play very well—for someone wanting to throw a touchdown pass in that situation. It was a selfish call, but not a dumb one. I could nitpick and say he should have put a little more 'touch' on the pass, considering how wide open his receiver was. Threw it a little too hard, maybe. But the throw was on the money, and Ronnie should have caught it. He would have nine times out of ten, at least. What's sad is that, if he'd simply dropped it, we'd have won the game."

Hoch nodded but said nothing.

"Also, being new to our school, Tony didn't look at the Waverly game the same way the rest of us did. I think it was his ego that beat us...that and bad luck."

The deputy stood up. "Thanks for your time, Mike. You think of anything relevant, let me know." They shook hands.

"Uh...by the way," Mike asked, "have you been to the crime scene?"

"No. Why?"

"Well, I was just thinking what a great place it would be to shoot somebody."

"How's that?"

"Well, that alley is so full of potholes—some really deep ones—that cars almost never come through, and—even with the back door closed—when people are bowling, it's so noisy you could...have a St. Valentine's Day type massacre and no one would hear it. No houses nearby, and it's very dark. Dad's been talking about putting a light on the back of the building but hasn't gotten around to it. We use a flashlight when we take out the trash at night."

"Was it dark enough that you might have missed a red Corvette?"

"How close to the dumpster was it?"

"Fifteen—twenty feet."

Mike shook his head. "No car there."

"Maybe I'll stop by there and check it out some night. Thank you."

Wednesday, December 6

Mike arrived at work at six PM. "Cops talk to you?" He asked his father.

"Earl Hoch came by yesterday."

"And...?"

"And nothing, really. Asked where I was; I told him."

"You weren't home?"

"No. I was out."

"With someone."

“Yes.”

“Guess that’s all I’m gonna get, huh?”

‘It is. Think you can change a sweep motor in twenty minutes?”

“Sure. Which one?”

“Five. It kicked out on me twice today. Overheated.”

Mike headed for the back.

Friday, December 8

More details had come out in the paper about the murder. The time of death was determined to be between two and four AM, and a single .22 slug, fired into his right temple at close range, had killed him. His body had been dragged behind the dumpster. His wallet was missing, but the key was still in the ignition of the Corvette. Evidence pointed to robbery as a motive, but no one could explain why the killer hadn’t taken his car.

The funeral service was at the Holy Trinity Catholic Church on Route 73 at Pond Creek Road. School was canceled to allow students to attend. Reluctantly, Mike decided to go.

A handful of classmates were there, including John, Tim, and Eve. Both football coaches were there, but Mike made a point of avoiding them.

John and Tim approached him before the service started. “The football banquet is still scheduled for next Saturday night," John said. "We’re thinking that, considering all the shit that's happened, we should talk to the powers about canceling it. What do you think?"

Mike shook his head. "Remember back in the summer when we talked about leadership? That's not me anymore, John. I'm totally out of the leadership business. Not the *Pied Piper* anymore."

"Yeah. With all the shit that's happened..."

"And, if they do have one, I won't be going. So it doesn't really matter to me. You two should get the guys together and see what they want to do, and then go to the coaches."

John nodded and clapped Mike on the back. Wordlessly, Tim and Mike shook hands.

Mike found Tony's parents, introduced himself, and offered his sympathy. Sal and Marie Duvardo were an attractive, middle-aged couple. He was an older, somewhat softer and heavier version of Tony. She was tall, slim, and dark.

"We considered taking him back to Michigan; we have family buried there," she said. "But we're committed to this area for the foreseeable future, and I'll be able to visit his grave more often." Tearfully, she squeezed Mike's hand.

"Tony talked about you," Sal said. "He said you were a good player and seemed like a good guy. I was kind of hoping the two of you would become friends." He sighed.

Mike didn't respond.

Sal continued. "Part of the reason we moved here was to get him into a safer and more wholesome environment. We didn't like the crowd he was hanging out with in Detroit."

Belatedly, Mike asked, "Were you at the Northwest game?"

Looking into his eyes, Sal said, "We were at all the games, Mike."

Mike nodded. "I'm sorry." *Sorry I was such a prick to your son.*

"We actually wanted to buy a house in Portsmouth and have him go to Notre Dame, but he talked us out of it. Said he wanted to live in the country for a change. He still could have gone to Notre Dame, but I don't think he cared much for nuns." Sal looked at his wife. "I think we were all beginning to like it out here." He massaged his chin and looked away with tears welling in his eyes as Marie sobbed. Mike hugged her and shook Sal's hand before turning away.

The church was crowded; the service was long. Mike stood along the back for a while, and then went outside, putting his hands in his pockets, and hunching his shoulders against the brisk wind that made the forty-degree temperature feel much colder. *Why am I even here?*

When the service ended, Eve Phillips approached him. "May I ride to the cemetery with you, Mike?" They hugged.

"Actually, I wasn't planning on going to the cemetery."

"Well, I'd like to talk to you about Tony."

"Okay," he said, with zero enthusiasm.

As they waited in the Chevy for the procession to move, Eve spoke up. "I just...don't want people thinking he was a horrible person."

"And I'm supposed to tell everyone he wasn't a horrible person?"

"Okay, I don't want *you* to think he was a horrible person."

"I don't think that much about him one way or the other, right now. I have problems of my own. His have been pretty much... Sorry. I guess that was insensitive."

"He wanted to be your friend, Mike; just didn't know how to go about it—and you didn't let him. He needed friends, just like everyone else. But, because you shunned him, everyone else did, too. If Mike Harrison doesn't like you, there must be something wrong with you."

"You didn't shun him."

"Only because I was pissed at you."

"Why?"

"You quit calling me."

Mike didn't respond. He was thinking about Tony so proudly showing off the Corvette back in August, which seemed like years ago.

"He told me about trying to impress you with his car. About his 'nigger' remark, and about his Jack Spratt remarks. How bad he felt because you disapproved. Shit, Mike, you know as well as I do, that racist jokes, queer jokes, and ethnic jokes aren't uncommon at school. I remember you telling the one about the Polish couple who couldn't consummate their marriage because they kept waiting for the swelling to go down."

"That was just a joke."

"Where do you draw the line?"

Mike shrugged but said nothing.

"He also told me about smoking marijuana with you."

"You think that was some sort of a cry for help?"

"Could have been."

"So, if I'd been his friend, he wouldn't have gotten himself killed?"

"Maybe. And maybe he would have simply handed the ball off to you on that last play of the Waverly game."

"You think?"

"Maybe. You know what he called you after the Northwest game? Humpty Dumpty."

"That's about right. I go from the Pied Piper to Humpty Dumpty."

"He also said, 'I know that, except for Coach Hauser, Mike owns this school—the students, the teachers, and the coaches. I didn't want to compete with him. I just wanted in'. You should have just let him in."

Mike looked at Eve as though seeing her for the first time. She wasn't exceptionally attractive—not like Mary and Norma. Her nose was just a bit too big, and her upper body didn't quite match her lower. She was small breasted, with a slightly larger posterior. But to him, she was very sexy. Her smile would get anyone's attention; her blue eyes sparkled; her teeth were pearly white and nearly perfect; her natural blonde hair fell halfway down her back; her legs were long and shapely.

She tugged at the hem of her dress. "You've seen all this and more. Besides, we're at a funeral."

"I've always liked what I saw. But you know the story, there."

"I know. I spent a lot of years trying to pry you away from her."

"I guess I should have told you it wasn't going to happen."

"Yeah, you should have. You know...you always called me. I never called you."

He grunted his agreement.

The procession began to move out onto Pond Creek Road.

"You've heard the 'Easy Eve' thing?" she asked.

"I've heard it. Never called you that."

"You know how many guys I've been with? Three. Ricky Sloan got me drunk on cheap wine sophomore year, and then bragged about it. Wasn't even enjoyable. Two minutes of pain and a mess to clean up after. Then there was you, of course, and then Tony."

Mike said nothing. *What qualifies a girl as easy? Three guys, four guys…ten guys?*

The car in front of them moved.

"Did Mary find out about you and me?" she asked.

"Yeah."

"And that's why you quit calling me, and took up with Norma."

"Makes me sound…"

"Shallow, self-centered, heartless, devious? That's what was so unique about you, before. You were none of those things. You were like a god to us. The guys all wanted to be your best friend; the girls all wanted to be your girlfriend. I swear, Mike, you could have deflowered half the virgins in our class by freshman year."

"Including you?"

"Especially me."

The whole procession was finally moving. "Did Tony rat me out on the bowling thing?"

"I'm pretty sure he didn't. And…by the way, he didn't put the dildo on Jack Spratt's desk. It was Ricky."

"How do you know that?"

"Ricky? Ricky, who can't keep his mouth shut? He bragged about it."

They were now on Pond Creek Road and moving toward the cemetery, some two miles away.

"Mike, I can't remember you being judgmental about anybody but Tony."

"Well, there was Billy…somebody."

"Oh, Billy Cooper." She laughed. "I remember him."

"Tony called me Mister Perfect."

"Well, you never were *that*." She laughed again. "I remember once, in tenth grade, you coughed without covering your mouth."

The car in front of them stopped.

Her tone turned serious, again. "You know what I think?"

"Looks like we'll be a while. Tell me what you think."

"You looked at Tony as a rival—on the football field, and for Mary's affection."

Mike grunted. "He was my teammate."

"Yeah, but you weren't 'Cock of the Walk', anymore."

Cars were moving. He felt a headache coming on.

"And," she continued, "you're not the same person you were. It's like Tony changed your personality."

"I quit being the Pied Piper?"

"Yeah. We all miss him." She smiled.

"You happen to have an aspirin on you?"

She dug in her purse and presented two capsules. "Midol."

He looked at the pills, grunted, and swallowed them one at a time, nearly choking on the second one.

She slapped him gently on the back. "What's sad is that the only person who could have screwed things up with Mary was you."

"And I did."

"And hanging out with Norma isn't helping."

"I know."

They were on the cemetery grounds. Cars began parking alongside the road.

Mike pulled over behind the last one.

"So, this conversation wasn't really about Tony, was it?"

"Not entirely. I guess it was about all of us." She sighed. "Time to grow up, I guess."

He toyed with the gearshift knob, and then looked at her. "So...if I hadn't stopped calling you, would this conversation have even happened?"

She met his eyes. "Maybe not. But maybe if I'd said something sooner, all this *shit* wouldn't have happened." She found the door handle. "You can go. I'll get a ride back." It sounded like a dismissal.

Tuesday, May 29, 1962
Ocean Beach

Debbie stopped him and went to the refrigerator for more beer. After handing one to Mike, she asked. "Have you ever read the story of the *Pied Piper*?"

"Not really. Something about a charismatic person who got rid of rats."

"Well, it's been used as a metaphor for a charismatic person, but the real story is more complicated than that. It's based on something that happened in Hamelin about the time of the Plague."

"He got rid of the rats that caused the Plague?"

"Well, he lured them away with his magic pipe and was supposed to get paid for it. When the mayor of the town refused to pay up, he lured the children out of town the same way. They were never seen again. That makes the Pied Piper a vindictive person, not a hero."

"I never pictured myself as either."

"You're not. Anyway, it's apparently a historical fact that a bunch of children disappeared from that town during that time. Some historians speculate that he was a pedophile and/or a mass murderer."

Saturday, December 9
Portsmouth, Ohio

"Mike Harrison, right?"

Mike turned from putting away a pair of rental shoes. On the other side of the counter was a heavy-set, fortyish man sporting a comb-over that started less than an inch above his left ear. He was dressed in a wrinkled, brown, polyester suit and a blood-red tie.

"That's me. May I help you, sir?"

The man flashed a badge. "Detective Sergeant Waters, Portsmouth Police Department. You have time to talk?"

"Long as we can do it between customers."

"No problem. I was wondering if you have some record—or recollection of who was here after midnight the night of the murder?"

A group of four plopped their rental shoes on the counter. Mike took the scoresheet and turned to the detective. "I could write down the names, but it would be better if you just came back at one. They'll likely all be here. Pretty much the same guys every Saturday."

The detective nodded, hesitated, and drummed his fingers on the counter. "I'll be back then."

When he was gone, Penny came out of the bar. "What'd the cop want?"

"How'd you know he was a cop?"

"I dated him 'til I found out he was married."

"He'll be back."

Mike looked around as Sergeant Waters walked in shortly after one AM. "They're all here—plus a few others," he said.

Waters interviewed them all, in turn, spending more time with Penny than any of the others. His interview with Mike was very short: "What time did you take out the trash?" "Did you notice anything unusual when you did?" "What time did you close?"

With all the distractions, the pot games broke up early, and Mike was out the door by three AM.

Friday, December 22

Last day of school before Christmas break.

There was no news about Tony's murder, and Mike had had no further contact with the police. While the story was still front page news, it no longer dominated. The *Portsmouth Times* and its readers seemed to be losing interest as Christmas approached.

At the end of the school day, he stopped Mary in the hallway. "Let me take you home," he said. "I have your Christmas present."

She leaned against the wall. "You got me a Christmas present?"

"I could return it, but I don't want to."

"Okay. Actually, I have one for you, too."

"When were you going to give it to me?"

She looked away. "I was just going to stick it in your mailbox."

In the car, he handed her a large poorly wrapped package. She took a small neatly wrapped one from her purse and handed it to him.

"We should open these," he said.

She opened hers and smiled. "It's the sweater I saw at Marting's. You remembered."

He recalled how much she had admired it when they window shopped on their way back to his car after the movie.

He opened his; it was a new Timex.

"I remember yours quit on you," she said.

He took her hand and said, "Thanks."

She squeezed his and said, "If you'd like, maybe you could come over during the holidays. The family misses you."

"And you...?"

She sighed. "Of course I do, Mike, but..."

"Yeah, I understand. We're divorced. I know Dad has some work planned for me at the bowling alley, but I'll have some free time. Maybe I will come over one day."

In front of her house, she said, "Come here." They hugged for several minutes. Tearfully, she finally said, "I have to go in. Merry Christmas, Mike."

Sunday, December 24

Mike went to his grandfather's house and insisted he pack some clothes, and spend at least a couple of days with his family. Reluctantly, he also invited Aunt Margaret and her drunkard husband, but, to his relief, she declined.

Don closed the bowling alley at four PM and was home by four-thirty.

There was no Christmas tree. In previous years, Mary had helped Mike decorate. This year, without her, he'd had no enthusiasm for it.

The three Harrisons spent the evening watching an old black and white version of Charles Dicken's *A Christmas Carol* on TV, and drinking eggnog with extra bourbon.

His father seemed almost cheerful. *Must be the booze.*

Monday, December 25

The bowling alley was closed.

After breakfast, Don put on his coat. "Andy and I are going to screen and coat the lanes, today," he said, looking at his watch. “He’s meeting me there in twenty minutes. We should be done by six or so.”

“I can help you,” Mike said. “Maybe Andy wants to spend Christmas with his family.”

“Andy wants the overtime pay. Besides, you and your grandpa have to make Christmas dinner.” Without waiting for a response, he held up his hands. “Wait. Here’s the deal: We have ham at the bowling alley; I’ll slice some up and bring it home. You and your grandfather can mash some potatoes, and maybe heat up some canned vegetables, or something.” He grinned at Mike before heading for the door. “Sophie will bring the apple pie. There’s ice cream in the freezer.”

“Stop!” Mike exclaimed as he got up from the table. “Who in the hell is Sophie?”

His father turned and smiled again. “A lady I’ve been seeing at the bowling alley—and after work a few times. She’s nice; you’ll like her.” *It wasn’t the eggnog.*

Mike had never seen any of his father’s dates or known any of their names. He looked at Gramps who looked back and shrugged.

At five PM, Mike and Gramps were playing checkers and listening to Christmas carols on the radio. Mike was debating with himself about calling Mary when the phone rang.

“Maybe Dad got done early,” Mike said, picking up the phone.

It was Andy Mershon, screaming into the phone. “MIKE, YOUR DAD’S HURT—BAD! THE BOWLIN’ ALLEY’S ON FIRE!”

As calmly as he could, Mike asked, “Where is he, Andy?”

"HEADIN' FOR MERCY HOSPITAL. THE AMBULANCE JUST LEFT!"

"Okay, take it easy, Andy. Where are you?"

"Phone booth by the drug store," Andy said, more calmly. "What should I do, Mike?"

Without replying, Mike hung up, grabbed his coat, and helped his grandfather into his, explaining on the way to the car.

Mercy Hospital was located on Scioto Trail, on the north side of Portsmouth. Mike and Gramps arrived at 5:20 PM. Don Harrison had been pronounced dead ten minutes earlier. The emergency room doctor explained that there were burns, some of which were third degree, and there was a bump on the side of his head. Apparently he had fallen and struck his head on the corner of the desk, but he had died from the inhalation of smoke and noxious fumes from the lacquer. He had stopped breathing in the ambulance and couldn't be revived.

Gramps was shaking. Mike led him to a chair. In a daze and not knowing what to do, he called Aunt Margaret, collect, from the pay phone. "I can be there by noon tomorrow," she told him. *Probably has to wait for the drunkard to sober up.*

His next thought was to call Mary, but he changed his mind and called Norma, who agreed to meet him at the house.

"I'm okay, Mikey," Gramps said when Mike came back. "Let's go home. Nothing we can do for him now."

Norma was waiting at the house when they arrived.

"Gramps, this is Norma," Mike said. "Will it be all right if she stays with you while I go by the bowling alley and see what I can find out?"

"I'll be all right. Don't need a babysitter."

"I'll just feel better if someone's here with you."

"I should go with you."

"And do what? It's two degrees."

Gramps grumbled some more but took Norma's hand. "Pleased to meet you, Norma."

Mike parked two blocks away on Gallia Street, as close as he could get, and walked to what was left of Harrison Bowl. The fire department was there dousing the still-smoldering building. Andy was standing across the street, his nearly bald head bare, hugging himself and shivering.

"Are you all right?" Mike asked.

"Yeah, I'm okay," Andy said. "How's your dad?"

Mike told him; Andy sobbed.

"Tell me what happened. You weren't smoking, were you?"

"You know better'n 'at, Mike." He wiped his eyes with his thumb and forefinger. "Your dad and me, we done this a dozen times. And I quit smokin' years ago. We even made sure to turn off the pilot lights for the furnace and kitchen stove."

"Tell me the story, Andy."

"We was done an' gittin' ready to clean up, and turn the heat back on so the lacquer'd dry before tomorrow. Your dad was in the kitchen; said he needed to slice up some ham. I decided to call home from the phone booth by the drug store to tell 'em I'd be home in a little bit. Wuden there more'n a few minutes when I heard the 'larm go off. The buildin' was on fire. Your dad come hobblin' out. I hung up the phone and went to see if he was okay; he said he was. Then he said, 'I gotta go back in there', and went hobbling back in. I couldn't stop him, Mike."

"Why didn't you call home from the bowling alley?"

"I was gittin' light-headed from the fumes, Mike; needed fresh air. The fire department was here in jist a few minutes time—mebbe five or six minutes. They went in and got him. God, Mike, there was smoke rollin' off his clothes when they brung him out. I think he was in the office when they found him. I don't know what he was after, but nuthin' in there was worth dyin' fer."

Mike looked at what was left of Harrison Bowl. The domed roof over the lanes had collapsed completely, but part of the flatter roof in the front was still standing. He spotted Frenchy Bernard, who was a regular league bowler and a lieutenant in the Fire Department. Turning to Andy, he said, "Go home and warm up. I'm gonna talk to Frenchy."

Frenchy asked about Don. When Mike told him, he shook his head and put a hand on Mike's shoulder. "God, I'm so sorry, Mike."

"Thanks," Mike mumbled.

Frenchy lifted his hat and ran the back of his hand across his brow. "Fires like this don't usually happen unless you are actually sanding. Sparks from hitting nails with the sander can ignite the stuff. Even then, it's usually a smoldering fire that starts under the lanes or the pinsetters and eventually ignites the wood. Pine ignites pretty quickly."

"I know. They were just screening and coating."

"Well, we know that lacquer is highly flammable. And being an old building with wooden trusses and all that pine, it didn't take much to get it going. Anybody smoking, you think?"

"No, they both quit years ago."

"Back door was open, right?"

Mike nodded. "And they had the big exhaust fan blowing out. Fumes get to you after a while."

"Yeah, but, even with the fan blowing, the office is such a small cubby hole, the fumes could have gotten to your dad before the smoke did." He shook his head. "He should have known better than to go back in there."

"I know. Can't imagine what he was after."

"It may take some time to figure out what happened. Could have been arson, I suppose."

"I can't imagine anyone wanting to burn it down."

"Me, neither."

"When will I be able to get in there?"

"We're probably going to have to pull that roof down. I don't know. Maybe we can let you in tomorrow; maybe not." He shrugged. "The police will have somebody patrolling to keep looters out, and I'm sure they'll have someone out here to look at the office area. You had a fireproof safe, right?"

Mike nodded.

"So, whatever was in it is probably okay. Go home, Mike; nothing you can do here. I'll call you." He put a hand on Mike's shoulder, again. "Your dad was a great guy, and I'm really sorry." He looked back at what was left of Harrison Bowl. "This was like a second home to me—and a lot of people. Poor man's country club, we called it."

Norma greeted Mike at the door with a cup of coffee. Hugging her briefly, he said, "I really appreciate this."

"You know I'll do anything I can for you, Mike."

He turned to his grandfather who was looking expectantly at him. "You okay, Gramps?"

"I'll be all right, Mikey." He patted the couch cushion beside him. "Sit down and tell me about it."

Mike told him what he knew, and then turned to Norma. "Can you stay?"

"As long as you need me," she replied.

"Will your mom need the car?"

"She can use her new boyfriend's pick-up."

Tuesday, December 26

As she was preparing to leave, Norma kissed Mike on the mouth and said, "You need anything at all, you call me."

He thanked her and watched her drive away. As he headed back into the house, Aunt Margaret drove up, alone.

"Couldn't get his drunken ass out of bed," she explained, as she tearfully hugged Mike.

"So, what do we do now?" Mike asked, taking her coat.

"We'll need to call a funeral home and have him picked up." She eased herself down onto the couch.

Mike looked at his aunt. She seemed to be aging and expanding at a rapid pace. *Probably has something to do with the drunkard she lives with.*

"I know the people at Emrick," Gramps said. "I'll call them."

"We have to figure out what he wanted," Margaret said. "I know he wasn't religious. I also know he has a plot at Scioto Burial Park next to your mother. He's had that ever since she died. But he's also a war hero, so he's entitled to..."

"He didn't want a funeral service," Gramps interrupted. "He said several times, 'Just put me in the ground'."

Margaret shook her head. "We can't do that."

Sounding agitated, Gramps said, "We should honor his wishes."

Margaret was adamant. "We can't just put him in the ground, Dad. He was a war hero. Won a Silver Star."

"Bronze Star," Gramps corrected.

Mike looked out the window. It was snowing hard and beginning to stick on Hope Run. The grass was already white. "What difference will it make to him?' he asked. "He's dead. Would you like some coffee, Aunt Margaret?"

She nodded.

"I'll make a fresh pot."

"Listen, Mike," his aunt said when he returned, "funerals, wakes, whatever, are not for the dead. They're for the living—the survivors—family and friends. A chance to say goodbye—commiserate. I know you and your dad weren't as close as some, but...I know he had a lot of friends at that bowling alley."

Mike rubbed his eyes. "How about this? We can have a visitation—wake—whatever, at the funeral home. That'll satisfy his bowling friends. I'll see if I can find somebody to say something religious at the grave site." The only person he could ask to do that was Joe Bryant.

"No flowers," Gramps said, shaking his head.

"Right. He didn't like flowers," Mike agreed.

She sighed but nodded her approval. "Okay, I'll get something put in the paper. I'll say they should donate to a charity in lieu of flowers, but you know a lot of people will send flowers, anyway."

"Will anybody donate to a charity?" Mike asked.

"Probably not."

The phone rang. It was Mary. "Mike, I just heard. I'm so sorry. What can I do?"

Take us back to October before the shit hit the fan. Tell me you don't really want a 'divorce'. "I think we're okay. Aunt Margaret's here. It would be nice if the family would come to the visitation. Probably Thursday night."

"Of course we'll be there. Mike, do you need me to come over?" It almost sounded like a plea.

Mike exhaled slowly into the phone. "No, thanks. The weather's getting nasty. But I'd like to talk to your dad if I could."

He could hear her breathing into the phone. Finally, she said, "Sure."

Joe Bryant came to the phone. "I only talked to your dad a few times, but he seemed like a good man. I'm sorry, Mike."

"He liked you, too. You know, he didn't go to church or anything, so I don't know any...clergy. I was wondering if you could say a few words over his grave."

"I could get you Elder Tackett. He's a real preacher."

"I'd rather you did it. Maybe just a couple of Bible verses."

"All right. I'll come up with somethin'."

Wednesday, December 27

Frenchy called Mike at nine AM. "I'll meet you out there if you want to look around. Just in the front—like the office and bar."

"Have you figured anything out?"

"We know the fire originated back by the pinsetters somewhere. May take a while to determine the cause."

"Cops been there?"

"They came, looked around, took some pictures—mostly of the office area—and left."

An hour later Mike was at what was left of Harrison Bowl. The flat roof had been pulled down, exposing everything to the elements. Frenchy was waiting at the front of the building. "I just want to go into the office," Mike told him as he made his way through the debris, carefully avoiding the patches of ice.

"I'll wait here," Frenchy said.

The office seemed to have been damaged nearly as much by water as by the fire. Partially burned papers, some of which were obviously money, lay on the floor, partially covered with snow and ice. He spotted some ones, some fives, at least one twenty, and some of indiscernible denomination. It was impossible to tell how much money had burned. *Would he have come back in just for the money?*

He opened desk drawers. Most of the paperwork inside was legible but wet. The same was true for paperwork in the file cabinet.

He went to the safe; it was locked.

Having opened it only a few times, he had to look at a piece of paper he kept in his wallet for the combination – L32-R36-L9.

The dial was on 36. Thinking maybe his father had been in the process of unlocking the safe, he turned the dial left to 9, and tried the handle; it didn't work. After going through the combination twice, he finally got it open.

Inside was cash drawers for the two registers, which likely contained fifty dollars each, as that was what they started with each day. There was a cloth money bag with rolls of coins and small bills. He recalled that it should contain a hundred dollars for making change. He didn't count it. There was also a bank bag with a deposit in it. He looked at the deposit slip. Five hundred, twenty dollars and some change, which would have been receipts from Saturday and Sunday.

On the top shelf was the petty cash box with some small bills, a few coins and a receipt from the hardware store. The next thing that caught his eye was the pistol. Though he knew very little about guns, he could tell it was a revolver. He opened the cylinder. Six shells, one of which had been fired. The bases of the casings were marked .22LR, leading Mike to assume the gun was a .22. With crazy thoughts running through his head, he stuck the gun in his coat pocket and dumped all the money into the cloth bag.

In a desk drawer, he found the company checkbook, which contained several undamaged checks, and a pad of undamaged deposit slips, which he also stuck into the bag.

"Thanks, Frenchy. I'll have to come back with boxes to get what I can salvage of the files."

"Think you'll rebuild it, Mike?"

"I don't know. I'm seventeen, and I know nothing about being a businessman; couldn't do it by myself." He shrugged.

"It would be nice if you could. Most of us don't like bowling at City Lanes."

Mike started to leave but then turned around. "Maybe I can figure out a way to do it…if that's what people would want."

"That's what they would want, Mike. But you have more important things to concern yourself with right now. Sometimes we forget you're just a kid."

Leaving his car in the parking lot, Mike walked four blocks to Jerry Hutchinson's Waller Street office and dropped the bag on his desk. "I'm in the dark here, Jerry. Help me out."

A thin, blond man in his early thirties, Jerry was Harrison Bowl's accountant, and a regular league bowler. He quickly came around the desk and shook Mike's hand. "I'm so sorry, Mike. Your dad was a good guy; we'll all miss him."

"Thanks."

"Did you call the insurance company?"

"I don't even know who that is."

"I have the information; I'll call them. Your dad had his mail delivered to a post office box. I have the number—and a key. Bills will be coming in, and we need to do the payroll."

"Is there enough money to give the employees a couple of weeks' severance pay?"

"I'm sure there is. Your father made the last payment to the bank on the business loan in November. There should still be a couple thousand in the business account. I have employees' names, phone numbers, and pertinent information, so I'll take care of it. Your grandfather is authorized to sign checks, so he'll have to come in periodically—or you could pick them up and take them to him. At some point, we can set you up as an authorized signatory on the account"

"What else?"

"This is all pretty complicated, Mike, being that you're not of legal age. You and your grandfather need to talk to Ben Abel."

"Who's that?"

"Your dad's lawyer. He used him for company business as well as personal stuff. I'm sure there's a will." Jerry pulled out a business card. "Give him a call. Between the two of us, we can get you through this. Again, I'm so sorry about your dad."

Thursday, December 28

The visitation was from six to eight PM.

Mike had never seen so many flowers. He and his grandfather exchanged looks. Aunt Margaret seemed pleased.

The first to arrive were the Bryant family. They all hugged him, in turn, even little Mark, who hugged Mike's leg and smiled up at him as Mike mussed his hair. Mary hugged Mike fiercely and whispered, *"We have to talk. Not now; maybe next week."*

He looked into her eyes, seeing either desperation or panic. "Okay."

She broke away as a line of people began to form.

Both coaches were there. Coach Hauser squeezed Mike's hand and hugged him. "Anything I can do, Mike, just call me. Anything at all."

"Goes for me, too, of course," said Coach Riley.

Hundreds came and went, mostly regular bowlers and business associates, along with a handful of Hope Run neighbors. Then came Eve and Norma. Eve pointed her thumb over her shoulder at the line of students behind them. "We all still love you, Michael Harrison," she said.

He blinked away the tears as nearly the entire senior class, including John and Tim, along with the rest of the football team and dozens of underclassmen paraded by. Behind them was Al Lewis, sans cigar. Tearfully, he took Mike's hand in both of his. "Mike, I'm so sorry about this. And I'm *really* sorry about the other thing. That was my fault."

"I came to you, Al. That wasn't your fault."

"I put the idea in your head. And, considering what was at stake, I should have said 'no'. God, I could've even lent you the money."

"Wasn't your fault," Mike repeated.

Al started to move on and then turned back. "By the way, it wasn't the Duvardo kid who ratted you out. It was the Jensen brothers. Apparently, they thought we hustled them."

Mike looked past him at his father's closed casket. "Didn't we?"

"I guess maybe we did." He pulled out a cigar, patted Mike on the back, and left.

Mike turned back, finding himself face-to-face with a tall, somewhat thin, fortyish woman, with dark, shoulder-length hair and high, prominent, cheekbones. She reminded him of Katharine Hepburn. When she spoke, her low, quiet, throaty voice sounded nothing like Katharine Hepburn. More like Lauren Bacall with a head cold. "My name is Sophie Reese."

"Dad's Sophie?" Mike blurted out.

"I wouldn't put it that way, but I really was looking forward to Christmas dinner. I was actually waiting for him to call me when I heard the sirens.

After recovering, he cleared his throat. "So, when did you find out?"

"Six o'clock news." She teared up. "I'm so sorry."

"Could we...get together and talk, sometime?"

"I'd like nothing better." She wrote her phone number on a scrap of paper and handed it to him. "Call me when things settle down."

Friday, December 29

Only a relative handful of mourners were at the gravesite. It was cold—near zero—and overcast, with gusty winds blowing through the bare trees, and kicking up snow that was still covering the ground. Mike looked around for Sophie Reese; she wasn't there.

The entire Bryant family was there, bundled up and stoic. Joe Bryant quoted several Bible verses that Mike neither recognized nor understood, but hopefully, made his aunt feel better.

"Do you think you'll be coming back to school, Tuesday?" Mary asked him as they were leaving.

"Haven't thought about it. Probably not 'til at least Thursday; I have a few things to clear up."

"Maybe you could give me a ride home, Thursday. I need to talk to you."

"Can't we talk now?"

"You have enough to deal with now, Mike." She smiled weakly and hugged herself. "Besides, it's freezing."

She climbed into the station wagon without looking back. Mark slipped onto her lap and waved at Mike.

"Either of you ever heard of Sophie Reese?" Mike asked on the way home.

Gramps and Margaret simultaneously said, "No."

"Didn't either of you see the tall, good looking lady at the visitation?"

Silence. He waited.

"Sophie Thornton," Margaret finally said. "That was her maiden name. We spoke briefly."

"Is that all I'm gonna get?" Mike asked, exasperated.

Gramps finally spoke up. "We knew her during the war. So did your parents. She moved away years ago, and just moved back a couple of months ago after her husband died. There's no mystery."

Mike glanced at his grandfather, and then in the rear view mirror at his aunt in the back seat. *There's a mystery.*

Saturday, December 30

Margaret left at nine AM, saying she needed to get back to her drunken husband. After saying goodbye and promising to do better at staying in touch, Mike went back into the house and called Sophie Reese.

"That was quick," she said. "Why don't you come to my place? I'm renting a small house on 22nd Street, just off Scioto Trail." She gave him the address.

"I'll be back in a couple of hours, Gramps," he said, after hanging up. "Your turn to make lunch."

Her house was a small, neat, bungalow with a driveway leading to a detached garage in the back. There was a single spruce tree in the center of the front lawn.

She answered the doorbell immediately. "Coffee? I just made a pot."

Mike nodded. "Thanks."

They sat in her eat-in kitchen, silently sipping coffee. He watched her face, noticing the laugh lines that were barely visible around her eyes, and trying unsuccessfully to envision her on a date with his father.

"How old are you, Mike?" she finally asked.

"I'll be eighteen in February."

"I should have known that. I remember when you were born."

"Oh, yeah?"

"Yes, Valentine's Day. You seem…very mature for a seventeen-year-old. And it seems like you're handling your father's death almost…calmly."

Getting irritated, he asked, "How am I supposed to handle it?"

"I don't know. I would think you'd be more devastated?"

Mike said nothing. *Hardly knew the man.*

"Won't you miss him?"

Can't miss what you never had. "Can we just skip the..."

She sighed. "Okay. There were the four of us, your parents, Charlie Spradlin, and myself. We graduated from high school together. After your father came home from college in the summer of'41, we all hung out together—went out together several times. Spent many hours playing cards, mostly euchre. We all loved to play euchre." She smiled wistfully and sipped her coffee.

Mike grew impatient. "What was going on that Gramps and my aunt don't want me to know about? Something happened between my parents that caused them to get a divorce before I ever had a chance to be part of a real family."

He stopped, breathed deeply, and then continued. "My mother died before I had a chance to know her, and my father wouldn't talk to me about any of this. And since what's left of my family clammed up at the mention of your name, it seems to me you're the one with the answers."

She held up her hand. "Mike..."

"Did they not want a child? Is—was Don Harrison my real father? Were you screwing him? Was this Charlie Spradlin screwing my mother? I'm only seventeen, but, unfortunately, I know a little bit about people screwing people they're not supposed to be screwing... "

She held up both hands. "Young man, you'll let me tell the story my way, or I won't tell it at all."

"Sorry," he muttered into his coffee cup.

"Your father and I talked some about you. He mentioned your problems with your girl—Mary, is it?"

He simply nodded.

"And the football thing—and the bowling thing. Obviously, it's been a rough couple of months for you, so I'm going to—as honestly as I can—tell you everything I know about your parents' situation."

She poured them more coffee, and then brought out a bottle of amaretto and poured a shot into each cup. "That'll loosen up my tongue, maybe."

He took a sip, didn't like the taste, but didn't complain.

"The four of us were close friends all through high school. At some point, we paired off. Your parents became a couple, and Charlie and I became a couple. Your parents married in late '41, right before Pearl Harbor, but Charlie and I never even discussed marriage."

Calmer now, he asked, "Why not?"

"I think it's possible we paired up wrong." She stopped and sipped her coffee. "No, that's not exactly it. I was very much in love with your father. And Charlie really was in love with your mother. The problem was that your parents loved each other. What does that make the situation…a love rectangle?

"Anyway, your dad joined the Marines in...I think...February of '42. Your mother was not happy about that. In fact, she was very upset; seriously pissed off might be a better way of putting it." A smile came and went.

"During this time, Charlie and I saw less and less of each other. And rumors were flying that…" She paused, took another sip and looked up at him. "There were rumors about your mother and Charlie. I can't say that anything happened between them, but they did spend some time together. Both her parents had passed away while your father was off to war, which, I guess, left your mother lonely and vulnerable."

"Yeah. Gramps told me about that. She died of some type of cancer, and he drank himself to death. And...mom was an only child."

"Yes, unfortunately. Well anyway, Charlie got drafted and went off to boot camp just a few days after your father came home. The rumors, of course, got back to your father. So, I guess in retaliation, he...he began an affair with me." She looked away, and then back at him. "Yeah, I was a tramp, taking up with a married man, but...truth is, I was still very much in love with him. And there was a war on; good excuse for bad behavior." She shook her head, sipped, and then held his eyes briefly before continuing.

"Your father never got it out of his head that his wife had cheated on him with Charlie. And yes, he did question whether you were his child. I heard he hit her a few times. Anna wasn't the kind of person who'd put up with that.

"Before long, he stopped seeing me; said he wanted to try to fix his marriage. Shortly after that, I met an older man, Doctor Elliott Reese, and, looking for security, I married him. He got a position at Walter Reed and was still there when he died this past summer. I moved back here specifically to try to strike up a new relationship with your father."

"No kids?"

She shook her head. "After two miscarriages, we gave up."

She poured another shot of amaretto into each cup and poured coffee on top, and then gazed at Mike, waiting.

"What happened to Charlie?" he asked.

"He went to England, took part in the D-Day invasion. I don't know how much you know about the war, but he went in with the first wave on Omaha Beach."

"I've read about that. He's lucky to be alive, I guess."

"Yes, he is. He was also at the Battle of the Bulge. After the war, he came home for a couple of weeks, but I saw him only once. We agreed that we had no future together. He moved to Seattle, got a job at Boeing, and married some woman from up there."

"Still there?"

"As far as I know."

Mike sipped and then asked, "Did Dad ever talk to you about the war?"

"Not really. I brought it up a couple of times, but he simply said, 'You don't want to know about that'. But he did second-guess his decision to volunteer. Said he should have simply waited to be drafted—like Charlie and so many others did."

"Yeah. I kinda gathered that."

"Something else he told me was kind of disturbing. He said that, on his way home after he mustered out of the Marines, he planned to get off the bus, walk to the Second Street Bridge and jump off. Fortunately, Anna and your grandparents were waiting for him at the bus station."

Mike contemplated this. *Would I not exist? Or would I be living in Seattle with Charlie Spradlin?*

"Don't judge him too harshly, Mike."

"I don't judge him."

She looked sharply at him. "Don't you? He thought you did."

Mike shrugged. "Doesn't matter now, does it? You planning to stay here?"

"I don't know. I have a little bit of money, but since I'm not rich, I'd have to find something to do. Too young to sit around doing nothing, anyway."

"Do you have any family here?" he asked.

"A sister who lives up around Jackson, and a brother in Columbus. Haven't had much contact with them, lately. Christmas cards every year is about it. Now that I live closer, I might see more of them."

Mike drained his coffee cup and got up to leave. "Would it be okay if I call you once in a while?" He asked. "We could just talk."

"I think that would be wonderful. Call me anytime you want."

Tuesday, January 2, 1962

Ben Abel was a short, round, balding, man with a large nose and a bushy unibrow. After introducing himself and offering sympathy, he pointed to the two leather chairs in front of his desk.

"Okay," he said matter-of-factly, "here's the situation. I have your father's will, and I am the executor. He left all his assets to you, Mike—except for a few items of sentimental value, which he left to your aunt. Officially, the court is supposed to appoint a legal guardian, which would likely be your grandfather. Unofficially, you can just hang in there 'til you turn eighteen."

He looked down at the paperwork on his desk. "You'll be eighteen next month. That will make you an adult in some ways."

He looked up and smiled. "You'll have to register for the draft. You'll be legally allowed to drink three-two beer. There are some contracts you'll be allowed to enter into. But some—such as a liquor license, assuming you'd want to rebuild—require you to be twenty-one."

He looked at Gramps, and then back at Mike. "Your grandfather could get the proper licenses if you want to go that way. In any case, it'll take several months for the insurance company to come through—maybe more if they suspect arson. They tend to stall sometimes and have to be prodded, so don't expect any money from them until at least May or June.

"Your father had a life insurance policy of ten thousand, which it shouldn't take long to get. In the meantime, if you need money to live on while all this is taking place, as executor, I can provide that out of the assets of the Company." He looked at Gramps again.

"I can take care of Mikey, no problem. I've got a few bucks," Gramps told him, smiling at Mike. "Also, I'm moving in with him and selling my house, so we'll be fine."

"That simplifies things," Ben said as he stood up. "Don't worry about the red tape, Mike. Your accountant and I will work through that and keep you informed."

In the car, Mike asked, "You're really moving in, Gramps?"

"You're only seventeen, Mikey. You shouldn't be living alone. I'll have to put a lot of my stuff in storage, and take a lot of crap to the dump. I'll put the house on the market after you and I do a little painting and fixing up."

"You got it, Gramps. When do you wanna start?"

"How about right after you make lunch?"

Thursday, January 4

Mike was back in school. Several of the students who hadn't made it to the visitation offered their condolences. Mary was quiet; the day dragged.

Finally, when school was out, she met him in the hallway. "Where can we go?" she asked, as Mike watched her eyes, reading nothing.

"My house. Gramps will be out shooting pool with his buddies, and won't be home 'til six or so."

"Is he going to live with you?"

"Yeah, we're moving him in gradually."

"At least, you won't be alone."

WIOI was playing the Shirelles new hit, 'Baby It's You'. As Mike downshifted and turned onto Hope Run, he glanced at her. She was gazing blankly out the window at the bare trees and muddy, brown grass along the banks of Hope Creek.

He took her coat and offered to make hot chocolate; she declined and sat on the couch.

Taking a deep breath, she exhaled slowly and looked up at him. "I might as well just get right to it. I'm…I'm pregnant."

Mike stared, feeling like he'd been kicked in the crotch. Of all the things he'd thought might be wrong, somehow this one had never found its way into his brain. *Why not?* He stared at her but didn't see her. Nauseated, he walked to the window and looked out, but saw nothing.

"Look at me, Mike," she pleaded. "Say something."

"*Tony?*" he managed, in a hoarse whisper, still staring out the window.

"He raped me. Please look at me, Mike."

He dropped into a chair across the room, and took several deep breaths, but couldn't rid himself of the suffocating feeling. "Tell me."

Tears streamed down her face. He went to the bathroom and returned with a box of tissues, and stood in front of her as she dabbed her eyes and blew her nose.

"The night of the Waverly game…" she started.

"You were there?" He was still feeling nauseated.

"Yes."

"You left with Tony; that's why he left Eve stranded?"

"I told my father you were bringing me home. I really wanted to see the game, and figured I'd get a ride with someone…hopefully you."

He closed his eyes. "Why didn't you wait for me? I needed… Mary, you could have made that night a whole lot less awful."

"I know. But I was still very mad at you, Mike. No…more than mad. I…"

He couldn't resist asking, "Was it rape? Or was it, 'Put out or get out'?"

She stood and hit him flush on the chin with a roundhouse right. Surprised, he staggered backward, fell over the coffee table, and landed flat on his back. By the time he recovered, she was out the door and running up Hope Run toward Bryant Holler. He caught her after several hundred yards and grabbed her arm. She jerked free and continued running.

"Stop, Mary, please…I'm sorry…I said that… Just… come back," he said while bending over, hands on hips, trying to catch his breath. "Besides…you…forgot your coat."

She stopped and walked back to him. "Will you…help me?"

"I'll do what I can if you'll just come back in out of the cold."

Back at the house, they both sat on the couch.

"Where?" he asked.

She dabbed her eyes some more. "The Neumann place."

"It's empty. They moved out in September."

"I know. Obviously, he did, too. I got the impression he'd been there before. Just let me tell you the whole story, please."

He sat back. "Go ahead."

"I was really mad at you, but I knew that, at some point, I was going to have to just let it go. All those years together. But I wasn't ready to just let it go—not yet."

Mike started to speak, but she held up her hand. "Don't say it. After what you did at the Northwest game, he began asking me out. I told him dad wouldn't let me go out. Then he started bugging me about just taking a ride in his Corvette.

"After the game—the Waverly game—I headed toward your car, but Norma was there. I just...couldn't...be around her."

"Did she see you?"

"I don't think so. Tony was parked around the corner, close to the building. He came out still sweaty; with his hair all messed up, and offered me a ride. I thought it would be okay, and maybe a way to get back at you. I didn't think anything was going to happen. And...I felt sorry for him."

"Sorry for *him*? He cost us the game."

"That's why I felt sorry for him."

"Excuse me, but if nothing had happened, I would never have known about it. How, exactly, were you getting back at me?"

She contemplated the carpet. "I know it's silly, but I thought that, when you came back begging, I'd tell you about it as a way of punishing you. I'd casually let it slip that I'd ridden in his Corvette. I'm so stupid."

He struggled to keep his voice even. "There may have been a point where I would have come back begging, but that went away when you said you wanted a *divorce*."

She looked at him bleakly. "Screwed up with that, too, didn't I. Same day you blew up your car, wasn't it?"

"Yeah." He stood up and paced back and forth in front of her. "Finish your story."

"Anyway, we were on Hope Run, and he pulled into the Neumanns' driveway. Said he wanted to show me something, and took a flashlight from his glove compartment."

She held up her hand again. "I know. I know. I was starting to get a little uncomfortable, but still had no idea anything was going to happen. Naïve little Virgin Mary.

We went into the house; it wasn't locked. There was a mattress on the floor in the living room. When he grabbed me and started trying to kiss me I finally realized..." She stopped and looked at him.

He rubbed his chin. "Please don't hit me again, but did you try to fight him off?"

"Of course, I did. I kicked; I screamed; I bit him on the arm. I tried to scratch him. I kneed him in the crotch; he punched me in the ribs and threatened to kill me. Then he choked me 'til I almost passed out."

She paused and massaged her temples. "Now, let me ask you a question, Mike. What would have happened if I'd fought long enough to get myself a black eye or two and a broken nose? I would have had to tell you what happened. What would you have done?"

"I would have killed him," he replied, hoarsely.

"If my father didn't get to him first. I certainly didn't want either of you going to prison over my stupidity. Anyway, after he...after he was done with me, he said no one would believe me if I reported him—and I'd just be ruining my reputation."

He sighed but said nothing.

She dabbed her eyes again. "Did you know, in some countries in the Middle East, they kill girls for allowing themselves to be raped?"

"No, I didn't."

"They call them honor killings. You, or Dad, or even Jimmy could do it. In fact, you'd be expected to do it."

"Makes no sense. Why not kill the rapist, instead?"

She sat back and closed her eyes. "Well, in this case, somebody did."

He tried, unsuccessfully, to blink away the image of her lying on a filthy mattress with Tony Duvardo on top of her.

He went out the back door, and breathed deeply, feeling the cold air stab his lungs. He was shivering, but not from the cold. *What have I done?*

Upon returning, he stood in front of her again. "Your parents know nothing, right?"

"Mom suspects something; Dad's clueless."

"So…is that why you missed those days of school?"

"My ribs were so sore I could hardly breathe, and I had bruises all over. Mom saw some of them, but I told her Babs accidently slammed me into the barn door. I don't think she believed me, but she let it go."

"How about your dad?"

"Just told him I was sick. All I have to do is mention 'cramps' or 'period' and he leaves me alone for days; almost like it's some contagious disease."

He sighed loudly; his shoulders sagged. "What do you want me to do?"

She closed her eyes, massaged her face with both hands, and then met his eyes. "I…want you to help me…get rid of it."

"An abortion? Since you were raped, couldn't you…?"

"Couldn't I tell the world? Couldn't I tell my father? I'd rather stick a coat hanger up there. And…how would it look, anyway, accusing a dead guy who couldn't defend himself?"

He shrugged. "After what he did at the Waverly game…?"

"I thought maybe Eve or Norma might know somebody."

"Norma might. But I can just hear her now: 'So, you knocked up Virgin Mary, huh?'."

"Maybe somebody else."

"Contrary to what's been going through your head, I don't have connections..." He studied her face as she looked expectantly at him. "Look...I'll talk to Norma and tell her it's some bowler friend's daughter. She may not know anybody, but it's a good bet her mother does."

She sat silently on the couch looking at the knuckles on her right hand.

"Hurt you more than it hurt me, huh?" he asked.

"Probably. How's your chin?"

"Gonna be sore." He rubbed it. "Remember the story you told me about your father hitting you... "

"You're not getting that promise from me, Mike." She stood up. "Do you hate me, now?"

"I could never... Are you sure you want to do this?"

"I've told you I want to be more than another teenage mother on Hope Run. I have that scholarship to work on. I want to get a degree and have a career; maybe see my byline under a newspaper headline. I just want to...do something meaningful with my life, but I can't do much of anything while lugging a rapist's baby around. I love my family, but I just don't want to spend the rest of my life on Hope Run. Besides...I'll never be able to look my father in the eye if he finds out what happened."

"Are you sure you're pregnant?"

"My periods have been like clockwork since I was thirteen. I've missed two in a row, and I've had morning sickness. So yes, I'm sure."

"Even if I find somebody, it'll cost money."

"How much? I have about fifty dollars saved."

He took her hands in his. "Honestly, I have no experience in this, but I'm sure no one would do it for fifty dollars. Don't worry about it, though. I'll get the money…if I find somebody."

She put on her coat. "Please drive me home, now. I have a cow to milk."

In front of her house, he hugged her briefly, and then watched her eyes as she looked at him. *Desperate and vulnerable, but strong and defiant.*

On the way back home, he listened to Gene McDaniel singing 'Tower of Strength'.

Can I talk her out of this? Do I want to?

Tuesday, May 29
Ocean Beach

Debbie stopped him again. "So…she got in his car to get back at you, and he raped her to get back at you. Is that what you're thinking?"

"Yeah."

"Seriously, Mike? The world doesn't revolve around you."

"I never thought it did."

"They both may have had other motivations." She waved a hand as if shooing away a fly, and drained her bottle. "More beer?"

He showed her his half-full bottle. "I'm fine."

Friday, January 5
Scioto County

He offered Norma a ride home from school; she quickly accepted.

"We need to talk," he said as he parked in front of her house.

"Why don't you come in? Mom won't be home for a while—if she comes home at all."

"What's that about?"

"She gets off work at five, usually goes to a beer joint. Sometimes she comes home after a couple, but sometimes…" She shrugged. "It's Friday night."

He looked around. Books, newspapers and magazines were piled high on the coffee table. A half-empty coffee cup sat on top of the TV. The carpet was stained, and apparently hadn't been vacuumed lately. *Mary would have a heart attack.*

Norma picked up a pile of clothes from the couch, and took them into another room. Upon returning, she turned on the record player, which was stacked with 45's. Brenda Lee's 'Fool #1' was playing.

"Sit," she said. "Sorry, we're such lousy housekeepers. What's up? Wanna fool around?"

"No," he said, emphatically.

"Well then, what?"

"Uh…I'm looking for someone who does… abortions. I thought maybe…"

She snickered. "So…you knocked up Virgin Mary, huh? I thought she hated you."

"I didn't knock anybody up. And it's not Mary. Friend of a friend." He told her the lie. "And Mary doesn't hate me."

She left the room and came back with a scrap of paper. "If they're still doing it, it'll cost three hundred—unless the price has gone up in the past year."

"Thanks a lot, Norma. Uh…not to get personal, but did you…?"

She sighed heavily. "Me once; Mom twice that I know of."

"I'm only asking because I wonder if it's a clean place…a safe place."

"It seemed okay. It wasn't the kind of shit-hole you see in the movies."

"Where is it?"

"I don't know. I met them in the Kroger parking lot. They put me in a car and made me lie face down in the back seat. They parked in a garage about five or six steps from the back door of a house. No idea where it was. When they were done, they took me back to Kroger's.

"Did it hurt?"

"Like hell." She leaned in and kissed him. He pulled away and said, "Honestly, I'm trying to be good, and I just need friends, now. Will you be just my friend? And can we keep this between you and me?"

"I understand. If I'd behaved myself back in October…" She cupped his face in her hands. "You've been through a lot, Mike. I'll be the best friend I can possibly be, which means you can tell me anything and I promise I'll keep my big fat mouth shut, and won't ask anything of you."

"Thanks." He got up to leave. "How about I start picking you up for school every day? It's not far out of my way."

"What about Mary?"

"Mary will just have to deal with it."

She stopped the record player in the middle of Ray Charles' 'Unchain My Heart'.

Saturday, January 6

He called Mary at four PM. "I have a phone number for you."

"Will you call, please? I don't know what to say."

"No, I will not," he replied, not trying to hide his irritation. "I have no experience with this, Mary." *And I didn't knock you up.*

"Will you take me, and stay with me?"

"Of course."

"You and Gramps could come to supper if you're not doing anything."

"We've been working on his house all day. Gramps is napping, and I don't know how long it'll be."

"Mike, I really miss you…us."

"Me, too. I'll see you at school, Monday." He hung up the phone.

Friday, January 12

It was set up for seven PM.

They made the excuse that they were going to the basketball game in New Boston. Joe Bryant, obviously happy to see them back together, had smiled and shook

Mike's hand enthusiastically. Stone-faced, Rose just hugged him.

In the car, Mike asked, "Does your mom know—or suspect?"

"I think she suspects something, but she hasn't said anything."

"If she knew what you're about to do would she stop it."

"Probably. Did you get the money?"

"Yeah. Gramps gave it to me, and didn't even ask what it was for."

She put her hand on his forearm. "I'll pay you back."

The instructions were to park in front of a used furniture store on Eleventh Street. When they arrived at six-fifty-five, he looked at Mary. She was staring straight ahead, shivering, her hands clenched in front of her stomach.

"Mary, you don't have to..." Mike began.

"Yes, I do," she interjected. "I have no choice."

They watched several cars pass before a '59 Pontiac Bonneville parked behind them. A large woman got out and approached on the passenger's side. Her gray hair was tied back in a bun. Her glasses were half-way down her very long nose. Mary rolled down the window.

"Do you have the money?" the woman asked.

Mike counted out three hundred dollars in twenties.

The woman looked at him and said, "You'll have to wait here."

"No!"

"Only way it's gonna happen, sonny."

He looked at Mary; she nodded solemnly and got out. He watched in the rear view mirror as she disappeared into the back seat of the Pontiac.

After some time, he looked at his watch. Seven-fifteen. The second hand seemed to be moving at half-speed. Five minutes later, he turned on the engine and the heater to warm up. At seven-thirty, he turned off the engine, got out and paced back and forth on the sidewalk. A young, thin, black man in an older model Cadillac parked in front of him and got out.

"Lookin' for something, Jim," the man said.

His first impulse was to say 'I'm not Jim'. Instead, he said, "No, I'm just waiting for someone."

The man pointed at the passenger side of the Cadillac as a black teenage girl opened the door, displaying long, bare legs. "I got someone right here, Jim. Ten bucks'll get you an hour, but I bet you won't need the whole hour." He laughed, showing several missing teeth.

Mike shook his head. "Not looking for that; just waiting for someone."

The man stepped closer. His breath smelled like an outhouse. "Okay, man. How about five? You can do it right here in the back seat of my Caddy. With her, you won't last more'n five minutes, anyway."

Am I gonna have to fight this guy? He took his hands out of his coat pockets and said, "Not what I'm looking for, tonight.

"Shee-it." The man waved the girl back into the car.

Shaking, Mike watched him drive away.

Back inside the car, he started the engine and waited.

Fifteen minutes later, the Pontiac parked behind him again. Mary emerged alone, looking pale and walking gingerly.

"Are you okay?" Mike asked as he opened the door for her.

"No. Cramps, worse than any I've ever imagined. Let's get out of here before I puke."

He looked at his watch. Just after eight. Mary sat leaning against the passenger door, shivering.

"I shouldn't take you home 'til after the game's over," he said. "Let's go somewhere and get coffee, or something to eat."

She winced. "I couldn't eat. Could we go to your house?"

"Gramps will be there. Let's go to Patsy's Inn and get coffee.

At Patsy's Inn on Clay Street, they sat across from each other in a booth. She put her hands on the table and he took them both in his.

"Mike, did we just murder a baby?" Her voice was trembling.

"Don't talk like that, Mary. He raped you. It shouldn't have been."

"But maybe it was God's will."

"It wasn't God's will; it was Tony Duvardo's will."

"Maybe it was our date."

"Our date?"

"Yes, our one and only date—on Friday the thirteenth. Maybe God was telling us we shouldn't be together. Maybe our kids would have been demons or something."

"Mary, you're the smartest person I know. You can't possibly believe that crap."

"No, I don't," she conceded as she squeezed his hand and winced in pain.

The waitress brought coffee for him and hot chocolate for her.

"I'd give anything to be able to go back to October and re-do this," he said, "but I can't...we can't."

She absently stirred her hot chocolate. "Will things ever be the same between us, Mike?"

Looking down at the table, he shook his head. "Probably not."

In the car, he tuned the radio to WNXT to catch the basketball scores, in case someone asked. The Shawnee had lost 56-51, but Mike was pleased to hear that Tim Crabtree was the team's leading scorer with sixteen points.

When he parked in front of her house at ten o'clock, she moved closer to him and said, "Hold me, please."

He held her for several minutes, with neither of them speaking. Finally, she broke away and said, "I have to go in."

"Will they be able to tell that something's wrong."

"Cramps, remember? I won't be lying. But it might be better if you'd come in and say 'hi' to the family."

Inside, Mary simply said, "I'm not feeling well; going upstairs." Her mother followed her.

Though the Bryants had updated their house of late, they still had no central heating. In the corner, a large fireplace blazed and crackled. Joe sat near the fireplace in a recliner. He acknowledged Mike with a smile and a wave, and then concentrated on *77 Sunset Strip* on TV. On a large couch, the three smaller kids were sharing a blanket. Mark and Joshua were sound asleep. Esther smiled at Mike, and then returned her attention to the show. Jimmy, who also seemed to be engrossed in the show, greeted Mike, and then made space between himself and Becky on a love seat.

"How's Paul?" Mike asked Becky.

Sharing her blanket with him, she whispered, "*He's on the basketball team. You didn't see him, though, did you?"*

He looked up at Joe, who was still concentrating on the TV.

Rose came down after a few minutes and whispered, "*Cramps".* Joe nodded.

Halfway home, listening to The Impalas doing an *oldie* called 'Sorry (I Ran all the Way Home)', it hit him. *How did she get home that night? The Neumann place was nearly six miles from her house. If she had walked, it would have taken her, at least, two hours, and by then her father would have been out looking for her. Did she lie, or just leave something out?*

Sunday, January 14

She called him at eleven AM.

"How are you feeling?" he asked.

"Better," she replied, "but not great. The family's at church and I'm all alone. Please come over."

He sat at the large dining room table. She poured him coffee, poured herself half a cup, and finished filling it with milk and sugar.

"What did your mom say when she followed you upstairs?" he asked.

"Not much. But I think she knows something's wrong."

"What would she do if she found out?"

"She'd be upset."

"Would she tell your dad?"

She shrugged.

They sipped silently, occasionally glancing at each other.

"What's the deal with your scholarship?" he finally asked.

She perked up. "I have everything in. There's just an in-person interview, which is this Wednesday. They'll announce the winner February 15th."

"I sure hope you win; you deserve it."

"What about you? You can't play football, but you can still go."

"Right now I have zero enthusiasm for school. I'll probably take some time off after graduation and travel. Just get in the Chevy and go—maybe check out the world's fair in Seattle." *Maybe I'll check out Charlie Spradlin.*

"It would be nice to have you in Columbus with me if I get to go." She massaged her temples with her index fingers and looked down into her coffee cup.

He looked at her face, thinking back to their date in October. Her eyes were the same dark brown, but they no longer sparkled. She still had the same nearly perfect facial features—high cheekbones, flawless skin, perfect nose—but she looked thin and pale. The enthusiastic, happy, optimistic, Mary Bryant of their October date was no longer there.

"How's Babs?" he asked.

"Seven months pregnant. We're in the process of letting her go dry. We'll have to start buying milk."

He looked out toward the meadow. With the leaves missing from the trees, he could just make out the log they had sat on. "Well, I should go. Gramps is probably ready for lunch."

Monday, January 15

After school, Mike called Deputy Hoch.

"I was wondering if I could come see you this afternoon," he said.

"Sure. I'll be here 'til at least five, but if you have anything on the Duvardo case, you should probably talk to the Portsmouth Police. It's their case."

"I feel more comfortable talking to you."

"Fine, I'll be here."

Hoch led Mike into a small windowless office, sat down behind a beat up desk, and motioned him to the folding chair in front.

"Sorry about your father; and sorry about missing the wake. I was out of town over the holidays visiting relatives."

"That's okay; he'll never know. There's something I forgot to tell you that might be important."

"What?"

"Two weeks before he was killed, Tony was in the bowling alley at about one in the morning."

"That would be the night of the big bowling match—when you destroyed your football career?"

"Yeah, that night. He came in, used the pay phone, and left."

"And you're wondering what he would have been doing there. Well, let me tell you a story. Your father mentioned to me on a couple of occasions that he thought there was drug dealing going on behind the bowling alley. I passed it on to the city, and they said they'd look into it." He pulled out a cigarette. "Do you mind if I smoke?"

Mike shook his head.

After lighting up and taking a long drag, he looked at Mike for a few seconds. "I probably shouldn't be discussing this with you, since you haven't been totally ruled out as a suspect, but…the investigation is focused mainly on a couple of guys who deal drugs—small time—mostly marijuana and pills. I've already been informed that Tony was a pot smoker—as I think you already knew."

He held up his hands as Mike started to speak. "Now, dealers don't generally shoot their clients, but there could have been a dispute over money. Or maybe Tony flashed a wad of cash that the guy couldn't resist. Of course without the murder weapon…" He shrugged and took a drag.

After debating with himself, Mike asked, "Would you be able to identify the murder weapon?"

The deputy didn't reply immediately; just looked at Mike. "Not my area of expertise," he finally said, "but ballistics tests could probably determine that, if we had the gun. Why?"

"Just curious. Do you know what kind of a gun it was?"

"The bullet was a .22 long rifle."

"So, he was killed with a rifle?"

"No. The forensics people say it was a pistol, at close range. It's not the kind of weapon a professional killer would use, but, fired into someone's temple, it's more than capable of doing the job."

"So, I'm not really a suspect?"

"I don't think they're looking at anyone associated with the school. And…there are about fifteen witnesses who will swear you never left the bowling alley between twelve-thirty and five the morning of the murder. I know they're all your friends, but I can't imagine that many would be willing to lie under oath."

"Wouldn't the police consider the possibility of some connection between a murder and the fire at the same place?"

The deputy looked sharply at him. "I don't think they see a connection. Do you?"

"Not really. But wouldn't you think that they'd have looked a little closer at my dad's death. Maybe wonder why he went back into the building?"

"You'd have to ask them. But with the burned money—which they photographed—it seemed logical that was what he was trying to save."

"They're probably right." *They're probably wrong.*

Deputy Hoch stood up. "We done? I gotta get back to work."

"Yes sir, I appreciate your time."

"Look, Mike. I like you, and I feel bad about all the shit you've had to deal with lately, but I think the Portsmouth

Police have a pretty good handle on what happened. And...the Fire Department seems to think the fire was nothing more than an accident. And going back in there was just a tragic mistake on your father's part."

"Okay." Mike stood up.

"Appreciate you coming in. And, again, I'm really sorry about your father." He crushed out his cigarette and winced as he burned his fingers.

Wednesday, January 17

Mary was out of class for her interview during fifth period. She walked into the sixth period classroom as the bell was ringing, talked briefly with Mr. Devers, and then caught up with Mike in the hallway.

"That was a long interview. How'd it go?" he asked.

"Really well, I think. Give me a ride home and we'll talk about it."

"Sure, I have to take Norma home first."

"I'll take the bus." She quickly headed for the exit.

He caught up and took her by the arm. "Mary, we're divorced. Remember?"

She pulled her arm free and kept walking. "Yeah, I forgot."

"Dammit, Mary!"

"Don't swear at me, Mike!"

"Norma will take the bus. You're riding home with me."

She shrugged. "Okay."

In the car, she said, "I think they really like me. They asked me all kinds of questions. And I think I gave them some good answers. Seemed to be impressed with some of the essays I've written."

"How much is this scholarship worth?"

"It's a full ride—tuition, books, room and board. Four years, if I keep my grades up and stay out of trouble."

"What about living expenses?"

"I won't get much from my parents, but I won't need much. Maybe I'll try to get a part-time job at the Dispatch."

"I really hope you get the scholarship. You deserve it."

She smiled as she turned toward him with her back against the door. "It'd be much better if you were there, too."

He decided not to wait any longer. "Mary, how'd you get home that night?"

Her smile disappeared. "I…walked."

"Six miles, after being raped and beaten? That means you got home around two in the morning. Your parents didn't have a problem with that?"

She stared through the windshield. "They thought I was with you, which meant I was perfectly safe. They're pretty naïve about that, you know."

He pulled the car off the road, closed his eyes, and pressed his index fingers against the bridge of his nose, as his head began to throb.

"Mary, why are you lying?"

"I'm not…" She glanced at him, and then looked away. "Okay, I got a ride. A man picked me up after I started walking."

"Who?"

She stared out the window.

"Look at me, Mary. And please don't say it was a stranger. You'd have had to explain why you were all beat up and disheveled. It was either someone you knew who would keep his—or her—mouth shut, or it was Tony. I can't picture him saying, 'Okay, I'm through raping you now, so I'll just take you home'. I can't picture you getting in his car after what he did. So will you please just tell me the truth?"

She opened the car door. "I'll walk."

He grabbed her arm. "Mary, just tell me what happened!"

A car passed; the driver honked. Mike looked up but didn't recognize the car.

She closed the door. "The school bus will be along in a few minutes. Take me somewhere."

"Okay, we'll go to my house."

Gramps greeted them at the door.

Mary hugged him. "Hi, Gramps."

"Good to see you, Mary. Good to see you two together."

Mike looked at his grandfather. "Why are you all dressed up?"

"Got a date." He pointed toward the phone. "I left you a note."

"Should I wait up for you?"

Gramps laughed. "If I'm not home by eight, you should probably send out a search party. It's just dinner, and you know how early we old people like to eat."

"Have fun, Gramps."

Gramps smiled at Mary. "You too, Mikey."

"Okay," she said, as she sat on the edge of the couch, "I guess it doesn't matter, now. Here's the rest of the story: Tony did offer me a ride home afterward. He actually tried to apologize, but I told him to get away from me. That's when he said no one would believe me, and just took off. I was walking home when your…father came along and…"

"My father?" *It's starting to make sense.*

"He said he saw me get into Tony's car after the game, and thought about following us right away, but decided to wait for you. After several minutes—too many minutes, as it turned out—he decided to leave anyway and make sure I got home okay. I probably hadn't taken more than a dozen steps down Hope Run when he picked me up, brought me here and let me take a shower and straighten myself up the best I could. Then he took me home and said I shouldn't tell anybody because, if you found out, you'd kill Tony, and he didn't want you going to prison."

Mike's head was still throbbing. "So, what happened when you got home?"

"Nothing. My parents were sound asleep; blissfully ignorant because they thought I was with you."

Mike stood up. "I guess I should take you home."

"We sure made a mess of our little fairy tale romance, didn't we?"

"Mary, I realize I really screwed up, but I can't get past the fact that you flirted with Tony."

"I'm not sure I know how to flirt. When did I flirt?"

"That day in the cafeteria. For someone who didn't know how to flirt, you were doing pretty well at it. I know I overreacted, but still…"

She stood up and picked up her coat. "Don't forget, you're the one who cheated, Mike."

"Maybe you should have just knocked me on my ass, then."

"Maybe—in hindsight. But would that have stopped you from cheating again?"

He didn't answer.

As she opened the car door in front of her house, he spoke up. "Considering how bad I felt after what I did, I think the answer to your question is 'yes'. But I have a question for you. Would you even be talking to me right now, if you hadn't gotten yourself knocked up?"

She stepped out of the car, and then turned back toward him. "You immature, self-centered, insecure, phony..." She stopped and stared at him.

Their eyes locked. "And you're none of those, right?"

She slammed the car door.

When Gramps walked into the house at seven-thirty, Mike was waiting for him with a cartridge from the pistol. "What is this, Gramps?"

"Looks like a bullet to me, Mikey."

"Yeah, but what kind?"

Gramps took the cartridge and spun it between his thumb and forefinger. He looked at Mike, suspiciously. "Twenty-two long rifle. Where'd you get it?"

"Found it. I was just curious." Mike took the cartridge back and put it in his pocket. "How was your date?"

"Fine. She's a nice lady."

"Did you kiss her—or anything?"

"No, I did not."

Mike debated talking to his grandfather about the rape and the gun, finally deciding that now was not the time. *Maybe the cops will arrest some drug dealer.*

Saturday, January 20

Mike called Frenchy at the firehouse.

"I'm not supposed to say anything 'til the investigation is done," Frenchy told him. "But—keep this to yourself, for now—they're concentrating on the area where your dad had plugged the big exhaust fan into an extension cord. Looks like that's where the fire started, but they are still looking at other possibilities."

"Thanks. I'd appreciate it if you'd keep me posted," Mike said.

"It'll take some time, Mike."

Mike and Gramps spent most of the day working on the house on Front Street. "We need to lay new linoleum in the kitchen," Gramps said, as they were leaving. "That should do it."

"Maybe paint that ugly, baby shit yellow, bedroom."

Gramps smiled wistfully. "That was your dad's room—way back when. He didn't like it either."

In the car, Mike said, "Gramps, I think I'll invite Sophie over for dinner sometime,"

"Why would you want to invite the woman who broke up your parents' marriage to dinner?"

"Obviously, Dad wasn't innocent; maybe Mom wasn't either. Besides, I like her."

Gramps shrugged. "I guess I could put up with her for a couple of hours."

Mike and Gramps stayed in and listened to the undefeated and top-ranked Ohio State basketball team, led by All-Americans Jerry Lucas and John Havlicek, beat Minnesota 90-76. The Buckeyes seemed ready to redeem themselves after losing last year's NCAA championship game to the University of Cincinnati.

Gramps went to bed shortly after the game. Feeling lonely, Mike sat in front of the TV for a while and considered calling Norma. Finally deciding against it, he went to bed. Two sleepless hours later, with thoughts of Mary, his father, Tony Duvardo, and Sophie Reese bouncing around in his head, he got up. Looking around for something to read, he discovered Mary's copy of *Of Mice and Men*. Reminding himself that he needed to get it back to her, he sat down and began reading. Within ten minutes, he was sound asleep.

His father, engulfed in flames, was crawling up lane three. Mike tried to move, but couldn't. On lane six, Mary was lying, naked, on a filthy mattress. 'It's all your fault, Mike', she said. Tony was standing naked over her with an enormous erection. Mike tried to move, but still couldn't.

Norma appeared in front of him. "She's not worth it, Mike. Just love me, instead."

Forcing himself to move, he woke up and went to bed.

Saturday, January 27

Mike invited Sophie to dinner, and after some thought and consultation with Gramps, he invited Norma, as he seemed to be her only friend. Boys had asked her out, but she showed no interest in anyone but him. "They all want the same thing, and I just don't want that, right now," she had told him.

He and Gramps decided that, together, they could make spaghetti and meatballs. Sophie volunteered to bring the wine.

He was at Norma's house at six PM, and met her mother for the first time. Jean West was of an indeterminate age—maybe thirty-five, maybe fifty. She wasn't unattractive, though she used too much makeup and, judging by her complexion, spent too much time in the sun, smoked too much, drank too much, or some combination of the three. *Rode hard and put away wet.*

"I have a date," she announced, as a pick-up truck pulled into the driveway. "Nice meeting you, Mike." She took his hand and held it uncomfortably long as she looked into his eyes.

With an exasperated look, Norma grabbed Mike's arm and said, "Let's go."

In the driveway, they said 'hello' to a greasy looking middle-aged man with long, bushy sideburns.

In the car, Mike asked, "Who's he?"

"Never saw him before in my life," Norma replied. "Considering the way she goes through boyfriends, I'll probably never see him again."

Sophie was already there, talking to Gramps when Mike and Norma arrived. They each had a glass of red wine in front of them.

After introducing Norma to Sophie, Mike said, "Started the party without us, huh?"

"Do you like merlot?" Sophie asked him. "I brought two bottles."

"I wouldn't know merlot from cooking sherry," Mike said, "but I'll try it."

She laughed. "I'll bring cooking sherry next time."

He looked at Norma.

"I like merlot," she said simply as she sat down at the table and looked back and forth between Sophie and Gramps. "Hi, Mr. Harrison."

"Good to see you again, Norma. You can call me Gramps."

In the intervening silence, Mike watched Norma as her gaze alternated between Sophie and the table.

"So...Norma, I hear you're a new student at Central High," Sophie finally said. "How do you like it?"

Norma seemed nervous. "It's okay. Not much different than any other, I guess." She smiled at Mike. "I've met some nice people, though."

"You lived in Portsmouth, before?" Sophie asked.

"Yeah. It is nicer living in the country." She was still looking at Mike. "It's quiet."

"Let's serve dinner, Mikey," Gramps said as he headed for the kitchen.

In the kitchen, he whispered to Mike, *"That girl's got it bad for you."*

"Yeah, I know," Mike whispered back.

Gramps shook his head. *"You know you're going to mess things up with Mary."*

Without replying, Mike took the bowl of spaghetti into the dining room.

Sophie and Gramps finished off the wine. Mike could tell they were both tipsy. He had finished one small glass and cut Norma off after two.

Gramps and Sophie began reminiscing about the war. Gramps, who hadn't seemed to want anything to do with her before, now seemed mesmerized.

After clearing the table, they moved to the living room. Gramps broke out some World War II memorabilia he had saved. He showed Mike and Norma some leftover ration stamps for sugar. "That's when I stopped putting sugar in my coffee," he said.

There were also pictures; of him and Grandma Molly; of Mike as an infant; of Don Harrison in uniform. One picture was of Don on an island in the Pacific, in full combat gear, his M-1 rifle, with a fixed bayonet, in his right hand, his camouflaged helmet, cocked off to one side, seeming too big for his head. He would have been about twenty-two, but looked sixteen.

Mike looked at medals, ribbons and citations his father had earned. "So, what did you and Grandma do during the war, Gramps?"

"Well, I worked at the steel mill twelve hours a day; sometimes more. Your grandmother worked her victory garden; did some charity work. We all gave blood; participated in paper and scrap metal drives; did what we could."

Mike came across a grainy picture of two young couples, all dressed up. He recognized his father, but no one else. "Who are these people?"

Gramps looked at the picture, and then handed it to Sophie.

"That's your parents with Charlie and me," she said. "Dressed up for a wedding, I think."

Mike stared at the picture; his eyes going back and forth between Don Harrison and Charlie Spradlin, concluding that neither really looked like him.

"You didn't recognize your mother?" Norma asked.

"Haven't seen many pictures of her. I remember her, but I don't remember her looking like that." What he remembered was a thin, gray-faced woman, lying very still in a casket, as a room full of adults talked in hushed tones. He also remembered touching her ice-cold face.

"She looks really happy." He looked at Gramps. "Did he really beat her up?"

"I think he hit her a few times," Gramps responded, after a pause. "Not to excuse him, but he was a very frustrated man."

"About what, exactly?"

"Well, we've already talked about the war, and his injury, but there was the other thing."

"You mean Mom and Charlie?"

"Jealousy can be a powerful thing, Mikey. Just the thought that your mother may have...been with someone else..." He shrugged. "He couldn't get that out of his head, even though..." He looked at Sophie. "I talk too much when I'm drinking."

Sophie stood up quickly. "I need to go home, now."

"You're not driving," Mike said, firmly. "Norma can drive you home in your car, and I'll follow and take her home."

"Fine, let's go." She picked up her coat. "Goodnight, Tom. Maybe we can get together again, sometime."

"You bet." Gramps smiled and nodded.

"So, what was that about?" Norma asked as Mike parked in front of her house.

"What was what about?"

"You know. Your mom and this... Charlie person."

"Nothing. Uh...Norma, have you met Sophie before?"

"No, I haven't. Why?"

"No reason."

"Can we, maybe, start studying some together?" she asked as she got out. "My grades are starting to get kind of crappy."

Since Mary had stopped helping him, Mike's own grades were slipping. He'd gotten his first 'D' ever. "Yeah, mine too. We'd have to do it at my house, though, since I don't feel comfortable here."

"Me neither."

Wednesday, February 7

When Mike arrived home from school Gramps handed him a ten thousand dollar check from Nationwide Insurance.

"You should open a savings account and a checking account, Mikey. Spend this wisely and it'll last you several years."

"I need to pay you back. How much do I owe you, anyway?"

"We'll figure that out." Gramps waved at him. "No hurry."

"Did you have lunch?"

"Yep."

"What do you want to do about dinner?"

"I'm having dinner with Sophie. You could join us."

'No, thanks. I'm supposed to pick Norma up later. We're doing homework together."

Gramps frowned. "I thought Mary always helped you with that."

"Let it go, Gramps." Mike flashed a smile. "So...you and Sophie are getting to be real buddies, huh. Or is it more than that."

"Just friends. She's a nice lady."

"Kinda sexy, too."

"Let it go, Mikey."

"Okay."

Wednesday, February 14

It was Mike's eighteenth birthday. Mary came by his desk in homeroom and said, "I'd like to bring you a birthday present tonight after school."

Their recent conversations had been brief and uncomfortable. They had communicated primarily through fleeting glances.

Somewhat confused, he said, "I could give you a ride."

She smiled. "No. I'll walk over later since it's a warm day. Will Gramps be home?"

"I think he'll be at Sophie's house by then."

"He has a girlfriend?"

"I think you could call her that."

"I got you a new set of floor mats for the Chevy for your birthday," Gramps said. "Sorry, there's no cake."

"Thanks, Gramps. Don't need a cake, but I did need new floor mats."

"Sure you don't want to go to Sophie's with me? She could cook us a nice dinner."

"Mary's coming over."

"Well, that's even better." Gramps patted him on the back and mussed his hair.

She knocked on his door shortly after five. It was nearly dark. "Sorry. I had to finish my chores," she said. "Gramps home?" Her face was flushed.

"No, he's with Sophie. Probably won't be home 'til around eight." Their eyes met briefly.

She turned her back to him, took off her coat and tossed it onto the couch. When she turned back toward him, he gasped. She was wearing the same jeans and tee shirt she had worn that day in August.

She came to him, put her hands on the back of his head, and kissed him hard on the mouth. Putting his hands on her forearms, he gently pushed her away.

"Mary..."

She turned away and pulled off the tee shirt, tossed it onto the couch, and turned back to him. "Your birthday present—and valentine. You have a rubber, I presume."

He stared, but then turned away. "Mary, please put that back on. You don't need to do this."

"Don't you like what you see? Don't I look as good as Norma?"

"Better," he croaked. "But would you, please, just put the shirt back on."

She looked down and saw the effect she was having on him. "Nothing to save now, Harrison. That little piece of skin is gone forever; not gonna grow back. And I'm probably going to hell, anyway, for killing my baby."

"Mary, we're divorced, remember?"

"People in my family don't get divorced. It's against our religion." She pressed against him.

"And this isn't?" He didn't wait for a response. "We're not doing it, Mary. And by the way, I don't have a rubber, and haven't had any use for one since October. And...you're not going to hell."

She backed away and folded her arms across her bare chest. "Am I damaged goods? Don't you like me anymore?"

"I love you more than anything, Mary, but we can't do this now. We can talk, eat, watch TV, or just sit and look at each other—with our clothes on, of course—but we're not going to do that."

"Why not?"

"I'm...not good enough for you, Mary. I can't just..."

"Good enough for Norma, though?"

"Mary, have you ever even seen a rubber?"

She sat down on the couch and picked up the tee shirt. "No, but I sure wish my rapist had used one. Of course, I think they're against our religion, too."

He went to the kitchen and poured himself a glass of water. After taking a large gulp, he closed his eyes, but the image just wouldn't go away—two perfect, pear-shaped breasts with very long nipples. His mind flashed back to October, sitting on the log...

When he returned to the living room, she was fully dressed. "I guess I should have just gotten you a card."

He nodded. "Yeah."

"Will you drive me home, now?" she asked. "It's dark."

There was no conversation as he drove her home, listening to the Everly Brothers' 'Crying in the Rain'. In front of her house, she looked his way as she opened the car door. He looked back, expecting her to say something. She didn't. He waited until she was in her house before driving away.

He stepped onto the back porch and looked down at her. She was sitting on the glider reading a book; she didn't look up. He glanced up toward the potato patch and saw his father engulfed in flames, his arms stretched toward Mike. 'Help me, son', he said, calmly. Next, he saw Tony, laughing and pointing. 'See, Harrison, we should have been twins. We're both assholes'.

He turned back toward the glider. Mary was no longer reading, but instead was lying naked on a filthy mattress, her eyes closed, her mouth open, her face contorted in pain, or was it…

He looked for his father, who had disappeared and been replaced by Coach Hauser, standing with his arms folded across his chest, his stomach protruding cartoonishly. 'I knew you'd screw it up', he said.

Mike sat up in bed and looked at the clock. It was four AM. He lay back and closed his eyes, but couldn't get rid of the image of Mary lying naked on a filthy mattress.

He got up and quietly roamed the house until it was time to get ready for school.

Tuesday, May 29, 1962
Ocean Beach

Debbie stopped him. "So…why didn't you just screw her?"

Mike sighed. “I don’t know. I got the impression that she was just testing me, but...”

“What else?”

He fidgeted. “I really didn’t have a rubber.”

“Come on, Mike. You can do better than that.”

He leaned back in his chair, laced his fingers behind his head, and closed his eyes. “It just...seemed too simple. We have sex, everything’s fine, and we live happily ever after.”

“You didn’t like the idea of living happily ever after?”

“That only works in fairy tales.”

“Admit the truth, Mike. You’d have been compelled to dump Norma. And you weren’t ready to do that.”

Mike grunted.

“Same reason you called Norma instead of Mary when your dad died.”

Mike grunted.

Friday, February 16

During homeroom, Principal Thomas announced that Mary had won her scholarship. Mike immediately went to her desk to congratulate her. She said, “Thank you”, but didn’t look at him.

The Principal also announced that John Breech had been awarded a football scholarship to Kent State. Not the Buckeyes, but it was still college football. Mike had learned earlier that both Tim Crabtree and Eve Phillips had earned academic scholarships to Ohio University at Athens. He felt left out. *At least, there’s Norma.*

At lunch, Mike sat alone in the cafeteria, looking across the room at Mary and Eve. Eve was talking rapid fire; Mary was mostly listening. Occasionally she would sneak a peek at him and then look away. Eve caught his eye and smiled, which got Mike to thinking how wrong she'd been about Tony. He'd have raped her, too, if she hadn't put out voluntarily. *But maybe not. Maybe everything would be different…* He shook his head, violently. *Don't look back.*

Saturday, March 24

Over the past five weeks, his conversations with Mary had been rare, clipped, stiff, and formal. 'How are you?' 'I'm fine; the family's fine. How are you?' was a typical conversation, with both avoiding eye contact.

Becky called at ten AM to inform him that Babs had just had a calf—a boy—and to reiterate that Mike should just come over and grab Mary by the face. He declined, but thanked her.

Frenchy called at noon to tell him it was officially determined that the faulty extension cord had caused the fire, and there was no evidence of arson. The insurance company had authorized the cleanup of the site. Mike was still debating whether to look into rebuilding or just selling the lot. He decided he should talk to Ben Abel.

He called Tim and John to see if they wanted to watch the NCAA championship game with him. Both had dates. Gramps was out somewhere with Sophie.

After rejecting the notion of calling Norma, he made himself a huge batch of popcorn and watched the game alone. The Buckeyes blew it again, losing to U.C. 71-59. Though he, obviously, had no control over the outcome of the game, it made him feel even more like a loser.

He looked at his watch. Ten o'clock, and Gramps wasn't home. He called Sophie's house. "He just left, Mike. You shouldn't worry about that old fart; he's just fine."

Monday, March 26

"You don't have to make the decision to rebuild right away," Ben Abel told him. "They'll pay you replacement cost, which, according to the policy is ninety thousand. That's replacing everything with brand new. Of course, the cleanup of the property will cost you a few thousand. You'll have a sizable vacant lot that would have some value if you decide to sell it. Or you can hang onto it and pay the property tax, which would be lower without a building on it. If you invest it right, you can live a long time on that money.

"Given the official report from the fire department, I would expect a check within the next couple of months. I'll do my best to hurry them along."

"That's fine," Mike said. "I appreciate your help."

Ben smiled and shook his hand. “You’ll get my bill when it’s over.”

Andy Mershon lived a few blocks from Sophie on 18th Street. Mike decided to pay him a visit. “You get a job yet?” he asked, as they sat on the couch in Andy’s living room, surrounded by his three small children and his plain, but pleasant looking wife, Alice.

“Naw, still drawin’ unemployment. I’m lookin’, but not much out there.”

“How about City Lanes?”

“Said they didn’t need nobody. Brunswick machines, anyway.”

Mike told him about the Fire Department’s assessment of the cause of the fire.

“That don’t make no sense, Mike. Your dad had me buy that extension cord brand new jist a couple days 'fore Christmas. The fan was no mor’n a few months old. Nuthin’ wrong with them cords.”

“Rats could have chewed them.”

“Never seen a rat in there. You’d think they’d be in the kitchen if we had ‘em.”

“Well, keep this between you and me, Andy. If the insurance company suspects arson, they’ll use it as an excuse to hold up payment of the claim, I’m sure.”

“But...what if that Duvardo kid’s parents somehow...? You know, I heard his daddy had mob connections.”

“Just because he’s Italian?”

“No. I jist heard the Detroit mob... Maybe they think you or your dad killed the kid.”

“I don’t see that; doesn’t make any sense, Andy.” He held up his hands as if to surrender. “I just wanna drop the whole thing—let it go.”

"Okay." Andy's voice brightened. "We still thinkin' about rebuildin'?"

"Still thinking, but don't hold your breath. If you get a job offer, you'd better take it. Have you talked to Penny or Marsha?"

"Penny's tendin' bar at a dive on Second Street. Hates it."

"Oh, the hillbilly place?"

"Yeah. Marsha's like me, still unemployed."

"I should go see both of them."

"They'd appreciate it, Mike."

"How about the part time people—George, Tiny, Karen, Judy...?

"I ain't seen any of 'em. They all had regular jobs, though. Should be okay."

They shook hands. "I'll let you know what's going on, Andy. In the meantime, don't turn down any job offers," Mike reiterated.

Marsha lived alone in a small house on Scioto Trail. After hugs and small talk, she asked the same question Andy did, and he gave her the same answer.

"Are you doing okay," he asked. "Need money?"

"I'll be fine 'til my unemployment runs out. It would be nice to go back to work, though."

"I'll keep you posted," he told her.

Friday, March 30

It was Norma's eighteenth birthday.

"You and your mom celebrating?" Mike asked as they left school.

"She probably doesn't even remember it's my birthday."

In the car, she eyed him, flirtatiously. "I could think of a way to celebrate."

"Not that. But I know a place where we can drink three-two beer and listen to hillbilly music."

"Where?"

"Silver Slipper, on Second Street. We won't see your mom there, will we?"

"I doubt it. She usually goes to a place on Scioto Trail."

"Good. How about I pick you up around seven?"

"Could we go to that place by the river afterward, and act like teenagers on a date? Watch submarine races again?"

"I'd like that, but we're not going there."

She sighed but smiled her enthusiasm. "Okay, I'll be ready at seven."

The Silver Slipper was already busy when they walked in at seven thirty. The jukebox was blaring Leroy Van Dyke's 'Walk on By'.

Penny saw them immediately and rushed around the bar to hug Mike. He introduced her to Norma as they took two empty seats at the end of the bar.

"I have to look at her I.D., Mike. Sorry. I know you were a Valentine baby, but I don't know her," Penny said.

"It's fine, Pen. Just doing your job," Mike replied as Norma produced her drivers' license. "It's her eighteenth birthday."

"Well then, let me buy you a birthday beer. It's three-two, you know."

"Yeah, we know," Norma said.

Penny sat two Hudepohls on the bar. "They're both on me." She studied Norma briefly before heading to the other end of the bar.

"Got any change?" Norma asked Mike. "I wanna play some Patsy Cline."

After taking a sip of beer, he fished around in his pocket and found two quarters. Norma went to the jukebox.

As Norma studied the jukebox, Penny deserted a muscular patron with exceptionally long sideburns, and glided back to Mike. "This your girlfriend?"

"Sort of."

"What about Mary? You two ain't back together, yet?"

"No, we ain't, nosy woman."

"That's too bad." She went to the other end of the bar and served two men in cowboy hats and boots, and then returned quickly to Mike. "Are you re-building the bowling alley, Mike? Please say 'yes'."

"Maybe. It's still up in the air. It would be toward the end of the year, at best, so don't plan your future around it."

"Whatever I'm doing, I'll quit and come to work for you—if you'll have me."

"You'll be the first one I call."

"Promise?"

"Promise."

"Mike, I feel so bad about your dad. He was such a good boss. You know...I saw him Christmas day, just a few hours before he...died. I'd never seen him look so happy. You know what I think? I think he found himself a woman, and..."

"Wait! You saw him?"

"Yeah, I thought about mentioning it at the wake, but there were so many people, I just didn't wanna bother you."

A customer at the other end of the bar waved at her. After serving him a beer, she came back. "I happened to drive by the bowling alley and saw him and Andy in there working. Stopped and paid him the money I owed him."

"What money?"

"I'd borrowed a hundred and twenty dollars from him to buy Christmas presents for the kids. Finally got a child support check from my ex. I had the cash in my purse, so I figured I'd better pay your dad before I wasted it on something else."

"Did you happen to see what he did with the money?"

"Not really. He just took it into the office. Why?"

Mike frowned. "Denominations?"

"Some twenties, some fives, and some ones, I think. Why?"

He shook his head. "Just curious." *Wouldn't have gone back in there for a hundred and twenty dollars.*

Norma had found Patsy Cline. 'Crazy', came blaring out of the jukebox. She grabbed Mike's arm. "Let's dance."

"You know I'm not much of a dancer."

"Please."

They danced—sitting out the ‘shit kickin’ songs—and drank beer for nearly two hours. During the last Patsy Cline song, ‘I Fall to Pieces’, Norma whispered into his ear, “I love you, Mike.”

“Time to take you home.”

“I’m sorry, Mike. I couldn’t help it,” Norma said as he parked the Chevy in front of her house.

“It’s okay, but you remember what we talked about.”

“Yeah, but there’s no law…” She stopped and eyed the pickup truck in the driveway.

“Don’t wanna go in, huh?”

“It’s just… I know that guy. He ogles me all the time. Makes me uncomfortable; makes Mom jealous.”

“Why don’t you just stay at my house? You can sleep in Dad’s room.”

“You serious?”

“Why not?”

“Okay. I should tell Mom I’m going… No, I’ll call her from your house.”

“She had a cake for me,” Norma said when she hung up the phone. “Now I feel bad.”

“You wanna go back?”

“No. I don’t feel that bad.” She laughed.

“Well I don’t have a cake, but I could make us a sandwich. Beer for dinner just wasn’t enough.”

“Okay. Peanut butter and jelly? I’ll make it.”

He eyed her cautiously.

“I know.” Her head bobbed as she emphasized every syllable of each word. “Mix-them-to-geth-er-first-and-cut-the-sand-wich-di-ag-o-nal-ly.”

Mike smiled. *It would simplify things if I just loved her back. Or would it?*

Gramps called at eleven. "I'm staying overnight at Sophie's house, Mikey. Too tired to drive home."

"She's wearing you out, huh,"

Gramps laughed into the phone. "Shut up, Mikey."

Mike hung up. "Gramps isn't coming home, but that doesn't change our sleeping arrangement."

"I know. Maybe one of these days."

"I really don't think so."

"I really don't understand why. I know you're still hung up on Mary, but that horse is already out of the barn."

"Let's watch some TV. And please don't sit so close to me. You know how long it's been."

"Same for me."

"That shouldn't be a problem for you. Half the guys in school..."

"I don't want half the guys in school. You know what I want."

He didn't reply.

She studied him. "I think I'm finally starting to understand what you're trying to do, Mike."

"What am I trying to do?"

"You think that...what we did that Sunday in October..."

"We had sex. We screwed. We..." He stood up and moved to the recliner. "Drop it, Norma."

"No. We should talk..."

"NO! We shouldn't." He got up and headed toward his room. "I'm going to bed. You know where Dad's room is—was. Good night."

She stared at the floor. "Good night, Mike."

He came back, kissed her on the forehead, and said, "Happy birthday."

Saturday, April 7

Mike and Gramps sat eating their PB&J lunch at noon.

"You going to Sophie's, today?" Mike asked.

"Yep."

"Don't feel like you're cheating on Grandma anymore, huh?"

Gramps put his sandwich on his plate and contemplated the ceiling. "Not so much," he said. "You know, when your grandmother and I were married, it was a…well…we were counting on growing old together and taking care of each other. She can't do that for me, now. And now, with your dad gone…" He picked up his sandwich, took a bite, and chewed slowly. "I just don't want to be a burden to you down the road, Mikey. You have way too much to deal with already."

"So…Sophie's just a substitute for Grandma…or Dad…or me?"

"Yeah, but I really like her; I like her a lot."

"Apparently you really 'liked' her last Friday night," Mike smirked.

Gramps's face reddened, but he said nothing.

"I'm really happy for you, Gramps. I was thinking about taking a trip after graduation, now that I know you're in good hands…"

"Where?"

"Out west."

"Seattle?"

"Yeah."

"I figured. Sophie's talking about moving back to Maryland. Says she has friends there."

"Sounds like she's trying to get some sort of a commitment from you."

"Whatever she wants. Of course, I'm too old for her."

"Not if she doesn't think so."

Saturday, April 21

Mike convinced Gramps and Sophie to go to a Reds game with him and Norma. Gramps insisted they leave early and visit Margaret.

The Reds were off to a slow start at 4-6, but the season was young. They were playing a night game against the Giants. The weather was expected to be perfect tonight—clear and in the mid-sixties at game time—after last night's rainout.

Mike and Sophie sat in the living room, waiting for Gramps to get ready. They were to pick up Norma in a half hour.

"Are you making any progress with Mary?" Sophie asked.

"No, not really. We're not even talking." He sighed. "She thinks it's all about sex, like I'm some sort of pervert who can't keep it in my pants. And she thinks I'm doing it with Norma—which I'm not," Mike replied.

"So, why do you keep hanging out with the girl who helped you wreck things with Mary?"

"I don't know, exactly." He shrugged. "I think she needs me. The girl doesn't have an easy life."

"And she loves you, of course."

"I know."

"That feeds your ego, doesn't it?"

"I guess."

"Not still doing it with her, huh?"

"Not since I got caught."

"If you hadn't gotten caught, would you have kept doing her?"

"I don't think so; I hope not."

"It's all about self-control, then."

"I'm working on that. I can't expect Mary to trust me if I can't trust myself."

"Before you get too down on yourself, you need to understand that it's all about sex. Sex is all around. Dogs sniff butts; bulls chase cows. It's how we propagate the species. I read somewhere that the average teenage boy thinks about sex about twenty times a day.

"Sex is used to sell cars, beer, cigarettes... Sex is why men volunteer to go off to war; why they hunt for sport; why guys like you play football."

"How's that?"

"It probably goes back to cavemen. The aggressive guys—the ones who kept the women safe by fighting off neighboring tribes—came back to the cave and got laid a lot. The guys who slew the savage beasts and brought them home for dinner got laid a lot.

"Football players date the cheerleaders...or girls like Norma. Playing football makes you sexy to women. And cheerleaders wear those skimpy outfits as a motivation for the players. That's about sex, even if nobody admits it."

"Never thought about it that way."

"And...of course, having money makes a man sexy, even if he's ugly."

"Did you think your husband—Mr. Reese was sexy?"

"Yes, I did." She laughed. "He was five-eight, weighed two hundred pounds, had a pot belly and a receding hairline, but he was sexy. Obviously, I thought your father was much more so."

Mike watched her eyes as they took on a far away, almost trance-like look. "And Gramps...?"

"Of course." She smiled. "Mike, do you have any idea why women wear red lipstick?"

"No. I've never thought about it."

"Ask someone who does."

"You're not going to tell me?"

"No, I'm not." She laughed and then continued. "People prepare for sex, even when they're not looking for it. Your grandfather, right now, is in the bathroom combing his hair and making himself as attractive as possible. Not necessarily thinking about sex; but it's there, somewhere in his brain. He wants to look good for somebody; me, I hope."

"I'm sure it's you."

"My point is that you're a normal kid who acted like a normal kid. And you've had so much crap thrown at you lately, I'm surprised you're even functioning. I know what you're trying to prove, but if you want Mary back you should probably just ditch Norma, and pick up the phone."

"Like my dad ditched you?"

"Exactly."

"Can't do that, right now. Norma needs me—and I need a friend."

"Mary won't even know you're being faithful to her."

Mike didn't respond immediately. "But I'll know," he finally said. *Then I can look her in the eye.*

Sophie got up from her chair, sat next to him on the couch, and gave him a hug. "You need a mother."

Gramps came out of the bathroom, hair slicked back, closely shaven, smelling like Aqua Velva, and wearing a brand new shirt. Sophie winked at Mike and smiled at Gramps. "You look great, Tom."

Ted McMahon was actually sober when they arrived at his house at one PM. Margaret, looking even heavier, chided Mike and Gramps for not coming around more often. "We're here, now," Gramps grumbled at her. "And 52 goes both directions."

Margaret greeted Sophie warily, and then hugged Mike.

"I think you met Norma at the wake," Mike said.

"Oh yeah. Good to see you again, Norma."

After lunch, Mike, Gramps, and Ted sat on the back porch talking baseball. Surprisingly, Ted was pleasant when sober. It turned out he was a huge Reds fan, quoting statistics and telling stories that even Mike was unaware of. He showed them an autographed picture of Ewell Blackwell, a pitcher, who had been inducted into the Reds Hall of Fame in '60.

"I was at Crosley Field when he pitched that no-hitter," he told them. "Almost pitched another one in his next start; took one into the ninth. Only Johnny Vander Meer has ever had two in a row."

Mike considered inviting him and Margaret to go to the game with them, but decided that Ted would probably be drunk and obnoxious, by game-time. *Am I being judgmental? Add him to the list.*

The Giants won the game 8-6, with Don Larsen, who had pitched a perfect game for the Yankees in the '56 World Series, getting the win in relief.

"I have one hell of a headache," Gramps said as they got into the car. Sophie dug a bottle from her purse, and dumped two aspirin into his hand; he swallowed them without water.

They were on Route 52 and heading home by eleven PM. Mike picked up WLS on the radio. Arthur Alexander's 'You Better Move On' was playing. His thoughts kept drifting back to Mary. *Sophie's probably right. I should ditch Norma.*

Fifteen miles from Portsmouth, Gramps spoke up from the back seat. "Something's wrong," he said.

"What is it?" Sophie asked.

"Left arm's going numb; head's killing..."

Mike pulled off the road and turned on the dome light. Sophie looked at Gramps's face and said, "God, Mike, I think he's having a stroke."

Mike turned and looked. Gramps's face was ashen, and the left corner of his mouth was drooped. "Say something, Gramps," he said.

Gramps mumbled something unintelligible as spittle trickled down from his mouth. Mike immediately hit the dome light and peeled away, burning rubber for fifty feet.

The Chevy wasn't quite as quick as before, but reached a hundred by the time he hit fourth gear.

"Don't kill us, Mike," Norma said through gritted teeth.

"Just close your eyes, Norma." He downshifted on the curves, never touching the brakes until they came to the Second Street Bridge. They were at Mercy Hospital in Portsmouth a few minutes later.

The three of them sat close together in the waiting room, with Norma beginning to doze against Mike's shoulder. He looked at Sophie, who was staring straight ahead, expressionless. *Will she help me with him if he's a cripple?*

As if reading his mind, she said, "We may have to spend a lot of time taking care of him if it's bad."

"You'll help me with him?"

"Of course. You didn't think I'd desert him, did you?"

He took her hand. "Just hoping you wouldn't."

The doctor came in and found Mike. "It looks like a mild stroke—if there is such a thing. It has affected his left side; slurred speech, numbness. We have him on oxygen, but we won't know the extent of the damage for a couple of days." He looked at Sophie. "You are…?"

"Just a friend." She introduced herself.

"Best-case scenario, he'll need a lot of attention for the next few weeks." He looked at Mike. "School?"

"I'll skip school—or drop out if I have to," Mike said.

"You don't need to do that," Sophie interjected. "I'll take care of him if he's allowed to go home."

"Can we see him?" Mike asked.

"Let's wait. Why don't you all go home? It's late and we'll know more tomorrow," the doctor told him.

Sunday, April 22

Mike and Sophie were back at the hospital at eight AM. After learning that Gramps was still asleep, they went for breakfast. She was wearing a matronly looking black dress, no make-up, and her hair in a bun. "You look like a widow dressed for a funeral," he told her.

"Really? I was just going for a more mature look."

"More motherly?" He chuckled.

"Maybe. Maybe I should adopt you since you're an orphan."

"Being eighteen makes me an adult, not an orphan."

"Are you saying you don't need a mother?"

He looked at her but didn't reply.

"You're stuck with me, kid. At least as long as your grandfather is around."

He reached for her hands and she gave them to him.

"Couldn't feed myself, Mikey," Gramps slurred as drool escaped the left corner of his mouth.

"They say you'll be all right, Gramps. It'll just take time."

"I'll feed you 'til you're ready to feed yourself," Sophie said as she dabbed his mouth with a tissue.

"I don't want that." He shooed her away, motioned Mike to come closer, and, struggling to enunciate each word, whispered, *"Remember what we talked about before? Where's my gun?"*

"What gun? Mike whispered back. *"And what did we talk about?"*

"You know."

The doctor came in and looked at the chart. Mike patted Gramps's hand. "We'll talk about it later."

"Things look pretty good," the doctor said. "If we don't have any complications, he can be out of here in a couple of days. We'll get him a wheelchair and line him up with a physical therapist. There's still a lot we don't know about strokes, but there's a fair likelihood that he could have another one. There are pills he needs to take to lessen that likelihood."

Tuesday, April 24

When Mike arrived home from school, the house smelled like a bakery. With Gramps scheduled to come home tomorrow morning, Sophie had moved in, cleaned house, and made herself at home.

She greeted him with a hug and a cookie.

"Hi, Mom," he said. They both laughed.

"You'll tell me if I'm overdoing it, right?"

"You're overdoing it, but I'm not complaining, yet."

"We need to re-arrange the living room."

"What? You just move in and..."

"You don't understand. Your grandfather is going to be in a wheelchair for a while, so we have to open the space up a little bit to give him room to maneuver. We may have to make some changes to the rest of the house, also."

"Oh...sorry." He finished his cookie. "So, why are you doing all this?"

She studied his face for a few moments, and then went to the couch and sat down. "I guess...partly because I've gotten to feel like part of the family. But...I need to make a confession and I hope you don't hate me after I do." She patted the couch cushion beside her; he sat.

"I've been debating about this since I first met you. And…I've finally decided that…you need to know. All this stuff…between your parents. The divorce, the abuse, the fact that your dad questioned whether you were his—it's my fault."

"*Your* fault?"

"Remember our conversation back in December when I mentioned the rumor about your mother and Charlie?"

"Yeah."

"You can smack the crap out of me and throw me out if you want, but I…started the rumor." Her eyes moistened as she looked anxiously at him.

His face hardened. "*You…*started the rumors?"

"It was accidental…sort of. I was at a party. I'd had too much to drink, and Charlie and I weren't seeing each other much. This was just before your father came home from the war. Someone asked me about Charlie, and I said…" She stopped and picked at lint on the couch.

Mike stood up. "You said what?"

"I said…'I'm sure he's with Anna'."

He stood over her; she looked up at him. "Like I said, I'd had too much to drink, and was feeling sorry for myself. But there's no good excuse. There were about twenty people at the party. They all heard it. Even afterward, I could probably have put a stop to the rumors, but I didn't. I could have told your father the truth then, and everything…might have been fine between them. But…I didn't want things to be fine between them." She teared up. "I'm a horrible person."

"What was the truth?"

"The truth was that your mother and Charlie spent some time together, but there was no...evidence it was anything but platonic. Charlie told me there was nothing going on between them. Of course, he'd have said that, either way."

"Dammit, Sophie..."

"Mike, I didn't come back here just to renew my relationship with your father. I came back to...at least try to help repair what I had broken. Your father was miserable; he asked me to come back. I thought..." She looked up at him and blinked away the tears. "Shit, Mike, I'm not sure what I thought."

Mike didn't know whether to give her a sympathetic hug or punch her in the face. Finally, deciding neither was appropriate, he went out the back door, went to the shed, grabbed his bat, and sprinted up the hill, barely making it to the top before collapsing, his quads burning.

He absently batted rocks in the general direction of Mary's house, as he tried to make sense of what he had just heard. *Charlie Spradlin could still be my father.*

Half an hour later, he walked back down the hill and into the house. Sophie was still sitting on the couch dabbing her eyes with a tissue. He sat down and, wordlessly, hugged her. *Judge not.*

Wednesday, April 25

Mike took the day off from school.

Gramps sat in his wheelchair facing the TV. He'd been able to walk with the help of a cane but was still unsteady. His speech was coming back to normal—slow but barely slurred.

"Where's Sophie?" he asked Mike.

"Kitchen."

"Where's my gun?"

"What gun, Gramps?"

"You know what gun. The one you took from the bowling alley safe."

"That was *your* gun? Tell me how it got there."

"I'll tell you the whole story if you get me the gun."

"What would you do with it, Gramps?"

"I'd wheel my sorry ass into the bathroom and blow my brains out."

"Why?"

"Because it'd be easier to clean up the mess there than in the living room."

"That's very considerate of you. Maybe I could just wheel you out to the back yard where we could just hose the mess down."

"Remember back in the fall when I said I wanted you to kill me if I got like this...?"

"You were just talking out of your ass, Gramps. You're going to be fine. A little physical therapy and you'll be as good as new...well as good as you can expect, considering how ancient you are."

"I don't want you to do it, now. Just put the gun someplace where I can get to it."

"You're not serious."

"Deadly."

"Not funny, Gramps."

"Not trying to be. I told you I didn't wanna be shitting my pants and having someone else clean it up."

Sophie walked into the room. "What's up?"

Mike went to his bedroom, retrieved the pistol from his underwear drawer, brought it back, and handed it to her. “It's loaded. He wants to shoot himself.”

Sophie looked shocked, but recovered quickly, popped open the cylinder, emptied it, handed the gun back to Mike, and said, “Hide this thing somewhere.”

Gramps looked up at Mike. “You'll never know how it got into the safe, now.”

“Price I'll have to pay. Gramps, you're gonna be fine, so stop the bullshit, okay?”

Without replying, Gramps turned his attention to the TV game show, *Concentration*.

Friday, April 27

The word was out about the stroke. Mary asked Mike how Gramps was doing and if there was anything she could do. After he thanked her and told her everything was under control, she nodded and turned away, ending the conversation.

He wanted to ‘grab her by the face and fix it’, as Becky had suggested, but realized their relationship had deteriorated beyond that. *May never fix it.*

Sophie was in the kitchen doing dishes when he arrived at home. Gramps was sitting in his wheelchair, dozing.

Sophie dragged Mike into the kitchen. “He's got physical therapy scheduled for Tuesday,” she said. “But I'd like to get him off his ass and get him moving around here. I don't think it's as bad he lets on. He's been going to the bathroom by himself."

Mike hugged her and said, "Thanks."

"I assume you don't hate me for what I did," she said. "I was young, stupid, and in love..."

"I'm in no position to be throwing rocks," he replied.

"You know, I'd love to go back and change things if I could, but I can't. This is the best I can do."

"I'm glad you're here, but you shouldn't feel obligated."

"I want to be here, Mike. What do you want for dinner?"

"Norma and I are going to Patsy's Inn after we finish homework."

She seemed disappointed. "I'll find something to stuff into your grandfather's mouth."

Mike went back into the living room. "Still pissed at me, Gramps?"

Gramps looked up at him, trying not to smile. "You let me down, Mikey. I could be dead by now."

"I hear you went to the bathroom by yourself. Did you shit your pants?"

"Of course not."

"Wipe your own ass?"

"Yeah."

"Well then, it's not time to shoot yourself."

"Fine. Will you get me the gun when it is?"

"Speaking of guns, I heard a joke, today. Wanna hear it?"

Gramps nodded.

"So...this Polack comes home early from work, and finds his wife in bed with another man. He grabs his pistol and puts it to his own temple. The wife starts laughing. He says, 'Laugh all you want, bitch, but you're next.'"

Gramps managed a chuckle, and then wiped the spittle from his chin with his sleeve. "Will you get me the gun...when it's time?"

"If you'll tell me why it was in the safe—before you put the gun to your head."

"When the time comes." Gramps held out his shaky right hand and Mike took it.

"Your house has been on the market for two months now, and you haven't had any offers."

"Overpriced, you think?"

"I'm thinking you and I should go there tomorrow and do a little bit of landscaping—maybe put some flowers in the bed out front. Plant a couple of shrubs. Curb appeal, I think they call it."

"Think it'll help?"

"Can't hurt."

He looked at Norma across the table at Patsy's Inn, noticing how much more conservatively she was dressed—blouse buttoned to the neckline, skirt longer and looser.

Following his gaze, she said, "If you can be like a monk, I can be like a nun."

He laughed. "Sorry. You still don't look like a nun. And you know it's not necessary."

"Sure it is; you're my hero."

"You know, there are days when I'm sorry I'm so hung up on Mary."

"That's every day for me."

"You deserve better."

"Maybe." With her elbows on the table and her fists under her chin, she gazed into his eyes. "I talked to my dad on the phone last night."

"And...?"

"He wants me to come visit this summer. Says I can even stay if I want."

He tried to read her face. *Does she want me to ask her not to go*? "Are you going?"

"Gonna hop a Greyhound as soon as school's out."

After some deliberation, he said, "I could drive you there if you don't mind going by way of Seattle."

Her eyes widened as she continued to stare. "You *serious*?"

"Yep. Blink now, please; you're scaring me."

"What's in Seattle?"

"World's Fair for one thing."

"What else?"

"Charlie Spradlin." He summarized the story.

"So...that's what that was about. You really think he's your father?"

"I don't know. I just want to look at him...and ask him."

"If he wanted anything to do with you, wouldn't he have contacted you before now?"

He shrugged. "I don't necessarily want anything to do with him. I'd just like to know."

"So...I guess I won't need a prom dress, huh?"

"Has anyone asked you to the prom?"

She laughed. "No. I think I'm getting into the same category as Mary with that."

"How's that?"

"They all think of me as your property."

"Sorry."

"No, no, no. It's not your doing; it's mine."

When he parked in front of her house, Norma asked, "Are you serious about Seattle?"

"Uh-huh. But it depends on how Gramps is doing. He seems okay right now, but you never know."

"Fine. I'm going to plan on it, so please don't change your mind."

Back home, as he opened the front door, he heard the radio playing Glenn Miller's 'In the Mood'. Gramps was sitting in his wheelchair facing the couch. Sophie was sitting on the couch with her bare right foot in his lap, bobbing her head to the music, while Gramps clumsily massaged away.

"It's a good physical therapy for your grandfather's hands," Sophie explained.

"Shut up, Mikey," Gramps said. "The music beats the hell out of that rock 'n' roll crap you listen to."

Mike held up both hands. "As long as that's all you two do in the living room, it's okay."

Sophie changed feet. "There's cookies. Home-made chocolate chip."

Saturday, April 28

Mike awoke at eight AM to the sound of Gramps thumping the floor with his cane. "Mikey, wake up! She's gone!"

"What...?" He sat up and rubbed his eyes.

"I heard her start my car and drive away. My wallet's gone."

"How much was in it?"

"About seven hundred."

"Why so much, Gramps?"

"You just never know when you need it; but that's not important, now. I just know she's gone, and so's my Buick."

Mike slid out of bed and got dressed. "I'm sure there's an explanation. Doesn't make sense. Seven hundred dollars and a '61 Buick LeSabre? How far could she get?"

Gramps shrugged. "Car's worth at least a couple thousand. And…I can't find my checkbook, either."

"She could write checks out of it?"

"Probably forge my signature."

"You want me to call the cops?"

"I don't know. Let's see if anything else is missing."

After searching the house, they determined that nothing else was missing. "She didn't take her clothes," Mike said.

Gramps snorted. "Probably in Cincinnati—or somewhere—buying new ones, with my money."

"You want me to call the cops?" Mike repeated.

"I don't know." Gramps was back in his wheelchair.

"The longer we wait, the farther she'll get."

"Make us breakfast and we'll think about it."

As they were finishing breakfast, Mike said, "You don't wanna catch her, do you?"

Gramps sighed. "I should have known she was too good to be true."

"Geez…Gramps. She was married to a doctor. You'd think she'd have money of her own."

"That what she told you?"

"Uh…yeah."

"Same story she told me. I don't know that it's true."

"You didn't know her husband?"

"No. She just disappeared right after the war." He limped into the bathroom. Mike decided to clean up the kitchen.

With the water running in the sink, he didn't hear the car, but looked up to see Sophie pass by the kitchen window, looking exceptionally beautiful, holding two bags of groceries.

When he opened the door, she asked, "You gonna stand there and gawk, or help me with these bags? They're heavy."

"Hey, Gramps!" Mike yelled as he took the bags, "Sophie's home!"

"Where is he?" she asked.

"Bathroom."

"There's more in the car. There was practically nothing left to eat here." She threw Gramps's wallet on the table. "Sorry I snuck out, but I didn't want to wake you guys. Took the Buick because my car's almost out of gas."

Gramps emerged from the bathroom and casually asked, "Sophie, have you seen my checkbook?"

"Very back of your sock drawer, left corner. Why? Do you need it?"

He shook his head and grinned at her.

"And why in the world do you carry so much cash in your wallet?" she asked.

With a sigh of relief, Mike went out the back door.

Sunday, April 29

"I found Charlie Spradlin's phone number, if you still want it," Sophie told Mike as they cleared the breakfast table.

"Great," Mike said. "Will you call him and tell him I'm coming; somewhere around the third week of May?"

"Sure."

Gramps spoke up. "What, exactly, do you expect to accomplish, Mikey?" The wheelchair now sat back in the corner, rarely used. Gramps sat in the easy chair with his cane as his constant companion.

"Just have to satisfy my curiosity. If you're really my grandfather, I'll have to resign myself to looking ugly and decrepit like you in about fifty years."

"You'd be lucky to look this good, you little shit."

"I'd be lucky to have a hot babe like Sophie looking after me."

Sophie smiled her thanks at him as she dialed the phone. Gramps looked warily at her.

"C'mon, Gramps," Mike said. "Let's go out back and let her catch up on things with her *ex*-boyfriend."

Fifteen minutes later when Sophie came out the back door, Gramps was pretending to read the paper, and Mike was engrossed in the sports section, catching up on the pennant races.

"He'll be expecting you," she said to Mike.

"Does he know why I'm coming?"

"Yes. I had to tell him."

"What'd he say?"

"He said he was looking forward to meeting you."

"That's it?"

"That's it. Here's the phone number. Don't lose it."

"How is old Charlie?" Gramps asked as he looked up at her.

She bent down and kissed him on the forehead without replying.

Tuesday, May 1

When Mike arrived home from school to an empty house, there was a note from Sophie. "Took your grandfather to physical therapy. Call Ben Abel."

"Good news, Mike," Ben told him. "We've got everything. I just need you to come in and sign some paperwork. Then you need to get together with Jerry and figure out where to put the money."

"How about I come in now?"

"Come on in; it won't take long."

After meeting with Ben Abel, Mike went to see Jerry Hutchinson, who punched numbers into his adding machine and said, "You have a hundred thousand and some change, plus whatever you have left from your dad's life insurance. After you clear up some bills, you'll still have over ninety. You have some options as to where to put it. You could invest it and..."

"I'll just stick it in a savings account 'til I figure out what to do," Mike told him. "I'm leaning toward re-building the bowling alley—if I can count on a lot of help from you, Mr.

Abel, and my grandfather. I feel like I owe it to the employees and the bowlers."

Jerry's eyes registered his enthusiasm. "That's great, Mike. I'll start looking into it, right away. I have several building contractors as clients. Uh...Brunswick or AMF?"

"AMF is all I know—and all the employees know."

"We can play them off against each other, maybe get a better deal."

Mike shrugged. "Fine, as long as we end up with AMF."

"Okay."

Mike told him about his plan to drive to the West Coast.

"How long are you going to be gone?"

"Don't know, but I'll keep you posted."

Saturday, May 5

At ten AM, the phone rang. Sophie answered, and handed the phone to Mike. It was Joe Bryant.

"Mike, we need to talk." It didn't sound like a request.

"About what, sir?"

"Why don't I pick you up, if you're not busy? Maybe take a ride."

"You gonna shoot me?"

Joe laughed. "Probably not. There some reason I should?"

"Matter of opinion, sir. You coming right away?"

"If it's okay."

"I'll be ready."

In the station wagon, they headed back up Hope Run toward Bryant Holler. Joe sighed deeply and then began. “My daughter's hidin’ somethin’ from me. And Rose knows somethin', but won’t tell me. Got any ideas?”

“Uh…no, sir.”

Mike expected him to turn onto Bryant Holler, but he drove on past. Mike didn’t know whether to be concerned or relieved.

In an even voice, Joe asked, “You get her in trouble, Mike?”

“You mean pregnant? No, sir.”

“Look, I know what happened with the other girl.”

“That was…wrong and stupid, what I did.”

“Happens. But there’s more goin’ on than that.”

Mike shook his head. “I don’t know, sir.”

“I don’t expect an honest answer, but have you and Mary…” He hesitated.

“Have we what, sir?”

Silence.

Feeling braver now, Mike said, “You want to know if Mary and I have…had…sex, right? No, we haven’t; that’s the honest truth.”

Joe concentrated on the road as a car passed. “You love my daughter?”

“More than anything, sir.”

“Mary says you sound like Eddie Haskell on *Leave it to Beaver* when you do that.”

“Do what, sir.”

“That. Call me ‘sir’ all the time.”

They both laughed, and then went silent.

Joe spoke again. “I thought I had it all figgered out, Mike. Mary was gonna be in good hands in Columbus.”

"I know. I messed that up, but Mary can take care of herself."

"I don't know 'bout that. The girl's never even been to a big city, let alone on her own. I'd jist feel a whole lot better if you was there with her. And I know she still wants you there."

He turned left into the Neumanns' driveway. Mike looked at him apprehensively. He looked back with no discernable expression. "Jist turnin' around," he said. "I hear there's a family movin' in here in a couple of weeks. Good thing. I hate to see vacant property; it invites all kindsa mischief."

As they sat in Mike's driveway, Joe said, "I hear you're goin' out west when school's out."

"Yes, sir."

"And takin' this...Norma with you?"

"Taking her to her father. Mary doesn't understand, but it's...it's an obligation."

"I don't understand either, son, but I know about obligations. Gonna be gone long?

"Not sure. I just have some things to work out."

Joe re-positioned his John Deere cap, displaying more gray hair than Mike remembered. "This game you and Mary are playin'...you play it too long it'll come back and bite you both in the rear ends."

It already has. "What game?"

"I think you know. Your car in decent shape?"

"It will be. New tires, new battery. Elbert's gonna check belts and hoses."

"Well, good luck. You're always in our prayers."

They shook hands.

Friday, May 11

Last day of final exams.

Mike and Mary played glance tag all day long, but neither made the effort to strike up a conversation.

"We're leaving Tuesday morning," he told Norma.

"We're not staying for commencement?" she asked.

"Nope. Got some things I need to clear up. Gotta get the Chevy worked on, Monday. They can mail our diplomas. Have you talked to your dad?"

"Yes. I told him we'd be there before the end of the month. Have you talked to Mary?"

"Mary isn't talking to me."

"Gramps going to be okay?"

"I think so. Between Sophie and his physical therapist, it's under control; they don't need me. I told them to call Joe Bryant if there's a problem they can't handle. What about your mom?"

"I think she's feeling guilty about being such a crappy mother, but she'll be fine."

"You think?"

"Yeah. She can always console herself with a couple of beers and a greaser with a pick-up truck."

Tuesday, May 15

With five hundred dollars in his wallet, another thousand in a plastic bag taped under the front seat, and his checkbook in his suitcase, Mike left at eleven AM promising to call every chance he got. Gramps was getting around without his cane, a slight shuffle in his gait and an almost imperceptible sag in the left corner of his mouth the only noticeable evidence that he'd ever had a stroke. He and Sophie stood on the front porch, holding hands as they waved goodbye.

Jean West, who had taken the day off work to see Norma off, was crying. *Crocodile tears? Maybe just feeling guilty.*

Mike loaded Norma's two large, heavy, suitcases into the trunk. "What the hell have you got in there?"

She looked back at her mother, who was standing on the front stoop. "Every stitch of clothes, and everything else I have of any value. I'm not coming back."

They headed west on US 52 toward Cincinnati.

"I would like to make it to Chicago, today," Mike told her. "There's a road atlas in the back seat. You can navigate."

"I don't know how to read a map," she said as she reached for the atlas.

"Not a big deal yet, since we'll be on this all the way to Indianapolis. Once we get there, it'll be uncharted territory for me. I've never driven farther than that, so we'll have to map out a route from there."

"I would help with the driving, but I can't drive a stick."

"That's okay. I wouldn't be a very good passenger, anyway."

"We gonna just get one motel room?"

"One room—probably one bed—just for sleeping."

"I know. I'm a nun. Ain't had *nun*, and ain't getting' *nun*.

"Don't blame me for that."

"I'm not blaming... I'll be good, I promise. But what if they wonder what two teenagers are doing renting one room? What if they think we're just going to get a room and... screw?"

"I'm sure someone will take our money. Don't tempt me by snuggling, by the way."

"What if I get cold?"

'Don't."

Along the way, Mike caught up with the hits. "You can be the 'radio girl', he told Norma. "When one station fades, find me another. If you can't find anything, you have to sing to me."

"Okay, I will." She smiled her enthusiasm.

And she did. In dead spots between Portsmouth and Cincinnati, she sang Patsy Cline tunes. To Mike's surprise, her voice was pleasant and soothing. When she started on Elvis' 'Can't Help Falling in Love', he told her to shut up. She changed to 'Good Luck Charm'; he didn't protest.

They listened to Mary Wells' 'The One Who Really Loves You'. It was the first time he had heard it. Norma sang along without taking her eyes off him.

After catching the partially completed Interstate 74 to Indianapolis, they took 421 to 30 to Interstate 80 in northwest Indiana and headed west into Illinois. Finding a reasonably clean looking motel near Moline, they stopped for the night at ten PM.

The room was small, but clean, with one double bed. Norma came out of the bathroom with long flannel pajamas, buttoned all the way to the top. Putting the spare pillow in the middle of the bed, she said, "There. You can't blame me if something happens."

"Nothing will happen," he replied.

Wednesday, May 16

Mike awoke at six AM to find the pillow gone, and Norma snuggled against him with her arm across his chest. With a severe case of *morning wood*, he eased himself out of bed and went to the bathroom. When he returned she was sitting on the edge of the bed.

"Who moved the pillow?" she asked, innocently.

He shook his head, but couldn't keep from smiling. "You need to stay on your side."

"I'll try."

"We should get ready to go. We're burnin' daylight."

"We're what?"

"Never mind. Just shower up and let's get on the road. We'll find breakfast somewhere along the way."

After exhausting her repertoire of rock 'n' roll and country songs—and making up a few bawdy ones of her own—Norma said, "We need a camera."

He found a drugstore near Omaha, and bought her a Polaroid.

"Film's really expensive," she said.

"I can afford it," he replied. "Grab as many packs as you want."

She bought all the Polaroid film in the store. The bill was over a hundred dollars.

Exhausted from maneuvering through road construction on Interstate 80, and barely able to keep his eyes open, Mike stopped in Rapid City, South Dakota at one AM. They went to bed immediately.

Norma put the pillow between them and situated herself on the extreme edge of the bed, facing away from him, her knees hanging off.

"What are you doing?" he asked.

"Staying on my side," she said, with just a hint of a pout.

"You really think you can sleep like that?"

"Probably not."

With an exaggerated sigh, he tossed the pillow onto the floor. "Sleep however you want."

She quickly snuggled up to him and was asleep in minutes. He watched her face for several minutes before turning out the light. *So innocent looking; so trusting.*

Thursday, May 17

They slept in until nine AM.

"We need to slow down and be tourists for a couple of days," Mike said, as they were finishing breakfast. "Mount Rushmore is right here, Yellowstone is kind of on the way, and you have all that film to use up. I drove almost nine hundred miles yesterday, and I'm not doing that again. So...let's plan on being in Seattle...say...on the 20th."

She reached across the table and grabbed his hands. "I love you, Mike, and don't you dare bitch about it."

He gently pulled his hands free and picked up the road atlas. "You're going to have to learn to read this thing."

"I can figure it out as long as I turn the map in the direction we're going. We're going west, right?"

"What you just said makes no sense at all. But yes, we'll be going mostly west."

"Makes sense to me," she pouted.

Tuesday, May 29
Ocean Beach

He drained his beer and gave Debbie the safe sign. "No more of that. Don't want to get plastered again."

She smiled at him. "You were having the time of your life with Norma, weren't you?"

He nodded. "I was having fun. Feeling guilty at the same time."

"Weren't tempted?"

He scoffed. "Constantly."

"Being hard on yourself?" She giggled.

He laughed. "Not constantly, but..."

"I get the picture."

Sunday, May 20
Seattle

After spending three days stopping and taking pictures of everything touristy along the way, they arrived in Seattle at four PM and spent the next two hours looking for a place to stay, finally ending up in Bremerton, across Puget Sound, an hour ferry ride and a short shuttle bus ride to the Fair.

The motel room was nice but pricey. Norma couldn't hide her disappointment when she saw the two double beds.

"Which bed do you want?" Mike asked her.

She shrugged. "Doesn't matter, does it?"

He called Charlie Spradlin, and they agreed to meet for lunch on Tuesday. That gave them the whole day Monday to do the Fair.

"So…after you talk to this guy, what happens?" she asked.

"I take you to your dad."

After dinner and some TV, they went to their separate beds at ten PM.

Monday, May 21

Awakening at seven AM, Mike was neither surprised nor disappointed to find her bed empty and her warm body spooning his.

She awoke and looked over at her bed as if it had somehow betrayed her. "I got cold," she said.

He slapped her gently on the rear end. "Supposed to be a warm and sunny day—unusual for Seattle, I hear. Let's go fight the crowds."

The closest he came to giving in to temptation was when she emerged from the bathroom in a tight pair of white short shorts and a red halter top that exposed her belly button and lots of cleavage.

But, somehow, Mary would know. "You gonna wear that?" he croaked.

She looked at his face and then allowed her eyes to travel downward. Putting her hands to her face, she said, "Okay, I'll change." Grabbing clothes from her suitcase, she went back into the bathroom. Two minutes later, she came out in a tight pair of jeans and a top that covered marginally more cleavage.

"Better?" she asked.

"Some," he replied, shaking his head. "What happened to the *nun* look?"

She simply giggled.

Three hours later, they were riding the monorail. "We're not gonna see everything in one day," he said. "I want to see the futuristic cars at the GM exhibit, and then we can do whatever you wanna do."

"I wanna do whatever you wanna do," she replied, hugging his arm.

He glanced at her cleavage. "We're not gonna do what I wanna do."

"I know."

They took a simulated trip on the 'Spacearium', ate, stood in line for two hours to go up the Space Needle, ate some more, went to the GM exhibit, bought postcards, took pictures, and browsed some foreign exhibits.

Looking at a map, Norma said, "Let's go to the 'Gayway'."

"You mean like, 'Don we now our gay apparel'? Or do you mean *gay* way?"

She backhanded him in the stomach. "It's where the rides are, silly. We can just act like teenagers for a change." She gave him a wistful look. "You can kiss me at the top of the Ferris wheel…or not."

Exhausted, they caught the nine PM ferry back to Bremerton and were in their room by 10:30. Norma immediately fell asleep on her bed, fully clothed.

Tuesday, May 22

He was awakened at eight AM by her snoring into her pillow. Smiling at his disappointment that she hadn't crawled into his bed, he went out for coffee and a newspaper.

When he returned she was sitting groggily on the bed.

"I thought you'd left me," she told him, as he handed her coffee in a Styrofoam cup.

"You know better than that."

She got up, headed for the bathroom, and then turned around. "You *will* leave me, Mike. We both know that."

He sipped his coffee without replying.

They took the ten AM ferry across the Sound and headed north toward the Boeing plant, planning to meet Charlie Spradlin at a diner two blocks from the main gate. With Norma reading the scribbled directions, they got lost twice before finally finding it at 12:30 PM.

Looking around the diner, they spotted a middle-aged man who raised his hand with his forefinger pointing in their direction. He stood and greeted them. “Charlie Spradlin,” he said, with a firm handshake. “I assume you’re Mike.” After introducing Norma, Mike checked him out. He was tall—about Mike’s height—and slightly overweight with a healthy head of light brown hair. His complexion was medium, as was Mike’s—and Don’s. *Doesn’t look like me, though. Thinner lips, longer nose, higher forehead.*

The waitress came by; they quickly ordered.

After a few minutes of small talk, Charlie looked at his watch. “I only have twenty minutes left,” he said, looking back and forth at the two of them, and then concentrating on Mike. “I could have answered your question over the phone, but I wanted to meet you—and offer my condolence for your father.”

“Thank you.”

“You look a lot like your mother, Mike.”

Mike filled Charlie in on what was going on *back home.* Their food arrived; they ate silently.

Charlie spoke first. “Getting to the point, Mike, I couldn’t possibly be your father,”

“Because…?”

“Well… you know how that works. A man and a woman get together and… Your mother and I didn’t. So you see it’s not biologically possible.”

“You didn’t?”

"To be honest with you, it wasn't for a lack of trying on my part. But your mother wouldn't have it. If Don Harrison isn't...wasn't your father, it's someone I don't know. Definitely not me."

"But the two of you hung out together—you and Mom?"

"Some, while your dad was overseas, yeah. She was very lonely and I was in love. But nothing happened."

"And Sophie...?"

"Pined away for your father. Under different circumstances, your mother and Sophie could have been best friends. But given the fact that they were in love with the same man, they weren't comfortable around each other." He smiled ruefully and shook his head. "We were a screwed up bunch."

"I heard you took part in the D-Day invasion."

"Yeah. First Infantry Division—the 'Big Red One'."

"And the Battle of the Bulge?"

"Froze my ass off."

"I guess Dad came back from the war a lot different than he was before."

"We all did, Mike. You can't experience all that and not be changed in some way. Some just handle it better than others."

"You handled it better than Dad?"

"Apparently." He looked at his watch and stood up. "It was nice to meet you both." He looked at Norma, and then at Mike. "I hope you both find whatever it is you're looking for." He picked up the check. "I got this."

In the parking lot, he said, "You know...I cried when I heard about your mother's passing. She was a wonderful person, and I loved her very much. And, if I *were* your father, Mike, I'd be proud to acknowledge it."

"That guy's not your father," Norma told him as they drove away.

"I suppose he could be lying, but I don't think so. I'm gonna assume he isn't, and let it go." He hit second gear and peeled rubber. "That means I have no parents."

"But you have Gramps and Sophie."

"That reminds me, I have to call them."

He found a pay phone and called collect.

"About time," Gramps scolded. "You've been gone a week and you're just getting around to calling. For all I knew, you could be dead, or lying in a hospital—or a ditch."

"Sorry, Gramps. How are you?"

"Fine. How's Norma."

"Fine."

"Still platonic?"

"Yes. How's Sophie? Don't say that's platonic."

Gramps chuckled. "She's fine."

"If everybody's fine, why are you pissed at me for not calling?"

"For one thing, Jerry Hutchinson called, and said he had a couple of building contractors chomping at the bit. Says they can get a building up in three months, and have us up and running within six weeks after that. He even has an architect lined up."

"You and Sophie can get the ball rolling on that. I should be home in a couple of weeks. Hey, Gramps…I need to ask you something. Did Dad tell you what happened to Mary last fall?"

Silence. Mike waited.

"Yes he did," Gramps finally muttered.

"When?"

"Couple of days after it happened. Terrible thing. I don't suppose you've called her?"

"Mary isn't talking to me. Is Sophie available?"

"Of course."

After exchanging small talk with her, he asked, "Did you tell Dad you started the rumor about Mom and Charlie?"

"Yes, I did."

"When?"

"The Saturday before he...the Saturday before Christmas."

"He get pissed?"

"No. He seemed...almost...relieved."

Heading south, they reached Portland, Oregon during rush hour. Amid stop-and-go traffic, Mike squirmed in his seat.

"My back itches. We should have an arm back there to scratch with."

She reached underneath his shirt and found the spot. "Maybe that's what other people are for."

"Maybe in the shower, too?"

She giggled. "Yep. Back *and* front."

He tried not to laugh. "Quit that."

She giggled some more. "You started it."

At length, he asked, "You ever been in love?"

"Stupid question, Mike."

"No. I mean before..."

"Yeah, let's see...there was Elvis, and then Ricky Nelson, and I'm kind of in love with David Janssen, right now..."

"No. I mean for real."

She sighed. “Only went back for seconds once. That answer your question?”

He nodded but said nothing.

They turned southwest and caught the Pacific Coast Highway near Lincoln City, where they stopped for the night.

“Ever swum in the ocean?” she asked him as they settled in for the night.

“Nope.”

“We should find a beach tomorrow.”

“Let me guess. You have a skimpy bikini you just can’t wait to wear.”

“Of course.”

“You can be very cruel, Norma.”

She giggled. “Maybe you should just wear really baggy trunks. Or tape it to your belly.”

Wednesday, May 23

They found a nice beach just south of Lincoln City. Norma’s bright yellow bikini was even skimpier than he had imagined. The water was much colder than they had anticipated. After splashing around a while and using up most of the Polaroid film, they headed south, planning to make Eureka, California Thursday, and San Francisco by Friday.

Looking across the bench seat at Norma, Mike couldn’t stifle a laugh. She was studying the atlas, which she had turned backward in her lap.

She looked up at him and frowned. "What? We're going south, right?"

"Yes, we are." He grinned. "Why don't you take some pictures? I'd never seen the ocean before this trip—or a palm tree."

"Me neither," she said as she grabbed the Polaroid from the back seat. "We're about out of film, though."

Friday, May 25
San Francisco

They crossed the Golden Gate Bridge at eleven AM, and by noon were at Fisherman's Wharf having lunch.

"Wanna just stay here overnight or keep going?" Mike asked her as they sat eating, freezing, and watching the boats.

"Lot to see here," she replied, looking at a brochure.

"Giants are playing at Candlestick this afternoon. Wanna go?"

"Sure. I'm not much of a baseball fan, but I can eat hotdogs—and take pictures if you buy more film."

When the waiter brought the check, Mike asked him for directions to Candlestick Park. The waiter, who couldn't seem to keep his eyes off Norma's cleavage, drew him a map on a paper napkin and said, "Better take a jacket or you'll freeze."

"I've heard stories," Mike said.

"All true, I assure you." He took one last glance at Norma's chest before going away.

It was—as the waiter had told them—cold and windy at the game. They arrived in the third inning, just in time to see Willie Mays hit a home run. The Giants beat the Phillies 10-7.

Still cold, Norma snuggled up to him in the car on the way back, making it difficult to shift gears. He didn't mind.

Saturday, May 26

Remembering that Gramps had had a doctor's appointment Friday, Mike called him at eight-thirty AM.

"When are you coming home, Mikey?"

"Don't know, Gramps. What'd the doctor have to say?

"Could have another stroke—maybe the big one—tomorrow, or I could be around another twenty years. I could also get hit by a bus. How's Norma?"

"Fine. I'm dropping her off in a couple of days."

"We're ready to start on the bowling alley as soon as you give the okay."

"Shouldn't be more than a couple of weeks. Say 'hi' to Sophie for me."

They had done some sightseeing Friday night. This morning, they took a trip back over the bridge to Sausalito where Norma bought souvenirs and more postcards.

"Who're you gonna send all those postcards to?" he asked.

She smiled up at him. "No one."

"We could make L.A. by tonight. It's only about four hundred miles."

She picked up the road atlas. "Or…we could take our time, and get to my dad's house sometime tomorrow afternoon. Besides, we need to find a laundromat. How about Santa Barbara?"

"Not anxious to see your dad?"

"Not anxious to be dumped off by you." She continued staring at the backward road atlas. "And not anxious to wear dirty underwear."

"You know you don't have to stay."

"As much as I'd like to continue our road trip, and snuggle up to your warm ass in a hotel room every night, I see staying with Dad as my best option. I don't want to go back to her if I don't have to."

"You're eighteen. Get a job and an apartment."

"May do that if things don't work out with Dad. I really am looking forward to seeing him; just not tonight."

"Santa Barbara tonight, then." He glanced at her.

She looked up from the map and said, "Don't worry, Mike. Nothing's gonna happen tonight, even if you want it to."

He glanced her way, again, but said nothing.

Sunday, May 27
Los Angeles

As Mike maneuvered through light traffic on the freeway near downtown L.A. looking for the Whittier exit,

Norma spoke. "I heard a joke about this. You wanna hear it?"

"Sure."

"Okay. Do you know why traffic in L.A. is so light on Sunday morning?"

"Why?"

"Because...the whites are in church, the blacks are in jail, and the Mexicans can't get their cars started." She cocked an eyebrow. "Kinda racist, huh?"

He chuckled. "Yeah, but kinda funny, too."

"What's your dad's name?" Mike asked as they headed southeast on Whittier Boulevard, looking for Penn Street.

"Leonard. They call him Lenny." She consulted the paper in her hand. "Turn right on Penn Street and right again on Comstock Avenue."

Lenny West was a handsome, but somewhat greasy-looking man, about forty, wearing a faded Hawaiian shirt, blue jeans, and deck shoes. A couple of inches shorter than Mike, but stockier, he had thick, dark hair combed back in a D.A., and long sideburns. His girlfriend, who introduced herself as Diane Hunter, was tall, blonde, and attractive, looking to be in her mid-thirties. They both greeted Norma with an enthusiasm that seemed to be somewhat forced—insincere. *Maybe not. Maybe that's just how California people are. Maybe I'm paranoid.*

Norma seemed to have no doubts about her father, as she continually hugged him and chatted away at him.

"We have your room all ready," Diane said.

After Mike and Lenny lugged Norma's suitcases into a small bedroom, Diane began making sandwiches for lunch. Mike asked for peanut butter and jelly instead of the ham and cheese the others were having. Norma giggled at him and said, "I'll make it."

When she returned with his perfectly made sandwich, she giggled some more. He faked a slap to the back of her head. She cringed and ducked, but giggled again. Lenny and Diane looked puzzled. "Don't ask," she said.

"Thanks for bringing my daughter to me, Mike," Lenny said. "I've really missed her." He smiled at Norma.

"You're welcome," Mike replied, still not sure about the man. To Norma, he asked, "You staying?"

Norma looked at her father. "Am I staying, Dad?"

"Of course you are. I'd like to get you enrolled in college for the fall session if you want. Rio Hondo is a junior college right here in Whittier. It shouldn't be any problem getting you in. Or you can just hang out all summer—maybe bum around at the beach—while you're figuring out what you wanna do."

Norma smiled quickly at Mike. "Looks like I'm staying." The smile faded just as quickly.

Trying not to show any emotion, Mike finished his sandwich and stood up. "Nice meeting you folks. I'm gonna head south. I'd like your phone number so I can touch base with her before I start back to Ohio."

Lenny scribbled down the number and, apparently sensing Mike's concern, said, "Thanks again, and don't worry about Norma. I made a mistake not bringing her with me when I left Portsmouth. I'll take care of her, I promise."

Norma walked Mike to the Chevy. "It'd be easy for you to talk me out of this," she said, looking glumly at him.

"How?"

"You know; me, not Mary." She shrugged. "Of course, we both know that's not gonna happen."

He shook his head. "You don't have to stay here, you know. You can just keep going with me for a while."

"Then what?"

"Eventually, we'll end up back in Scioto County. Don't know when."

She shook her head. "I'm staying."

He watched her eyes as they began to tear up. "Norma, will you do me a favor?"

"Anything."

"Don't… I don't know how to say this. Promise me you won't end up…"

"Like my mother?" she finished. "I promise. I'll just stay horny 'til the right one comes along. And I won't date anyone who drives a pick-up."

He managed a smile. "It's not the vehicle. I'm sure there are lots of nice guys who drive pick-ups."

"I guess."

"I just worry, Norma. I remember when you came to the house…"

"The day I ruined your life. I remember it, too."

He hugged her. "I'm not proud of what we did that day, but—looking back—I'm glad you came to my house. And...hey, there's got to be more to life than football."

She squeezed his hand with both of hers. "Listen, Mike…I'm not your responsibility. I can take care of myself."

He took the camera from the back seat and handed it to her. "This is yours," he said.

"Wait a minute," she said. She went into the house and returned several minutes later with a handful of Polaroid shots. "These are for you. Sorry. That's all you get."

He shuffled through six pictures, one of the mountains, one of a palm tree, and four of her on the beach, frolicking in her bikini.

"To remind you of what you're missing out on, asshole." She put her head to his chest. "Funnest twelve days of my life."

"That's not a word, but I had fun too. I'll call you when I get somewhere."

They hugged.

In the car, Mike revved the engine twice, mustered a weak smile at her, and drove away.

Heading south toward San Diego, he found a 'Top Forties' station and heard the Beach Boys for the first time, doing 'Surfin' Safari'. *Maybe I'll take up surfing.*

Not sure where he wanted to go, he stopped in Oceanside and registered at a beach hotel. After spending two hours walking on the beach, he went to bed alone for the first time since the trip started.

Tuesday, May 29
Ocean Beach

"Yesterday, I drove here. The end," he said.

"Have you called Norma?"

"No."

"You should."

"Yeah. You're right."

"So, let me see if I have this straight. You cheated on Mary with Norma, setting off a disastrous sequence of events, and that makes everything your fault, right?"

"If I hadn't done it ..."

"Stop! Let me think of a comparison..." She looked out at the ocean, and then back at him. "Okay, let's say you're in your car and, because you're in a hurry, you pull out in front of another car, causing the driver to slow down. Now...you make it through the next traffic light but he doesn't. Two blocks later he runs over a pedestrian. Is that your fault or his?"

"Depends. Is he still pissed off because I pulled out in front of him?"

She shook her head. "You're such an idiot. What if Mary hadn't reacted the way she did? What if she'd just fumed for a while, made you feel like shit for a couple of weeks? Not asked for a *divorce?* The chain of events would have been broken right there. So it's all her fault."

"It's not Mary's fault."

"Okay, let's go the other way. It's Norma's fault for coming to your house and seducing you. It's her mother's boyfriend's fault for hitting her. It's her mother's fault for being a slut. It's her father's fault for not bringing her to California with him. How far back do you want to go, Mike? How about we go back to Adam and Eve, and the forbidden fruit. Was it her fault for tempting him, or his fault for not being disciplined enough to keep his peter behind his fig leaf?"

"It's my fault for not trying to...establish a relationship with Tony. For being an asshole to him."

With a sigh of exasperation, she said. "Stop it! You can't blame yourself for what Tony did! There's absolutely no proof that you could have changed him—

and you had no way of knowing what he was about to do. He wasn't your responsibility." After a pause, she added, "Nor was your father."

"What…?"

"You obviously feel guilty about not going to work with him on Christmas. You think you could have saved him. But it's likely that, if you had been there, you'd have gone in after him, and there would have been two dead Harrisons instead of one."

He shrugged. "Maybe."

"You didn't mention the aftermath of your mother's death. Did your father talk to you about it? Console you? Comfort you? Hug you? Reassure you?

"No. He didn't do any of that, but Gramps did—sort of."

"Didn't you find that strange?"

"I was six.

"All the more reason…"

He said nothing.

"You've had a strange childhood, to say the least. But I'm particularly intrigued by your relationship with these two girls. Do you have pictures?"

He showed her one of the pictures of Norma posing on the beach, and then a yearbook photo of Mary.

She held up the picture of Norma. "Wow! Shit! Looks a little bit like Natalie Wood—except for the big tits. So you have this gorgeous girl who worships you, apparently is fun to be around, and would probably make beautiful babies with you." She put the picture on the table but continued looking at it. "Can't you just imagine coming home from a hard day's work and have her greeting you at the door, with your favorite drink in her hand, wearing nothing but a smile?"

He cleared his throat and nodded, vigorously. “Yeah, I can imagine that.”

“It’s kind of funny. You’ve spent the last…what…seven months doing penance—punishing yourself—by hanging out with her and not screwing her?”

“I guess.”

“But, even though you weren’t screwing her, you enjoyed her company. Don’t kid yourself.”

“Yeah. She’s kind of fun to be around.”

She held up Mary’s picture. “Here’s another beautiful girl—taller, isn’t she?”

“Yeah, about five-eight. How would you know that?”

“Taller girls tend to be more independent; more self-assured.”

“Is that a statistic? Did you take a class...?"

"Shut up. From what you tell me, she’s very smart and independent—and ambitious. You’re not ever going to be the only thing she’s going to want. She’s not going to be willing even to talk about making babies with you ‘til after she’s established her career. When she does, she’ll probably be out on assignment for days at a time, or working late, while you’re home changing little Mikey Jr.’s diapers, and wondering what she’s doing. And who she’s doing it with.”

Whom. He shrugged. “Maybe.”

“And…she’s punched you out once. Chances are she’ll do it again if you say something stupid.”

“Yeah, she might. You’re saying I should be with Norma?”

“Of course not. You’re eighteen. My advice would be to grow up a little before you get serious with either of them. But it’s too late for that.”

He felt a headache coming on.

"In a different world, you could have them both. That won't work here." She flipped Norma's picture over. "From what you've told me, the Norma you dropped off in Whittier is not the same Norma you screwed last fall, but I suspect she's still a bit of a partier and probably always will be. Mary isn't. Nor was your mother."

He massaged his temples but said nothing.

She put Mary's picture down. "When I was a kid, we had this dog. Got him when he was a puppy. We had a large, fenced, backyard—never let him out. One day, when he was about...three, someone left the gate open, and he ran away. We searched all over; tacked notices on every utility pole in the neighborhood; pestered the pound every half hour. No luck. We gave up, assuming we'd never see him again. Three days later, he came prancing up the driveway, head held high, proud of himself. It was as if he was saying, 'I had my little adventure, now I'm ready to go back to being a prisoner'. He died ten years later, never having tried to run away again."

"So, I'm Mary's prisoner?"

"Yes. But not just Mary; the whole Bryant family owns you. I remember you told me about Mary saying you two were a 'unit'. Well, big boy, that's what you are. And it's not necessarily a bad thing."

He shrugged. "Maybe not."

"You and Norma had your little adventure. Something you both will remember for the rest of your lives. Something most of us never get to have. Revel in the memory."

His mind flashed to Norma dancing suggestively and giggling on the beach. He smiled but said nothing.

"At first, I thought it was kinda strange—almost creepy—that everybody was pushing you toward Mary. I hate to pile on, but they were right." She took the phone from the counter and sat it in front of him. "Quit feeling sorry for yourself and just call her. It's time. Be contrite, but don't grovel."

Reluctantly, he picked up the phone and dialed, but got a recording telling him that the circuits were busy.

"Call her back in a few minutes," Debbie said.

"No. I'll call her tomorrow. Let's do something fun."

"Fine. You're calling her in the morning."

"Okay. Okay. I will."

"Let's go to Knott's Berry Farm."

They spent the evening there with Debbie acting like a teenager on her first date. Laughing, hugging, and hanging onto his arm, she made him feel like he was the only man on the planet. *Frank is such an idiot.*

Wednesday, May 30
Memorial Day.

He called at nine AM, Pacific Time. Becky answered on the first ring.

"I thought it might be you," she said. "Are you okay?"

"Fine," he answered. "How's the family?"

"Everybody's okay except Mary. She's being a—you know what—starts with 'b' and ends with 'i-t-c-h'. I'm telling you, Mike, just come home and grab her by the face."

He laughed. "How's Paul?"

"Paul's fine. Don't change the subject."

"You think she'll talk to me?"

"I'll see."

There were several seconds of muted conversation, and then Mary said, "What?"

"Mary, can we talk?"

"How's Norma?" Her voice was cold.

"I left her with her dad, as was my plan."

"So, it's back to me now, huh?"

"You know it's not like that. It was never not you."

He thought he heard her whisper '*Double negative*', but wasn't sure.

"I gotta go," she said. "We're decorating graves this afternoon." *Click.*

They spent the morning on the beach, with Mike becoming more comfortable with—and less fearful of—the ocean, even bodysurfing with some success. After lunch, they went to Disneyland—with Debbie acting like a teenager on her second date—and were exhausted when they got back at eleven PM.

Thursday, May 31

He called Mary at nine AM.

"Who are you with now, Mike?" she asked, too casually.

"Uh…nobody." He shooed Debbie away. "Mary, I'm not gonna beg, but I *am* sorry for what I did, and I'll cut my pecker off if I ever cheat on you again."

She didn't laugh. "Wouldn't that be punishing both of us?" After a brief pause, she said, "If you call again, tell me who you're with." *Click.*

At eight PM, Mary was propped up on pillows in her bed, wearing Mike's blue and white shirt, reading *Great Expectations,* and imagining herself as Miss Havisham. Patsy Cline's 'She's Got You' was playing on the radio. The family was downstairs watching a re-run of *The Donna Reed Show.*

Her mother knocked gently on the bedroom door and entered. "Mary, we have to talk."

"About what?"

Rose toyed with her chin. "Mary, I…know you got an abortion. Did Michael get you pregnant?"

Somewhat taken aback, but not surprised, Mary replied, "No, Mom, Mike didn't get me pregnant. How did you know?"

"Just tell me what happened, Mary. You know you can tell me anything, and it'll go no further."

Mary looked at the door; Rose closed and locked it, and then sat on the edge of the bed, waiting.

Mary told her everything, beginning with Mike's indiscretion with Norma.

"Am I going to hell, Mom?"

"God will forgive you—if you ask him to."

Mary pleaded with her eyes. "Will you tell Dad."

"No. There's no need. But you should try to make things right with Michael. We all miss him—even little Mark asks about him."

"I hate him."

"No, you don't. Mary, what if he never comes back? What if he just stays out West?"

"I don't care. Let him stay there. I hate him."

"Let's see...you're wearing his shirt, his picture is still on your nightstand, you've been miserable since last fall. But you hate him."

"Did Dad ever cheat on you?"

"I'm sure he didn't, but..."

"Did he ever take a road trip with another girl?"

"It was a different time, and you know..."

Mary put up a hand as a stop sign. She took off the shirt, balled it up and threw it into the corner. She then took Mike's picture out of the frame, tore it into several pieces, and dropped it into the wastebasket. After looking defiantly at her mother, she returned to her book.

After dinner, Debbie and Mike retired to the patio with a bottle of wine.

Mike spoke first. "What's your brother majoring in?"

She shrugged. "I...don't know."

"Is he a good student?"

She frowned. "Don't know."

"Does he have a girlfriend?"

"Don't know." She was staring at him, now.

He silently sipped his wine.

"You're a strange kid, Mike."

"How's that?"

"When we talk about my problems, or baseball, or life in general, you sound like a mature adult. But when we talk about Mary, you sound like a ten-year-old. Or maybe a six-year-old."

He nodded. "So...?"

They sat silently, listening to the ocean, for several minutes.

She finally spoke. “I took some psychology classes at San Diego State when I was trying to figure out what to do with Frank. A professional would have a field day with you, I bet.”

“How’s that?”

“Well, you’re so screwed up in the head.”

He could tell she was getting tipsy, but he topped off her wine glass and waited.

She sipped then continued. “As I recall, your father assumed your mother cheated on him, and then retaliated by sleeping with Sophie, and then beating your mother up. You surely witnessed some of the beatings, but apparently chose not to remember.”

“I was four when they got divorced.”

“But still you saw it, I’m sure. Anyway, your mother died, and you started school…what…a couple of weeks later?”

“Yeah.”

“So, you latch onto Mary. What does that tell you?”

Mike said nothing.

“It seems to me that you don’t function very well without a girl—or a woman— around you. Norma, Sophie, me.”

“Substitutes for my mother?”

“You found that twelve years ago.” She leaned on him.

“Substitutes for Mary?”

“You’re fighting the inevitable, Mike. Just keep calling her, but don’t go back ‘til she asks you to.”

“What if she never does?”

"She will. And when you go back, don't bury your face in her bosom and ask for forgiveness. You hurt her; she hurt you back. Call it even."

They spent an hour walking along the beach, holding hands, and sipping wine. The longer they walked, the more he thought about giving in to temptation. *Maybe I don't need Mary.*

"Mike, I'm a little drunk, but I have some thoughts," she said. "Let's sit for a while."

He sat next to her in the sand.

"Okay, let's skip your early childhood for now and go to the day Norma came to your house. You've beaten yourself up about that ever since. So, how many seventeen-year-olds would have been able to resist an attractive girl who pulled his dick out of his pants? Maybe one out of a hundred?"

"I don't..."

"Shush. Rhetorical question. So now, Mary finds out and comes up with her 'I want a divorce' routine. That didn't just hurt your feelings. It pissed you off, right?"

"Was that a rhetorical question?"

"No."

"Okay, I was a little pissed, but I was the one who cheated." He leaned back on his elbows and looked at the stars.

"So now she comes to you with the rape and pregnancy thing. After the initial shock, your first impulse was to boot her out of your house, right?"

"Yes, it was."

"You didn't, but you certainly made your feelings known by asking the question that got you punched out. Geez...'Put out or get out'? That's so juvenile."

"I know."

She turned to him and leaned on her forearm. "That night...you're not sure if it was rape or...revenge sex, are you?"

He said nothing.

"And whether or not it was rape, you're struggling with the notion that, after you spent all these years with her, someone else got there first. Am I right?"

"Pretty immature on my part, I guess, considering..."

"Yes, but normal. Boys want to sow their wild oats, but still marry virgins. There aren't as many around as most of you guys imagine, by the way. I told Frank I lost mine on a bicycle."

He laughed. "Didn't he ask how you could have sex on a bicycle?"

She giggled. "I bet it's possible, with a little bit of imagination. But you know what I mean."

"Yeah, I know. Mary and I had that discussion. Sauce for the goose..."

"Let's say you're out looking for a new car. You find exactly the one you want, but it has...say...twenty miles on the odometer. You can lament the fact that someone else drove it first, or you can realize that, with proper care and maintenance, it's good for another hundred thousand miles or more."

"Maybe it's about who drove it."

"He's dead! Get over it!"

"I'm trying!"

"You know...you never once mentioned your father hitting you. Did he?"

"Not that I can remember."

"Or hitting anyone else?"

"No."

"So, he wasn't really a violent man. Only what happened—or what he thought happened—between your mother and Charlie, seemed to set him off."

Mike shrugged.

"So he had an issue with Charlie, in the same way you had an issue with Tony."

Mike shrugged, again. "I don't know. I never had any desire to hit Mary."

"Only with words."

"Yeah, I said some things..."

"Look, the selfish me wants you to just stay here—at least for a while. The pragmatic me knows that's not a good idea. The kind, decent, 'big sister' me says..." She paused.

"Says what?"

"Can you imagine how you'd feel if she went on a road trip with some guy?"

He closed his eyes and shook his head slowly. "Probably go nuts."

"That's proof you belong together." She sat up and hugged her knees. "I'll tell you this much, though, in case you haven't already realized it. You're going to have to do a lot of compromising if you're going to get along."

He nodded. "Yeah." *Happily ever after is for fairy tales, anyway.*

"I'd like to meet her, someday. Now let's discuss the other things you told me about."

"What other things?"

"The murder; the fire; your dad."

He hadn't thought much about any of that, lately. "What about them?"

"Okay, here's my take on the murder. It wasn't a drug dealer, probably wasn't random, and was very likely related to the rape."

Dad shot him. "How do you figure that?"

"First of all, kids who deal dope generally are in it to make a few bucks—maybe enough to buy their own dope. They're not hardened criminals who carry guns. Secondly, it happened shortly after he raped Mary. Coincidence?" She gave him an exaggerated shrug.

He chuckled. "You take a class in law enforcement—or drug enforcement—at San Diego State, too?"

"No, but I have a brain. And I've bought marijuana—don't act surprised. I'm telling you the kid got himself killed because he was a rapist—maybe a serial rapist. Did you ever think of that?"

He shrugged but didn't reply.

"Rape isn't about sex, Mike. It's about violence. Rapists tend to have issues with women—maybe mother issues. From what you've told me about that kid, he didn't have a problem getting laid."

"He had Eve."

"You think your father killed him. Maybe he did; maybe he didn't."

They sat silently, listening to the ocean.

"About the fire," she said, at length. "You told me they had a huge exhaust fan blowing fumes out the back door. If someone had flicked a lit cigarette in the door, it would have been blown back in his face."

"You remember a lot of details."

"Yes, I do." She paused and hugged her knees again. "And, from what Frank has told me about Italians and their vendettas, they wouldn't have been satisfied with burning down a building. They'd have gone after you, your father—and probably your grandfather. Most likely, Tony's parents are simply Italian-Americans trying to get through life, just like the rest of us. And…they wouldn't likely have known what was going to happen on Christmas Day. So the question is: Who would have known ahead of time that your dad was going to be applying—what was it—lacquer, to the bowling lanes that day?"

"Andy."

"So, if it was arson, there's only one likely suspect."

He rolled his eyes. "Andy? There's no way." *Why didn't he call from the pay phone in the bowling alley?*

"I'm just playing the devil's advocate, here. What if Andy had an issue with your dad? They go into the office for some reason. He whacks your dad on the head, starts the fire, and walks outside. I'm not saying that's what happened, but if anything sinister was going on..."

"I can't picture poor, dumb, Andy doing something like that."

"You're probably right, but—as I remember—you said your father whacked his head on something."

He shook his head. "Not Andy…"

"Just a thought. Whatever happened, I don't think it was related to you screwing Norma or Tony getting himself killed."

After another silence, Mike spoke up. "Mind if I ask you something?"

"Go ahead."

"Remember your scenario where you have Norma greeting me at the door wearing nothing but a smile?"

"Uh-huh."

"Did you ever greet Frank like that?"

Without answering, she stood up, grabbed the wine bottle, wiped the sand from her butt, and headed for home.

Inside, she looked at him through smoldering eyes. "Screw you, kid! You don't know me or my situation well enough to give me marital advice!"

"Sorry. I wasn't advising…just asking."

She headed for the bathroom. "I gotta pee."

When she returned, he said, "Sorry, I wasn't trying…"

She interrupted him. "It's okay. I really shouldn't be advising you either, since I don't know Mary. The difference is that you want Mary; I don't want Frank. You see, I was advising you on how to get what you want, but you're…" She poured the rest of the wine into her glass. "I probably drink too much."

Fighting off temptation, he said, "I'm going to bed, now. Good night."

"You're too old to sleep in the crib, Michael," his mother said, as she tucked him in and kissed him on the forehead. "We need to get you a real bed and put you in your own room."

Lying awake in the darkness, and wondering why she wanted him in a different room, he heard his father's voice as it became louder.

He climbed out of the crib, went to the door, and listened. It sounded like they were re-arranging the living room furniture. His mother cried out.

Mike put his ear to the door. He could hear her crying.

"I've had enough. I want you out of this house, tonight!" he heard her say.

His father mumbled something unintelligible. Mike climbed back into his crib and listened. The house got quiet. He went to sleep.

Friday, June 1

He called Mary at nine AM. She answered on the first ring. *A good sign?*

"Whom," he said.

"What?"

"Twice yesterday you used 'who' when it should have been 'whom'. Object of a preposition."

"What do you want, Mike?"

"You, of course; all I ever wanted."

"Whom are you with?"

"How do you know I'm with someone?"

"I know *you,* Mike. Who the hell are you with, now?"

"Don't swear at me, Mary. And it's still 'whom'."

He could hear the sadness in her voice. "Mike, I don't want to play that game, anymore." *Click.*

As Mary turned away from the phone, her mother took her by the shoulders. "How long are you going to keep torturing that boy, Mary?" she asked.

"Torture? He doesn't know the meaning of the word."

Rose hugged her. "We both know you're not innocent in this. You had three weeks from the day you found out what he did 'til the day you climbed into that other boy's car. You could have used that time to fix things. You could have forgiven him. Instead, you acted like a spoiled six-year-old. Now you're about to ruin the whole thing with Michael. Is that what you want?"

"What I want is for my family to stop siding with him."

"Michael isn't perfect, Mary. But it seems to me he spent a lot of years trying to be. Did you ever wonder who he was trying to be perfect for?"

"Not really, because I already knew he was trying to be perfect for his dead mother..."

"Maybe, in the beginning, but..."

"...or trying to get his father's attention."

"Partly, maybe, but...there's more to it, and you know it. You already told me he would have killed for..." She stopped and stared, wide-eyed, at her daughter. "He didn't, did he?"

"Mom, you're talking about Mike. Of course, he didn't."

"But, you said he would have."

As she began to tear up, Mary ducked underneath her mother's arm and said, "I have a garden to hoe, Mom."

After spending the day at the San Diego Zoo and Sea World, Mike and Debbie drove to Los Angeles to see a night game at Dodger Stadium. The Dodgers beat the Phillies 8-5, with Don Drysdale winning his eighth game of the season.

While most of the fans left in the seventh inning, Mike and Debbie stayed until the end of the game, not getting back to her house until after one AM.

It was barely daylight when he awakened in his crib and looked at his parents' bed. His father wasn't there.

He climbed out of the crib and crawled into bed with his mother. She opened her eyes and whispered, "Michael."

She hugged him fiercely. He hugged her back, and then looked at her face. She had been crying. There was a blue spot on her cheek. "Just you and me now, little man," she said as she smoothed his cowlick.

Saturday, June 2

Debbie looked at the clock at nine AM and asked, "Aren't you gonna call her?"

"I don't know what to say. She knows I'm with a girl—woman—someone."

"Now, how does she know that?"

He shrugged. "Reads my mind over the phone, I guess."

"You poor bastard." She laughed. "Why don't you just tell her the truth? You picked up some old lady on the beach because you needed a place to stay."

"She'll know that's not the truth."

"What is the truth, Mike?"

He shrugged and drained his coffee cup. "Where do we catch the ferry to Catalina Island?"

"Dana Point, about fifty miles north. You don't get seasick, do you?"

"Don't know, but I guess we'll find out."

She went to her room, and returned five minutes later wearing shorts and a halter top. "Let's go."

He looked at her.

"What?"

"Sunscreen."

They were back at nine PM, and, beers in hand, walked out to the beach. A bright full moon hovered over the water, highlighting the whitecaps and breakers. Looking south, Mike noticed a group of people sitting in a circle around a small fire, talking and laughing.

"College kids," Debbie said. "Probably passing a joint around. Here, hold my beer. I'll be right back."

She returned with a cigarette, which she quickly lit.

Mike gave her a quizzical look, but then recognized the smell.

She handed him the joint; he took a hit. It irritated his throat, but he was able to refrain from coughing by taking a quick swig of beer.

They sat quietly, listening to the ocean and watching the group of kids douse their fire and noisily leave the beach.

He watched her. She was sitting very still, cross-legged, with her eyes closed as if in meditation. *I could just stay here—if she'd let me. But, of course, there's Frank.*

At length, he spoke. "This place…Vietnam. You think we'll be going to war?"

She opened her eyes and turned toward him. "Sadly, yes. And Frank will be right in the middle of it."

"How do you figure…?"

"Well, let's see. The Generals always want war, as do the defense contractors. The President? Not sure, but since Khrushchev has already made him look like a wimp, a nice little war could give him a leg up on re-election. Of course, certain congressmen will push for war because the defense contractors have paid them to. Other large corporations wouldn't mind a little war in some foreign country, as wars are generally good for the economy. Not a real war with nukes; just a little one like Korea. Fewer than forty thousand Americans died in that one."

Mike watched her face in the moonlight. Their faces were a foot apart. *God, she's beautiful.*

"Depressing," he said.

"Eisenhower warned about that, but I don't think anyone listened."

"Oh, the military-industrial complex thing?"

She became more animated. "Yeah. And as far as the Military is concerned, it's not just the Generals. Junior officers—and even enlisted men—want war because promotions come much more quickly than during peacetime. Frank is a good example. It took him two years in Korea to make Sergeant E-5. In peacetime, it would normally take a Marine six to eight years for that, maybe more. If war breaks out, he could make Sergeant Major in a few years. In peacetime, it might take him another ten years just to get *one* more promotion."

"So…there's going to be a war?"

"Yeah. I know a little more about Vietnam than I told you. The North is apparently making a lot of progress toward unifying Vietnam as a communist country, mainly because the government in the South is unpopular and corrupt. The North Vietnamese, along with the Chinese, and maybe even the Russians, are supplying weapons and training to the rebels in the south—the Viet Cong. Officially, there are no North Vietnamese soldiers doing the actual fighting, but apparently that's bullshit. So it's just a matter of time before the whole thing escalates. And…then, there's the 'domino theory'."

Their faces were six inches apart.

"What's that?" he inquired, with a catch in his throat.

"Basically, it's the theory that the countries over there will fall to communism like dominoes, and that if we prop one up, the dominoes will stop falling." She turned her head away. "Stop looking at me; I can't concentrate."

He didn't stop looking at her. She continued. "South Vietnam is the logical place to do that. Of course, wars don't usually work out as planned, and there's no logic to the domino theory since each country has its own political situation. The war won't go as planned; they never do. People like you and me, if we survive, will be left to pick up the pieces, bury the dead, and take care of the crippled and maimed."

Unable to control himself, he began to giggle. "So, you took a class on this at San...?"

She interrupted. "Yes, I took a class at San Di—fucking—ego State." She began giggling, also.

Within seconds, they were rolling around in the sand together, giggling uncontrollably as she gently began boxing his ears, filling them with sand. Grabbing her wrists, he pinned her to the sand and was on top of her. Breathing heavily, they stopped giggling simultaneously.

He moved closer, feeling her warm breath on his face. She jerked her right arm free, rolled away from him, and stood up. "You're welcome, little brother," she said, still breathing heavily. "Ain't that just like a man? I talk about war, and you get turned on."

He sat back and began digging sand out of his ears.

She sat down beside him.

He looked at her. "San Di– *fucking* –ego State?"

"I think the Marines require the use of that word at least once in every sentence."

The giggling began once more.

Monday, June 4

At nine AM Debbie picked up the phone. "You didn't call her yesterday."

"It was Sunday. She'd have been in church."

She put the phone on the table in front of him. "Call her."

Mary answered on the first ring.

"She's a nice lady I met on the beach, and we're not doing anything," he said quickly.

After a long silence, she said, "You didn't call Saturday or Sunday. I thought something had happened to you."

"You were worried about me?"

Silence.

"Mary, can we just fix this?"

No response.

"Mary...?"

Finally, she spoke. "You're out there having fun on the beach with some 'nice lady', after taking a trip with Norma, while I'm here milking a cow, slopping a pig, hoeing corn, and being ostracized by my family. No, Mike, we can't fix this from two thousand miles away." There was a short silence before she hung up.

He relayed the conversation to Debbie.

She looked at him quickly, grabbed her coffee, and went out the back door. He sat and watched her for fifteen minutes as she walked back and forth along the beach, occasionally looking back at the house.

Finally, he joined her. Red-eyed, she looked at him. "You still here?"

"I could wait 'til tomorrow."

"No, you couldn't, because we might end up doing something you'd regret—we'd regret." She took his hand. "You'd hate yourself, and...maybe your paranoia is rubbing off on me, but I have a feeling that...somehow, she'd know."

He called Gramps to say he was on his way home.

"Sophie and I agreed we should tell you about the gun when you get here," Gramps said.

"What's the gun got to do with Sophie?"

"Tell you when you get here. Drive carefully, Mikey."

At the car, Debbie hugged him and said, "She'll make you miserable at times, but the rest of the time she'll more than make up for it, I'll bet you."

"What about you?"

"I'm trying to build some enthusiasm for giving Frank another shot. Maybe I can make him want to be home more."

"I hope it works." He grinned at her and quickly held up his hands. "But only if you want it to."

"You grow on people, you little shit." She grinned back at him. "You were a nice little brother for a week. I'll miss you."

"Me, too."

"And...I'm gonna call Sean and invite him down for the weekend. He and I should get to know each other better."

"I'm glad." He turned to leave.

"Listen, Mike, whatever happened, happened. You can't unscrew Norma, or revirginize Mary. You can't resurrect the dead, or your football career. Just go from here."

"Yeah, you're right, of course. Thank you."

"You're welcome."

Watching her face, he suddenly remembered. "Hey, I need to ask you a question. Why do women wear red lipstick?

Smiling, she whispered in his ear.

Blushing, he got into the Chevy and headed for Whittier.

Two hours later, Norma greeted him at the front door with a hug. "You were supposed to call me."

"Sorry."

"Did you come back for me?"

"Only if you wanna go back to Ohio with me."

She shook her head. "Only if Mary moves to Timbuktu. Anyway, I'm getting to like it here."

He watched her big, dark eyes; they registered an enthusiasm that made him just a bit jealous. "Is everything okay with your dad and…what's-her-name?"

"Diane. They both seem to really want me here." She shrugged. "And if that changes… well, I'm eighteen and I can take care of myself. Who knows, maybe I'll get discovered and become a movie star."

"Maybe I'll come visit sometime."

"Maybe you'll dump her and come back to me." She laughed. "Maybe a monkey will jump out of your ass, or a cow will jump over the moon."

She escorted him to the door, and they hugged again, briefly. "I love you, Mike. I can say it all I want, and there's nothing you can do about it. Say 'hi' to Gramps and Sophie—and Mary. I've tried to hate her, but I can't."

"You know, under different circum…"

She put a hand over his mouth. "Don't say it, Mike. Just don't say it."

He gently pulled her hand away. “Dammit, Norma.”

“Yeah, that about sums it up.” A single tear ran down her cheek.

“Is it all right if I call you once in a while?”

“You’d *better.*”

He kissed her on the forehead and walked away.

With the nagging feeling that he’d forgotten something, he headed home. As he turned east on Route 66, he recalled that there was a TV show by that name, but he’d never seen it. At midnight, struggling to stay awake, he stopped near Albuquerque for the night.

She was snuggled up to him with her arm across his chest. “Sorry. I got cold,” She said. He looked at her; it was Mary.

Across the room, standing by the door, was Norma in her flannel pajamas. “I’m not cold, Mike,” she said.

Friday, June 8
Scioto County

He turned off 104 onto Hope Run at ten AM, listening to Ray Charles’ ‘I Can’t Stop Loving You’ on WIOI. Somehow, the Blackburn’s Market commercial that followed didn’t sound as obnoxious as before. He tuned to WNXT and caught the baseball scores. The Reds had lost to the Cardinals 8-2, leaving them eight games behind the first-place Dodgers. Ten minutes later, he was welcomed home by the Mail Pouch Tobacco barn across the road from Bryant Holler.

After exchanging greetings with Gramps and Sophie, he called Mary.

"You home?" she asked, casually.

"I am," he said, just as casually. "What time can I see you today?"

Without hesitation, she said, "Five o'clock."

"See you then." He hung up.

The three of them sat at the dining room table drinking coffee. Gramps, looking better than Mike could remember, silently sipped his coffee, and watched Sophie play nervously with her chin.

Mike caught her eye and said, "Let's hear it."

Sophie looked at Gramps, nodded and said, "Mike, I…killed Tony Duvardo."

After nearly choking on his coffee, he looked evenly at her and said, "Keep talking."

She cleared her throat and continued. "Back in November, I was at Glockner Chevrolet getting my car worked on. He was there, apparently having something done to his Corvette. We struck up a conversation, which eventually got around to football—and you—and your father. He seemed like a pleasant fellow…"

Mike interrupted her. "He raped you."

She sighed and nodded. "Followed me home and forced his way into the house. Beat me, choked me, threatened to kill me."

"You told dad?"

"Yes. Remember that night in November when your father didn't come home?"

Mike nodded. “Oh…yeah.”

“That was the night. He told me about Mary the same night. And as it turns out, we weren’t the only victims.”

“Who…”

“I’m not telling you who, so please don’t ask again. Anyway, your dad wanted to go after him immediately. But I…came up with the idea of scaring the crap out of him, threatening him with bodily harm, and hoping that would be the end of it.” She looked down at the table, and then at Gramps, who looked away and toyed with his earlobe.

“How…?”

“I know it sounds stupid, but I came up with the idea of luring him somewhere and threatening to cut his balls off.”

Mike looked at his grandfather. “You went along with this shit, Gramps?”

Gramps looked away, turned back, and met Mike’s gaze. “I supplied the gun, Mikey—reluctantly, of course.”

Sophie continued, “Your dad hated the idea, but decided to help after he realized we were going to do it with or without him. Being aware that people were selling drugs behind the bowling alley, and knowing that Tony had been in there late at night, he picked the spot, figuring the police would look at the drug connection. The other victim lured the boy there with the promise of a bag of marijuana and a night of sex.”

She folded her hands underneath her chin and rested her elbows on the table. Seemingly unable to look at Mike, she continued. “Your dad stood watch at the back door of the bowling alley, and I hid behind the dumpster. When Tony got out of his car, I stepped out and pointed the gun at his head. I didn't even get a chance to say anything to him. He grabbed at the gun and it went off."

"You shot him in the temple."

"It happened so fast, I..."

She looked at Gramps who spoke up. "Must have turned his head, Mikey. They were wrestling over the gun."

"You weren't there, Gramps?"

"No."

He turned back to Sophie. "The other victim...?"

"She wasn't there—and didn't need to be; she'd already done her job. Anyway, your father and I dragged him behind the dumpster."

"And robbed him?"

"Spur of the moment. The money went to the Salvation Army, by the way. Your dad took the gun, and I assumed he was going to dump it somewhere. I have no idea why he put it in the safe."

Mike considered this. "He should have thrown it in the river."

Gramps spoke up again. "He told me he was thinking he might need it for self- protection?"

"From...?"

Gramps shrugged. "I believe he thought Tony's family might come after him, being Italian and all. Who knows? Maybe he planned to get rid of it, but just never got around to it."

"Sophie, why didn't you call the police when he raped you?"

She looked at him and shook her head. "I keep forgetting you're a teenager, Mike."

"I hear that a lot. I hate it."

"Back in Maryland, I served on a jury in a rape case. They put the victim on trial, making her look like the biggest slut in the state. The guy brought all his buddies in and had them testify that they'd had sex with her. I refused to vote for acquittal, so we ended up with a hung jury. But the case was never retried. Our justice system simply doesn't work when it comes to rape."

"You said Dad wanted to go after him. What did *he* plan to do?"

"I'm not sure, Mike." She looked at Gramps; he nodded. "He had a baseball bat with him."

As Mike massaged the bridge of his nose with his thumb and forefinger, trying to digest what he had just heard, it hit him. *Norma.* "I gotta go," he said.

He drove into Portsmouth and stopped at the sheriff's office. Deputy Hoch greeted him warmly. "What are you up to now, Mike?"

"Nothing much. Just got back from California. Can we chat?"

Hoch led him to the small, windowless office and, without asking, lit a cigarette, quickly filling the room with smoke. "How was California?"

Mike shrugged. "Different."

"Yeah, I was there once, several years ago—San Diego. I suppose you want to talk about the murder. There's nothing new, as far as I know."

"By chance, did anyone check to see if Tony was involved in anything in Detroit?"

The deputy took another long drag, looked at the ceiling as he exhaled, and then looked back at Mike. "Contrary to what you seem to think, the Portsmouth Police are actually pretty competent. Officially, I can't tell you anything about that. Unofficially…screw it." He shrugged. "Marijuana possession. The charges were dropped. He was also accused of rape by a girl who later recanted. You think there's a rape connection?"

"I just remember his dad telling me that Tony had been hanging around with the wrong crowd in Detroit. Maybe someone up there came after him."

"I guess that's possible. I really haven't talked to the city lately, but I'm sure they've considered that. Mike, just between you and me and… the haze…"

"Maybe you should have a window."

"Or an exhaust fan. Or just quit smoking. Anyway, there were two guys they were looking at. One, a seventeen-year-old grade school dropout, had an alibi. The other, a more professional guy in his twenties, wasn't dealing just marijuana and bennies. Hard stuff. He's disappeared. Even if they locate him, they need physical evidence—an eye witness—something. Barring some unforeseen development, I don't expect it to get solved anytime soon—if ever."

"Have you heard from Sal Duvardo?"

"No, I haven't. Surprisingly, he and his wife have both been very quiet. You'd think they'd be hounding the Portsmouth Police, but apparently they're not." He paused and pursed his lips. "Mike, do you remember, back last fall, the Clayton kid who got himself killed on Hope Run?"

"Yeah. Sad. I heard he was a helluva guitar player."

"He could sing, too. Lotsa people thought he'd eventually make it big in Nashville. Anyway, his dad is a highway patrolman. I had a conversation with him after the funeral. He told me about pulling the Duvardo kid over back in the summer. Remember? You were in the car."

"Yeah. I didn't know his name."

"Well, the guy was blaming himself for his son's death."

"Why?"

"There's more to the story. The first guy on the scene—literally seconds after the crash—said he was heading north on Hope Run, just a couple hundred yards from the bridge. Coming the other way was a red, late model, Corvette convertible. He said the car was doing about eighty and ran him off the road."

"Tony?"

"Can't say for sure. Not many red, late-model Corvette convertibles in Scioto County, though."

"Did anyone talk to Tony?"

"I did. He said he was home, but his parents couldn't verify that. Apparently, they didn't monitor his comings and goings very well.

"Anyway, there was nothing we could charge him with. Couldn't even give him a speeding ticket on someone's say-so. Couldn't prove it was him, anyway. But the general assumption was that they were drag racing; playing chicken with that bridge."

They don't want to find the killer.

"So…why does Patrolman Clayton blame himself?"

"He's thinking that if he hadn't gone so easy on Tony, maybe he would have gotten the message. He could have taken him to jail for doing a hundred in a fifty.

Mike shook his head. "Probably wouldn't have helped. Maybe he should have been a little harder on his own son."

"Young people tend to do a lot of stupid things against their parents' advice." A smile flashed and faded. "But I'm sure he's thinking that, too. I'm sure Tony's father is blaming himself for Tony's death. And…I'm sure you're blaming yourself for a lot of things."

Mike stood up. "I'm trying to quit blaming, sir."

Hoch studied him. "Mike, this is the third time I've talked to you about this. And I feel like I still haven't asked you the right question. Is there something you need to tell me?"

Mike smiled and shook his head. "No, but there's something I want to tell you. You remember Mary Bryant."

"Yes, of course."

"We have a…summit meeting at five o'clock, today."

Hoch stood up and extended his hand. "Good for you. I hope it works out."

On the way home, he recalled something Penny had said about Andy: 'He's such a nice guy that, if he caught you stealing his car, he'd ask you if you needed gas money'. Couldn't possibly be a murderer. The fire was an accident; maybe the new extension cord was faulty. And, his father had gone back in to retrieve the gun so that the cops wouldn't discover it. *Still doesn't make sense. The gun was safe right where it was. Cops couldn't have made him open it without a search warrant.* Finally, it dawned on him. *He wasn't trying to unlock the safe. He was locking it. Maybe locking up the gun. Maybe locking up the seven hundred dollars. Surely thinking he'd have time to get out.*

He remembered that his father was in the habit of leaving the safe open when he was there. *So…he probably went in, closed the safe, and spun the dial. It just happened to land on 36. Probably never know for sure.*

Obviously, Eve was very wrong about Tony. Even getting regular sex from her didn't stop him from simply taking what he wanted; for thinking his status as a football star allowed him to ignore the rules.

Do I have room to talk? Well…some. And, 'Judge Not', while a nice notion, doesn't work in the real world.

He thought about what Debbie had told him—that rape isn't about sex, but violence—violence toward women. *Maybe it wasn't Tony's father who picked on him for pissing the bed. Maybe it was his mother.*

Sophie's story was bullshit. She—with his father's help—had simply executed Tony. There was no struggle for the gun. It was cold-blooded murder of a seventeen-year-old kid. Vigilante justice. '*Shot him down like an egg-suckin' dog.*'

But Tony was doomed. If she hadn't done it, it's likely Dad would have. And I'd have been next in line. If she can live with it, so can I.

He drove to Scioto Burial Park. There were relatively fresh flowers on his parents' graves. *Gramps or Sophie—or both.* He stood over them for several minutes, but could think of nothing to say to one mound of dirt and two headstones.

Sophie greeted him apprehensively as he walked in the front door. Going directly to the phone, he dialed Norma's number. "Making a personal call. Go away," he said.

Gramps took Sophie's hand and led her to the back porch.

Sounding out of breath, Norma answered on the fifth ring.

"What were you doing?" he asked.

"Not what you're...thinking, dirty-minded boy." He could hear her take a deep breath. "I just got home and heard the phone from outside. Somehow, I knew it was you. I was applying to the junior college here in Whittier, and it looks like I can get in for the fall session."

"That's great."

"You home?"

"Yeah. The trip was no fun without you."

"No one to snuggle with, huh?"

"Yeah, I didn't sleep very well. And I had trouble reading the map facing the wrong way."

"All you had to do was turn it the direction you were going. East, right?"

"Right. Listen, Norma...I need to ask you something. Please give me an honest answer and I promise it'll go no further."

"Oh shit."

"I remember you telling me how aggressive Tony was on the date you had with him. Uh...did he rape you?"

There was no response. Finally, he asked, "You still there?"

"Yes, he did," she conceded. "I suppose you know the rest of it."

"I know almost nothing. Why didn't you report it?"

"You're not that stupid, Mike. School slut charges football star with rape. Where would that go? The whole school was excited about how the team was doing. Shit, Mike, can you imagine how people would have treated me? A slut can't be raped, anyway, since she's always asking for it, you know."

"You're not a slut, Norma. Stop that. So how did my dad know?"

He heard her sigh into the phone. "The night of the Waverly game... Oh shit, Mike. Tony raped Mary, didn't he?'

"Just tell me the story."

"When I got to your car, your dad was standing there. He introduced himself and—acting kinda weird—asked if I was Norma. When I said I was, he asked me if I knew Tony, and I said I did. He told me that Mary had gotten into Tony's car. That's when I told him what Tony had done to me."

"Dammit, Norma, why didn't you tell me about this before?"

"Your father also said, 'If you care about Mike, you'll keep this to yourself'. You have no idea how many times I wanted to tell you about it, to show you your precious Virgin Mary wasn't so perfect." She sounded near tears.

"You should have."

"It wouldn't have changed anything, would it?"

He sighed. "No, I guess it wouldn't have."

"God, Mike, was the abortion for her?"

"It was for the daughter of a regular customer at the bowling alley. Let it go."

"I didn't know they were gonna kill him, Mike."

"Listen carefully, Norma. We don't know who killed him. Could have been his dope dealer. Could have been somebody who was in the car with him. Maybe just an armed robbery that got out of hand. Who knows, maybe some other rape victim. Maybe even a Central High football fan. Hell, I probably wouldn't have blamed Coach

Hauser if he'd done it. Do you understand what I'm saying?"

"Yes. They can torture me and..."

"Don't be so dramatic about it, Norma. Nobody is going to torture you. The cops are clueless, and it's likely gonna stay that way. If by some chance they should ever ask, you know nothing. Simple as that. Okay?"

"Okay."

"So...how did you manage to lure Tony back there?"

"I wasn't sure it was going to work. In fact, I wasn't even sure I wanted to do it, but Sophie convinced me that it...would be okay. I told him I had a supplier, and that we could get a whole ounce for forty dollars."

"Is that a good price?"

"Someone told me a half ounce was thirty, so I figured it was a bargain. Anyway, he was such an egomaniac; he actually believed I wanted him, even after he raped me. I told him that if he would meet me and *my* dealer there with the money, we could go to a girlfriend's house there in Portsmouth and party with her, hinting that he could have us both."

"And he didn't question any of that?"

"I can be pretty persuasive with guys, you know."

He laughed in spite of himself. "Yeah, I've seen both your persuaders. Let's just leave it there, and pretend this conversation never happened."

"Okay, I'll try. But I'm an accessory to a murder or something, right?"

"Let it go, Norma! Please, just let it go. What else is new with you?"

Her voice brightened. "I have a date."

"Who is it?" He shook off a quick pang of jealousy.

"Not that it's any of your business, since you blew your chance—more like a million of them—but it's a guy I met on the beach. We're going to a Beach Boys concert in Anaheim."

"Oh, the surfing guys?"

"Yeah."

"Doesn't drive a pick-up, does he?"

"No. He drives this cute little sports car. MG, I think."

"No back seat?"

"No. And...I promise I won't screw him on the first date."

"Atta girl." He laughed. "I gotta go."

"Take care of yourself, Mike."

"You, too."

"Don't forget me."

"How could I?"

Sophie and Gramps were sitting on the back porch swing, holding hands, when Mike came out the door with the gun in his hand. He walked past them, went to the storage shed, laid the gun on the concrete floor, and hit it twice with a sledgehammer.

Holding the mangled weapon by the barrel, he came back and stood in front of his grandfather. "Can't shoot yourself with this, now, Gramps."

Gramps grunted. "Guess not. You forget our deal?"

"When the time comes, I'll buy you a new one. Is there a record of ownership of this thing—bill of sale—anything?"

"No. I won it in a poker game back in...'52—no '51, the year of Bobby Thomson's home run. Won it off ole Jesse Smart." He chuckled. "Guess he wasn't very. Carried it around in the pocket of his bib overalls. He was out of money and owed the pot ten bucks. Thought his two pair, aces up, was good enough. He said, 'I think my two pair is higher'n your two pair'. I said, 'Yeah, I got two low pair. But unfortunately, for you, I have two pair of fours'. When I laid four fours down, it pissed him off. When he pulled the gun out of his pocket I thought he was gonna shoot me."

"What happened to ole Jesse Smart, who wasn't very?"

"Died a couple of years back."

Mike handed him the gun. "If I were you, I'd get rid of this thing, just in case. I assume if they can't shoot it, they can't trace a bullet back to it, but I don't know anything about that stuff."

Both looked at him with anticipation.

Standing in front of Sophie, he asked, "Do you have a better story for me than the bullshit you fed me before?"

Gramps started to protest, but Sophie put up her hand, looked at Mike, and then down at the floor and began. "Your father was by the back door, wearing dark clothing, leaning on his baseball bat. Tony parked his car just a few feet away and got out with the motor still running and the headlights on. I remember he hit a pothole and knelt down to look at his front tire, swearing. At some point, as he walked toward your father, he must have sensed that something was wrong and realized that it wasn't...the girl. He whispered her name."

"Norma," Mike interjected.

"I should have known you'd figure it out. Guess it doesn't matter. Anyway, he hesitated and then turned around and, acting confused, headed back toward his car. I stepped out behind him with the gun pointed at him. He must have heard me, because he started to turn toward me. I pulled the trigger. Honestly, I didn't go there with the intention of killing him, but when I saw him… Mike, you have no idea what it's like to be assaulted like that and know the guy isn't going to be punished… And I panicked. Just didn't…"

"Let's just stop," Mike interrupted, putting his hands over his ears. "I haven't heard anything you've told me, today. And, as far as I'm concerned, Tony's murder is still an unsolved mystery."

He sat down between them on the swing with his head and eyes going back and forth. They both looked at him with apprehension.

"Here's the deal," he said. "We're gonna rebuild Harrison Bowl. It'll give you both something to do. Maybe keep you from talking about killing yourself, Gramps. But since I don't plan to be around much, we'll have to hire a manager—somebody who knows the business, and will treat the customers right. Maybe Al Lewis; he was there all the time, anyway.

"We'll coordinate this all with Jerry Hutchinson and Ben Abel. Ben will set up a corporation. I'll set up a business account and transfer eighty thousand to it. When that runs out, you two will have to dig into your own pockets. I'll do what I can for the rest of the summer, but won't be involved on a regular basis after that, since I plan to be in Columbus, attending classes, hanging out with Mary, going on dates with Mary, and doing whatever else Mary wants to do with me. It's only ninety miles away, so I can drive back some weekends. Will that work for you two?"

They both nodded.

"And…we have to get the word out to the bowlers…like…yesterday. We don't want our league bowlers signing up at the other place. Looks like we may be able to open the first part of November. Tell them that. All the files I could save are in my bedroom in boxes."

They both nodded.

"And, by the way, I read an article in *The Bowlers' Journal*. It seems the term 'bowling alley' has a negative ring to it. Harrison Bowl will be a bowling *center*. Not sure it'll matter in a town like Portsmouth, but..." He looked at his watch. It was four o'clock. "I'm going to take a shower and make myself presentable, and then I'm going to Mary's. Hopefully, I'll be very, very late getting home, so don't wait up." He stood, patted Gramps on the knee, kissed Sophie on the forehead, and went inside.

Sam greeted him with his usual enthusiasm and ran to the back porch.

Sitting on the glider with her long legs tucked underneath her and wearing her normal baggy jeans and shirt, she glanced up at him with no discernable expression, and then returned to her book. The ponytail was gone; the wind was blowing her hair into her face. She kept brushing it away.

He resisted the impulse to bury his face in whatever part of her anatomy she would allow, and apologize for everything that was his fault—and everything that wasn't. Instead, he walked past her and sat on the other end of the glider. Sam sat on the floor between them, panting and looking back and forth, as if expecting a show.

Looking to his left, Mike said, "Potatoes look...like beans." He thought he saw a crack of a smile around the corners of her mouth, but wasn't sure.

She tilted her head to the right but didn't look up. The potato patch was now behind the hog pen.

"Potatoes look healthy," he said, looking to the right.

"It's June. They should," she replied without looking up.

"Where's the family?"

"Piled into the car and took off about a half hour ago." She was still pretending to read.

"Knew I was coming, huh?"

"Yep."

He looked toward the barn. "How's Babs?"

"Fine. Knocked up again?"

"You take her?"

"Yep. Wham, bam, thank you, ma'am." She finally looked up and smiled.

"Whatcha reading?"

"Triple-Threat Trouble."

"Chip Hilton?" he asked, incredulously.

"Yes, and if you ask me what it's about, I swear I'll…"

"What's it about, Mary?"

She put the book down and turned slowly toward him. Her eyes sparkled. "Well, it's about this really good high school athlete, who doesn't cheat on his girlfriend."

"Shit, Mary, he doesn't have a girlfriend."

"Don't talk dirty, Mike." Her smile was genuine; her eyes still sparkled.

"Wanna take a walk?"

"I'll get the cow."

They stood simultaneously and engaged in a brief staring contest.

"Oh, I almost forgot." She pulled a sealed envelope from her pocket. "Becky insisted I give you this. I don't know what she could possibly have to say to you."

He took the envelope and tossed it onto the glider.

"Aren't you gonna open it?"

"I already know what it says." He grabbed her gently by the face.

The apple tree was loaded with small, green apples. The meadow was in full bloom with clover, wildflowers, and bees. He could hear water running in the creek. When he tied Babs to the stump, she welcomed him home with a look, and then attacked the grass with enthusiasm.

"We're going to fence this in this summer," Mary told him. "Maybe you could help."

"Sure."

They sat on the log, looking at each other. "So…tell me about your little road trip," she said.

He began by summarizing Sophie's wartime story. Then, holding her eyes throughout, he gave her every detail of the trip he could remember, except for his final temptation with Debbie on the beach. *Blame that on the marijuana.*

When he was finished she said, "Norma looked good in the bikini, huh?"

"You'd look better, I'm sure."

"Maybe one day you'll find out."

"I certainly hope so."

"And the 'nice lady'…?"

"It was just dumb luck that I met her. Might be in South America by now, if I hadn't."

"I wrote you a bunch of letters."

"Oh yeah? How many?"

"About forty. No place to send them to, though."

"Can I read them?"

"No. I ripped them up."

"Why?"

"Well, it was like this. One day I'd write about what a jackass you were. The next day I'd destroy that letter, and write about what a stupid bitch I was for not waiting for you after the Waverly game. Then it would be about Norma. Then about how much I loved you. Then about how much I hated you. You get the Idea."

"Yeah. Sorry."

"Me too. You think you and I could take a road trip, someday?"

"We can leave now if you want."

"Better wait."

He looked at his watch. It was after six. "You think the family will be home soon?" he asked.

"Don't know." She leaned away, arching her brow. "Uh…what did you have in mind?"

"That's always on my mind. But, right now, I wanna go to Portsmouth."

She looked out at Babs. "We'll have to take her in. She'll be disappointed."

"We'll make it up to her."

They parked in the Harrison Bowl parking lot, and, holding her hand, he checked it out. The lot needed re-striping but was otherwise in good condition. The eight thousand square foot area that was the bowling alley was now nothing but a concrete slab with several cracks that would need some attention. He looked at the alley. It had been repaved, and there was now a streetlight next to the dumpster.

"Let's go down to the river," he said.

They drove past Gramps's house on Front Street. With everything that was going on, Mike had forgotten about it.

There was a 'Sold' sign in the front yard. *The landscaping must have helped.*

They sat on the bench, holding hands, and looking across the river at Kentucky. "This is the exact spot where Dad and I had our only meaningful conversation, ever," he told her.

"Do you wanna tell me what he said?"

"The most important thing he said was that screwing around on you was a bad idea."

"Your father was a smart man."

"Yes, he was. The rest concerns no one but him and me."

"I understand."

"I'll always wonder how my life would have been different if…"

She watched his eyes. "It doesn't help to look back, Mike."

Satchel Paige said that.

He considered telling her the whole story, not wanting to keep any secrets. *But wouldn't that make her an accessory after the fact, like me. Maybe I'll tell her when we're old and gray.*

As if reading his thoughts, she looked at him and asked, "Do you think your dad had something to do with Tony's death?"

Avoiding her gaze, he concentrated on Kentucky. "No, I don't."

"Okay. I won't bring it up again." She moved in, snuggled against him, and whispered, *"Wanna go somewhere and neck?"*

"How about the Sunset Drive-In?"

"What's playing?"

"Does it matter?"
"Nope."

Saturday, June 9

At breakfast, Gramps said, "I almost forgot, Mikey, Andy Mershon called yesterday, right after you left."

"Asking about the bowling alley?"

"Didn't mention that; just said he needed to talk to you. I wrote down the number."

Mike dialed the number. Andy answered on the first ring.

"Mike, I killed your dad."

Thinking about his conversation with Debbie, he tried to keep his voice even. "Oh, yeah."

"You know how messy my car is."

"Yeah, I've seen it."

"Well, I was cleanin' it out the other day and under a bunch of crap, I found…a brand new extension cord. I'd bought a bunch of stuff at the hardware store that day and throwed it in the back seat. Guess the cord got lost under some crap back there."

"So you're saying the extension cord you and Dad used wasn't the new one."

"Yeah, I'm a stupid ass. The fire was my fault."

"Maybe it's time we just let that go."

"But I killed him."

"Andy, we can blame you, me, or God, but the truth is that Dad was the one who decided to go back into a burning building; that wasn't your fault. And if he knew the old cord was bad, he shouldn't have used it. Let it go, Andy."

"Thanks, Mike. Makes me feel a little better."

"Uh…Andy, did the cops talk to you after the fire?"

"Yeah. Tole 'em just what I tole you. All I could tell 'em. They asked me if I had any idea why your dad went back in. I didn't; still don't."

"Me neither."

"When's the bowlin' alley gonna be open?"

"Sometime in the fall. I'll call you."

He hung up and headed for Bryant Holler.

Jimmy greeted him at the car. "Hey Mike, guess what? Dad says I can play this fall."

"Well, I guess you and I have a lot of work to do this summer, huh? A lot more to quarterbacking than throwing a tight spiral. Uh…are your parents pissed at me for getting Mary home at two in the morning?"

"You probably shouldn't make a habit of it, but… they're just happy to have you back; we all are."

Becky stood on the front porch grinning at him. "Was Babs glad to see you?" she asked.

"I believe she was."

They hugged.

"You get my note?"

"Haven't read it, but I knew what it said."

"Did you do it?

"I did."

"Told you it would work."

After spending an hour with the family, Mike took Mary by the arm. "Let's go. I have a birthday present for you."

"My birthday's not 'til next week."

“Close enough. Let’s go.”

Back home he said to Mary, “I don’t think you’ve met Sophie.”

“It’s nice to finally meet you, Mary,” Sophie ventured. "I hope we can be good friends.”

“Me too.” Mary turned to Gramps and hugged him. “You’re looking good, Gramps.”

“I’ve missed you, Mary.”

“Okay, enough of that,” Mike said. “Let’s go.”

He took her by the hand and led her out the back door.

“I wanna be a kid for the rest of the summer, Mary,” he said as they stood on the back porch. “I wanna swim in our swimming hole. I want to take you to the movies. I wanna take you shopping for clothes that aren’t so…frumpy. I’ll even take you dancing, and you can teach me how to do the Twist.”

“The Twist is kind of passé. I’ll teach you the Mashed Potato—or the Watusi.”

“Okay. Can’t tell your dad about that, though. And right now, I want to go up the hill and bat rocks. Okay?”

She smiled up at him. “Yes. I’ve been looking forward to that.”

“Fine. Wait right here.”

He went to the shed and returned with two whittled bats, one of which was smooth and varnished. He’d written her name on it with a felt tipped pen. “Happy birthday,” he said.

“Looks like a cricket bat—or the paddle they used at school.”

“Well, it’s neither. It’s a rock bat. Come on.”

She inspected the bat. "When did you have time to do this?"

He cast his eyes down and away, and then back to her. "October."

She hugged him.

On the way up the hill, he said, "You weren't really reading that Chip Hilton book, were you?"

"What makes you think that?"

"Admit it."

"Okay, it was just a prop. I had Dad pick it up at the library a couple of days ago."

"Clever."

After a silence, she asked, "So…when are you gonna put your application in to OSU?"

"We could drive up there Monday and get things started; see if I can get in—unless your parents would object, or you have a cow to milk."

"Babs is Becky's job now. And my parents…well…I've never seen Dad so happy, and you already know what Mom thinks: that you can't do anything wrong, even when you do; that your…you know what doesn't stink."

"Shit?"

"Don't…yeah, shit!" She giggled. "What if you can't get in?"

"I'll move there, anyway, if you want me to. They'll let me in eventually."

"Of course, I want you to."

"Uh, I have a question for you. How'd you know I was with somebody when I called?"

"Lucky guess?"

"No."

"Okay, I just know you hate being alone. The 'nice lady' wanted you, huh?"

He closed his eyes, picturing Debbie on the beach with her book and her beer, staring out at the Pacific. "I think she just didn't like being alone, either," he finally said.

They embraced at the top of the hill. "Hey, what do you really want for your birthday?" he asked.

"Just you." Reaching behind him, she tucked the tag back inside his shirt collar.

Acknowledgements

I must thank a number of relatives and friends whose input, editing, criticism, and research contributed to this project: My wife, Chris ('Stop playing with it and publish it, already. I nearly have it memorized'), Joe Osborne (What's the sound made by a blown engine?), Karmyn Guthrie (Show; don't tell), Nate Schick, Ruth Schick, Sharon Mason, Matt Osborne ('Put John Grisham's name on it and it'll be a best-seller'), Theresa Krason, and Dan McRoberts ('Hurry up and publish it before your readership dies off').

While *Hope Run* is a work of fiction, several locations mentioned, do exist—or did exist at the time. There is no Hope Run on the map, but it could represent one of many narrow, two-lane roads—some paved, some not—that crisscross Scioto County, including such roads as Bloody Run, Slab Run, Carey's Run, and Duck Run—the boyhood home of cowboy star Roy Rogers. Scioto Central High School is fictional, but all the other high schools mentioned are real. To my knowledge, neither a Harrison Bowl nor a City Lanes ever existed in Portsmouth.

The results of college and professional games mentioned are as historically accurate as I could make them.

The only actual people presented in a fictional role are Woody Hayes and Bo Schembechler, who was Hayes' assistant at Ohio State from 1958 to 1962. Their relationship presents an interesting story in itself. From Ohio State, Bo went to Miami (of Ohio) University as head coach. Miami is commonly referred to as the

'Cradle of Coaches'. Many famous coaches, including Paul Brown, Woody Hayes, John Harbaugh, Jim Tressel, Weeb Eubank, and Ara Parseghian, coached there before going on to bigger things.

When Schembechler was hired as head coach at Michigan in 1969, an already intense rivalry with Ohio State was taken to a new level. Woody wouldn't call Michigan by name, referring to it only as 'that school up north'. At the end of a 50-14 rout over Michigan in 1968, he had his team go for two after their last touchdown. When asked why, he simply said, "Because I couldn't go for three."

The following year, the Buckeyes went to Michigan for their traditional final regular season game, unanimously ranked number one in the country, having beaten every opponent by at least three touchdowns. Schembechler's two loss Wolverines beat them 24-12, igniting what has been referred to as 'The Ten Years War', in which one team was knocked out of national championship contention by the other nearly every year. The rivalry, which is still going strong, is considered by many to be the greatest in sports.

A few words about bowling:

Bowling in 2016 bears little resemblance to the bowling in 1961. In the late 1960's and early 1970's, due to insurance company requirements, the flammable,'soft' lacquer finish was replaced by urethane. Because urethane was harder, it didn't track the way the lacquer did. This led to the prevalence of 'lane blocking' (heavier concentration of oil in the center of the lane) which the better bowlers took advantage of to create more room for error.

Technology then took over. Softer surface bowling balls followed, as did synthetic lanes. With the introduction of tacky resin balls in the 1990's, scores skyrocketed, as 300 games and 800 series' became much more frequent, even as the number of league bowlers dwindled. Prior to 1997, there had never been a sanctioned 900 three-game series. As of January 2016, there are twenty-nine. In 1961, a 300 game would get you a headline in the sports section of your local newspaper. In 2016, it barely rates a PA announcement at the bowling center. In 1961, 200 averages were relatively rare. Today 230 averages are commonplace.

This is not to, in any way, disparage the talent level of today's professional bowlers. In some ways, they are more talented and more athletic than the Don Carters, Dick Weber's, and Billy Welu's I used to watch on *Championship Bowling,* but, in 1961, bowling was considered a sport. in 2016, it's more likely to be a punch line delivered by a stand-up comedian, or something to be made fun of in a bad movie.

In 1961, keeping score was part of the game. Today, with automatic scoring, many bowlers don't even know how their scores are arrived at.

Yes, to me, the sport was much more fun and much more real in the old days, but...remember what Satchel Paige said.

For questions or comments:
steveosborne36@gmail.com

CPSIA information can be obtained
at www.ICGtesting.com
Printed in the USA
FFOW02n1827170416
23259FF